WHISPERING SKIN

J.D. ROBINSON

DEDICATION

For my family, both real and imagined.

INTRODUCTION

Whispering Skin wiki

In her travels, our heroine Olivia Jelani encounters both the familiar and the strange. But it's all new to us, so I've whipped up a supplementary wiki that explains many of the terms you'll find throughout this story, as well as characters and places. Feel free to check it out, but be aware that you're sure to find spoilers if you read it straight through. Here's the link: https://bit.ly/WS-wiki

Join my newsletter

The J.D. Robinson newsletter offers news, sneak previews from upcoming releases, plus oddments and ephemera. See the back of the book for details on how to sign up.

PART ONE
BIRTHDAY

ONE

DAY 1

THE EARTH RIPPLED under Olivia Jelani's feet as she pedaled her legs enough to keep her head above water, but easy enough to keep the worst of the pain at bay. The view through her polycrystalline-based pool—looking down from her home on the Vaix Orbital—never failed to give her a thrill. A mere projection of the planet would have lit her underground natatorium just as well. But a projection, no matter how lovely its light, could never match the live view, because it wouldn't be real. That made all the difference.

Her joints had been nagging her all day—all year, really—but the swimming helped. At least in the moment. A few hours from now she'd feel as she had a few hours ago, and just slightly worse.

A tone, brief and pleasant, filled the chamber.

Olivia wiped the water from her face. "Yes?"

"A man named Tanzig Sagaa is at your door," said the ambiont.

She ran the lyrical name through her mind several times, but came up blank. "Do I know him?"

"Not that I'm aware of. He's a Sovereign Alliance officer representing the General Polity."

Now her curiosity edged closer to concern. Why would the SA send someone all the way to the Vaix Orbital when a note would do? Unless this was some prank.

"Show me?" She pedaled over to the side of the pool to save her legs some strain as a face appeared above the blue wavelets. The man's prominent widow's peak was the most notable thing about him, a stranger after all. And apparently he'd popped over from Heliopolis.

She should at least find out why he'd gone to all the trouble.

"Tell him to hold on."

She grabbed the rail of the ladder and, bracing herself, gingerly climbed out of the pool.

———

In the lounge, Olivia sat across from the man in the navy-blue suit as he sipped the smoked black tea she'd set before him. Her hair, still wet, was tied back. The old basset hound Somtow had found a patch of sun, the light just peeking out from beyond Vaix's far rim, and regarded their houseguest with his big brown eyes.

Time to find out why he was here.

"This isn't about my bottomless pool, is it?"

She'd insisted on that bit of architectural whimsy back when she'd still had enough residual social capital to score a plot variance. Structurally her pool was fully to code, of course. But it was an indulgence that her nearest neighbors would never be permitted.

The man smiled. "Ah, no, Ind. Jelani." So now she was an "individual." Was the title of courtesy—the Sovereign Alliance's honorific of choice—a calculation? A note of formality to put her in the right frame of mind? He sipped at his tea, then set the mug on the low table. "Do you keep up with the news?"

"Enough to make small talk."

"Did you happen to see the footage of the small craft that emerged from the Accolla Sphere last week?"

Where could he possibly be going with this?

In 2967, Stellorg SE—a mining syndicate sponsored by the Accolla Polity—had discovered a construct of suspected alien origin: a faceted spheroid, nearly six hundred kilometers in diameter, in the Main Asteroid Belt between the orbits of Mars and Jupiter. The makeup of its hull prevented precise readings, but scans indicated that it was inert.

Then, almost a year ago, in 2994, the mass of the sphere had fluctuated without explanation, renewing the interest that had fallen dormant in the intervening decades. But no further activity was observed until just days ago, when without fanfare, a craft—little more than a spartan wedge—emerged from a fresh opening in the construct's skin and proceeded to make its way toward the Terran aggregation. With an official entourage of Sovereign Alliance patrol vessels, and an unofficial one of onlookers, the alien ship came to rest not far from Heliopolis, the home of the General Polity, within the Earth-Sun L5 Lagrange point.

"That news would have been hard to miss," Olivia said.

The man nodded. "The ship's crew call themselves 'teelise.'"

"Call themselves . . . ? You're saying the General Polity has met aliens?" That had been the initial assumption, but the feeds had dried up in the days following the encounter, with no new details, and life went on.

"In person. Yes."

The heat of Olivia's mug soothed against the relative cold of her fingers. "I hadn't heard about that."

"It's not a secret," Tanzig said with a hand flutter, "but the prevailing guidance is to be deliberate about how that information is made available."

"To people like me."

"It's a novel situation. It makes us cautious."

"Yet here you are."

"Here I am."

He was going somewhere with this, but he was taking his time getting there. Olivia wasn't about to rush him, however. His caution made her feel cautious.

"We've been meeting with them—the teelise—long enough now to have made it most of the way through the list of questions we've been holding on to for nearly three decades."

"This is a lot to take in." Olivia sipped her tea. "So why are *we* talking about this? Because I don't really have any—"

"Ind. Jelani, I'm here because I have an offer for you."

Just then, Somtow picked himself from the floor with a wheeze and headed out of the room.

"An offer for me, specifically?"

"For you."

The sound of the front door opening was met by the excited clacks of dog nails on biocrete, followed by a man's voice. "Who's *that* good boy, mm?"

Aleksi.

If Olivia had known where this conversation was headed, she would have waited for him.

"Excuse me a minute," she said, and made her way to the foyer stiff-legged, until her joints eased up.

Aleksi was giving Somtow one last deep-tissue mush before he stood and dusted off his hands. "Do we have guests?" He threw a thumb over his shoulder. "There's a cruiser out front with some kind of fancy livery."

"Yeah, we're talking in the lounge." She leaned in for a hug. Her partner had that smell again. It was innocuous—something resiny, like sumac—but unlike anything in the manor. "I mean, I don't know him. Tanzig something, from the SA."

Aleksi was suitably impressed.

"He says he has some kind of offer for me."

"You applied to something?"

"Uh, no." What interest could she possibly have with a bureaucratic alliance of the fourteen major polities, the self-appointed arbiters of cultural norms? She'd sooner go into sundiving.

"Well, if he's here in person, it must—"

"I don't know the details yet," she said, trying to keep the edge out of her voice. "You're just in time to hear his spiel."

"You want me to sit in?"

"Of course." Or did he not care? "Assuming you want to."

As she headed back into the lounge, Aleksi muttered something under his breath.

Olivia found her old spot on the sectional, right by the gash in its upholstery. When Somtow was a puppy he'd tried to jump up by himself, an errant toenail had caught in the fabric, and he'd opened a tear as he went tumbling to the floor. The dog had never attempted such a feat again, but the damage had remained, a reminder of youthful imprudence.

At the moment Somtow sat with his head resting on Tanzig's knee. The dog had given up any pretense of suspicion.

"This is my partner, Aleksi," said Olivia as he sat down beside her, close enough that she could smell that smell. "I hope it's okay that he's here?"

"Of course." Tanzig looked at Aleksi and put up a hand. "I only hope I didn't come at a bad time."

"No," Aleksi said, "this seems like something we'll both want to hear. Was it Tanzig . . . ?"

"Sagaa, that's right." Their guest gave a nod toward the table info-point, invoking his identity chit. The words illuminated the space between them.

```
Sovereign Alliance
Agency: SAFAS (Foreign Affairs)
Name: Tanzig Sagaa
Title: Outreach Officer
Polity: General Polity
Comm: H001-1cf77-1e (SLT)
```

"Outreach?" Olivia asked. "Reaching out to me or to the aliens?"

"A bit of both?" Tanzig gave Aleksi a quick brief to get him up to speed, and he listened in silence.

"So where would I come in?" Olivia asked once he'd finished.

"The General Polity has drawn up something we consider to be a vital initiative. A matter of state. If you agreed to lend your support, I'd need you to know that it would involve some travel."

She couldn't help looking at Aleksi, who was giving their guest his contemplative squinch. She turned back to Tanzig. "Is this how you normally recruit people?"

"We don't recruit people. No, this is what you might call a special circumstance."

"And I'd be traveling to Heliopolis?"

"Yes, initially. But then you'd head to the Accolla Sphere. The teelise have requested someone from our race to meet with theirs, in a more official capacity. Or . . . ceremonial, if you prefer."

"The *teelise*." She shook her head. "You've *already* been meeting with them."

"We have. But this would be on their turf. A regular citizen—which you are—to represent humanity at their introductory ceremony. I'm talking about a symbolic gesture."

His words were like dust motes in the sun—there but intangible. Why was he here?

Olivia eyed Tanzig's ID again, this time more closely. Sovereign Alliance. The identification couldn't be a forgery, because it was live-signed by the Orbital Centrum in conjunction with the Sovereign Alliance itself. Whatever this was, it was as real as the growing ache in her bones.

"Why me? I'm not a diplomat," Olivia said, and at her side Aleksi chuckled silently. "Or an astronaut for that matter." Her connective tissue disorder, untreated as it was, would be considered a disqualifying defect.

"No, you're not," Tanzig said, sitting forward, "but you are the *daughter* of one."

Olivia's stomach tightened. "What?"

"Max Mehdipour, Integrity Polity envoy."

"*What?*"

"Your father."

"I *know* that. What does he have to do with any of this?" The sharpness in her voice was unintentional. But the man's unexpected mention of her father had rattled her, possibly more than it should have.

"Ind. Mehdipour has been assigned to attend this ceremony I spoke of. He was selected by committee from among the active council members and representatives of the teelise faction."

Olivia was silent.

"He's going to the Accolla Sphere," Tanzig repeated, as if that provided more context.

"So then you have your diplomat," she said. "Your envoy."

"No, you don't understand: the teelise asked for a *single* representative —one human—a stipulation they seemed adamant on. But once your father was selected, proud and loyal citizen of the Integrity Polity that he is, an appeal was made to expand the team by one seat. And the teelise acceded, finally. They're willing to make an exception, for family. Which is good news for you. That's why I'm here, to tell you there's a seat for you, to help represent your people before a new race."

There was something in his voice, an invitation to tease out his true meaning. She looked at him with a dawning realization.

"The General Polity doesn't like it that the envoy is a member of the Integrity Polity."

Now it was Tanzig's turn to be silent.

"So this is *politics*?" She picked up her mug, then put it back down. "This is why you came all the way out here? To enlist me as a General Polity spy?" Just because Vaix was under the GP aegis didn't make its people duty-bound serfs.

Aleksi put a hand on her arm, and Somtow stood and made his way out to the other room. Olivia had assumed the SA had made a mistake, but this was worse. This lackey wasn't here for her at all.

"Not as a spy." Tanzig looked genuinely pained. "As an attaché."

"An . . . ?"

"A cultural attaché."

"You have this all worked out."

Tanzig sat back. "I have to admit, I thought you'd be more . . ." He struggled to find the word.

"Thankful?"

"*Receptive*."

"Hey, Liv?" Aleksi, ready to placate.

No, she had to nip this in the bud.

"Ind. Sagaa, I think you've made some unfortunate assumptions about me. So I thank you for your consideration, but this venture of yours isn't something I can be a part of."

Tanzig was silent for a good five seconds. "I don't understand. You'd pass something like this up without any consideration? Not even for—"

"Don't even think about saying 'for family.' My family is right here."

He blinked at her.

"Have you talked this scheme of yours over with Max Mehdipour?" she asked.

"We *would*, of course. If you agreed."

"If you had spoken with him about it already, you might find him as receptive to this father-daughter absurdity as I am. The two of us haven't spoken since my vocabulary consisted of strings of free-verse phonemes. And now . . . It's not that I lack that pioneer spirit. But what you're asking me is to open up a part of my life that is resolved and done."

Tanzig gave her a long look, then stood. "I'm sorry, we had no idea it was like that between you. Is there . . . anything I can say to convince you to think this over?"

A fair question. "If Max backs out, you let me know. Otherwise, I hope you enjoy your trip back to Heliopolis."

TWO
DAY 1

OLIVIA AND ALEKSI ate dinner as the sun was falling behind the crescent of Vaix's retaining rimwall—fresh halibut straight from the coast of the neighboring Apeiron canton. Aleksi had taken a few calls as he was preparing their meal—work-related by the sound of it—but by the time they sat down he was quiet.

Olivia dabbed the corner of her mouth with her napkin. "Would you have given a different answer?"

He looked at her.

"To the Sovereign Alliance," she clarified. "Would you have agreed to go?"

She hadn't intended it, but the question was a test of sorts. Would he leave everything behind to go after something like this? Would her partner leave her?

Sometimes she'd felt that they already had left each other, just not so formally. Lately she'd been putting more energy into the relationship, so maybe she noticed it more. Then again, she had more time in general these days. Aleksi, after nearly a decade of scripting and threading, seemed to be on the verge of real success as a storyguide. Most of his brand of immersive, self-propagating fiction was dreamed by dedicated dramaturges—Aleksi had labeled it "chains of derivative tropes with rare moments of accidental brilliance"—but he'd made it his mission to gain the attentions of a participant audience who didn't seek the extraordinary, and finally, the right eyes were on him. Only a select few storyguides were sought after for their unique voices, and Aleksi Tsang was now one.

But the promise of success had made him cautious, quiet. The better he was doing, the more hesitant he was to share about it.

"Well it's a lot to ask of someone point-blank," he allowed.

"To ask someone if they're prepared to drop everything and . . . break bread on an alien ship?"

He nodded.

"Yeah, it is," she said.

"Even though there's not really another way you can ask something like that, if it must be asked."

She considered that. It was a fair answer, but didn't really get to what she wanted to know.

"So you would have said what?"

He twirled his fork. "Well, our circumstances are different."

"Some things are the same. We're in the same relationship." That rang false as soon as the words passed her lips. Was that true of any relationship?

"But I can't pretend to know how being in close quarters with your biological father might make you feel, especially since it's not a topic we've ever discussed," Aleksi said. He'd always been close with his parents, which made sense, because they were perfect. At least from a distance. "But . . . was your decision based mainly on that?"

"I don't know."

"Would you have considered going if not for Max?"

Olivia's question had somehow come back on her, and maybe there had never been a way around that. Had Max's involvement simply . . . made her decision easier to justify? Made it not a decision at all, and therefore a good cover? Maybe. But did Aleksi have to zero in on that immediately?

He waved off the question. "Hypotheticals."

"Moot point," she added. "If not for Max, they wouldn't have asked me anyway."

As the patio fell into shadow, Olivia chalked the whole question up to a pointless exercise.

THREE
DAY 2

THE VAIX INSTITUT Polytechnique faculty center was an unassuming facility nestled in tree-lined campus grounds abuzz with crickets and sweet with the scent of honeysuckle. Olivia had done her best to put yesterday's interruption behind her by organizing some course notes for a peer workshop she belonged to.

Now she stared at the open file on the panel in front of her: *Language and Lyricism Beyond the Stanza.*

She was feeling quite a long distance beyond the stanza at the moment. She hadn't changed a word of her proposal since she'd sat at her desk nearly an hour ago. She looked down at her braces, their matte shafts following the contours of her legs like shallow question marks. Her first poems, scratched into a pad fifteen years ago—as she lay recuperating after a labral tear in her right hip—had felt as inevitable as a sneeze. When she received her first literary award she lied, telling those gathered that she'd been driven by a deep need to articulate the mystery of her own circumstances, of her own body. But in truth, her writing was merely one of the few uses of her body, and of her mind, that would never cause her agony.

Or so she'd thought at the time. By the age of thirty she had given up on poetry—less a conscious choice than a state of inertial standstill—only to find herself awarded the Art Next Universal Prize for her last poetry collection. Accepting the prize made her feel like an impostor, and ever since she'd found herself writing the same poems over and over. Inspiration became familiarity, and her writing process was more numbing than enlightening. She'd discovered the poetic equivalent of semantic satiation —the phenomenon in which repeating a word over and over causes it to lose its meaning.

In the end, she was left with a single harsh truth: she'd stopped growing. In stasis there could be no writing. At least nothing of merit.

She hadn't finished anything new in three years.

"In on your off day?" Siti, the adjunct foreign language instructor, sidled up to her desk, hiking her backpack higher on her shoulder. The two women sometimes ate lunch together.

Olivia's eyes flicked to the date on her panel. "Looks that way." Would she have known if someone hadn't said something? Her mind had been in a fog all day. "I needed to get out of the house."

"Fancy a stretch? I was going to do a circuit or two on the path to wake myself up."

Olivia's hip had begun to bother her on the fifteen-minute walk from home. She didn't want to push it. "I think I'm going to keep at it." She pointed at her panel.

"Your proposal?"

"Yeah."

"Maybe you can run it by me next week."

The younger woman was solicitous by nature, but especially where Olivia was concerned. Olivia had long suspected it was because Siti had lost a sibling in childhood—a sister in her case—which was something they shared.

"Sure, thanks for asking," she said, suddenly thinking of Ran.

She turned back to the dead words on the screen and chuckled to herself. The General Polity wanted this broken-down lyrical onanist to meet their aliens? Of course they were merely leveraging bloodline to try to slip someone in from their own team, but they must have been disappointed to discover she was their best option.

The thought gave her pause. Maybe her rejection had less to do with Max and more to do with her ego: *You don't want me for the right reasons.*

By the time the letters were burning themselves into her retinas, getting some air seemed like a good idea after all.

————

While walking through the park, Olivia connected to her half-brother. Despite his isolated presentation on her comm's display—technically he wasn't anywhere, even if he was presently engaged at some specific location—she'd clearly caught him in the middle of something. His projected visage was tight around the mouth, and he kept looking away. But his eyes lit up as she filled him in about her visit from Tanzig Sagaa.

At least until she got to the part about her ultimate decision.

"Are you *kidding* me?" he asked, his disbelief exactly as lifelike as it needed to be. "You don't turn something like this down, whether or not you're feeling chummy about your crewmate. It's not like you have to sit in your dad's lap."

"Oh, please, Ran. *Dad* is my dad. Max Mehdipour was never anyone's dad."

"For two years he was."

"Two years I barely remember."

The dull ache had crept up between her bones, back first, then legs. She found a free bench and sat at the shady end.

"You don't have to *forgive* the guy," Ran said. "But to pass up something like this just to avoid being in the same room with him?" He shook his head.

"It would feel like I was signaling to him that it's fine."

"So go and signal that's it's *not* fine. But don't let this idea you have of him prevent you from meeting *actual fucking aliens* in the flesh. Especially not after what the guy already did." He squinted at her. "Would this be broadcast, or would this be a secret meeting? Are we supposed to be discussing this on an open channel?"

"It's moot, okay? Can we not hash all this out now? I'm already exhausted." Had she expected anything different from him?

After a pause, he nodded. "Yeah, maybe it's for the best that you avoid the whole thing. Who needs the stress?"

She said nothing. The last time he'd tricked her into a conversation about her condition, he'd called it an "indulgence," to bait her. This time she wouldn't take the bait.

"Have you been taking care of yourself?" he asked, his eyes suddenly too piercing by degrees.

"Please." An ironic question coming from him.

"Seriously, you've lost weight."

"I'm sure it's a bandwidth issue."

"Funny. But I'm serious, and it scares me that you'd say no to meeting another race. Because that's really not a yes or no question, Olivia. The person who would say no to that really isn't—"

"We're done talking about the aliens, okay?"

"I'm talking about *you*. Because this is all tied up somehow with your refusal to deal with your condition. Connective tissue disorders don't have to be—"

"*Ran.*"

"If systemic revision was good enough for your dead brother, it's good enough for you. I don't like seeing you suffer, or miss out."

And there it was. She was being *indulgent* just by being alive. She should let the medics kill her off, then spawn some idealized version of her. Except that hadn't worked out so well for her brother, whose body had died on the operating table.

"I'm fine as I am," she said.

"Wait," he said. Now his cheeks grew red, and even though everything about him was little more than a glorified simulation, the effect was real enough to bring on that dull, heavy feeling in Olivia's stomach. "What was that?"

"I said I'm fine."

"No, I *heard* it. You can't get past your 'I'm fine as I am,' anti-Seconder bullshit."

"Anti . . . ? Ran, don't make this about that. I'm not prejudiced."

"You're *afraid*."

"It's not something I think about." Unless she was talking to him. "Not everyone can be perfectly healthy all the time."

"But most can, if they want to."

Her muscles were bunched like a network of macrame knots, and she forced herself to straighten. "Look, I'm not wallowing in self-pity, *or*

17

making some slight at you." She lowered her voice as a couple walked by with their two dogs leading them. "This isn't remotely what I called to talk about."

"No, but it comes out, Olivia. You don't even hear it: this idea you have that Seconders somehow aren't the same person as the originals. That we're some . . . distilled approximation."

"I never said that."

"You don't *have* to! And I take offense. It's a slap in the face. If I'm not me, why did you call me?"

"Of course you're you, don't be ridiculous. But people are complex." What was that old saying? The map is not the territory. "But when you casually suggest systemic revision . . . who's to say what else I might lose, along with the disease?"

"I think I'm qualified to say." He shook his head. "Sorry, but we are who we are, for better or worse."

Just because he'd gone through the process didn't give him any special insight. It only proved the illusion was convincing.

"I'm telling you, I've seen it from both sides, and I didn't lose anything," he continued. "Tell me I'm wrong." He waited, but she resisted feeding him. If he kept pressing her, she might say something stupid. "You've known me my whole life, Olivia. Come on, this fear of yours, is it grounded in anything, or are you playing the suffering artist because that's your thing now?"

"*Ran!*"

"You're the poet girl with the disorder, and if you lose that—"

"Like you lost your suicidal tendencies?"

Shit.

Ran was visibly taken aback. "What the fuck?"

His fault. "I'm sorry, but the Ran I grew up with . . . he killed himself. That's all I meant."

"And now I'm not suicidal. That doesn't mean I'm not *me*, Olivia. Fuck. Is that who you thought I was? Grow up. People change in all kinds of ways, all the time. That doesn't mean they've lost their identity."

But she was thinking maybe it did mean that, even if it had never bubbled up like this before. Why were they even talking about this? She was fine with who Ran was . . . no matter who he was.

18

"This isn't about you, Ran, okay?"

"It kind of sounds like it is."

"I'm really sorry it came out the way it did. This isn't what I think about when I think about you."

"Okay."

But he wasn't okay. It was clear on his face.

She would salvage what she could.

"Have you talked to Dad?"

Their dad. Nils, not Max.

Ran bit his lip, but allowed the moment to pass. "He wants us both to visit."

"Yeah, well you know I don't like going back."

"'Going *back*.' Like you're being forced to relive some trauma. You can see Earth from your pool, but somehow you're afraid to actually step foot on it. Anyway, he's not in Toronto, he's in Montpellier. You've never been there, right?"

"No." But Earth was Earth, and the idea of going back was suffocating. Their dad had fled back to his birth home eight years ago, after his wife—their mother—had died on Vaix. Lately they talked when there was something to talk about, but how long had it been since they'd seen each other in person? Years, for sure. He couldn't expect Olivia to just drop in regularly.

"I'm surprised you're still on Vaix, honestly," Ran said.

"What are you up to?" No way were they talking about her again.

"You know, working."

"I could tell you had something going on there. What's up?"

He released a lifelike sigh. "I've been working on the COI with my Seconders group, you know. Future leaders from lives of adversity. Or deaths. There's still a stigma about 'echoes' outlasting their welcome in society, so . . . it's ongoing. You can see why I'd be touchy."

"Progress?"

"Slow, but . . . yeah, it'll be going on long after I've moved on."

Had Ran's personality drifted over time? Seconders didn't tend to lose cohesion anymore—that slow death that had plagued the earliest trials. But the seconded did tend to evolve away from their initial engrams, the gulf between them and their loved ones widening over time. Maybe that was normal, and Ran was right. Maybe that was what bothered her.

But she was still the same.

"Have you really considered moving on?" she asked. Only a small percentage of the Seconder population chose to remain "ghosts in the machine" with no physical form, as Ran had. Of those, about half eventually opted for dignified dissolution.

"I don't *avoid* thinking about it, sister."

She nodded, but said nothing.

"Well . . ." he said, "I'm sorry the idea of change scares you so much."

FOUR
DAY 9

"HEY, LIV."

Olivia had nearly finished preparing their crudités platter, but only when Aleksi interrupted from the other room did it register that there'd been a jolt of pain up her arm every time the knife hit the cutting board.

"Yeah?"

"Some officials are about to meet the aliens. It's live."

The Sovereign Alliance's state affairs feed had been detailing the meetings with the teelise over the past week, but—save for rumors and fanciful sketches—the aliens themselves had yet to make an appearance.

"Be right there." So she could see what she'd be missing.

Grabbing some napkins, she took the tray out to the lounge and joined him on the sectional.

"Nice," he said, sitting forward to survey the spread. "Thank you."

Olivia massaged her hand, only half watching the projection as some SA minister addressed her colleagues about this great honor.

"All good?" Aleksi was watching her.

"Yeah, yeah."

"You didn't say much when I got home." He'd been out meeting with his fiction team and got home several minutes after her tears had dried. But he'd sensed something anyway.

Now the officials were speaking about this important moment in the history of humankind.

"I had a weird conversation with my half-brother today, and . . . it always turns into something."

"Ah. But it's cool now?" He clearly didn't want to talk about it. But neither did she.

"Yeah."

Aleksi nodded. He'd done his part. He dipped a carrot in the yogurt then sat back to watch the proceedings.

The view cut to a statue of some sort, positioned at the edge of the dais. It was an impressionistic figure, caramel-colored and clean of line, its contours just detailed enough to evoke anatomy. Except . . . it wasn't a statue at all. And it was moving of its own accord to center stage, alive and unfamiliar. The camera tracked its steady progress across the floor. Was this a teelise then? Was everyone watching as this entirely new life form mingled with the officials in their fancy suits?

The ache between Olivia's bones, for the moment, was a million miles away.

The teelise—there were three of them in view, she now saw—were roughly humanoid in stature, but that's where any similarities ended. Their eyes ringed their mushroom-like heads, each a dark sphere with a single point of white at the center. Their unblemished skin was a uniform brown, and each of them wore a gauzy white scarf draped haphazardly, as if they were making a gesture toward clothing but not really under-standing its purpose. They didn't appear to require any breathing appara-tus. They had no pockets or protuberances, and lacked even a suggestion of limbs when they stood idle. It was only when they moved that their limbs separated from their torsos, peeling outward as needed, translucent and thin, like—it struck Olivia now—the shaved skin of a carrot.

Do they have feet?

She chuckled to herself as the teelise contingent, all three of them identical, presented the members of the SA's High Council with what appeared to be an award. Floating within a glass-sided case was a massive urn made of smoked glass. What had humanity won? Had the aliens come untold distances and waited three decades just to bestow a trophy?

But as the camera zoomed in, it appeared that the object might not be solid at all. Within its volume was a cloud of glyphs sequenced along countless strips that extended, web-like, from somewhere within the nebulous suspension. Nothing about this offering was static—it was a living sculpture, essentially made of language.

"What are they saying?" she asked.

Aleksi increased the volume.

". . . at the presentation ceremony, attended by General Polity Secretary-General Lancau Sebatic and the teelise delegation. Here, they've presented the domain of humanity—as they refer to our Solar System—with a gift from their people."

One of the three teelise now stood at the podium, with other humans and teelise by its side. "Within this seed," it said, "we carry the language of our forebears."

Its voice had been modeled to use the same generalized parlance as any newsreader. Its tone was gentle, even plain . . . yet somehow utterly foreign.

"We share this part of ourselves with you as a symbol of our everlasting connection. For it is not ours alone, but the accumulated wisdom of children set to wandering the stars. Each seed is as unique and evolving as each species in the universe is different. Now, as you contemplate your own journey, we welcome you. Welcome. And thank you."

As the alien stepped away, the camera cut back to the artifact itself. "Their gift to all of humanity," said the voiceover, "which they earlier referred to as a 'Lore Seed,' is said to represent centuries of the teelise people's written history captured in physical form. We've been told that each word, each thought represented within, is in a constant state of recombination, forming new, emergent meanings."

Olivia didn't realize she'd been weeping until Aleksi handed her a tissue. She hadn't felt so transported by an expression of language since she'd discovered how her poetry led to insights she couldn't have reached through other modes of expression, similar to the way a new language could. What visions might such an artifact of entified knowledge provoke, even more than poetry?

And as she watched the brief ceremony wrap up and dissolve to endless commentary, she tasted for the first time the unmistakable bitterness of regret.

She'd made a mistake.

FIVE

DAY 10

"I WASN'T sure you'd take my call," Olivia said, gazing out over the sparsely populated foothills of the Piosey canton from her deck. She might have expected everything to look different after last night's event. It *felt* different. *She* felt different, or at least more anxious.

"I'm not in the habit of ducking people, Ind. Jelani," said Tanzig Sagaa. The communication delay between Vaix—sharing the Moon's orbit —and Heliopolis was barely noticeable. "I know I gave you a lot to think about."

"It's Olivia, please."

"You've thought through everything we discussed, Olivia?"

"I have." Did his eyes flick offscreen? Maybe there was someone there with him. No matter, as long as she wasn't too late, let them all hear. The thought of missing out made her shoulders tight, as though her initial rejection might yet come back to bite her. But she owed him at least some explanation. "I watched the ceremony with Aleksi. I didn't know what to expect, seeing aliens—real aliens, this time—up there on the platform. But there it was. I was watching history unfold in front of me, but . . . it didn't matter. I couldn't connect with it—couldn't connect with the *truth* of it. It took so much effort just to wrap my head around the spectacle.

"But that changed when they presented their gift. When the teelise unveiled that 'Lore Seed,' and I saw their language swirling like a flock of birds—even though I couldn't read the words—that's when I felt that the teelise were knowable. A people who can create such poetry *should* be known to us. And I . . .

"Ind. Sagaa, if your offer is still on the table, I would very much appreciate the opportunity to get to know the teelise myself."

"They're remarkable, aren't they?" Tanzig said with a grin. "It's an amazing time in our history. We're all feeling much the same thing."

"Right. So if there's still time to talk about it, I would love to take you up on your offer."

To her relief, there was still time to talk about it. The opportunity hadn't passed her by. And for the next ten minutes, in the broadest of terms, they spoke about her trip to the Accolla Sphere, the representatives she'd be meeting there, and how much of this information she should be sharing with those closest to her.

"So what happens next?" Olivia asked.

"What happens next is a series of necessary hurdles—low hurdles—before we can actually get you prepared and on your way. Briefings, nondisclosures, and signatures, as they say."

"Today?" Dignity, Olivia.

"Oh, no, you'll be meeting with the Sovereign Alliance in person, here at Heliopolis."

The General Polity's primary base of operations was a small but majestic ring located at the Earth-Sun L5 Lagrange point. She'd been there only once, for a middle school field trip. By far the one thing that had made the greatest impression was the Global Polity Social Charter, emblazoned in larger-than-life letters across every polity building in the capital. She had wandered off on her own just to read the buildings.

"Does that sound like a good place for us to start?" Tanzig asked.

"As long as I don't have to pass any physical evaluations," Olivia said. Maybe it was the adrenaline coursing through her system, but she immediately regretted saying it.

"No need to worry about that, Olivia. Let me make arrangements and get back to you with some dates."

This was really going to happen.

"Oh, speaking of dates," she said, "one thing I have to ask you . . ."

"Yes?"

"How long would this assignment be for?"

———

That evening, Olivia relayed everything to Aleksi. It was no surprise to him, of course; she'd told him about her change of heart the previous night. But now it was official, or soon would be. She'd fly to Heliopolis for her initial briefing at the end of the week.

"You'll be okay on your own?" she asked.

"I'll manage," he said, smiling. "Will you be reachable on the sphere?"

"I'm sure that's something we'll cover, but I'll ask them."

He led Olivia to the couch. She detected no foreign smell on him today. He hadn't visited the set.

"I'm glad you decided this was something you'd be okay with," he told her, holding her hand, light enough to avoid causing her pain. But her joints hadn't been bothering her today, not since her meeting with Tanzig Sagaa. Her reward for being proactive.

She squeezed his hand. "Do you mean that?"

"You deserve this. And I think it'll be good for you."

And for him? In his own way he probably wanted this as much she did.

"Since we're talking about it, what about us?" she asked. "They said I might be there for a month or more, depending on how this ceremony proceeds." It seemed like a long time for a ceremony, but the thought of being immersed in an alien culture for an extended stay only made the prospect more compelling.

He nodded, but took his time responding.

"Ultimately . . . I think it'll be good. Maybe because I don't think your decision was clouded by that question."

"Meaning what?"

"That you weren't thinking about an outcome. Right? That you're interested in an experience. That you're choosing this for yourself."

She had wondered where such a singular, solitary journey would leave them, but he wasn't wrong. More than the journey itself, it was the decision to go that she'd needed to make. And ultimately, wherever that left them, that would be good for them both.

SIX
DAY 18

THE LANDSCAPE OUTSIDE THE CAPSULE, with its sheer fjords and glistening falls, sped by like a living painting. It was an apt comparison, Olivia thought, given that the formations hadn't been hewn by centuries of erosion, but by a decade or so of terrafab processes. Still, the end result was no less spectacular.

The group picnic had been Olivia's idea, hatched in the wake of her mission briefing earlier that week, once the true scope of the operation had been laid out before her. Now, setting aside the lie at the center of this outing, she looked across the aisle at two of their closest friends, Whistler Droz and Ekel Pefkiev. Aleksi had commissioned a block of rail time to take them somewhere Olivia had never been. He knew the details of what would remain unsaid, along with Ran. They had both signed the appropriate NDAs.

As far as their friends knew though, Olivia's upcoming excursion was of a far more conventional type.

"I've heard of the Steropees," Olivia said, her nose practically touching the glass, "but this is the first time we've actually made it out to see them."

"You could tell me they were as high as the rimwalls and I wouldn't argue it," Ekel said.

"Look here," said Whistler, pointing out a fearsome line of black cliffs as their capsule passed over it. "This whole range was going to be a tie-in for a mission we were designing. The project never made it off the ground, but they wrote off the terraforming as an R&D expense."

"So *that's* how that works," Aleksi said. He was in a position to know, since they were in a similar line of work—she with her visual design, and he with his interactive narratives.

"Something like that."

"Hey, whatever works," said Olivia. "We're so lucky that all of this is practically in our back yard."

Aleksi sat back in his seat. "People dismiss it because it's unsettled. It's *rough*. They prefer places like Dajia—"

"Yeah, if you're super into crowds and guided activities and curated tracts," said Whistler. "They're afraid of anything that casts a shadow."

"Well I live for the crinkly bits," Olivia said, still staring out the window. When would she see such sights again?

———

DAY 14

(four days earlier)

The confusion had set in moments after Olivia signed her life away. At least that's how it had felt.

"It's just a precaution," said the man sitting across from her. That was Ioor Volkopp, the silver-haired member of the Sovereign Alliance's diplomatic security, who'd taken over from Tanzig Sagaa. Tanzig was in attendance at the other end of the table, but he'd remained uncharacteristically silent throughout. Also in attendance were Pola Penrose, the SA liaison officer, and Quv Vidalin, the head of mission.

The SA home office on Heliopolis was far less monumental on the inside than it was from the pedway outside, with neat, thick-walled rooms formed from restrained arrangements of biocrete slabs.

"I'm afraid to make one wrong step," Olivia said as Ioor flicked away the image of her signed contract, clearing the table for the first time.

"It isn't like that," he said, resting his arms on the table now that the formalities were out of the way. "This mission isn't secret, per se. But there is certain information that you'll be learning before we've reached a decision on how . . ." He trailed off.

"We want to have a holistic plan in place," said Quv, a thin man with a pockmarked face. It said something about him that he'd foregone any easy cosmetic repairs. It made him seem more honest. "We'll need to know a lot more ourselves before we convey every last detail here to the public."

"Is the information yours to control?" Olivia asked them.

"Well, I didn't say control," Quv said, his mouth drawn tighter. "This is about being responsible. It's a big responsibility, and the full picture here, it's still very much at an unfolding stage."

Olivia held her tongue.

"This is all new to us," said Ioor, taking another tack. "Is it surprising that we'd be extra . . . deliberate the first time around? It's like new parents with their first child . . ." He saw the look on Olivia's face. "The point is, please consider our conversation here today, and any that follow, as *Restricted* with a capital R. Your partner and brother are being told much the same."

Despite the high level of security the mission required, Aleksi and Ran—the two people closest to Olivia—wouldn't be left out of the loop entirely. Giving them security clearances, if lesser ones, was a measure the Sovereign Alliance was willing to provide, Quv had told her. As an outsider to matters of state, they'd deemed it beneficial to provide Olivia with a more familiar support team, outside of the professionals in this room. Her brother and partner wouldn't be apprised of her every move, but she'd been assured that a line of communication between Berengia and Sol would remain available to her—strictly monitored, of course—so they could be there for moral support if she found herself homesick. Aleksi, presumably, was in a nearby office, receiving a subset of the briefing she was getting now. Ran, being bodiless, would be casting in on a secure stage for his. As for her father down on Earth, Olivia had decided that he should know only what the public knew. Bad enough if he suspected his daughter had any interest in connecting with Max. No, she would tell her father something prosaic to explain her absence, and hold Ran to it. She could apologize to him after, once she actually had experiences worth sharing.

"People, we do have a lot of ground to cover," Pola said. "So we'll cover logistics first, and agenda second."

"Sound good?" Ioor asked Olivia.

"Logistics?" Olivia asked. "You mean beyond getting a ride to the Accolla Sphere?"

"There's a bit more to it than that," Ioor said, and threw a glance to Pola. "The sphere is not your final destination."

"Oh." Were the teelise hiding something else, perhaps outside of the Main Asteroid Belt? The feeds had made no mention of a second ship.

"Now, this part will require some explanation."

Olivia nodded. Why the buildup?

"You and Max *will* enter the Accolla Sphere," Ioor said, "which serves as a local outpost. But the sphere's primary purpose is to house something the teelise call a 'spring.' Which happens to be a nonrelativistic gateway of their own design."

And there he stopped, as if to allow his words time to flutter over to Olivia. She looked from face to face, all eyes on her.

"Am I supposed to know what that means?" she asked.

"It's a wormhole," said Quv, stealing Ioor's thunder. "It's a gateway that allows for nonrelativistic point-to-point travel."

How many documents had she just signed? Suddenly she was sure she'd been deprived of a key piece of context, like promising not to get angry at someone before they revealed what they'd done.

"I didn't think wormholes existed," she said. "I didn't think they were possible."

"We didn't either," Ioor said. "Theoretically, yes. But not in a stable state, let alone in a form that would allow for safe traversal."

"A gateway," she said. "To where?"

"Directly to Maffei 1, which is a galaxy nine million light years away."

Olivia looked down the table at Tanzig. It was understandable why he'd omitted this particular morsel at their first meeting, but an expression of compunction now wouldn't have been unwelcome. Yet his face remained neutral.

"The spring is the key to this mission," Ioor continued, "since our introduction to the aliens—*your* introduction—will take place in *their* system."

"This all . . . doesn't sound real."

"Indeed, it's put our science team on their heels. But to the teelise the springs are an old and reliable technology."

"The classic teleporter," Olivia muttered. She imagined the look on Aleksi's face when they told him. She could see him shooting up from his seat. That was most often how he expressed excitement: he would stand, and then . . . nothing. As long as he wasn't sitting. The rest happened in his head, betrayed only by a glimmer in his eye.

She didn't feel like standing.

"According to the teelise, travel from our system to theirs will be practically instantaneous."

"One thing though," Quv said. "The traversal process itself is fairly . . . involved. I mean physically."

They wouldn't have highlighted the fact if it weren't important. Yet another warning sign.

"Well as I'm sure you've noticed," Olivia said, "I'm not the hardiest of physical specimens." She indicated her leg braces.

"We're aware of your challenges," Ioor said. "But we've been assured by the teelise that your physical condition, such as it is, will not present an issue." So it had come up. "In fact, one of the reasons it took the teelise twenty-eight years to reach out to us was because they were conducting research to ensure that humans could make the crossing safely."

"*Any* human," Quv said.

"So then, what kind of process are we talking about, exactly?"

Quv and Ioor looked at each other.

"Well," said Ioor, "you're familiar with the procedures deep-sea divers follow to acclimatize to their environment?"

"Vaguely. They have to take their time adjusting to extreme pressure changes."

"Yes. It's essentially the same idea here, only . . ."

Olivia shook her head. Only what?

"Only more involved," was all Ioor seemed willing—or able—to say. Maybe he didn't know.

"If I'm going to be undergoing this process," Olivia said, "I do expect someone to tell me, at some point, what it is I'll be subjecting myself to."

"Of course. But right now let's focus on the high-level details—the where, the who, and the what. We'll let the experts take you through the *how* when the time comes."

"You're not the diving expert."

"I couldn't swim to save my life."

"Right." Olivia shifted in her chair, trying to keep her back straight. It would be the only way to get through these briefings intact. "You've already told me the where. Nine million light years away. And the who is the teelise."

"Actually, the teelise are only here to handle the technical details of your travel. But they're not the ones who sent the invitation. A partner race did that."

"Wait. What?" What was that whole ceremony she'd watched less than a week ago? Had that not been an invitation? "What does that mean?" Olivia asked. "A partner race? *Different* aliens?"

"Yes. On the remote side of the wormhole is a multi-species syndicate —what the teelise call a 'symbiotry.' And we—the human race—have been invited to join it. Provisionally."

"But not by the teelise. By this other race."

"We call them the 'remotes.' It's a generic name, I know. They don't have a proper name for themselves, like 'humans,' so we had to pick something, for convenience."

"Remotes" seemed more perfunctory than generic, a barely more polite way of saying "foreigners." It brought to mind *stranieri*, from the Italian—literally, strangers. Besides which, once she got over there, the word "remotes" wouldn't make any sense at all.

Olivia sipped her water. It was clean, but flat. "Okay. Just to be clear, the teelise aren't the remotes."

"They are not," said Quv.

Ioor nodded. "The teelise are the facilitators."

"And what do we know about these remotes?" Olivia asked.

"Not much so far—"

"Surprisingly little," Quv put in.

"—except through the actions and philosophy of the teelise," Ioor finished. "For instance, we believe the remotes aren't big on travel. See, this is the kind of thing you'd be finding out for us."

Olivia looked at the faces around the table. They were gravely overestimating her value to the mission. "People, look. I'm sorry, but I wouldn't begin to know how to evaluate whether humanity can join some alien version of the Sovereign Alliance."

Ioor held up his hands in a placating gesture. "We don't expect you to. That's Max Mehdipour's primary remit. For you, this trip is to be a gentle, low-stakes introduction, nothing more. Of course, once we're all agreed that a new alliance between our peoples is mutually beneficial, a more involved diplomatic operation can begin, with teams who specialize in assessing the prospects of these new alliances."

He'd let her off the hook. Mostly. "So what *do* you want me to do here?" Olivia asked.

Ioor smiled. "For now, your impressions of the remotes are all we're looking for."

———

DAY 18

The drop into the gorge, only meters away, took Olivia's breath away, and the mountain range rose up even higher on the far side. Fortunately, for all its majesty, the windward currents were mild, idly toying with the fluttering fringe along their picnic blanket's edge.

The food arrayed before them would have fed twice as many people.

"I'm a little ashamed that it's taken us so long to make it out here," said Whistler.

Her partner had speared a falafel ball at the end of a toothpick. "We get so wrapped up in our routines."

"It's amazing the kinds of things you see just before you leave for somewhere," Olivia said. Would she be homesick? She hadn't thought so, but she hadn't traveled to any real degree for nearly a decade.

"I don't think that's uncommon," said Aleksi. "It's not until something bigger interrupts our routine that we blink and actually look around ourselves."

Grounding, that's what his words were. But rather than tedious, she found it endearing. Maybe *because* she would soon be gone.

Whistler placed a friendly hand on Olivia's knee. "I like to think that the more amazing the things you see before a trip, the more amazing the trip will be."

Olivia gave her a genuine smile.

———

DAY 14

(four days earlier)

"I suppose I should know what a cultural attaché does."

Olivia's Sovereign Alliance team had ordered food in, but the sandwiches didn't make their discussion about aliens feel any less strange.

The head of mission dabbed at his mouth with a napkin. "Essentially, you'll be a diplomat whose focus is on promoting our culture." Quv gave his colleagues a glance, as if to make sure they were all on the same page.

"Is that all?" Olivia said, allowing her smile to show.

"Well, no," said Ioor. "Generally speaking, although cultural attachés may be creative people, they tend to be more the planner or the marketing expert rather than the actual talent. You know, designing a campaign of activities to convey the message."

"The message about . . . ?"

"About who we are. Look, we know this isn't your background—"

"No, it's not." She shifted in her chair to alleviate her sore hips.

"I can get you something if you're uncomfortable," said Tanzig from the other end of the table.

"I'm fine," Olivia said, waving his offer away. "Here's what I keep coming back to. I'm not yet feeling confident that you know who I am, besides the daughter of Max M." What was she saying? Was she trying to argue them out of this? Because if so, why had she come all this way? "I understand that you don't want the only face of humanity to be from Integrity. It's petty, but I understand it. So besides showing my face . . ."

"You're demonstrating to them that our people aren't a monoculture," Quv said.

"But you make Integrity sound like a band of ragtag bandits. They're part of the Sovereign Alliance!"

"Exactly," said Ioor, his voice so quiet as to be soothing, "and we would normally send a wide delegation to represent that breadth and diversity, especially to a new species. Unfortunately, the limitations inherent to this exchange have been made clear to us. So here we are. We get to send you. And as far as I'm concerned, that's a win-win."

The man presented his best infectious smile.

"So," Olivia said, "did you see me participating as a poet, or as a spy? Because I'm definitely not both." And she might not be either.

"Just as a daughter."

Olivia scoffed.

"As an equal representative of our species, who *happens to be* a daughter," said Quv. "You'll be by your father's—"

"*Max's.*"

He blinked. "Really?"

"If you want our discussion to remain civil." When were these people going to get it? "My father is the man who raised me."

"Of course," said Quv, putting up a hand. "You'll be by *Max's* side, and you'll see first-hand how he represents us, and perhaps the SA as a whole."

"So no Integrity Polity propaganda allowed?" Olivia asked, not afraid to give them a poke. And why shouldn't she? If there was even a hint of gamesmanship, she was prepared to walk. Or so she told herself.

"We don't expect anything like that," Quv said flatly.

"You're not rivals, Olivia," Ioor added. "As I said, if we could send a broader, more representative team from the start, we would. But that will have to happen in the near future, so we hope. For now, we're making the best of this. And we're glad you're a part of it."

———

DAY 18

"Speaking of amazing trips . . . ?" Ekel looked over at her expectantly.

All eyes were on her. Olivia couldn't take the bait, but neither could she tell them nothing at all. At her briefing earlier in the week, the suggestion had been to give people a straightforward, plausible cover story. Something she'd have no trouble keeping consistent.

Tell them something you're planning on doing, or something you should have done, Ioor had said.

"I'll be visiting my dad for a while," she said, dipping a pita wedge into the hummus, "in Canadia."

"Old world," said Ekel.

Aleksi nodded silently. He was probably enjoying her performance.

"Whereabouts?" Whistler asked.

"Spokane. I have some downtime as far as my lecture circuit, and my half-brother is free. Ran. So we're planning a little family reunion."

"That's great!" Ekel said.

"Yeah, well, I should have done it a long time ago."

"How long will you be down there?" Whistler asked.

Only Olivia noticed Aleksi's raised eyebrow.

———

DAY 14
(four days earlier)

"We've been referring to their home system as Beringia," Ioor said, "since the remotes don't use proper names."

Where had she heard that name before? "Was that a lost island, or . . . ?"

"A prehistoric land bridge."

"I sort of remember the name."

"It connected two great land masses. See?"

"I get it. Clever. So how long will Max and I be in Beringia?"

Outside, the sun's afternoon glare had made the windows dim, giving everything a twilight cast. How long had she been here? Five hours at least, including the waiting, the greetings, the signing, and the briefings. And the dull ache in her left hip was telling her they would be having words later.

"The exact duration of your stay will depend on several things, including some key externalities."

Olivia looked at the team. "I know an asterisk when I hear one."

"It's something to plan around," Ioor said. "This spring we talked about earlier is actually one of many such gateways, all of which feed into a central singularity the remotes call 'the Fountain'—a bit of a parent-child relationship. The Fountain is located in Beringia, the host system—think of it as a central station—whereas springs can be opened to different destinations, according to the teelise. A hub and its many spokes. But, though the Fountain is always open to traffic, its individual springs operate based on their own internal cycles and are accessible only at regular intervals."

Like the "back door" to the Lonely Mountain, Olivia thought.

"Soon after you've traveled through it," Quv continued, "the spring between Sol and this Fountain in Beringia will go into its dormant state —for nearly a month in this case. You'll have to wait for the next active window before you can return. Like waiting for the next shuttle."

A month. Could she really spend that much time with Max? That depended on certain quality-of-life considerations.

Ioor seemed to be studying her face. "Reservations?"

"No, but . . . well, this sounds weird, but where will we be staying?"

"All your needs will be met. Don't worry about that."

"An alien hotel?" What would an alien hotel even be? Did they have tourism? She would have to insist on separate rooms.

"We don't have all the details, except that you'd be spending the bulk of your time on one of their vessels, where this multispecies assembly is held. But they assured us you'll both be comfortable and looked after, from creature comforts to communications, and—"

"Food, what about food? Clothes? How will I communicate?"

"Everything's going to be taken care of. We're sending some provisions and fab cells along, but the teelise were very clear that you will not want for anything, including food."

"Put it this way," said Quv. "Their system is a hub for a syndicate made up of eight other species. We will be the ninth. Which means they're the most experienced hosts you could ever hope to meet."

———

DAY 18

The picnic had left them all feeling pleasantly lethargic. While Ekel and Aleksi napped on the blanket among the leftovers, Olivia wandered over to a stone wall that separated the relatively level meadow from the treacherous drop beyond. Whistler joined her, dangling her legs over the far side as she sat.

"How are things?" she asked.

Olivia cocked her head at the question. What was she really asking?

Whistler gave her a look. "An open-ended family reunion on Earth, and Aleksi's not joining you? Come on." She gave Olivia a friendly poke in the shoulder. "Feel free to tell me to butt out, but you can't blame me for thinking there's something else going on."

"It's nothing like that."

Whistler pursed her lips and waited for a proper response.

DAY 14

(four days earlier)

After bidding farewell to Ioor and Quv—the *capital-R Restricted* part of the trip had concluded—Tanzig and Pola walked Olivia down to the entrance level, where an indoor fountain cast undulating reflections across the walls and ceiling. It was nice to see the sky again after spending the better part of the day in a dimmed office.

"So what happens next?" Olivia asked.

"What happens next is you go home and prepare," said Tanzig.

She smiled. "Get my affairs in order, in other words?"

"Well, yes, but no one's dying."

"Oh, before we leave . . . any chance I can see the artifact the teelise presented to you last week?"

The request appeared to take them both by surprise.

"Seeing as that was actually a big part of the reason I agreed to join the mission," Olivia explained.

"We wish we could," said Tanzig. "Unfortunately, I'm pretty sure it's in quarantine at the moment."

"Ah." That made sense. Would they do the same with her when she returned from the trip?

Tanzig led them outside to the Capitol Plaza, a grand avenue bordered by government buildings. Each facade presented a section of the polity's Social Charter in words taller than she was. The wave of nostalgia took Olivia by surprise.

"We'll need you to be ready to go in about a week," Pola said, "depending on a few things we're still working out. We'll send you all the details, but expect three days' advance notice."

"We have a private berth at Port 270," said Tanzig. "You and your— Max, will meet at the Accolla Sphere, since he'll be coming from the General Polity Orbital."

"Shouldn't it be the Teelise Sphere now?"

"What?" The GP officer's eyes brightened. "Yes, I suppose you're right."

"We'll have a small team to meet you both there," Pola said, already edging away. "They've been working with the teelise and will be able to answer any remaining questions you have."

———

DAY 18

Olivia had met Whistler eight years ago, after she'd moved to the Piosey canton to be with Aleksi. Whistler was the closest thing to a sister she had, and feeding her a cover story now felt like an unforced betrayal. She would beg forgiveness afterward—there would be no shortage of apologies to dole out—but right now there was no getting around it.

"I'm thinking of this reunion as something of a personal retreat," she said, which was close enough to the truth. "Aleksi's storyguide project is his life's work. It's *the thing* for him, you know? And I don't have that. And don't say anything about the poetry."

"I wasn't."

The wind whipped up over the side and tousled her hair. She brushed it aside. "If Aleksi came with me, our dynamic would become the focus, at least part of the time. My aim is to remind myself who I am outside of our little union. It sounds like I'm talking about a separation, but I'm not. I want to recalibrate, but . . . I can't think of one song when I'm listening to another one. I don't know if I'm making any sense."

"Of course. A relationship isn't just about the relationship. Sometimes you have to get outside to look in."

Way outside, in this case. But wrapped up in this fib was a kernel of truth, one that Olivia never would have articulated for her Sovereign Alliance handlers. She'd barely thought it through for herself.

"My joints hurt," she said, looking back out over the yawning ravine to the distant peaks. "Not just right now, I mean in general. And I'm used to the pain, but I feel it more when I'm not engaged. When things are *too* quiet, it's like a signal that only I can hear, and it tells me that not everything is as it should be." She found her friend's eyes, and saw all the understanding she needed there. She wasn't talking about her relationship anymore. "While I still have the energy, I want to find a way to apply myself to this part of my life that's just mine. Does that sound selfish?"

"Only in the best sense of the word." Whistler leaned over and gave her a hug. "But if *I* can be selfish for a second: I'm sad that we're going to miss your big four-oh."

It took Olivia a moment to figure out what she was talking about. "I completely forgot." But Whistler was right: unless Olivia's departure got pushed for some reason, she'd be observing her birthday—or not observing it—alone this year.

Or at least very far away.

SEVEN
DAY 22

OLIVIA HAD SEEN no sign of the teelise yet, but the alien shuttle's accommodations were reasonably human-shaped, and even easy on her joints. She figured this interior must be little more than a set piece, like an extravagant prop from one of Aleksi's productions. But if this was a show, she was only the co-star.

She glanced across the aisle at Maksym Mehdipour. Her father. He looked older than the old photos her mother had kept, if not exactly frail. His suit was somewhat ill-fitting; either he was too large or his apparel was too snug. Would she have given him another glance in a crowd? No. Whatever their connection, the man was a stranger to her.

"What do you want me to say?"

Olivia tensed. "What?"

His eyes were impassive. "You're staring, like you're waiting for me to say something."

The years had softened whatever accent he'd had to the barest inflection, but even if she didn't exactly remember his voice, his dismissive tone felt somehow familiar.

"I was wondering who you are," she said.

"Oh, listen to her. Is that for one of your poems?"

She didn't dare to let on how his knowledge of her writing surprised her. Less surprising was that he didn't know she'd quit. Then again, poetry, after a fashion, was the reason she'd decided to come.

"Sorry," she said, and looked out her window, which might as well have been a black-painted disc. In its reflection she saw him looking over at her still.

"I'd prefer it if we could stay on task," he said, his voice a notch quieter.

"Sorry?"

"I'm here for one reason, and I intend to stay focused on the matter at hand. We don't need to figure each other out, or—" He stopped himself and shook his head. "They didn't even . . ."

"I'm not going to get in your way or anything."

He waved her assurance away. "The teelise asked for *one* representative. They could have picked anyone in the room, but they picked me. Now, for some reason, you're here. It's . . . not appropriate. And I don't mean that disparagingly."

"I didn't take it that way."

He pursed his lips, as if assessing how much energy he had for this conversation. "If we keep our eyes facing forward, not looking back, we can get to Beringia and back without . . . rehashing unrelated events."

"Farthest thing from my mind."

Was that resentment she'd heard in his voice, or fear? Either one seemed misplaced. She had half a mind to probe him on the matter until he was annoyed enough to move. She had nothing to lose. On the other hand, he was right: they weren't here to rake over old coals.

At least he'd confirmed that she hadn't missed out on anything for three-and-a-half decades.

———

Max and Olivia debarked from the shuttle unaccompanied—he with his duffel bag and she with her rolling suitcase—and made their way into a cavernous reception area.

While the main concourse and its support structure were conventionally rectilinear, once you looked beyond the immediate reception area—if that's what this was—there were no proper walls or floors at all. The surfaces there ran together, twisted upward like electrical arcs caught in architecture, and formed a kind of sinewy cavern made of luminescent yellow resin. Was this a glimpse of the environment they'd find on the other side of the spring?

Stranger still were the two figures waiting for them at the center of the floor: two of the teelise. It wasn't until they moved that the reality of them struck Olivia—living beings from another world, right here.

From another *universe*.

If that was possible, anything must be possible. But could such a foreign species really relate to humans? On *any* level? Humans relating to other humans was often challenge enough. Then again, they were all physical beings, with senses and thoughts and, presumably, desires, so there must be some basis for understanding.

"Welcome," said the one on the left as Max and Olivia approached.

"You are Maksym Mehdipour," said the other, in Standard Heliopolitan Interlish. Where were the words coming from? Its speech had been generated by no detectable anatomical movements.

Max only nodded, too wrapped up in the spectacle, perhaps, to vocalize at all. Could the teelise read nonverbal cues?

Olivia responded for him. "This is Max." Unsure where to focus, she settled on the ring of black eyelets around the figures' crowns.

Still without moving, the same teelise said, "And you are Olivia Jelani."

Starstruck. That explained the beguiled, vaguely intoxicated swirl in her head. An alien had said her name.

"Yes, that's right."

With a delicate limb, that teelise motioned toward a circular exit at the far side of the bay, an easy enough gesture to interpret. The four of them walked as a group, with the two teelise leading them on ribbon-like legs that made Olivia think of articulated pasta strands. It was hard to avoid staring, let alone to avoid being *caught* staring, given that the teelise eyelets circled their heads entirely.

Olivia forced herself to look away by directing her eyes to the edges of their platform and beyond, to the yellow, taffy-like fibrils, contorted into baroque fractals, that formed the mysterious skin of the interior structure. By contrast, the modest facade that the teelise had laid out for their human guests seemed an indulgence—a lie. Olivia had the sudden urge to stumble off the flat walkway, to lay her hands on that strange material. Was it warm to the touch? Was it solid?

". . . let me know if it doesn't," one of the teelise was saying.

They'd been talking, and she'd been a million miles away. Had she missed something?

"Yes, of course," Max said. "Thank you."

Olivia scolded herself. Two minutes on an alien ship and her mind was already adrift.

"You are the parent of you," the other teelise said, in a matter-of-fact tone.

Yes, the whole reason she was here at all: that unbreakable familial bond.

"Olivia is my child," Max said, admitting to them what he'd dare not say to Olivia.

"When do we get to Beringia?" she asked, urging the conversation away from that topic. Would they understand what she meant? She'd been informed at her briefing that the teelise didn't use proper names, but they had to have ways to refer to things that weren't immediate or in the present.

"First there are the procedures to observe," said the teelise on the right. "I require you for this before you are in Beringia."

"Okay," she said, not knowing what else to say. "Thank you."

"Given the time required for preparation," the other teelise added, "I am providing you with rooms. This is where we go now."

———

The interior of the Teelise Sphere—or at least what Olivia had seen of it on the short walk to their accommodations—was divided into smaller sections in the manner of an orange. Translucent membranes anchored by fibrous support struts provided an overall framework upon which habitable constructs were huddled, somewhat like grand hives.

Olivia's room was located within a multi-unit complex that looked more grown than constructed. But despite the murmur of foreign mechanisms, and the vague sweet perfume of the air, the interior of her assigned space was so conventional in appearance—so *human*—as to seem comically out of place. It featured a fully interactive beachside view, complete with sun, surf, and palms swaying lazily to some simulated breeze. With its tasteful, vaguely Scandinavian appointments, the room looked like it had been plucked from an interior design exhibit.

She was relieved that the teelise hadn't expected the two guests to room together. Their escorts had advised that she and Max be rested for the commencement of their preparations tomorrow, and then left them to their own devices.

It wasn't until Olivia stood over her open suitcase that the homesickness washed over her. If she could only talk to Ran once more before she left, she could tell him she was sorry. Her stance on the Seconds wasn't really about him, was it? And regardless of whether he was really himself anymore—if that was something anyone could truly know—that wasn't something she should take out on him. She wasn't cruel. She shouldn't have let loose on him like that.

As for Aleksi, she had to believe he would be okay without her for a while. Perhaps this really was exactly what they needed, to help bring clarity about their path forward. But what did it say about her that she needed to leave the entire galaxy to get some perspective?

Sitting on the edge of her bed, she took a deep breath. What had she gotten herself into? What if she died light years away from any human, save the one she wanted least to be around? Would this venture have been worth it?

She let herself fall back into the plush blanket and forced herself to rest. For the moment, this was no different from any foreign hotel. The only thing missing, really, was a pool.

EIGHT
DAY 23

OLIVIA SHOWERED and dressed after sleeping for an unknown period of time. The illusion that she was on vacation extended no farther than her synthetic beach view. Beyond her door were no pastoral sounds of families, no wafting smells of breakfast. But that was fine. Immersion was the best way to acclimate. In fact, the sooner they left the Milky Way for Maffei 1, the better.

There had been no signs of the teelise since they'd led her to her room, but the communications bay in her room had a message for her and Max from the head of mission, rendered in static text:

```
Max and Olivia, we hope your trip to the
Accolla Sphere was comfortable, and that your
accommodations are to your liking. Having
worked with the teelise for several months, we
are confident that your hosts can see to all
your needs.

Tomorrow we and the teelise team there will
hold a joint briefing to supply you with some
additional details of your mission. Until then,
take some time to get your bearings, and rest
```

up. And I just want to say, have patience with
yourselves as you face each new challenge. The
rewards, have no doubt, will be immeasurable.

Beneath the text was an unfamiliar insignia: a gold-and-blue oval with
the words "Sovereign Alliance" along the top and "Empyrean Symbiotry"
rounding the bottom. Between them were the stylized swirls of two
galaxies bonded together by threads of light.

Olivia's stomach protested. "What time is it?"

"Just after seven by Piosey-standard reckoning," came the ever-
familiar voice of the local ambiont. She'd asked without even considering
that there might not be an ambient intelligence present, but they—the
teelise or the SA—seemed to have anticipated everything.

"Max, you there?"

A moment of silence.

"He's not responding," the ambiont said.

"Is he in his room?"

"Sorry, I don't know."

It would have been nice to sync up with the man early, before their
briefings. But breakfast—she assumed it would be provided—would
probably be improved without him sitting across from her.

"Uh, is there a breakfast service?"

"One moment while I find your hosts."

Olivia slipped on her shoes. She'd go for a walk, then get something
to eat before she was set upon.

"Olivia," came the voice of a teelise, "you inquire about your food?"

"Yes."

"I bring it to your room soon. Is that fine?"

Sure, she could eat in. But first she'd get her walk, and maybe find a
way to get off the beaten path.

———

Max didn't answer his door, and if there was a system that could provide
information about his whereabouts, Olivia didn't have access to it.

So, fine.

She followed the main passage of the habitation construct, heading away from the front entrance to see how far the human habitat went. Not far, as it turned out. The passage led to a rear portal open to the relative grandeur of the sphere's open interior—which was as close to "outside" as the sphere allowed—and the path continued from there into a neighboring complex that was identical to hers in every way, at least superficially. The passage she followed offered no windows, no framed pictures, no plants or vents. Which made it all the more surprising when . . .

She stopped, cocking her head for a better listen.

Voices.

Somewhere nearby, though she could make out none of the words. Was it Interlish? Were the voices even human?

Her curiosity piqued, she followed the self-illuminated hall until she reached a featureless, teelise-height inset panel. A door. Someone— multiple someones by the sound of it—were just beyond that door, though the conversation taking place within was still too muffled to decipher. Placing her hands on the frame, Olivia gingerly put her ear to the surface, straining to make out the words.

The door slid aside so suddenly that she nearly fell forward. The man standing on the other side seemed as surprised to see her as she was to see him. He spun to face her and took a step back. What a face. He wasn't just unfamiliar to her, there was something . . . *off* about his face. Nothing lined up quite right.

"Um, hi," she said, her eyes flicking past him to the room beyond.

Without responding, he pulled the door shut in her face. Not quickly enough though. She had seen Max, seated at a table with several others— humans, if her fleeting glimpse could be trusted. Had they started the briefings without her?

"Hello?" Olivia tapped at the door. Why hadn't she been woken up earlier? "Am I late for something?"

Inside she heard nothing. The voices had gone silent. Did they think she'd just lose interest and wander away?

She was about to knock a second time when the door pulled aside just wide enough for Max to pass through.

"What's going on?" she asked.

But he hurried right past her, and she had to jog to catch up with him, wincing in pain as her knees cracked.

"Max, what the hell?"

A moth device flitted through the air just above his right shoulder. Such mobile attendants were not uncommon, especially among those for whom an ambiont would be ill-suited, either for environmental or privacy reasons. But this specimen was unlike any she'd seen before. It resembled a small squid more than a simple drone.

"Hey, Max? Are you going to wait up?"

He didn't slow.

"What was that about?"

"Nothing."

She'd been more curious than suspicious, at least until she'd seen the look on his face. Whatever was up with that covert meeting, it wasn't *nothing*. And now they were almost back to their rooms.

"Max, I'm a member of this team too."

Finally he stopped.

"You have no idea what you're talking about."

Where was this coming from? She'd done nothing to merit this animus. "Look, if this is some sort of Integrity Polity thing to—"

"Can you *please*—" He rubbed his eyes. "Just give me some breathing room, okay, Olivia?" More than exasperated, the man was exhausted. No, he was shaken. Even more reason why he needed to communicate. Wasn't that why he was here, after all?

"No, not until—"

But he was off again, passing his room and continuing toward the shuttle bay. Where the hell was he going?

Olivia caught up with him again and grabbed his sleeve. But something in her hand gave, the bones issuing a meaty *pop*. She yelped and winced in pain as she shook her hand. "Damn it!"

That, finally, got his attention. "What's wrong with your hand?"

"Bad genetics I guess," she said, massaging the meat of her index finger. "Same old story." He looked more wary than sympathetic. "Are you afraid of something? Because if so, I need to know why. Who were those people?"

He actually checked to make sure the coast was clear, as if the sphere police might emerge from the folds of the outer enclosure. "The teelise aren't who we thought they were."

The hairs across Olivia's neck prickled. "This is what you were talking about in there?"

"They're going to do something to us."

Where was this coming from? "You're talking nonsense."

"We'll see," he said, and stormed off.

She'd lost the energy to pursue him farther. He might as well have punched her in the gut.

Or . . .

Maybe that was precisely what this was about. Maybe the Integrity Polity really did want to have the only seat at the table, and this strange outburst was nothing more than an attempt to scare her off. Olivia cursed herself for feeling any loyalty toward the General Polity. They had assumed that she would comport herself as a patriot, and now she was thinking like them.

Whatever Max was doing, she wasn't going to allow herself to get tied up in his ego trip. If he wanted to run around hatching conspiracy theories, let him.

She returned to her room, where a food tray was waiting for her on the table by the door, as the teelise had promised. Fruit salad, eggs, and toast. The smell was jarringly familiar, making it even more difficult to square what Max said.

Not who we thought they were.

Do something to us.

She pulled out the chair and sat. On a full stomach, the words would carry far less weight. They'd only just met the teelise, so who else did Max expect them to be? As for their nefarious plans . . . if getting shoved through a wormhole wasn't already exotic enough, nothing was.

NINE
DAY 23

OLIVIA WALKED beside one of the teelise, close enough that she imagined she could feel its warmth. Her personal escort had shown up just as she'd finished eating. Seeing the alien standing at her door had somehow made today's proceedings real, and now she squeezed her hands tight to hide the tremor.

Rumor has it you're going to do something to us.

Fuck Max for putting that idea in her head, for weaponizing his own self-doubts.

She distracted herself with the exotic environs. Much of the sphere's interior was open air, though it was difficult for her to gauge how vast the space was without familiar structures against which to assess scale. Not to mention the gloomy lighting, which gave everything an indistinct, dreamy quality.

"Is it different from what you imagine?"

She looked up at the teelise's eyelet ring. "I honestly don't know. I'm having trouble convincing myself that any of this is real." Was that something the teelise could relate to? Maybe they should stick to particulars over perceptions. "You came here twenty-eight years ago—to our Solar System, I mean. A long time."

"Yes, I am busy."

An explanation, not a dismissal, if the tone of its voice was reliable.

"Busy . . . waiting?" She'd wanted to say "watching," but couldn't quite work up the nerve.

"I learn about you, as much as possible."

"You mean, you wanted to familiarize yourself with humans before inviting us to meet the other races?"

"Yes."

"So you've done this before? You, personally?"

"I meet many people from many places," said the teelise, never breaking its pace or veering from the path. "This is my role."

"Well I'm new to this."

"First contact is always the same, because it is always different."

Was that a play on words? She smiled, but of course that would be lost on the alien, wouldn't it? The teelise's orange-brown skin flexed and folded as they walked. Were there smiles of its own hidden in there, or other non-verbal expressions? If so, it was all a foreign language to her.

"That's funny," she said, just in case. "So how many times have you done this? Introduced a new race to those on the other side . . . ?"

"There are eight member races. I am involved with every transfer, from the beginning. I help the remotes. I am told that is your preferred term."

"Is that okay?"

"It's practical."

"What do they call themselves?"

"They don't assign self-titles as humans do. But a 'natal' is someone born to the home domain."

She nodded. *Natal* as a generic term meaning "born one." Maybe like *human* came from the Latin word for earth or ground. Or *aboriginal*, which meant "from the beginning."

"But though there are no self-titles," the teelise continued, "there are unique signatures that may become accessible to you."

What does that mean? Olivia's first thought was of the gift that the teelise had presented to the GP High Council, the sculpture that seemed to be made from a cloud of glyphs. Perhaps their approach to language was as foreign as their interior decor.

As they made their way toward parts unknown, Olivia watched the strange interplay of light over the walls and wished that the spectacle of it could distract her from the throbbing in her joints. She'd walked too far. Or maybe it was something about being here that had made everything flare up. The stress of it, perhaps, no thanks to Max. Talking with the teelise had helped, but Max's words were still bouncing around in her head. He seemed even more out of place here than she did. Why send *him* on a diplomatic mission? He didn't have the right disposition—he lacked so-called *soft skills*, as he'd just demonstrated in rather dramatic fashion. He'd looked like he was coming undone.

"I am ready to meet with you both," the teelise said as they approached a rounded complex that looked like it had bubbled up from beneath the surface.

Just ahead were Max—his moth was buzzing about silently overhead—and another of the teelise. How long had they been waiting? Hopefully long enough for Max's escort to talk some sense into him.

Max watched Olivia approach with dull eyes, but he said not a word to her.

"Lead the way," Olivia said, gesturing toward the entrance.

———

"Wait. No one told me about this," Olivia said.

She and Max sat across from seven of the teelise, all of them identical to her eye. At the center of the chamber was the projection of Quv Vidalin, the SA head of mission, presumably casting in from the relative comfort of a well-lit office on Heliopolis.

It was all a little too much like an intervention.

There was no getting comfortable now. Her body was preemptively responding to what the panel had just proposed to them. She hoped she'd misunderstood. She feared she hadn't.

"I know it's a lot to take in at first, Olivia," Quv said. "But the plain fact is that no living material can pass through the springs except for the remotes. And that's because the springs are tuned, essentially, to their physiology."

Olivia looked over at Max, but he appeared to be staring out into space. No help there.

"So they're inherently flawed," she said. She looked at the teelise. "What about them? How did they get here?"

"I am engineered by the remotes to bypass this limitation," one of the teelise responded.

"Engineered?" Olivia shifted in her chair. "As in . . . you're constructed?"

"Yes."

"So you're not biological?"

"I am a dedicated appliance produced of many components."

That had to be an unfortunate mistranslation. And it didn't address the reason they were talking about this to begin with.

"Look, I'm not trying to be difficult," she said. "But what's so special about the remotes that only they can pass through the springs? If the remotes crawled up out of the muck like humans did, their makeup can't be all *that* different."

"They are pure," said another of the teelise. Another unfortunate mistranslation?

"Because of the essential nature of the springs," said another, "any significant deviation from the standard configuration is lost to the singularity."

Olivia blinked. They had an explanation for everything, not that the explanations made any sense, and it was all geared to rationalize what they'd proposed. She had to be dreaming all of this. Right? If she waited long enough, surely it would go away and she would wake up back on Vaix.

"Olivia, Max," said Quv, "I think it might help to have something to look at, so let me show you what the solution entails."

The solution.

Olivia already liked her solution more, which was to cast to the intro ceremony from the comfort of her room. Because that didn't call for—

Before Quv's image, a new projection appeared, an animal of some sort rotating in space, walking in a looped cycle as if on a turntable. It was like something that had emerged from the depths of Earth's oceans, a lifeform the likes of which Olivia had never seen. It was hexapodal, with its four hindmost legs on the ground and the two front ones held close to its chest, mantis-like. The four frontmost legs each had long tapered fingers, like those of a bat, only without the webbed membrane, but the fingers coiled back around the forearms, leaving each wrist like a hoof capable of taking the creature's full weight as it walked. And its head . . .

Olivia had to peer closely to figure out what she was looking at. The head—it was also somewhat mantis-like—featured two rows of eyes positioned evenly around the dome of its skull. Below, its face terminated in a six-lobed star of a mouth.

"This is them?" Olivia asked, knowing the answer before Quv responded.

"This is a remote, yes."

She remembered what he'd said during her initial briefing: *the process is physically involved.* This is what he'd meant. The SA had known about this the whole time, but had deliberately not mentioned it until the eleventh hour.

And what about Max? Had he known? Was this what he'd been hinting about earlier? Was this communicated to him in the clandestine meeting she'd seen him leaving?

"No," Olivia said. "Something like this . . . it's not, it's *not* something you can ask of us."

"Olivia, the procedure isn't permanent."

"*Procedure!* How do I know that? How do *you* know that?"

"It's . . . listen, you wouldn't go into the cold without a coat, would you? You wouldn't send an astronaut into space without a suit."

"You're talking about *apparel,* Quv." Her fingers were balled so tight that her fingernails were digging into her palms. She forced her hands to relax. "It's not the same thing. You just proposed plopping our minds into alien bodies, so we can visit with them on their own turf."

"What about your brother?"

Where had that come from? "What does Ran have to do with anything?"

"He's a Seconder, isn't he?"

"So?"

"So, isn't the principle similar? Wasn't he essentially taken from his body and migrated to a versatile repository?"

"Yes, but to a *human*—"

"And what we're talking about here is a slightly more advanced form of substrate independence."

Right. Which was why they'd divulged not a peep of this until now. Olivia massaged the bones of her hand, which only made her other hand hurt. In fact she hurt all over.

She stared at the image of the multi-legged lifeform in front of her and imagined massaging *those* fingers. She tried to picture herself *as* one of those things, some entirely alien form.

It wasn't possible.

"If you know me," she said, "you know I had my omni removed. Because this, right here, is me." She tapped her chest. Without that cranial black box, there was no chance she could be seconded the way Ran had been. She had no backup. "For better or worse, this is the only me there will ever be. If you take that away—"

"We're not taking this lightly, Olivia." But Quv wasn't breaking a sweat either. He was as composed as someone discussing the change of seasons. "When the teelise first told us about this limiting property of the springs, of course we were as hesitant as you are. But you have to keep one thing in mind: the teelise—the team in this room, and the generations before them—have been at this process for *millennia*." He paused, as if to allow that to sink in. "Think about that. Think about where *we* were a thousand years ago."

At this point Olivia could barely conceive of where she'd be tomorrow, let alone what humanity was up to a thousand years ago.

"Please. At least let them explain it to you first. Let them tell you what they told us."

Olivia stared. Was any part of her actually entertaining this?

"My method is reliable," said the teelise on the end, or maybe the one next to that one. It was difficult to tell who was speaking, given they didn't move at all. It didn't help that they always spoke about themselves in the singular. "I guide your centers of being into an analog frame," it continued, "and there you remain, in your sanctified form, for the duration of your stay. After you return here we reverse the process."

"Centers of *being*, is that what you said?"

"Until the transfer is complete, yes."

"And our bodies?"

"I need only your mind."

"Your body is held in suspension," said a different teelise. Maybe they had different specialties. One for the body, another for the mind. "Even now the frame is waiting."

The frame. The words gave Olivia a chill.

She looked over at Max again, who was inappropriately silent. He was a cipher. "What do you think about this, Max?" She gave his shoulder a gentle shake. "Seem pretty straightforward to you?"

He was nodding his head in a way that told her exactly nothing, but kept his mouth shut. If this was acceptance, it was anything but reassuring.

The teelise were silent as well, waiting for her to respond. A group of teelise, she decided, should be called an "arrangement." Because wherever they were positioned, they appeared to have been placed there.

"How do we know this would even work?" she asked.

Quv visibly relaxed in his chair. He'd heard something in her voice—and so had she. She was considering it. She was actually considering allowing an unknown alien species to pluck her from the ruins of her own body and essentially "second" her into a body that was utterly foreign to everything she'd ever known.

"Human biology is compatible with the transfer rite," a teelise answered. "Though you would be the first members of your species to participate, many before you share your basic biological structures."

Olivia winced as a lance of pain shot up her spine. She'd been too tense for too long, and her bones had settled into that tension. If she didn't know any better she'd think her body was trying to tell her something.

"And this is all okay with the Sovereign Alliance?" she asked the head of mission. "Two of our own, turned into aliens?"

"These are novel circumstances, granted." Olivia stifled a laugh of disbelief. "Extreme, even," he continued. "But Olivia, every day we ask people to face risks—bigger risks than this—when it stands to benefit a greater cause."

She could practically hear his anthemic musical accompaniment, he sounded so SA.

"An introduction between two peoples is a heralded occasion," the teelise said, as if reading from the same script. Tag team. "This process is my purpose."

"I am a bioengineer for four hundred seventy of your years," said another.

Four hundred seventy years? She was a child. She might as well be talking to gods. The biggest challenge for them wasn't the procedure; it was convincing these two backwards hicks that they weren't going to graft her head onto the body of a monkey.

Was it really as easy as they suggested? Just agree to take a vacation from the torments of her human frame? And then . . . come back again?

"I hope you'll see how much good can come from this," Quv said. "Think about it: you'll be the first human to visit another galaxy, and history will show that. And you'll definitely not be the last."

Olivia could almost imagine going through with the process, if only to spite her traitorous body. But she couldn't escape one thought: Would the person who returned still be *her*?

Perhaps reading her silence as hesitation, Quv cleared his throat. "What else can we tell you, Olivia?"

She could believe anything at this point. "I think I need to close my eyes for a while."

"Of course. I understand. Is there anything else you need?"

She was about to answer no, but then stopped. "Would it be possible for me to send someone a message?"

Now there was a hesitation, if brief. "You are aware of the restrictions."

They'd made that clear during the initial briefing. But that was before she'd been told what this trip entailed. "It's my dad—Nils Rocklin. I assume I can't tell him anything we've discussed today."

Quv took a breath. "Eventually this will be common knowledge, and that will be thanks, in part, to you. But for now, I'm afraid this is privileged information."

Olivia nodded. "I just want him to know I made it here okay. I won't mention anything beyond that."

"We'll arrange an open channel for you. But for now, we would all appreciate it if you would please think through the proposal on the table."

Olivia waited out front for Max to emerge from the facility. Minutes passed, and she found herself averting her eyes each time a teelise made its way by her. As far as she was concerned, they were all in on this.

When Max shuffled out onto the walkway as if he were going on his afternoon constitutional, taking his moth along for company, she stepped into his path.

"What the hell was that about?" she asked.

He stepped around her, and the moth buzzed by her ear. If it came any closer she could take a swing at it.

She followed him. "Seriously, Max, what's going on with you? They drop a bomb like that on us and you're a thousand miles away. Is there something more pressing?"

Was that a shrug? Was he even hearing her?

"Max, look at me."

"I don't answer to you," he said at last.

"No, but I'm starting to get worried. I'm part of this—"

"For better or for worse." He stopped to face her. "Look, this is how it's done."

"Meaning what?"

"It's called diplomacy."

"You did hear what they're proposing, right? Were you around for that part?" She didn't like feeling that she was alone in this. She didn't like this strange passivity. He needed to say something, one way or the other.

"The teelise explained why it has to be this way, and how it works," he said. "If you need a hug because it's scary and different, I'm sorry I can't help you."

Olivia bristled. "I hardly think an emotional response is unwarranted."

"This is unprecedented, Olivia. That's kind of the point. You can't enter into something truly novel and not expect to have your assumptions challenged. You can't expect another culture to bend."

"Not even if they're talking about turning us into . . . something else?

And what's with this moth tailing you everywhere?" She was throwing everything she had at him now. "Is that an Integrity Polity thing?"

He shook his head, then continued down the walkway. "Sorry, I'm not interested in indulging your dramas."

She let him go. He was incapable of relating on a human level. Maybe that was why he was perfect for this mission after all.

———

A teelise—perhaps the same one who'd escorted her earlier—led Olivia to an open-air rotunda at the nexus of several exposed walkways. It had stopped by her room shortly after the briefing, and she'd been happy for the interruption. The afternoon bombshell had left her of two minds, and she'd found herself vacillating between existential dread at the prospect of losing herself and a profound desire to cast off her aching flesh.

Indecision would provide her no sanctuary.

The communications bay had been set up beneath a domed crystalline structure that offered no privacy. Olivia weighed whether she should request a more concealed location, but it wasn't worth pushing her luck. She thanked her escort as she took a seat, hoping the teelise would understand that as a dismissal. It apparently did, and she waited for it to move away before she turned her attention to the panel.

The rig was clearly human-made. The stylized "VC" Vearncombe logo in the lower right looked as alien as anything in this environment. The interface itself was about as pared back as anything she'd seen since primary school: just a flat panel with a tactile control strip.

"Message to Nils Rocklin," she said, curious to see what would happen.

On the panel a single open entry appeared—simple text in a minimalist form—already addressed to Quv Vidalin. There was no affordance to change it. The message to Olivia was clear: say nothing to outsiders that you wouldn't say to the SA head of mission.

"What time is it in Montpellier?" she asked the interface, and a message appeared on the screen:

The transfer time from the Teelise Sphere, assuming the message wasn't bounced to any backwater relays, would take about four-and-a-half minutes. But there was no telling how long Quv and team would take to comb her communiqué for security violations.

So be it. She'd take what she could get.

She examined the panel's control strip more closely, but the available actions appeared to be limited to accessibility and cosmetic settings. "Um, can I get an image?" she said.

"Sorry, this terminal has no video," the ambiont explained.

"So words only."

"Communications will be sent as text."

Text.

Okay, they really weren't taking any chances. What was she allowed to say? Aleksi and Ran had both been briefed that she would travel through the spring to the remote system in the Maffei 1 galaxy, but her father didn't even know that much—and *none* of them knew about this scheme to transfer her mind into another body. She would have to talk around it all, sticking to generalities.

It would have been easier to think if she had more privacy. But she cleared her throat and started her session.

"Hey, Dad. I know Ran told you, and it'll be on the feeds soon enough. But I wanted you to hear it from me: I'm in the Accolla Sphere now." The last time they'd spoken, he and his NGO, World One, had been overseeing the distribution of food and resources to a group of people who had ended a skirmish with . . . another group of people. It was in Hungary, she remembered that much. She searched her mind for the details, but nothing more surfaced. That had been over a year ago. "Sorry I've been so quiet lately. But I'm okay, and everything is going . . . well, to plan." Whose plan was another matter. "And now that I'm sitting here my mind is . . ." She laughed. "I feel like I've been running in high gear."

Olivia stared at her words. Not a bad start, even if she still had a better idea of what she couldn't say than what she wanted to say.

"I'm babbling. I'm glad you can't hear all my pauses. I do think about you, more than you think. I hope things are good for you there. More *normal* at least."

She pictured him somewhere in the south of France, sunburned, with dirt under his fingernails. Much of his advocacy centered around raising awareness of ongoing human rights issues on Earth, which he'd said was a particular challenge for those who didn't live on the planet. People could only focus on a handful of things at a time, and usually only if they were happening in the same room. All this teelise business couldn't be helping.

"Anyway, I may as well paint you a picture, since I'm here. They dressed up the interior of the sphere for us—the teelise did—I guess to make it feel less outlandishly different. And it's a thoughtful touch. It's stagecraft though. There's a certain superficial *placeness* to our quarters, but you can't hide the artifice. It feels like I've entered a mirage. Maybe, in a way, the forced familiarity is more disconcerting than immersion would have been. Or maybe I'm too on my guard.

"As for the pain, I'd hoped it might taper off so I could focus. But instead it's been like a stowaway who came along for the ride. Even now, sitting here, it's my skin. Maybe it's trying to tell me I've really overstepped my bounds this time." A warmth rose in her cheeks. "But I think it's having the opposite effect. There's a part of me that says . . . *fuck* it. You know? What would it feel like to look forward to something that I'm ill-equipped to take on? That's the question. And if I think of it that way, for a second . . . suddenly I *am* looking forward to it."

He would think she was talking about being on the sphere, which was fine. Eventually she'd tell him everything. For now, maybe it was enough to hear herself say it out loud, to see if it held together. Hopefully it didn't sound like a confession.

"This could be my only chance, Dad. Not just because this is a once-in-a-lifetime kind of thing, but because . . . I'm turning forty *tomorrow*. I may not be the ideal player in this game, but I can still try. It's not too late for me. Not yet."

The thought of going back home was suddenly suffocating. When had that happened? Maybe she was already changing. This Olivia had to see what was on the other side of the spring—whatever the risks. And that decision was hers to make. That was the truth of it. Hadn't Aleksi basically said the same thing? No matter the outcome, all of this would be hers alone.

Maybe it was the intoxicating effect of her decision that cast any doubt from her mind.

"Yeah, I want this." She nodded. "I want it. Let's go."

She stared at her words on the screen. Good enough. There was nothing more to say anyway.

"I'm going now," she said, and sat up straight, gritting her teeth as her backbone issued a series of soft reports. "Okay, Dad." Miss you? Love you? "I'm thinking of you."

TEN

DAY 24

AS SHE PUSHED TOWARD WAKEFULNESS, the shape of Olivia's first poem in years was already receding into loose and fleeting impressions, the feeling of fresh discovery fading into loss. She reached for the words, but found only the vaguest notion of . . . desire?

Her eyes opened to the glare of the artificial sun coming through her window. How long had it been since she'd dreamed in poetry? Years of technical creativity—if that was a thing—had long ago killed off what remained of her muse. This had been different though. Or at least it had *felt* different. Dreams could lie. Had her composition been an illusion? More stagecraft, meant to evoke the feeling of creation, but without any real substance?

A movement at the other side of her room made Olivia sit bolt upright.

Two teelise, standing silently by her door. Waiting for her.

It was happening, today. A new start. And maybe a kind of ending.

"It's time?" she asked them. Adrenaline coursed through her system. She wouldn't be ready. No one could be prepared for something like this. It didn't feel real. But on the table they'd laid out a tunic of some kind for her—yellow and plain—and the reality of her circumstances was suddenly inevitable.

"When you are ready."

She moved her legs around to the edge of the bed and sat there for a moment before attempting to stand. Feeling self-conscious, she got to her feet. But she managed to twist her left hip the wrong way, and she cried out as she hopped forward to catch herself.

"You are okay," said one of the teelise, who had managed to cross half the distance between them without making a sound. Was it telling or asking?

"Yes, sorry," she said. *So much for dignity.* "I never know whether this body is going to cooperate." She checked her leg. Nothing sticking out at least, only a general feeling of disjointedness—her body's final protest, perhaps, for being forsaken.

Moving to the end of the bed, she sat and grabbed her left leg brace.

"You may leave those behind," the teelise said.

The full truth of the assertion didn't dawn on her until that moment. It was time to cast off her supports. And soon, everything else.

———

After dressing, Olivia followed her chaperones to the end of the familiar corridor—the edge of the stage. Beyond, the last gesture toward human aesthetic and proportion ended, giving way to an exotic habitat she'd been catching glimpses of over the past days. She stepped out onto an open path that had a pleasant give under her weight, like a tatami mat.

Had Max already come this way? Would they all be traveling together?

Last night she'd been hoping to track him down for dinner, maybe to reassure herself that everything would be cool between them, but he had been nowhere to be found. Resigned, she'd eaten alone, taking time to savor the provisions sent from Heliopolis: an orzo salad with chickpeas and veg. As she watched the night view of her private beach she'd tried and failed to imagine what the remotes ate.

"Do you know where Max is?" she asked, favoring her right leg as they walked.

"His process will be separate from yours," said one of the teelise.

Oh. Okay. At least she wouldn't have to try to make small talk. The less talk the better. Her head was positively swimmy. Was she coming down with something? It would be just like her to come down with something before a major life event—*again*. She'd nearly thrown up on stage at the Art Next Universal Prize award ceremony and had to exit the stage with the urgency of a doctor called to emergency surgery.

The teelise led her into a well-lit chamber. Several trunk-like projections emerged from its otherwise unbroken floor, and a translucent tank was centered below the high dome above. There was a stillness here, almost an air of the sacred, but from the chamber's pale, curved walls a subsonic hum emanated, and it seemed to pass through Olivia as if she were a ghost. Maybe it was due to her groggy state, but she found the sensation more relaxing than intimidating.

One of the two teelise asked her to wait by the tank, and the other moved to the adjacent trunk. As its limb touched the trunk's surface, the projection's tip bloomed with a silent and ephemeral panel, upon which it immediately went to work.

Olivia considered the tank before her. Apparently this was where she, or her body, would undergo the *process*. The tank was waist-high, its top open, and she looked down at the gel-like padding inside. It was truly, objectively, womb-like, if antiseptic. She might even consider it welcoming. But the tranquility of this space only seemed to amplify the stabbing sensation in her hip.

"May I sit, please?"

"You may lie inside," the teelise by her side told her, extending one of its limbs toward the tank.

"Now?"

"Now is a good time."

She wobbled on her feet. This was really happening. She was about to endure some unknown procedure. Up until now it had just been a proposal, an idea. Now it was *imminent*.

A procedure that would change her life forever.

How could she possibly proceed?

"This is your transfer hull," the teelise said.

"This is how I get to Beringia?" she asked, the words so far away.

"Yes."

"Okay."

Okay.

She looked at the teelise, somehow the most familiar thing in the room. "It's just, I wasn't expecting it to be like this." What had she expected? Something less *clinical*, maybe. Maybe a wall of energy for her to walk through? A true spring, with fish? Would it have made a difference in the end? Finding the courage to make the decision was one thing, but acting on that decision required something—grit, maybe—that she didn't possess.

"You lie inside," the teelise said, "and I take care of you as you sleep."

Sleep.

"And that's it?"

"Then you're awake in Beringia, to complete your transfer rite."

"Will it hurt?" she asked. A child's question.

"There is no pain," it said.

A sweeter promise than it could know.

Don't think.

Olivia approached the tank—the *transfer hull*—and the teelise offered her a limb to hold on to for stability. A flutter in her stomach was like her body's last, desperate reaction to her imminent betrayal. Cold feet, that's what this was. Nothing more. The teelise had been at this for a thousand years. If they told her now to clap her hands and spin around, that was exactly what she should do.

Inside the tank, sitting back on the gel pads, she looked up at the alien. "I'm nervous." What could that mean to it?

"A new experience is intimidating."

"Exactly right," she said. "Thank you for understanding."

As the other teelise pulled the instrument panel beside the hull, Olivia took a deep breath. The tank was so comfortable—taking her weight and distributing the pressure evenly—that she might fall asleep before they were ready to start. She laid her head back and listened to them as they worked, and allowed her eyes to close, only for a moment. Her muscles relaxed, and the pain in her joints receded into a dull soreness.

Alone.

She was alone. But that was okay. Such was death. Death, and—

A shadow fell over her, and her eyes snapped open. The teelise standing over her was a blur.

"Today is my birthday," she blurted out. "I forgot to tell you that."

"I don't understand."

"It's the day . . ." But her eyes were already so heavy. "Never mind. I'm just . . . afraid."

"Don't be."

PART TWO
SECOND SKIN

ELEVEN
DAY 31

LIGHT.

It had been there the whole time, so faint that Olivia had missed it. Except . . . it wasn't light, exactly. She wasn't seeing it. No, it was part of the darkness, lending it form, urging her forward from a disorienting obscurity.

What is this?

The spring. That's right. The exhaustion had overtaken her, and she'd dropped off while they—the teelise—were preparing things for her trip.

Now she heard no one. Maybe they were waiting. She was no longer groggy, but a dullness seemed to have settled around her, dampening her senses. Were her eyes even open?

"Olivia Jelani."

The voice was like a spotlight in the gloom.

She was awake, but . . . stuck.

Hello?

The word never made it past her lips. Curious. Maybe her throat was dry. Her throat . . .

She couldn't feel her throat.

"Olivia."

Something was wrong with her, but she could muster nothing more than the vaguest curiosity. That was odd. She should be more concerned about the feeling of . . . not numbness, but detachment. On the other hand, at least her joints had quieted down for now.

"Please concentrate on my voice." Spoken in perfect Interlish. "And be patient."

Yes, that seemed like the rational approach. Help had surely arrived. A response of some kind seemed warranted, but in this all-consuming murk her resolve to speak could find no purchase.

"You travel through the spring to Beringia," the voice said, "and all of your focus is required as this body continues to acclimate."

Was it implying that the passage hadn't worked? Had the spring done something to her?

"Your senses and motor functions are slow to respond. Now I can help you find your way."

Why can't I . . . ?

But her thoughts remained hers alone. There were no words, no throat, no body. They had put her under for some reason—like putting a sack over someone's head before taking them to some undisclosed location. Was that it? And if so, why did she feel no sense of panic? The mere concept of alarm was something distant, removed. The only thing to do was listen. So that's what she did.

She opened herself to her surroundings. Beneath the background hum was a sustained but muffled chatter, like a conversation of whispers filtering in from another room. It didn't seem meant for her though, and she couldn't pick out any individual words from it anyway.

Then she *saw*.

The interior space around her coalesced from a scatter of misaligned images into a single, almost panoramic view of a well-appointed lab lit by a network of distorted lights. It was similar in layout to the chamber she'd been in before her nap—complete with a teelise standing at its nearby console—but . . .

Why did it look so different? The odd geometry of the room was fairly wrapped around her, as if reflected in a spherical mirror.

Hello?

She might be able to see now, but it was still no use.

"Please attempt to communicate," said the teelise, and it was followed by a whisper, almost like a call and response:

74

Attempts . . . the words . . . the first . . . words . . .

But while Olivia's body was still beyond her ability to sense it, the teelise's instruction was so confident and assured that she tried her best to respond in kind.

"Where . . ."

Was that me?

"Where is . . . this?"

Her words, but not her voice. It was as if an intermediary had stepped in to articulate them for her. And her mouth . . . she had felt movement, but nothing like her mouth. Her lack of coordination ran deep, through flesh, into muscle, into bone.

The more she sensed, the more she sensed was off.

"You can see where you are?" the teelise asked.

Followed by the whisper:

Sees . . . the first . . . the bead . . . Max . . .

The room before her was growing more distinct with each passing moment, to the point that her field of view now included not only the teelise, but a good part of what passed for the ceiling. It was a lot to take in, but focusing on a subject of interest allowed her to ignore extraneous input, like staring through the eyepiece of a telescope with both eyes open.

"I see you. I see the room."

"Very good. You sound good."

"It's . . . so much. Why is my voice—"

A flood of memories stopped Olivia cold, as if some internal gate had fallen away. Travel through the spring meant porting their minds into those aliens, those six-legged things. Had that happened already? Did that explain the disjointedness? She still felt like herself, to the extent she felt anything. That much she was sure about, at least; beneath everything else, that base truth remained.

"Please describe your state of mind."

Good question. And each response she gave seemed to lead to a flurry of activity at the teelise's console.

"Curious, mainly."

The teelise stepped away from its workstation and approached Olivia with something tabular in one of its hands. Only then did she realize that the physique of her attending teelise differed notably from the ones she'd seen before. It had six legs and a flatter, more coronal head.

"Please describe your stress level."

Right. That's what was confusing. Who wouldn't feel stress after waking up with most of their senses gone or altered? And yet . . . there was nothing immediately threatening about this situation. Just a growing list of unanswered questions.

"I'm not worried. I want to see what's happened to me."

"Yes," the teelise said, tapping something on its tablet. "I can answer your questions now, as you finalize. You are in a receiving bead in Three Twenty Belt. You are aboard a Third Case construct, the home of the Empyrean Symbiotry."

As the teelise mentioned the structure's designation, the ever-present whisper rose up and delivered a complex response in the form of static electricity across Olivia's skin:

. . . *wave-tick-wave-beat* . . .

What?

The pattern, though it had run its course in less than a second, was made up of distinct parts, like the syllables in a word. Was the teelise producing these stray words and structures, or were they endemic to this setting, like a radio signal?

Before she could ask what she was hearing, something entered the room through a doorway. It was an alien lifeform of the type Quv Vidalin had previewed for her and Max: a hexapod, with its complex head, its sinewy fingers, and . . .

Another electrical tickle played out across Olivia's skin—this one a *tick-tick*—as the new arrival froze in its tracks. Then, just as abruptly, it turned and exited the way it had come in.

"I'm on the remote side of the spring," she said to herself. And it was worth saying. Even though it was obvious, even though the voice in her ears wasn't hers, it was something she needed to hear.

"Yes, you are now in the Home system."

. . . *beat-beat-tap-thud-burst-tick-wave* . . .

The Home system evoked its own electrical signature, an accompanying murmur lighting across Olivia's nerve endings like an ever-running narrative.

"Is there a reason I can't feel anything?"

"The process must be gradual. Tell me what you do feel."

She was about to tell it *nothing*, but that wasn't quite true. Somewhere within her, the slightest trace of warmth had flickered into existence. "Oh. Yes, I think there is something." It grew stronger as she concentrated on it, seemed to radiate from its small place, ever outward. "It's spreading."

Indeed, the indistinct heat had taken form, conveying more structure with each pulse of what must be her heart. It quickened around fine anatomical structures and fanned slowly outward as it moved down and down and . . .

Olivia's attention was called to two creatures at the far end of the lab —she sensed them before she saw them, as if the electrical breeze blowing over her skin had presaged their appearance. Two of the remotes this time: six legs each, and moving toward her, like dancers, across the floor's gentle concavity.

Neither was clothed, though one of them wore a kind of utility belt.

Shoulders . . . arms . . . fingers . . .

Their overall form was spider-like, if she was pressed to say, but not like any spider she'd actually seen. Their smooth skin had a waxy appearance, with blueish and black markings that fluctuated as she watched. Like a cuttlefish, she thought. Running along the crowns of their heads were two rows of eyes, dark and expressionless, like blisters.

They were beautiful in a way, yet somehow opaque to her. Their body language was indecipherable, and she could discern no facial expressions. Yet those shifting skin patterns of theirs—as detailed as terrestrial maps and as ever-changing as clouds—must reveal some interior sentiment or intention.

As the pair stood before her—assessing her?—she watched the patterns of dark and light playing across their skin. The dynamic markings certainly weren't random. No, there was a sense to it, or so it seemed. An order. She saw now that of the remotes had a mottled appearance, a Rorschachian pattern Olivia intuited as puzzlement, whereas its companion's skin displayed a far more regular pattern, like wavelets breaking around stones. Reassurance was what Olivia saw there.

You're reaching.

She should have known better than to trust such baseless notions. If she was right though . . . was Thing Two reassuring its colleague, or her?

"Olivia?"

The quality of its voice was almost identical to hers, tonally neutral, and in flawless Interlish. The sound seemed to be emerging from beneath two delicate flaps just above the six-lobed opening she'd initially assumed was its mouth. Dedicated speakers. The articulated speech must rely solely on internal structures.

"I'm Olivia," she said in that voice that wasn't hers. *At least on the inside.* She was reasonably sure that this wasn't something they should need to have confirmed; how many other humans had come over? What about Max? Was he going through this same procedure?

The second remote spoke to the teelise. "We'll handle the rest."

The teelise retreated, and the remote stepped up to the instrument panel by Olivia's side. Had the teelise been dismissed? She hoped not. She liked those statuesque appliances with their quiet dignity.

The first remote came up to her for a closer look, and Olivia observed it back. She scrutinized its elaborate skin patterns, its dark eyelets, and the grace of its long fingers as it touched the panel before it. *Who are you?* she thought.

A confusion of electrical sensations played across her skin, as if in response:

. . . burst-tick-static-tap-pulse . . .

Had the remote read her mind, or was she experiencing some perceptual lapse?

"Sorry, I don't understand you," she said aloud.

"We said nothing."

That was true, they hadn't vocalized anything. But the subvocal message was there still, consistent, insistent:

. . . burst-tick-static-tap-pulse . . .

"There's something I'm feeling," Olivia said.

"We are transfer stewards from the outreach and external affairs body," the remote said. Its voice was nothing like the teelise's soft, almost synthesized voices. This voice was more articulated, more *wet*. It spoke using its body parts. "You may call us elders if it suits you."

Elders. Titles, not names.

Olivia looked at the other remote, and another electromagnetic tingle spiced the air, different from the one before:

. . . static-pulse-thump-burst-tap . . .

The sensation was as distinct as the first, plainly not from her imagination. The two remotes might not be articulating the strange patterns, but perhaps they were emitting them.

She was reminded of a time years ago, when she'd awoken from eye therapy to find her vision plagued by gossamer auras. The side effect had lasted for the better part of a week before eventually fading away. This constant whispering—it was closer to a persistent articulated disturbance than an actual sound—was a similar distraction, and hopefully it too would fade.

Or maybe it was just some peculiarity of the ventilation system.

"Ours is a branch of Symbiotry security that oversees the transfer rites," the remote said. "We are here on behalf of the First Seat, to see to your wellbeing until you've properly acclimated."

The details washed over Olivia. It was challenging enough just accepting that she was here, that this was happening. But despite the intimidating appearance of the aliens—*aliens*—Olivia would think of them as Elder One and Elder Two.

"We imagine this information doesn't mean much to you now, but as a courtesy we like you to understand who we are."

"It's different with this one," said the remote standing at the panel.

Its colleague joined it. "Show us?"

"Here. Nominal."

"What's that?" Olivia asked.

They spoke quietly to each other, poking at the panel and generally ignoring her. Olivia watched their skin patterns, which had synchronized somewhat into crawling terrain maps of light and dark.

"Right now we need to get you moving," said the second remote— Elder Two—with a sense of fresh urgency.

Yes, that seemed like a good idea. It hadn't struck her that she was confined until that moment, but she hadn't been able to feel her body before.

As Elder One returned to its instrument panel, Elder Two approached once more, this time close enough that Olivia could feel the warmth of its body. It used its array of thin, multi-jointed fingers to release her constraints—not physical straps but luminous restraints, six of them in total. One for each limb.

She was looking down at the body of a six-legged alien.

A remote.

She was a remote, just like the elders.

They had really done it. This was what it felt like to be one of them. She was seeing the world, right now, through the eyes of a different body . . . which might explain her expansive field of view and the amber cast across everything in sight.

Yet as alien as it all was, most extraordinary of all was her unshakable sense of calm about it.

"We need to return," Elder One said to the other.

"We'll be there soon."

The first elder departed, and the second elder returned its attentions to Olivia.

"How is this possible?" she asked it.

"This is a complex process, as you might imagine."

"Tell me everything."

"We'll tell you what you need to know."

"Whatever you can." It would have helped to be able to read Elder Two's mood.

The remote made a gesture near its console, and the body of one of its kind appeared suspended in the air between them. As she watched, its head came into a closer, isolated view, and its flesh vanished to reveal bone, then brain.

"The transfer process is arduous because it involves a full migration of the brain and its supporting systems to a portable energy map."

"A . . . copy?" The idea struck her as less than ideal.

"No. A duplication would achieve nothing. No matter the fidelity of a copy, it's only ever a copy. The only way to achieve a true transference is for there to be a gradual, unbroken migration of the centers of consciousness." A translucent yellow shield formed around the exposed organ, then contracted into a small glowing dot, until nothing of the brain remained but a ghost image. "The benefit of this process is that once the consciousness is ported, it remains portable for any future transfers."

Olivia ran the explanation through her mind. It sounded somewhat similar to omni technology, only instead of a spooling one's identity to a backup store, the remotes had transferred the entire consciousness to an independent repository.

"We imagine this is disorienting," Elder Two said, waving away the diagram. It had fished something from his utility belt, an instrument of some kind, which it now held out between them. Was it taking a reading, or offering it to her? Not that it mattered in this body: the mechanics of it were well beyond her. The numbness from earlier had gone, but in its place was a sensory flood that would require some untangling.

"I shouldn't be feeling this calm," Olivia said, ignoring the instrument. "I'm in an alien body, and I have almost no control over it."

"Inhibitors," said Elder Two, after pausing for a second to check the device, then stashing it away. "Each analog frame incorporates a number of physical and emotional inhibitors to ease the process." Analog frame? "We will deactivate those in due course. And before you ask, it's the transliteration bud that allows us to understand each other, and we've mapped several senses innate to your analog frame such that they should make more sense to you."

The feeling of immersion was an illusion after all, if a convincing one. If she focused, Olivia could hear the foreign words the remote was actually speaking, but it was easier to accept the augmented reality.

"Now we must test your motility actuators, to help your brain translate executive function into action."

"Is it difficult?" It had been difficult enough getting her own human body to cooperate, let alone a body as foreign as this.

"Not for you. Each of these assistants will adjust over time in accordance with your needs. You won't notice when they're working. If you do notice, let us know and we can call the teelise in for an audit." Elder Two appeared to be looking her over. Satisfied, it returned to its console. "Do you have questions before we continue?"

The same question that had been nagging at her from the start. "Can you tell me why this is necessary? The transference, I mean. I know the spring gateways have some inherent limitation, but wouldn't you focus on fixing that rather than going to the trouble of modifying every visitor who comes through?" Offensive or not, she couldn't help but ask.

"This is a privilege—" Elder Two began, before stopping short and issuing a subvocal double-tick that tweaked Olivia's flesh, like a *tut-tut*.

Privilege, eh? Assuming it was working correctly, the transliteration bud had conveyed disdain in the remote's words.

"This sanctified form is a requirement for all those making the pilgrimage to the Empyrean Symbiotry at Zero Pole."

It must be talking about the multispecies assembly. No shirts, no shoes, no service.

"Is that what this is? A pilgrimage?"

"That is why you are here."

"And Max? My . . . father?"

"That is why you are both here." It waited for her, but she had too many new questions to select from. "We can go over any details later, Olivia Jelani."

"Yes. Okay."

"Right now we need to get you on your points. Your body needs to be active."

Her body.

Her *alien* body.

———

Elder Two took several steps back, its four hindmost legs remaining on the floor for support as it beckoned her with its front two, thin fingers splayed. But despite its stance, it struck Olivia that the transfer steward was only passingly mantis-like, given its more mammalian appearance. Overall it seemed a rather sturdy design, even elegant. Then again, at the moment she couldn't be sure any aesthetic appreciation was truly her own.

"Now, come forward to us."

She looked down at herself, at the oddly short torso supported by six knobby limbs. She wasn't wearing a stitch of clothing, but didn't feel particularly exposed. Her skin was practically flashing with activity, a purely involuntary response to her skepticism. "I don't know how."

"How would you ambulate normally?"

"Well . . . normally I don't need to think about it." Not unless the pain was bad.

"Exactly so. Don't concern yourself with how. Let your actuators work that out. Assume your limbs will move, in concert, in accordance with your intent."

Olivia gave her new body one last glance before switching her focus to the space between her and Elder Two. She would have to trust that she wasn't going to topple forward.

She envisioned herself moving toward the alien; imagined herself moving with its grace. And her body complied, the air almost thick enough to buoy her as she waded forward. Each limb registered its presence in turn, their kinesthetic sense of orientation, the flesh of each point pressed between bone and floor. The sensations came from all directions at once, from the panorama of the lab fed to her from a dozen eyes to the squeeze and release of fluids throughout her body.

"You're too much in your mind."

Elder Two was still waiting for her, its segmented arms out as if beckoning a child to cross the distance. She had stopped. Despite the technological assistance, she couldn't rely on autopilot. She would have to stay focused on her immediate goal.

"Sorry, it's overwhelming."

"Not if you remain focused."

Olivia might have laughed just then if she physically could.

TWELVE
DAY 31

OLIVIA FOLLOWED behind Elder Two to the best of her ability, feeling every bit as shaky as a newborn fawn. Her companion took its time, but their pace was only a small part of the challenge.

They emerged from the receiving complex into an open-air space, like the Teelise Sphere's, only far more vast. Despite the sun-like light source high above—yellow and rippling, as if seen through oil—there was no sky to speak of, just land curving upward in all directions. It was like being in a planet turned inside out. But despite the perilous appearance of their path's inwardly curving contours, they remained feet-down—*points-down?* —at all times. Nucleus-like interior hubs like the one they'd just left hung seemingly unsupported, connected together by axon-like walkways that gave no indication of gravitational direction.

"Where are we going?" she asked the elder.

"To meet with your father," it said, staying a few steps ahead of her. "They've complained of some difficulty since their activation, so we'll get you both some practice before we disengage."

They've, meaning Max and who? Was there someone else?

"How do you fare?" asked Elder Two.

Walking. Keep walking.

"This is very different from what I'm used to. It takes a lot of work just to move."

"Right now we imagine everything feels potentially significant, which will come with a temporary cognitive burden. Beyond sensory saturation, your initial goal should be to learn what's available to you and how to use that to your benefit. In time you gain a sense for the feedback you can safely ignore, and internalize the rest."

Again, it had referred to itself as *we*. From what she could tell the same was true for everyone.

"Stay on the fareline, concentrate on your immediate goal, and your points will know what to do."

Fareline—that was the word she'd heard transliterated. That must mean the path they were following along the massive suspension cables that connected hub to hub. They shared the fareline with other remotes, none of whom, as far as Olivia could tell, paid them more than passing glances. Some wore utility belts or other such task-related adornments, but she saw no clothing intended purely for concealment.

Though she managed not to get her legs in a tangle, her altered sense of balance was just one of the senses competing for her attention. When she turned her head, her surroundings became subtly diffracted, giving everything in her field of vision a halo. This effect vanished as soon as she faced forward again, in the "right" direction. The result was an internal sense not just of alignment, but guidance, like a series of invisible conveyors all around her. Was it a side effect of the artificial gravity? Or maybe it was an additional safety mechanism employed for new transfers, like training wheels.

"What is going on here?" she asked, without meaning to give voice to her puzzlement.

"We're afraid you'll need to be specific."

"I wouldn't know where to start. I guess . . . why is the organization of this place so . . ." What? Confusing? Non-linear? "Why is it the way it is?"

"We'll need more context to answer. We don't know what you're used to, but the Symbiotry Sphere—"

. . . *wave-tick-wave-beat* . . .

"—presents a rather traditional topography, in accordance with the electromagnetic lines of force."

There was that electrical pattern again, like an undercurrent to Elder

Two's words. The signal, if that's what it was, seemed to accompany the naming of people or places of note. Assuming it was intentional, was she meant to be remembering the sequences?

What was it she'd sensed? A wave followed by a kind of tick, then another wave, then a beat. Wave-tick-wave-beat. So . . . maybe *Wa-ti-wa-be*? The poetry of it made it easy enough to remember.

Watiwabe.

That she could remember.

"Honestly," the elder continued, "we prefer a terrestrial setting to the artificial fields implemented here. There's a lot to be said for proper poles, some sense of the archetypical orientations, and a sun that pulls across the skies. We yearn for it . . . but we're boring you."

"Not at all, no. It's just very different from what I'm used to." Based on the elder's description, the remotes' perceptions were profoundly tied to the underlying electromagnetic fields permeating their environment. The architecture was structured accordingly.

As their walkway arced toward another hub, they passed several other groups of remotes, all of whom gave them a wide berth. Perhaps they were all going through their own onboarding routines. Could Olivia distinguish between a native remote and a transfer like herself? Would they all move with her faltering cadence?

She thought of Max.

"My father's not doing well, you said?"

"They'll be fine. Some require more attention than others. You, for instance, are doing quite well."

Was she? "It feels like I'm piloting some exotic vehicle."

Elder Two gave her a look. "You're not struggling."

"No. It's fine." But it was alien, in the most intimate sense.

"Any dissociation you feel will pass. By the time you and your father are preparing for your regress, your sanctified form will be first nature to you."

Regress? Sanctified? More words to ponder, assuming the words Elder Two was speaking were similar to the ones she heard.

———

As soon as they entered Max's receiving room—the teelise had called it a bead—it was apparent that something was off with him. He'd been transferred to a remote body, as she had, but he didn't look at all well. His skin was an incoherent series of patterns that was distressing even to look at, and while she'd learned to move with a certain intentional reliability, he was by turns completely still or flailing about as if his nervous system was short-circuiting.

While the elders conferred with each other, Olivia approached him. "Are you in some sort of pain?"

"I'm fine," he assured her. While his voice was not quite his own, she recognized the characteristic graveness of it. And if she had any doubts that this was him, there was his moth, hanging dutifully over the ridge of his left shoulder—or, she should say, the foremost of his three left shoulders. The remotes must have paired that thing with him to help him with some aspect of this mission. Whatever its purpose though, it was not helping him now.

"I'll be fine if you—"

He froze, then convulsed as if his body was attempting to shake him out of it. Was he fighting his physical assistants? Several of the teelise hurried to straighten out his limbs, by which time he had gone slack. Meantime, the elders had returned.

"As if any of this is necessary," Max said, catching his breath. He turned to the elders. "But apparently you've made our torture into some kind of perverted theater."

Olivia quickly moved between him and the elders. The impolitic remark wasn't out of character, but he could surely exercise some impulse control. Perhaps whatever was causing his physical struggle was also be affecting his mind. "Hey," she said. "Try to relax. That seems to be working for me."

Elder One coaxed her aside and splayed its—their—fingers at her in a gesture that required no translation. No need to interfere here.

"Is your body moving as you intend it to?" asked Max's elder.

"Clearly not," Max said. "One minute it is, and the next—" His frontmost legs shot straight out, nearly sideswiping Elder Two. "I can't do it. I suppose you're enjoying this."

The elder ignored him. "Could it be interference from that thing?" they asked their colleague, pointing at Max's moth.

"It's . . . my aid," Max managed to say. "Provides information . . . about protocols, culture, hist—"

"That is *our* role," Elder One interrupted, "for as long as you're here."

"It will remain by my side." Despite the risk of causing offense right out of the gate, Max was unwilling to consider giving up his precious moth.

Olivia glanced over at Elder Two, tucked in behind their console. They seemed content to remain quiet on the matter, their skin rather dappled and static.

They definitely had the right idea.

THIRTEEN
DAY 31

THE TRICK to moving efficiently in her new body, Olivia discovered, was working out the unique rhythm of its gaits. In her early adolescence, dance had taught her how to express herself through her physicality, how to master her overall presence through the heft of bone, the control of muscle, of flexion, of rotation. She had assimilated that sense of physical presence into her self-identity. And not just the presence, but also the *power* it carried.

Once her connective tissue disorder fully asserted itself—once it had forced her to quit her beloved pursuit of dance—her relationship with her body had become more guarded, but no less studied. Frailty, through the attendant vigilance it demanded, had been a cruel teacher. But in time her ailment had offered her a new type of mastery.

She'd proven herself adept at driving her own body, no matter the circumstances. Now her body had changed once again, more radically still. But no matter how strange, she would master it again.

Max, however, appeared unable to grasp even the basics of operating this alien anatomy. His juddering, shambling movements looked like a string of barely controlled seizures. And yet, slowly, and with a great deal of assistance from the remotes, he moved forward with Olivia as their chaperones led them from their hub and through the open-air space.

They paused at a bridge suspended between a branch in their fareline and a second one—its mirror image—across a chasmal gap. "We can stop here to allow you to rest," said Elder One.

"*No*," Max said, his voice loud enough to startle Olivia. "No, I have to make sure . . ."

But his legs had gone rigid before he could complete his thought. This time the elders made no effort to assist him, which seemed negligent, given their remit.

Cursing herself, Olivia went to him. "Are you okay?"

"No cooperation."

He must mean his body. "Don't fight it. Let it do the work for you."

"What do you think I've been *trying* to do?" He pulled away from her, and his moth whirred to follow. "You have no idea," he said over his shoulders.

After several minutes they were on the move once again, and Olivia turned her attention back to the other pressing issue. Despite being in the open air now, the whispering—an incessant chatter of electric phonemes, more tone poems than words—hadn't diminished in the slightest. Olivia's senses were as keen as they were alien. The whispered words were impossible to ignore, and it required only the slightest focus to summon them.

Testing herself, she moved closer to Elder One and opened her receptors to whatever the phantom signal deigned to dispense. Sure enough, a single distinct whisper, seemingly from nowhere, broke from the chatter and whispered across her skin:

. . . *BUrst-TIck-SStatic-TAp-PUlse* . . .

Butisstapu, Elder One's own signature, as Elder Two's had consisted of a *SStatic-PUlse-THUmp-BUrst-TAp*. *Ssputhu-buta*. As good as names, should she ever find herself in need of them.

In the meantime, the whispering returned to its more indistinct babbling. The elders' conversation had turned to the upcoming forum, scheduled to take place the day after tomorrow.

Olivia had grave doubts about Max's attendance. "Isn't that too soon, considering . . ."

"It may be sooner than is ideal," Elder One said, "but we can walk Max in there by executive direction if we need to. As long as they're cogent."

"We have a full cycle," said Elder Two, managing to sound less imperious than their colleague, "which is plenty of time for you both to acclimate to your surroundings and sanctified forms. We've done this many times before."

How many?

"More practice is what's called for," said Elder One.

"An escort will be by to pick up you and Max tomorrow," said Elder Two. "They'll shuttle you around the outer loop to the best medical facility we know. Not just labs, but a full physical therapy hub."

It was almost hallucinatory to be talking schedules with aliens on an alien ship. But hadn't they skipped over the basics?

"Do you sleep?" she asked them.

"Sleep?" Elder One asked.

"They mean torpor," said Elder Two.

"Oh yes, recuperative inertia."

Torpor.

"Toward the approach of local night you should feel the lethargy setting in. Then you must seek the support netting in your beads."

"A comfortable place to relax until the next cycle," Elder Two explained. "We'll show you when we return."

But for all the questions Olivia had, she realized the remotes had never expressed curiosity about humans. They seemed, in fact, entirely uninterested in anything about the lives of their two transfers up to this point.

After crossing a high suspension footbridge over a meadow below, Elder One stopped them. "Wait here, please. We need to speak with our duty manager at the First Seat."

As the transfer steward moved away for privacy, Elder Two came close. "How is Max managing?"

"Well enough," Max said, while failing to suppress the trembling of his limbs. He moved away from them toward the fareline's edge, perhaps to take in the great concavity of the sphere's interior.

Olivia wanted to apologize to Elder Two for Max's performative reticence. They were the more personable of the two stewards, after all. But Max wasn't her problem.

"We'll see to your father," Elder Two said, "in case that was a concern. In the meantime, how are you faring?"

"The less I think about it, the better," she said without consideration. "Sorry, I didn't mean that to sound . . . I want to be able to appreciate everything around me. This experience. But I'm still very much focused on mechanics and minutiae."

Starburst-like blooms appeared across the silent elder's skin. Approval, if Olivia's intuition was accurate.

"It is beautiful though." She turned to the eerie beauty of the interior space. "The quality of the light here is fascinating."

"Being the host construct for the Symbiotry—"

. . . *WAve-TIck-WAve-BEat* . . .

"—has its advantages. It's not quite like Home—"

. . . *TAp-PUlse-WAve-THUd* . . .

"—but it's better than most."

Watiwabe the sphere and *Tapuwathu* the planet, respectively.

"Where is home?" she asked them.

"Home is the second planet in this system. I understand you designated it as a Beringia?"

"I can call it whatever you call it." Could she? Would she be able to mimic the electrical patterns she'd been sensing in her very pores? If only her transliteration bud could help with those.

"Well . . . it's only ever been Home to us."

No acknowledgment at all of the whispered name.

"Have you been away from your Home for long?"

"Twenty circuits almost."

Years, maybe. Cycles seemed to mean days. But the terms were only transliterated literally.

"Do you miss it?" She pictured the look Aleksi had given her when she'd told their friends her cover story. Would he miss her? What would he make of her now?

"We miss a time in our life more than a place," Elder Two said. "But that time exists no more, and the work we do here is important."

Maybe some things were universal. That, or Elder Two's cover story had been tailored for relatability.

Elder One joined them once again. Olivia read fresh agitation in the distinct rings along their skin. "Where's Max?"

Olivia's field of vision immediately widened, giving her a nearly three-hundred-sixty-degree view of her surroundings. And there he was, several meters up the fareline, struggling against the balustrade.

"There," she said, pointing. He was in danger. Not only had he gotten himself tangled in the tension cables, his squirming was likely to send him tumbling over the side, gravity or not.

Tick-tick, tick-tick

The elders' electromagnetic interjections required no translation. Olivia was surprised that she didn't feel as panicked. Her inhibitor must have had that dialed down to a mild curiosity.

The remotes were much faster to Max than she could have managed, and immediately set to work extricating his limbs from the cabling. They dragged him back to safety and laid him by her.

"What were you thinking?" she asked, unable to stifle her curiosity.

"That I want nothing to do with their pool," he managed between breaths. "I can't. I can't *do it*."

"What are you talking about?" Had he heard her? Was he even lucid? His eyes were all open, but she couldn't know what those dark beads were seeing. Regardless, he seemed to be getting worse. "This can't be normal," she said to the elders. "Is there something you can do? Did his procedure not work?"

Tick-tick

"Not all are strong," Elder One answered with a tone Olivia had no trouble deciphering.

Did they think she was overreacting? Max had clearly been struggling since his arrival here. Had they never seen this before, even with all their experience? Or maybe they were just reluctant to talk about it. That would be a new concern, on top of whatever Max was experiencing.

The elders now walked with Max between them, each with a hand on his shoulders as they retraced their path back to the administration hub. After several minutes of careful progress the four of them entered the facility and followed a passage whose gentle arc must have reflected the underlying electrical fields. Those fields caressed her skin as they walked by a row of portals—fluctuations like faint tugs, as if each door was coaxing the air from the passageway.

The elders stopped before one of the portals, and only then did they release Max. Elder Two checked something on their device while their colleague popped the portal open with a touch.

Olivia sidled closer to Max.

"You had me concerned back there."

"I can't seem to . . ." His skin flashed dark, then returned to pale. "I'll be fine. It's a new experience, isn't it? Of course it's going to be difficult."

A change of heart then. Good. But really, had it been *that* difficult? Maybe she'd been lucky.

"I need more time to figure out this contraption," he said.

"Here we introduce you to your torpor beads," Elder One said, stepping between them.

Max peered through the open portal. "What's this?"

"They mean our rooms," Olivia said.

"For your recuperation," Elder One added. "Everything will go well once you're rested and focused."

"Okay," he said. "Fine."

"You've taken on a lot for your first cycle," Elder Two said.

"Fine, yes, I understand."

The entrance to the bead had seemed tight, but Max's actuators eased him through without problem, and his moth was inside just behind him. Olivia went to follow, but Elder One moved in front of her.

"We'll be staying with them tonight," they said, "so that we and our team can continue to monitor their progress."

"We'll reconvene for the high moment," said Elder Two, as if to reassure her. What were they talking about? "Your bead is a few ports down. You can link with your father from there if you need to, but we would advise you to leave them to their rest for now."

"Sure," Olivia said, backing off. They knew best. And there wasn't much good she could do for him anyway. The elders had done this before. They'd seen it all.

Following Elder Two's lead, Olivia approached her own portal with curiosity piqued. What kind of cubbies were these torpor beads?

It turned out that only the opening was small. Beyond it was a roomy, even comfortable space, if somewhat plain. It was comfortable, but . . . something else. Under her elder's watchful gaze, Olivia strode around the periphery of the main chamber, growing more aware by the second that something almost beneath perception was imbuing the space with a sense of profound calm. No point fighting it.

Elder Two took their time showing Olivia the highlights of her bead, which appeared decidedly low-tech. The sole exception was a curved window that overlooked the expansive landscape of the sphere's interior, where murmurations of drones caught the dusk's waning light.

"Your affordances generally follow the precept of discretion," Elder Two said, their words pulling her away from the view. They drew her attention to an inset panel in the wall, where a quick wave of a hand over a hieroglyphic label revealed a hidden display. "You see a message waiting for you here." Rows of hieroglyphics glowed on the screen. She would have to figure them out later. "We would presume this communiqué is from your people. Know that any response you make—should you respond—will be conveyed back through the Fountain to the spring in your system with minimal delay. Though the spring will become inert in the next cycle, this channel of communication will remain accessible."

Good to know. "Are all the amenities hidden away like that? How do I find what I need?"

"Your transliteration bud extends to the room, so if you find yourself thirsty, cold, or in need of the waste chamber, simply ask. Like this: hygiene access." One wall faded away, revealing a seamless stall with a basin below. "Use whatever terms you prefer—your intention will be inferred."

Their own version of ambionts. That would ease the culture shock.

The centerpiece of the room was a sunken tub that closely resembled the tank that human Olivia had lowered herself into back in the Teelise Sphere. Within the soft basin was a web of netting, clearly meant to accommodate one remote body. But surely there were no transfers in her future.

"How do I use this?"

"It is your torpor hull," Elder Two said.

"My bed." But before she could ask why it was positioned at the room's center, the answer asserted itself, as subtle as the current in a stream. Whatever mood-altering fields were at work in that room weren't blanketing the room evenly. As with the farelines outside, a clear sense of directionality made its presence known here, and all fields led in one direction. "It's intentional."

"What is intentional?" asked the remote, its skin pattern oscillating, speckled.

"There's a feeling of balance here, centered at the hull."

It sounded like nonsense, but her assertion earned her starburst blooms across Elder Two's skin. She read it as approval. "Your perception appears to be keen."

So she was right. But what was she picking up on exactly? Was it purely aesthetic, like the soothing soundtrack at a spa? "There's a feeling when I stand near it that . . . everything sort of culminates here."

"As it should, by the end of a cycle," the elder said. "A harmonious composition is the desired outcome here. Less optimal living conditions do exist, of course, but that's not something you'll encounter." They made a sweeping gesture. "This is to your satisfaction?"

"Sure." It was surely nothing to complain about. "It's just not something I'm familiar with."

Elder Two moved toward the portal. "Now we're sure you must be feeling the fatigue of your cycle."

"Is Max going to be okay?"

Elder Two's skin mottled slightly. "You don't have to worry about them."

"The way he was behaving earlier—you've seen that before?"

"We've seen all manner of reactions to the transfer rite, if that's what you mean."

"Not with humans."

Skin darkening, the patterns growing knottier. "Everyone is different, it's true. Every species has different obstacles, different sensitivities."

"But the transfer works for everyone, eventually?"

"For most."

"And for the others?"

Now Elder Two's skin took on the appearance of fresh loam. "Those who are not sanctified are not invited to stay."

What did that mean for Max? If his sanctification didn't take, would he be put on ice until the Sol-side spring opened back up? That wouldn't bode well for the mission. She wasn't his understudy. No, he'd need to pull his weight . . . once he figured out how to stand up straight.

"There's a lot I need to learn," Olivia said. "Basics, like about food." How did a thing like this eat? Would it be like trying to work a docking crane?

"You shouldn't be hungry."

It wasn't the response she'd expected. And she *wasn't* hungry—at least as far as she could tell. Surely she would know. "No, but we haven't talked about food." Not to mention what constituted food . . . and how to eat.

"The feed is a semi-formal occasion at the start of every cycle. Here on the Symbiotry Sphere—"

. . . Watiwabe . . .

"—it occurs shortly after you rise from torpor. If you were planetside it might be different, but here the population falls into synchrony in short order."

"I think I'll need some help with the basics. The mechanics."

"Of *course*," Elder Two said, as if to a child. "You will not starve. The tradition is to cover such basics as part of the first orientation, but we've had to deviate from the usual procedures today."

"Totally understandable." Max's antics had derailed whatever the remotes had had planned for today. If he didn't pull himself together by tomorrow, it might be worth asking if she could strike out on her own. Olivia Jelani, Cultural Séparé.

"Tomorrow we'll cover everything else you'd need to know," said the elder as they stepped toward the portal. "We'll collect you here, shortly after the high moment."

"The high moment, you mentioned that earlier. That's a specific time?" Another thing she was supposed to know about?

"Yes. Early. You will feel the call, just as you've managed to feel the orientation of your bead. It will be more distinct."

Another unique signal. Fine, as long as it wasn't drowned out in the whisper's continuous din.

"I'll try to be ready."

Alone, Olivia surveyed her room—her very own bead aboard an actual shellworld. *Watiwabe*, she reminded herself. Its unique signature. Its interior must have the surface area of a good-sized orbital, and its miraculous architecture favored the lines of force of countless underlying electromagnetic fields over gravity.

Those fields were evident even as she paced her bead, like a compass needle gently orienting her. Between the phantom push and pull, and the remotes' creative approach to gravity, and the whispering in her head even now, it was a wonder she'd fared as well as she had. But despite the fact that she was in far over her head, her sense of resolve never wavered. Surely it must border on the delusional. Was the feeling genuine, or the product of her many corrective augments? Just because she felt something didn't mean it was *hers*. After all, her tranquility was in the best interests of her hosts, too.

The still-glowing display that Elder Two had conjured from the bead's wall caught her eye. Despite her curiosity, it was too late in the day to be wading through some alien interface. But the elder had suggested she need only ask for what she wanted. So she gave it a try.

"Anyone there?"

"I can hear you, Olivia."

The voice of the natal ambiont was quiet and calming, and seemed to originate from everywhere at once.

"Can you play the message for me?" she asked it.

"The message from Sovereign Alliance head of mission Ioor Volkopp is in text form. I can dictate it to you."

Of course. She'd almost forgotten the SA's preferred mode of communication. "Yes, please."

"Message follows:

"Ind. Jelani, first let me congratulate you on behalf of the entire team here. It's our understanding that the transfer process takes about a week, but all indications are that your visit is going to plan. I'll keep this short, as I'm sure you have enough on your plate already.

"Ind. Mehdipour and you are doing a great service for humanity. You've heard us say it before, but right now the words feel different.

We're on the cusp of something that will change us forever, to the benefit of all. And it all begins with your first steps, as all journeys do."

Olivia ambled across the slight concavity of her bead to the floor-to-ceiling mirror.

Olivia the alien.

"We will be checking in regularly," the ambiont continued, "and we'll look forward to hearing of your experiences whenever you're inclined to share them. For now, I'll let you get back to your task. Good luck, Olivia. And enjoy the experience.

"Message concludes."

The message was a variation on a theme. A prosaic string of words meant to encourage? To inspire?

"Thank you," she said to her empty room.

Far more interesting than the message was the alien in the mirror—and not because of its foreign architecture, but because she was the one animating it. The creature standing before her was as opaque to her as any of the others, its expression—if there was one—beyond her ability to read. She might as well be wearing a costume; the confusing flesh topography provided no hint as to what lay beneath. Glassy dark eyes, like rows of beads, stared into themselves, then to the large mouth at the center of her face. Concentrating, she imagined the six lobes of her mouth pulling back like a flower in bloom, and the figure in the mirror complied, its open mouth revealing . . . not so much teeth, but two pearlescent ridges, one left, one right. If this was a smile, it didn't work on the face of a remote.

"Happy now?" she asked her image, the words emerging from her two expressionless speaker flaps. "Are we still Olivia, or are we something else?"

Her impulse to laugh displayed itself in wavy spirals across her arms and shoulders. She and Max were the only *remotes* here, not the elders. What was it Ioor Volkopp had said the aliens called themselves?

"Natals."

The native-born.

———

A rising whir—the chance passage of something flying by outside—lifted Olivia's attention from some fathomless recess. How long had she been standing in front of the mirror? Night had fallen. She'd lost time. Part of her brain had simply turned off.

It might still be off, judging by that sense of disconnection as she moved toward the webby bassinet at the center of her bead.

Off to a great start.

The truth was, even after only a single day she was already getting the hang of it, but still—too many things continued to feel deliberate. Including going to bed, apparently.

She lowered herself into her webbing, trying to work out how to position her too-many limbs and joints as she settled in. She prepared for the pain of shifting bones and distressed ligaments and tendons. Only . . . there was no pain. None at all. She allowed her muscles to relax.

Would she dream? And if she did, would the dreams be hers? Would she ever feel at home in this body? Or would she wake up tomorrow and shit on the floor like a new pet?

No, the hard part—those wobbly first moments—was surely over. Already she had a better sense of herself. She was steady and strong.

And for the next month she would be free, finally, of the physical pain.

FOURTEEN
DAY 31-32

OLIVIA FINDS *herself in Aleksi's story development volume, a virtual stage fashioned after the home they shared together. How has she found her way inside? He's facing away from her, sweeping his arms like a conductor as he removes the back wall, opening their home up to the rolling foothills beyond. He might not welcome her unannounced presence, so long after they've gone their separate ways.*

. . . pulse-tap-tap-tap . . .

Someone is at the front door.

The ambiont announces an unfamiliar name, but Aleksi waves it away. No distractions right now, not until . . .

But he's seen her now. "You're back." *He approaches, puts a hand on her shoulder as if to reassure himself she's really here. His smile is genuine.* "So? What did you think of the production?"

That's pride she's hearing. She was meant to see this—his creation has been tailored for her after all.

"It was so real. Like I'd stepped into another life." *But that doesn't quite capture it.* "I think I discovered something new about myself."

He's nodding, satisfied. She gets it. But why has he gone to all the trouble just for her? She didn't ask for his help. She wouldn't have.

A breeze, surprisingly cool, falls across her skin. Is she naked? She looks down at her six legs. This may be a problem. But it's something she'll have to face sooner or later. "I was going to tell you," *she says.*

"I know," he replies, and the look on his face—

. . . pulse-tap-tap-tap . . .

That incessant knocking again. "Just a second!" she calls. The urgency of it worries her though.

"Go ahead," Aleksi says. "I can wait."

He won't though. He won't be around after.

. . . pulse-tap-tap-tap . . .

How did they even find her?

———

. . . pulse-tap-tap-tap . . .

Olivia's dream was gone, and in its place was her room, quiet, still, and lit only by the ambient light leaking in through the window. Had something changed? Was she imagining that vague sense of turbulence in the air?

"Hello?"

Had she overslept? Elder Two had said she'd know when it was time to get up. She glanced out the window. The light coming in was no brighter than when she'd gone to sleep.

. . . pulse-tap-tap-tap . . .

She froze. The silence was unbroken, but from somewhere close came an electromagnetic disruption, persistent enough to have interrupted her dream.

. . . pulse-tap-tap-tap . . .

Olivia set about extricating her legs from the netting, bracing herself against the edge of the hull with one leg while pulling—

. . . pulse-tap-tap-tap . . .

"Shit," she said as she freed herself. She strode to the portal and reached for a handle that wasn't there. Placing a hand on the partition, she gave it a nudge. It pulled aside.

Max's moth buzzed into the room, circled Olivia twice, then exited back out to the fareline. There it flittered at her eye line, refusing to be ignored. Thus far it had never indicated any interest in her, nor any capacity for communication. She had assumed it was autonomous, in possession of a level of intelligence sufficient only to provide Max with contextual matters of protocol. But now it was unstable, frenetic, in a state of agitation.

The moth repeated its routine once more, circling her twice—as though roping a lasso around her—then flitting back outside.

"You want me to follow you?"

This it appeared to understand. It retreated slowly down the corridor as though coaxing her to follow. It must be heading toward Max's room.

Olivia stepped out into the fareline, noting how much easier it was to walk than it had been yesterday. On the other hand, she was feeling something new, too. Not pain, but a feeling of internal discomfort. Probably nerves.

Max's portal opened for the moth, and it disappeared into his room—his bead—as Olivia approached. Unbelievable. Max had sent the moth to fetch her like an errand drone. After a day of myriad tribulations, had insomnia finally made him snap?

She ducked into the open bead. It was exactly like hers, only without the spectacular view hers offered. It was also a mess, with blue-gray fluid sprayed across the walls and furniture. Had he and his elder thrown some kind of members-only party after she'd left?

"Max?"

No response. The moth zipped around into the bath alcove, and Olivia followed hesitantly, loath to breach his privacy.

"Max, did you want to see me or not?"

She stared at the limb for several seconds before it registered what it was. Mainly because the leg wasn't attached to anything.

"*Max?*"

But only as she came around the partition could she fully appreciate his predicament. Max—or the body he'd been inhabiting—was most likely dead. And unless she was miscounting appendages, there were two natal corpses splayed with him. The hard floor of the washroom was strewn with entrails and that blue-gray goop.

One of the natal bodies had been torn open from mouth to . . . thorax? The second wasn't nearly as savaged, but the damage in evidence must still have been fatal. Most of the eyes had been excised or burst, and the lacerations to the head had exposed a gray lobe of the brain.

As Olivia assessed the tangle of limbs and gore, she found herself more detached than the circumstances should have warranted. Indeed, the immediacy of her first thought pushed away all else:

It's not a pain in my abdomen—I have to relieve myself.

That would have to wait. She'd walked in on a scene of carnage, and now . . . well, she was standing in it. She'd managed to get blood on her own points, had tracked it across the mat floor. And though she understood why, Max's predicament elicited only the vaguest sense of disappointment. It was those mood-dampening governors the teelise had implanted in her. A similar sense of cool resolve had settled over her after she'd had her cranial omni removed, when she'd awoken from the procedure on strong painkillers. Even so, it was difficult to imagine the old Olivia taking in such a sight as this without some trauma.

The gravity of the situation was clear: Max was dead, and so was his elder. Whether murder, suicide, or assassination—or some combination of those—there must be a reason. Was this a part of some plot? How well did anyone really know the natals? How well did she really know her father? An international incident on day one.

Not international. Intergalactic.

It was well out of Olivia's hands at this point. The implications of this remained to be seen . . . as did the implications of failing to deal with certain biological imperatives. Tragedies notwithstanding, she was going to need to figure out what these bodies did to relieve themselves in short order, or she would most likely find herself adding to the mess.

She turned to the moth, which was haplessly drifting over the remains of its charge. "I'm sorry, but I don't know what to tell you." How much could it understand her? "Thank you for letting me know. I think it's time to appeal to the authorities."

The drone settled on a table in the corner of the room, looking as resigned as such a device could.

"Uh, room?" Olivia said. "I need to speak to Elder Two. And . . . maybe contact the authorities?"

"The operations ward has been notified," said the ambiont.

"Oh. Okay. And is there anything I should be doing?" Besides peeing?

"Please wait for your escorts."

"Right," she said. "I can do that." But for how long?

She stared at the ruined bodies. It wasn't yet daybreak, so most would be asleep still. Yet it was never fully quiet here. The whispering was her constant companion, that insistent electromagnetic susurrus unheeding of Max's defiled torpor bead. If not for her emotional inhibitor, Olivia might have found its continual prattle disconcerting.

And not just the whispering. The pressure in her abdomen continued to build unabated.

"Come on, where is everyone?"

They were taking too long. Surely she could see to some pressing matters without harming the scene of the . . . whatever this was.

———

Olivia crossed the hall and headed for her bead, Max's airborne pest in tow.

"I don't need another chaperone," she told it, stopping at her portal. She eyed the moth dubiously. Maybe it had seen the whole incident play out. Maybe it was in shock. "I don't know if you can understand me, but you probably need to stay in the area until the authorities get here. Right now I can't have you breathing down my neck."

The moth didn't respond, but it allowed the distance between them to grow.

Back in the privacy of her bead, Olivia tried to remember what Elder Two had called the toilet. Waste something? "Room, I need to relieve myself."

As it had the first time, a section of the far wall faded away revealing a small chamber with a mesh floor and seamless walls. Olivia entered and looked for any indication of what she should do. Markings on the floor? Explanatory labels? Stirrups? She was essentially an infant again, unsure of what to do, or even where the action was supposed to take place.

But she must have relaxed enough to allow nature to take its course. A stream of something warm exited her.

Elder Two entered the bead, saw her, and immediately turned away. "We're . . . sorry. We didn't . . ."

"It's fine, it's fine."

From the other side of the room, Elder Two called, "We need to speak as soon as possible." Several new voices drifted in from the fareline.

"I'll be right out."

I think.

Elder Two left her alone, and Olivia listened to the chatter as she allowed her body to conclude its business.

"This should all be arranged through the consulate."

"Sorry, but this is out of their jurisdiction. Everything on a Third Case construct is under—"

"*Not* everything. And definitely not this."

"We don't know what *this* is yet. Have you been in there?"

"Not yet, but from what we heard—"

"Elder, tell your Affairs Chancery what we told you, then let the highest ridges argue it out. But for now . . ."

"Yes, we're cooperating."

A fine mist filled the lavatory, and Olivia was treated to something not unlike a bidet. After a moment the process concluded, and she glanced down at herself. She was dry, at least. *Not bad for her first time.*

She emerged from her bead to find the fareline full of strangers, most of whom sported colored garters on their forelegs. One of them had Max's moth in hand, but the device appeared to be entirely inert. And though the squad looked virtually identical, Olivia was able to pick out Elder Two a moment before they turned and joined her.

. . . *Ssputhu-buta* . . .

"How do you fare?" they asked her.

"Fine, I think. Calm." Artificially so.

But as the others drew more closely around her, Olivia was suddenly self-conscious. Was she doing this body correctly? Did she look like a foreigner? A child? Was it apparent to all that she wasn't one of them?

"The constable here—"

. . . *WAve-SStatic-WAve-TAp* . . .

"—is from the operations ward."

Wass-wata, Olivia decided. The constable was the big one with the green stripes on their forelegs.

"You are not immediately implicated, they tell me. But you'll need to be available for questioning," Elder Two said. Then added, "We'll be here the whole time."

That seemed fair. "Sure, anything I can do to help."

"This is the common prime, the Olivia?" the constable asked.

She looked at Elder Two. "Common?"

"A stranger," the elder explained.

. . . *BEat-BEat-THUmp-TIck* . . .

Or *bebethuti*, if the whisper had anything to say about it.

"Olivia is their title," Elder Two said to the constable.

"The Olivia and the Max are . . . ?"

"They're guests of the First Seat, yes. As we noted."

The constable looked Olivia up and down—made a show of it, by her estimation. "Well, Olivia, this should be . . . enlightening."

FIFTEEN
DAY 32

ON FINDING Max in the earliest morning hours, Olivia had contemplated the implications of his death for mere minutes. But the interrogation that followed, conducted by the natal authorities, took several hours. She couldn't have sailed through the ordeal as effortlessly if her emotions hadn't been kept in check. The proceedings came across as a test more than anything, designed to trip her up by exploiting any variations in the answers she gave to their directed questions.

"You did well," Elder Two said once the authorities had left them alone in her bead.

Olivia made an attempt to shrug, but it didn't translate to her natal configuration. "I guess so."

The investigation was now fully underway in Max's bead. But constable *Wass-wata*—as Olivia thought of them—had made it clear that no one was to leave the premises until clearance had been issued by . . . someone.

Olivia's head was still spinning from all the titles and associations. But her biggest question seemed more immediate.

"Is Max really dead?"

Elder Two's wordless response came as another electromagnetic signal:

Beat-beat-beat.

She took it as a "huh?"

"I mean, his body," she clarified. "Did its death also take him—"

"Unfortunately so," said the elder. "The transfer rite process is a true electrical and biomechanical migration, not just a translation or transmission. The donation from their natal form . . . We're afraid that their essential being has been rendered unsalvageable, given the damage." They clasped their hands together as their skin went pale and marbled. "We can't express how sorry we are that things have taken this turn. We've never seen anything quite so grave. But we assure you that our team will work diligently to discover the cause, and to prevent any harm coming to you."

They were in uncharted territory, but what else were they going to tell her? "I'm sorry about your colleague, too. Whatever happened."

Elder Two's head dipped a bit, which could have meant a lot of things. They moved to the window, and Olivia followed. The artificial sun at the sphere's core had brightened in the intervening hours, casting a murky orange glow across pasturelands of exotic flora, low-set dwellings arranged in concentric rings, and connecting farelines ascending to countless floating hubs overhead. It was futile to take it all in, and this might be her last view of it.

"Do we know what happens now?" she asked. "Is our assignment canceled?"

"How do you mean?"

"Well . . . my understanding was that Max was going to sit at our introduction to the Symbiotry."

"Yes. But an outright cancellation is unlikely, in our view." After some seconds of silence, they added, "Perhaps to your point though, if Max themself did commit this act, there will be questions about whether a sanctified form can be culpable for such actions."

Olivia puzzled over the elder's choice of words. Was it important for them to hold the natal body beyond reproach even if Max was found guilty? That seemed backwards. As little as she'd known about Max, she was pretty sure it wouldn't have come to this if not for the natals' enforced transfer rite. That was where the investigation should focus.

"I suppose some answers aren't so clear-cut," she said.

"Precedents will be set."

Was the elder talking about some kind of retaliation? Would they take back their gift sculpture? Or . . . worse?

Olivia didn't give voice to her thoughts.

A long *thump-wave-sstatic-thump-wave-sstatic* played across her skin, forcible enough to make her flinch.

"Do you feel that?" she asked the elder as the pattern repeated once again.

"The high moment," said Elder Two, turning away from the vista. "Time for the feed."

———

With *Watiwabe*'s artificial sun undulating overhead, Elder Two brought Olivia to an expansive open market with more natals than Olivia had ever seen in one place. Colorful vendor booths, most with smoke billowing from the tops, were arranged at the periphery of an open court, with communal dining patches at the center, and the rich medley of aromas reminded her of the farmers' market in the Rinpoche Station canton back on Vaix, though here she had no basis for identifying any of them.

As for breakfast, Olivia was happy to go with Elder Two's recommended fare, which appeared to be a smoked protein of some sort bound with bamboo-like sticks. At their dining patch—really just a low stone slab—she welcomed the elder's help in unbundling her meal, feeling like a child once again. She marveled at the sight of her own long tapered fingers wrapped around her spatula handle. She counted five joints in each of her six fingers, but though they resembled tentacles, they weren't so exotic that she had to learn their particularities from scratch. They worked, generally, as fingers worked.

"Your limbs and digits are performing as you expect them to?" Elder Two must have caught her gazing at her own hand.

"Oh, yes. They're not so different from the human versions." Four hands—twenty-four fingers—had proven to be surprisingly manageable, thanks to whatever internal remapping they'd performed on her.

"Very good."

Max's moth landed on the patch's edge, and Olivia suppressed the urge to wave it away. The constabulary must not have found it worth keeping in custody, and it had tracked her here. She thought of Somtow sitting at the periphery of the dining room, looking as pitiful as he possibly could with the hope of earning scraps.

"Were you not briefed about human physiology at all?" she asked Elder Two, her spatula balanced in her fingers.

tick-tick

"The information was provided to us, it's just not our area of . . . expertise."

Or maybe *interest* was the more appropriate word. It wasn't the first time she'd sensed a certain apathy from her hosts toward the lives of their guests.

"Anyway, that sort of thing is best left to the teelise," the elder concluded.

"Right."

Considering the food on the slate before her, Olivia couldn't help musing that Max had never gotten the chance to eat.

"We don't mean to interrupt your high moment."

. . . WAve-WHIir-HIss-TIck-TIck . . .

A stranger—*Wawhihititi*, according to the whisper—had sidled up to their dining patch. At the same time, Max's moth zipped away. Olivia made note of the green rings around their visitor's forelegs, the standard constabulary dress code.

"Constable," said Elder Two. "Are we concluded?"

"Not quite. We need to check one thing from our notes with the Olivia."

At this rate she might never get the chance to eat either. "Something I can help you with?" She'd already answered their questions every which way, so one more variation couldn't hurt.

The natal slouched in a way that their head was nearly level with Olivia's. A courtesy, she thought. "Did your Max express to you any misgivings about their ambassadorial role, post the transfer rite?"

If anything he'd seemed even more insistent that things go to plan after that clandestine meeting he'd had on the Teelise Sphere. "Never," she said. "He believed in this cause. The only thing he questioned was the rite itself."

"What does that mean?"

Elder Two stepped in. "They mean that it was a novel experience for them. Max was moved by it."

The constable was silent. Then, "Is that what you meant?"

Olivia considered what she could say. It wouldn't help anyone to get into that debate now. "Yes, that's it. The transliteration, it's . . . regrettably approximate."

"Is there anything specific you can tell us about the investigation?" asked the elder.

The constable straightened up again. "For the moment the only thing we can say is that we've cleared you to leave the habitation belt. But you'll need to remain aboard the Symbiotry Sphere—"

. . . *Watiwabe* . . .

"—for now."

In other words, the investigation, though still ongoing in some undisclosed capacity, had turned its many-eyed gaze away from Olivia. For the moment, anyway. Fortunately, any surveillance would show the authorities that she'd arrived at the scene well after the terrible events had concluded.

After the official left them to their meal, Olivia waited for Elder Two to upbraid her for her rash disclosure. Fortunately, they exercised restraint.

"Now observe," said Elder Two. They ladled some veiny dumplings to their slate, then used their fingers to single one of them out. "Before you consume, you'll let the air out." The elder peeled back a small flap on top, and the morsel deflated with a *puff*. They leaned forward, demonstrably taking in the aroma before popping it into their multi-labial mouth. "Savor it. Engage all your senses."

She reached for the ladle before she could reconsider.

———

Olivia couldn't help gawking at the fractal monument through the transparent skin of their shuttle—Elder Two called it a line runner. The colossal reticulated structure outside was easily the size of a municipal spaceport.

After the high moment, Elder Two had whisked her to a rapid transport hub, where they'd boarded the single-car vehicle with Max's moth tagging along—she presumed because Max's departure from the scene had left the drone without any other purpose. The ride had offered Olivia a grand, if fleeting, view of *Watiwabe's* equivalent of suburbia, with its architecture of twisting spires nestled among low-lying blue and green shrubs. The flora tended to grow in concentric rings around single towering wood tusks, like petals arrayed around a flower's central pistil.

"I thought you'd mentioned an appointment at a rehabilitation center," she said. Surely it wouldn't be housed in the glorious constructs outside.

"For you, no," the elder said from their saddle opposite hers. For most of the trip the elder had been swiping at a small constellation of glowing micro-motes suspended in the space between their hands. Whether a form of communication or a means of creation, Olivia didn't know. Now, with a flick of their fingers, the points of light vanished. "Some physical therapy is the usual course as we conclude the transfer rite, but in your case . . . we've been impressed by your natural facility with your sanctified form. We've been part of this mission for at least one gross arrivals, and physical coordination tends to be the primary challenge at first. But your somatic mastery leads us to believe that there are better uses of our limited time. Especially given the state of your colleague."

Mastery? They've got to be kidding, Olivia thought. Sure, the act of walking no longer required brute concentration, but less than an hour ago she'd painted her face with her breakfast. She wouldn't have objected to a little PT session; she could use all the help she could get. But if they thought otherwise . . .

"Okay, I guess," she said. "If you think it's advisable to skip."

"In favor of some real-world orientation, yes."

She returned her attentions to the lush biomes of the sphere's interior. Occasionally she'd caught glimpses of diminutive forms darting in and out of the foliage, or among clusters of natals, but whether pets or pests she hadn't had time to assess.

As the vehicle finally decelerated, she gazed up at an architectural behemoth on the far side of the fareline. It must be important, given its prominence. "Is this where the assembly takes place?" she asked.

"Come, we'll show you," said Elder Two, inviting her to follow as they moved to the aisle.

Olivia sensed a new, distinct electromagnetic signature as soon as she emerged onto the platform. In contrast to the calming alignment of her personal torpor bead, the feeling in the air here was one of urgency, of motion, as if she were being ushered forward. Could the alignment of local fields explain why everything seemed brighter and crisper, or was she reading too much into it?

She and the moth tagged along as Elder Two led the way from the station to the gleaming building that wouldn't have looked out of place on the Capitol Plaza of Heliopolis. On closer inspection, the skin of the building was made up of small metallic facets that shifted with the currents, fracturing *Watiwabe*'s odd yellow sun. Standing in its shadow, Olivia peered up at its radial array of supports, massive and drooping under their own weight, which rose from the ground and pierced the intricate shell of the structure. Judging by the number of natals traversing them to get inside, these were no mere supports, but load-bearing truss bridges.

"What is this place?"

"This is the outermost belt of the Zero Pole."

"The . . ."

"The seat of the Empyrean Symbiotry."

Elder Two mounted the nearest bridge and beckoned for Olivia to follow. As she approached the near edge of the ramp, the fareline's gentle clutch impelled her forward with ever greater urgency.

"It all feels so different from what I'm used to," she said as she ascended. "The interactivity of it, I mean. Like I'm part of something in progress."

"Is it such an uncommon arrangement?"

Only in dreams had she felt such an animation in the air. "I'm not even sure how I'd describe it, except maybe . . . euphoria."

"It's an old orchestration," the elder allowed, "but quite appropriate given the venue."

Clusters of natals—tourists perhaps—traversed each span, gawking or meandering, seemingly as rapt by the urban vista as Olivia felt. Elder Two had already gotten a head start on her, and Olivia took the rear with some reluctance, following the path ahead as it grew ever steeper with relation to the ground far below, until it met the skin of the hulking construct. She was sure she'd fall, but some active force kept them both perpendicular to the span, no matter its angle of incline.

Within the Zero Pole facility, the inner landing curved upward until it was perfectly perpendicular to *Watiwabe*'s surface. Vertigo threatened to stop Olivia in her tracks, but she pushed on, stifling her fear of plummeting before it had a chance to take root. She didn't have to understand how the natals had accomplished this feat of engineering, she had only to put one leg in front of the other.

Between two swooping internal buttresses, they came to a portal guarded by a row of natals that Olivia had initially taken for statues—until one of them broke formation.

"Your deeplink will not be permitted," said the natal with the black sleeves.

"Sorry?" Olivia said. "I don't—"

"Your deeplink," Elder Two repeated, extending a hand toward the moth. "The interior is closed to the public."

"Oh, that. I don't know if it's a 'deeplink,' but it came here with Max." It was as much a visitor here as she was. She might have felt badly for it, too—it had been abandoned after all—were it not so doggedly conspicuous. Maybe Max was accustomed to such airborne assistants, but if it insisted on tailing her it would have to learn to give her some breathing room. "Can you just occupy yourself out here for a while?" she asked it.

After several seconds of inaction the moth apparently decided the matter wasn't worth fighting. The device zipped away, disappearing into the crowd.

"Thank you," said Elder Two, and made a hand gesture toward the guards before approaching the portal. Olivia peered past them to the black-and-silver enameled finish of the entryway. Around its inner lip was a string of foreign glyphs, which resolved themselves as she scanned them:

Internal belt access for ??? designees only.
Facilities — Service Beads — Transmission Nodes

As Elder Two approached the portal, the gate parted for them. Being an emissary had its privileges.

———

Hundreds of terraced seats—empty for the moment—filled the grand space within, fully encircling a central dais. The arrangement, made possible only by the natals' creative deployment of gravity, exceeded anything Olivia might have expected to see within a general assembly hall. But more remarkable still was the feeling she experienced as she crossed the threshold. Not elation exactly, but a sense of heightened clarity. It was electric.

Literally.

Olivia caught Elder Two's eye and indicated the nearest aisle. "May I?"

"Please do look around. This is why we brought you here."

She made her way down toward the dais, paying attention to the shifting of the signal as she approached it.

"This space was constructed nearly five hundred cycles ago," came the elder's voice, echoing through the hall, "during a period of general reconstruction we call the Lesson of the Fold. The architects are quite well known. I'm sure you'll see many marks of the Prepotent influence throughout your stay."

The whispering undercurrent actively responded to Elder Two's words, wrapping around them like vines through a slatted fence. But soon the electromagnetic discourse deviated, wandering off into its own inscrutable stream, as if it had its own matters to discuss. And the closer she got to the dais, the less she could tune it out. It was as pervasive as the call of insects in the summer.

When she was nine, her parents—Dalia and Nils—had taken her and Ran camping on Earth, and the first thing she'd noticed was how different it *sounded*, and how those sounds of life were ever-present and all around her. Were the sphere's original architects responsible for the way the magnetic fields were making her feel right now? Or was it a natural phenomenon, simply part of being natal?

Listening to the chatter, Olivia picked out one of the signatures she'd already sensed several times:

. . . syssiffliss . . .

Word, phrase, or symptom, she'd never know if she didn't ask.

Elder Two was still watching her from the periphery. She called up to them. "Can I ask you the meaning of . . ." She was on the verge of reproducing the pattern, but the more she thought about the mechanics of it, the more flustered she became.

"*What are you asking?*" Elder Two approached her, their skin displaying a rolling stipple pattern that Olivia read as satisfaction. They were proud of their assembly chamber, and rightfully so.

Without dwelling on it, Olivia imagined herself reproducing the signature, hoping her transliterators would take care of the details:

. . . syssiffliss . . .

Only it didn't work. It must look like she had fallen into a stupor— she was making a spectacle of herself.

But Elder Two's skin had gone pale. "*What?*"

"Did I do it right?"

"*Who told you that?*"

They'd definitely sensed something then. Good. Now, was there a way to explain what she'd been sensing without worrying them? "I want to know what it all means. Not just the feeling, but the *words*. There's a lot—"

But the elder's *burst-tap-burst-tap* was clear. More than reluctance. Objection.

"*Please try to stay focused on the task at hand.*"

Had she crossed a line? But how would she know if she'd never been told?

"I'm . . . staying on task. Is there something else I should be—"

"*Tomorrow you'll fill the role your Max left open.*"

What?

"No. That was never part of the plan."

But neither was his untimely death.

"*You need to make an appearance in his stead.*"

"I—I can't. Something this important shouldn't be left to an attaché." *Shouldn't be left to* me.

But Elder Two wasn't having it. They assured her that her appearance would be purely ceremonial. Her mere presence would be all the symbolism the body needed.

Or were they throwing her in the deep end to achieve some unknown end? Did they want the human race to come off as clueless, ungainly? First impressions mattered.

"There's so much I don't know," she said. And so much they weren't telling her.

"Which is why we're giving you this preview now." The elder came close, and for a moment Olivia was sure they were going to give her a shove. Instead they put a reassuring hand on her arm, a jarring intimacy. "You are exceeding our expectations."

"Oh," was all she could manage.

"Now we should go."

Could they sense something was wrong with her? Despite their reassurances, the mood had certainly shifted as soon as Olivia had made mention of the whispered word. Could her sensitivity to the whispering be a bad sign? Was there something seriously wrong with her? Had Max experienced any of these phenomena before his demise?

If so, she didn't know how much more of it she could take.

———

As Elder Two led the way to the park across the avenue, Olivia threw her field of view wide—her twelve eyelets now simultaneously contributing to a greater whole—to take in as much of her strange surroundings as possible. It was a mistake. The sheer scale of the full panorama was more than all-enveloping; it tipped toward overwhelming. Better to keep her attentions forward, for a keener, more focused view.

The moth emerged from the teeming afternoon crowd and remained close to her as they approached the edge of the fareline. Beyond it a clearing stretched, the grounds furrowed and ridged and covered in bluish ribbons of vegetative lace—the local version of grass. Small, six-legged animals moved in intricate formations among clusters of natal picnickers, like a complex dance. Most likely, Olivia surmised, their movements were in direct response to the magnetic fields sweeping over the terrain.

But the elder seemed wholly disinclined to step off the fareline. Perhaps they were "staying on task."

The silence between them was like a fog.

"It's still hard to believe what happened to Max and the other elder," she said, then second-guessed. Was she not allowed to ask about that either?

She anticipated the whispered signature before she heard it:

. . . *Butisstapu* . . .

"Let's hope we get answers," Elder Two said. Then added, "The transfer steward's role isn't known for its risk factor."

Olivia emitted a sound not unlike a chuckle.

"We weren't close to our colleague," they went on, "but we worked together for several circuits. Their line will be taking many lights down."

A memorial rite, she assumed. Would there be a funeral?

Olivia looked up at the fractured gleam of *Watiwabe*'s sun. "Do you think there could be some basic incompatibility between human physiology and your transfer process? I mean, as far as—"

"We don't think you have anything to worry about," Elder Two said, understanding her meaning. "You are operating, as they say, within expected parameters."

So then why the reluctance to discuss what she was sensing? "You seemed quick to dismiss my electromagnetic sensitivity. I don't think I'm hallucinating, am I? When I focus on someone, I sense a specific sequence across my skin, in my head." She looked at Elder Two.

. . . *Ssputhu-buta* . . .

"I'm hearing one for you right now."

She attempted to repeat the signature by thinking with as much projection as she could muster:

SStatic-PUlse-THUmp BUrst-TAp.

The elder turned from her and made their way along the fareline's edge, never once stepping onto the grass. Olivia hurried to keep up.

"It is possible that this predisposition of yours relates to some unique aspect of your makeup," they said.

"That would explain the words I'm sensing?"

"Words?"

"Like. . ." *Syssiffliss?*

Elder Two's flesh, now a dull labyrinth of dead ends, was the picture of disapproval. When they spoke, their voice was hushed. "We're sorry you're fixated on something so frivolous."

Fixated? "It's hard to ignore something when it's right in your face."

"Not everyone is susceptible to it as you seem to be. We suspect this is the one unfortunate drawback to your otherwise . . . impressive skill. You'd do well not to make mention of it. We tell you as a courtesy."

Courteous words betrayed by the pattern on their skin, which failed to conceal their irritation. What *was* this whispering that it evoked such antipathy?

The natal stopped under the shade of one of the many wooden spires that rose from the park. They paused, perhaps collecting themself—or finding the right words.

"The old vestigial doggerel does exist, unfortunately," they said at last. "It's a consequence of our proximity to the Fountain, if you must know." Olivia recalled the Fountain from her briefing with Quv Vidalin—the great singularity that all the springs fed into. "It's not unlike the reverberations of words spoken by the mouth of a cave. It's a torment. An agitant. And we're sorry about that. But to express it as you are—to articulate such epithets in polite society—is a vulgarity. It's not seen as polite, Olivia. This is understood. And better we teach you this now than you embarrass yourself later."

They spoke of the whispering as if Olivia had come down with an offensive form of synesthesia.

"I'll be discreet," she said. "I promise I won't embarrass myself, or you. But I have to ask where it's coming from."

Darkening skin, growing ever knottier. "Olivia, do you know people who read fanciful messages in nature's dance?"

Where were they going with this? "You mean like people who see patterns in the chaos?"

"Not just patterns, *instructions*."

"I don't know."

"If you fixate long enough on something—on anything—eventually you'll begin to discover things that aren't there at all."

But she hadn't been looking for anything, had she? Certainly not *fixating*.

"Trust us when we tell you that deriving meaning from that babble is the fetish of charlatans to dazzle the superstitious and the lost. Don't lose yourself to it."

Wow.

"I hear you, Elder," she said, sorry she'd brought up the topic. "I didn't mean to offend."

"It's not something you asked for," they said, walking on. They had reached another line runner hub. "If this is a flaw in your sanctified form, we'll see if there are ways to lessen the disturbance. Until then, we would urge you to exercise some self-discipline."

Before they entered, Olivia caught one last glimpse of the animals rippling like waves over the floral filigree, their dance an embodiment of the patterns beneath the chaos. Should they be blamed for their response to the invisible fields around them?

———

Back in her bead, a notification token on the otherwise blank surface of her comms bay notified Olivia of a waiting message. It was from Aleksi.

Straddling the saddle by the terminal, she touched the illuminated icon.

```
Hey, Liv. Text only, eh? This reminds me of
that prose game I developed in the early days,
My Next Dream. The epistolary one. Not sure if
I told you about it, now that I think of it.
Anyway, I guess dictating this to a blank panel
helps distract me from the fact that I'm
sending this to my partner in another galaxy.
That's still a little hard to fathom, and even
harder to keep secret.

It's hard not to be a little envious actually.
A lot envious. Even though I know basically
nothing. For all I know you're still in hiber-
nation, or however that works. Our pal Tanzig
```

hasn't been super-forthcoming with the details of your itinerary. Maybe you can fill in some of the blanks. Whatever you're up to out there, I hope your joints are behaving.

Speaking of adventure, I'm having one of my own, sort of. My team submitted our story "Wonderful Disarray" for review—fingers crossed—so we're at a natural break point. We all got to talking after you shipped out, and a group of us decided to head down to Avignon, since it features in the game. In France, you know. There's a decent hab here not far from the ruins of the old town. It's still a commercial polity—or I guess it's not a polity at all. Alpes Region. So we had to have credits on us at all times. You can see how different it is when everything is arranged around that transactional expectation.

Chapman's here, and a few others you know. Ged. Yellen. Really, it's just good to get away, whatever the excuse, since it's been a while. Not because travel is hard for us, I mean.

Anyway, it's been quiet here, but pretty hot. I've been sneaking in some work on that side project at night, from my rooms. When it's hot I basically revert to a night creature. A babbling night creature who easily loses his train of thought.

I should get going. There's some kind of food festival at the palace—air quotes, palace. But I hope you're doing important stuff. And I hope it's not too arduous being around you-know-who.

Okay. Hope you get this. Thinking of you.

Olivia stared at his words, tiny glyphs aglow across the panel. Aleksi seemed upbeat, but he was clearly concerned. And he deserved something. She should have written to him before now, even the briefest update. It wasn't like she'd avoided it. But the thought of slowing down enough to articulate everything, right now, seemed like work. Of course she'd only be making things harder for herself by putting it off.

But . . . tomorrow would be a better time to compose a note. She'd be able to tell him about the Symbiotry then.

SIXTEEN
DAY 33

IN THE ZERO Pole assembly hall Olivia sat among strangers, close enough to feel their heat. She'd greeted them as they'd been shown to their assigned saddles, feeling every inch the alien, sure they'd soon observe precisely how out of her depth she was.

There'd been no sign of Elder Two that morning, nor any of the other natals she might have recognized. After waking and taking care of her biological functions, Olivia had pinged the elder, only to be informed that they were occupied. She made do with the food that someone had left in a bulbous container by her bead's portal, and in time two escorts from the so-called External Affairs body arrived at her doorstep to usher her to the line runner hub. They'd been cordial enough, if not overly forthcoming as to her transfer steward's whereabouts.

Now, with the hall nearly full, the din of voices wasn't unlike the sound of the audience before a dance recital. The air churned as the cooling systems struggled to keep up, treating Olivia to a mélange of scents, some natural and others likely not. She looked around at the nearest natals, and it occurred to her that maybe some of them were transfers like her. For all she knew, *everyone* seated around her was a transfer, representatives of other races wrapped up in natal skins. She would have no way of knowing. How might they look on their own worlds? Perhaps similar to her. Perhaps even stranger than the natals themselves.

Did any of them look as out of place as she felt? If so, she couldn't read the signs, but it seemed *they* could. She caught several attendees looking conspicuously away from her. Maybe they were picking up on some cue too subtle for her to detect—her electromagnetic signature, or lack of one. Maybe it was the moth—originally Max's, and now possibly hers by default. The local varieties of drones, now buzzing overhead and throughout the great hall, looked nothing like the moth, which at the moment seemed content to rest on her shoulder ridge.

And was she the only one within the Zero Pole whose legs were entirely without stripes? Possibly. Or she was just being paranoid.

Most importantly, where was Elder Two?

I've been orphaned.

The double meaning of the thought struck her a moment too late. But this couldn't be how they usually ran things. Her assigned transfer steward had promised to brief her on anything she was likely to encounter, not pawn her off on their lackeys. Doubly so now that the designated human delegate was dead and she was being thrust into a role she had no business inhabiting. She'd been cast adrift. If not for her emotional inhibitors, she could never have faced the situation with such a cool head.

Then again, the elder had assured her that her appearance here was purely ceremonial. She just needed to be present and be herself.

She looked down at herself, all legs and restless fingers and over-expressive skin. Whatever it meant to "be herself," it had never been this.

———

At this range the whisper seemed disinclined to identify the speaker now addressing the forum from the dais. Olivia tried to pay close attention, suppressing the persistent thought that she was here not as a representative of anything, but as a stranger. An infiltrator.

Stay in the moment.

No human had ever seen anything like this before. Everything she was experiencing now was unprecedented. At least she could understand the words. There'd been no mention of humanity yet, or hers or Max's names. The first speaker spoke only of revitalization efforts with regard to the initiatives of the Symbiotry. The second had much to say about cultural speciation with regard to certain prevailing mores. Olivia could imagine a similar agenda being laid out at any Sovereign Alliance assembly. Maybe the two species weren't so different after all.

She nearly missed the first mention of "Sol" because the word hadn't been transliterated for her. But now the natal with yellow armbands invoked the name a second time, drawing it out like a steel brush against a pan:

"*Sssolll . . .*"

As if for emphasis.

"This is the domain of humanity," they said. "We have waited for this day with great anticipation, to greet them, to welcome them. Now the human delegation has arrived in this clean domain, as you all have. And their voices will join ours, as yours did before them. We know we speak for those gathered, for those *aligned*, when we say that we look forward to—"

"*Olivia.*"

She snapped to attention just as Elder Two was sliding into her row. They took the empty saddle seat next to her.

"Elder," she said, doing her best to modulate her speakers.

"We do apologize for being so late. It was not by choice."

"I'm glad you're here now." Her emotional inhibitor allowed her the mildest sense of ease. "I've been feeling a little out of my depth."

"We understand your meaning. But you're perfectly equipped to be here." Olivia followed their gaze to the speaker down on the floor. "The addresses made in this cycle are an essential part of your introduction, but the proceedings in this belt will be largely procedural."

She could have used that information prior to attending. "You understand that it'd be hard to know whether I was missing a cue, or maybe something important."

"Everything important—our agreements, our agendas, our promises— those will happen in small, shadowed beads among those whose arms are more colorful than eclipse clouds at end of cycle."

Olivia sat back in her saddle, satisfied for the moment with their assurances. "Are the others here?"

"Which others?"

"Representatives from the other . . . domains?"

"Other domains, other systems, yes, all. This is the Empyrean Symbiotry."

As if that should be self-explanatory.

"I'll introduce some of them to you after this," said Elder Two, as if anticipating her next question. "In fact that's one reason I rushed to get here."

Olivia kept her thoughts to herself and turned her attention back to the speaker, who sounded like they were making their closing remarks.

"As each participating domain has done before it, the domain of humanity now brings its own traditions and cultures into ours." And now the speaker looked straight up at Olivia, the house lights picking her out from the crowd as her skin went almost grid-like with a reflexive, detached acceptance. "You will benefit, as those before you have, from the wealth of the collective, for you will share in our symbiotry. So let us say, to this new member of our great Empyrean Symbiotry . . ."

Now a thunder of voices chanted in unison:

"Welcome, welcome, welcome."

———

Stately music played throughout the hall as Elder Two rushed Olivia out with the moth close behind.

"We know you're probably disappointed to miss the rest of the ceremony," they said as they emerged onto the suspended platform. Olivia held her silence, well aware of the eyes on her as they made their way up and past the outermost rows. "But we have some friends we want you to meet before we return to the habitation hub. We assure you that you don't want to be caught up in the exodus."

With the proceedings still in session, the outer area was nearly empty. But instead of continuing to the external support ramp that they'd crossed to enter the building yesterday, Elder Two took them on an ascending fareline that twisted back around to some kind of brightly lit space ahead.

"Now, just so you know," said Elder Two, never letting up their brisk pace, "the assigned constable—"

... *Wass-wata* ...

"—got back to us—the one you spoke to the other day?"

"I remember."

"According to them, the operations ward is now exploring the possibility that Max's failure was due to foul play."

Olivia ran that through her head again before she could respond. "That's not what I expected you to say." Alarm bells would surely have been ringing were it not for her technologically dampened emotions. But what good would panicking do anyway?

"But since you're no longer a suspect—"

No longer.

"—they don't think it would be fruitful to detain you or keep you in custody."

"Okay." Surely that counted as a vote of confidence. But it didn't explain how the investigation would proceed. Should she be watching her back?

"What did they say had happened?" she asked.

"With Max?"

"Yeah."

"Only that his new analog frame might have been compromised somehow, which would have to have happened sometime before your transfers, at the hands of someone who had prior knowledge of the time and location of your scheduled arrivals. Well, at least Max's."

Had she been overlooked? Or maybe it had been someone's goal to cause an intergalactic incident. She could only speculate.

"The Affairs Chancery and First Seat will be figuring out how to prevent these unfortunate matters from becoming a scandal. In the meantime, instead of bringing you in, they've asked if we might facilitate an excursion for you while they complete their investigation, in case someone decides to target you next."

Olivia considered the elder's situation. They couldn't march her back to the Fountain, since the Sol-side spring would be inactive for the better part of a month—the elder had called it "springstir" during her orientation. And given the added overhead that would be demanded of them by the ongoing investigation, it would simplify their life to have her off their docket, if temporarily.

So what kind of excursion did the elder have in mind? A trip to the countryside, or perhaps ushering her off *Watiwabe* completely?

"Where would I go?"

"We have an idea," Elder Two said. "Follow, please."

———

Beyond the main floor was a verdant confusion of flora, growing as if without regard to gravity. As Olivia followed Elder Two across a garden lounge alive with pearlescent gnats flying in intricate formations, *Watiwabe's* knotty sun mass high above streamed through the open atrium, and the air was hot and thick—and of great relief after the antiseptic atmosphere inside the Zero Pole. The moth seemed less enthusiastic though. It took to the air, zipping off to parts unknown.

From somewhere off to one side came a musical catcall. Two natals—one with red armbands, one with none—stood by a glass balustrade at the periphery of the lounge. Friends of the elder, perhaps?

"This won't take long," Elder Two said, as if Olivia were in some particular hurry. She followed them across the floor, where they greeted the natal with the red armbands using a gesture Olivia didn't manage to catch.

"I thought I recognized you," they replied.

The singular pronoun marked them as a visitor—another common prime. Or *bebethuti*, as Olivia had sensed from the whisper. She examined them for any outward indication of being a transfer, but apart from the lack of an electromagnetic signature, there wasn't one.

"Lequiquin, you're looking well," said Elder Two. "We haven't seen you since . . . when?"

"Not since the Qlin Cooperative Forum, certainly." Lequiquin turned to their naked-armed friend. "As we recall, you never attended our final physical therapy session."

Olivia was starting to think Elder Two didn't like physical therapy. A point in their favor.

"Well, we're glad to see everything worked out." Elder Two moved to the side to usher Olivia forward. "Olivia, these are Lequiquin and Laguayli from the Qlin domain."

"Good to meet you both," she said.

"Friends," said the elder, "we'd like you to meet one known as Olivia, from the domain of humanity."

"Oh, I didn't realize!" said Lequiquin. "Of course."

The two natals before her clasped the hands of their forelimbs together and held them there until Olivia thought to do the same. "We're glad you found the day."

Interesting they hadn't said "cycle."

"That's a traditional greeting," said Elder Two.

"Oh! I . . . thank you. I'm glad too."

Laguayli stepped closer. "Our two peoples—the Qlin and the syss— were neighbors since the Originid first dusted our homes."

"I . . . think I understand." She turned to Elder Two. "The syss are . . . ?"

But their skin displayed markings Olivia read as disparaging. "Don't listen to Laguayli. 'Syss' is an old epithet, as they're quite aware."

Laguayli tried again. "I speak, of course, of the great preceptors of the Fountain, and the aboriginals of this system!"

"So you've known each other for a long time." Could *syss* be related to *syssiffliss*? Olivia didn't dare ask.

"Yes!" said Lequiquin. "You can actually see our home from—" They turned to point out the window, but lost their balance in the process. Only then did Olivia realize that Laguayli had been clinging to the handrail for dear life the whole time, as if standing on rollers.

Nearly as interesting was the fact that Elder Two took no action to help Lequiquin back to their points.

Olivia stepped in to help them back up.

"I'm sorry," they said. "I'm a menace to my own dignity."

"I was a little shaky too when I first woke up," Olivia offered.

"First . . . ? No, my delegation has been living here for three circuits."

Three years? That couldn't be right. How could they still be so clumsy?

"The Qlin were the first to join the symbiotry, a dozen biqua-circuits ago," said Elder Two. Then, to the Qlin, "Olivia and her progenitor arrived here only two cycles ago."

"Two *cycles*? Never would I have guessed that. They move as well as you do!"

"We're pleased with their progress," the elder said, their skin displaying the rolling stipple of pride. "And of course we're excited by the breadth of knowledge and experience the domain of humanity will bring to the Empyrean Symbiotry."

"You sound like your friend with the yellow bands."

Elder Two ignored that.

"Is it true," asked Laguayli, "that their spring is located outside . . . *behpu . . . behpu-mu . . .* Sorry, but I have to keep trying."

Now Elder Two's skin was the picture of agitation. Could the Qlin read such cues? "Speaking the naming tongue aloud is rather pointless."

"Sorry."

Lequiquin tried a more straightforward tack. "She means to ask if you've come to us from outside the galaxy."

"So they tell me," said Olivia.

"'So they tell me!' Such a turn of phrase."

Elder Two's attentions, meanwhile, appeared to be outside the conversation. At the moment they were looking out over the amassed crowd that had been pouring in from the Zero Pole, as if to find an excuse to leave.

"Who else here is an exotic?" Lequiquin was saying. "The aanaati-imaa, I believe, yes?"

"That's right," Laguayli agreed. "You must meet with them while you're here. And of course there will be ample opportunity for the human delegation to meet with each of the others in a more formal capacity."

"That would be lovely," Olivia said. But how long would she be sticking around?

"Sorry to interrupt," Elder Two said. "We must attend to other diplomatic matters."

"Of course," Lequiquin said. The Qlin pair offered a parting salutatory gesture, hand clasped to foreleg. Olivia pantomimed the same.

"Please accompany us," the elder said to Olivia, setting off into the crowd, and she had to hurry to follow. Their departure seemed abrupt, but if the elder was determined to move things along, what choice did she have? "We want you to meet an old colleague of ours," Elder Two said, leading her across the lounge, where three natals appeared to be anticipating their approach. "That's why we're here."

The largest member of the trio—the one fitted with a mechanical black exoframe on their back four legs—had a signature that Olivia sensed from twenty paces away:

. . . *TAp-SStatic-BEat-WAve-SStatic-POp* . . .

Or *Tassbewasspo*.

The other two natals stood out in clothing that almost fully concealed their bodies. That was a first for Olivia, making them look as conspicuous as nudists might on Heliopolis. As with the Qlin, Olivia sensed no signatures from them. They were clearly transfers like her.

As they drew nearer, the elder said, "They're an assembly organizer for Home's fifth ward—"

. . . *POp-SStatic-TIck-BEat-WAve-TAp- SStatic* . . .

Posstibewatass.

"Home," Olivia repeated, trying to keep all the new signatures straight. "Your home planet."

Tassbewasspo greeted them with the *tap-wave-tap-wave-tick* signature Olivia had sensed previously.

"Um, welcome to the day," she said to them, unable to remember the actual greeting the Qlin had used. Was that a Qlin greeting? Were these even Qlin? The two of them clasped their hands before them, and Olivia followed suit.

Before the introductions, *Tassbewasspo* placed a hand on Elder Two's foreleg. "We were sorry to hear of your colleague—"

. . . *Butisstapu* . . .

"—and the loss that will surely be felt by all those they shepherded across. And the loss of your colleague as well," they said, addressing Olivia. "It is such an unfortunate turn of events on this otherwise historic occasion. Our lights come down for them both."

Their skin, in unison, depicted gentle light and dark bands of solemnity. A social convention, Olivia guessed.

"I appreciate that," she said, unable to conjure anything more profound. How should she respond when she didn't know who she was addressing?

"Truly a shocking and senseless tragedy," Elder Two agreed with a quiet voice as they turned to the other two. "You'll surely hear of it, but we'll spare you the details, except to say that the Affairs Chancery has the matter well under control."

"I leave matters of statecraft to those who profit from such things," said the natal on the left, with a tone Olivia might take for scorn. "But we did hear of the incident in question, and can only offer our condolences."

"This is Su-jinda," said *Tassbewasspo,* indicating the natal on their left. Then to the other, "And Su-povoi."

The two of them clasped hands before them, and Olivia returned the gesture.

"We represent the Silu-dou domain," said Su-povoi, "as sponsored by our faithful assembly organizer."

. . . Tassbewasspo . . .

"Did you come down from the Zero Pole?" Su-jinda asked.

"Yes, I'm . . . new here."

"This is the one called Olivia," Elder Two informed the group, "a pilot delegate representing the domain of humanity."

"Very good to meet you."

"We join our voices in welcome of this new delegation," *Tassbewasspo* said.

"Good to meet you all," Olivia said. "As I said, I'm new to this, so I apologize in advance if I address you incorrectly."

"It took me a full circuit before I could remember who was who," Su-povoi confessed.

A laugh suggested itself to Olivia then, but her ability to show it proved elusive. Her emotional inhibitor, it turned out, could be a drawback in social situations. She would have to ask Elder Two to dial it down later.

"Did you enjoy the introductory forum, all things considered?" *Tassbewasspo* asked, their voice sharper and more forward than Elder Two's.

Olivia wasn't even sure they spoke the same language. The words felt different.

"It was enlightening," Olivia said. "I was . . . humbled. To be there. Or maybe overwhelmed is more accurate."

"We imagine it's a lot to take in. Even for someone well versed in foreign affairs."

"Oh, but I'm not really a diplomat."

As she made her admission, the moth returned from its impromptu tour, landing in its usual spot on the ridge above Olivia's frontmost left shoulder. It issued a *tap-tap-tap*, then again once more. Was it trying to alert her to something?

She ignored it. "I was taking the place of my colleague—my father." She looked at Elder Two. "But as he was unable to be there, I was merely standing in, despite my relatively limited experience."

The Silu-dou had both moved in closer. "What is your capacity then, when you're not standing in for people?"

"Oh, well, I'm a poet." That was a stretch. But less so than saying she was an attaché.

"What is a poet?"

Olivia did her best to explain what it meant to be a poet, telling them of language and lyric and the musicality of it all. But she had her doubts as to whether her meanings were translated correctly, not just across language but across culture. But wasn't that a poet's enduring challenge?

"'Olivia,' did your colleague say?" asked Su-jinda.

"Yes, my given name. Or . . . title?"

"Our classification fashions are similar," they said. "While our arts tend more toward the tangible and kinetic, many of our names are the final results of language tournaments. As in 'Su-povoi,' I believe?"

"That's right," their colleague said. "My title emerged from our Hash-vin interactive meet, which runs in my family. Not so much for 'Su-jinda.'"

"No, no such provincial exhibitions among my kin, I'm afraid. Perhaps owing to the distracting dazzle of electricity?"

"That's probably true," said Su-povoi, with a fractal amusement spelled across their skin.

"Would we assume too much," *Tassbewasspo* said, slouching on their mechanical frame, "to suggest that your creative language pursuits might lend to a keener interest in the arts than in the particularities of statecraft?"

Olivia looked at the natal, trying to read between the lines. "Did you have something in mind?"

Tassbewasspo indicated Elder Two, as if they'd already discussed the matter. Because of course they had. "Our friends here are about to set off for the second planet of the Inceptive Expansion—"

. . . *PUlse-THUmp-BUrst-TIck-SStatic* . . .

"—to pay a visit to the Chronicle Library—"

. . . *HIss-SStatic-TIck BEat-SStatic-THUmp WAve* . . .

"—there. It houses a collection of rare books and manuscripts."

So, the *Hissti-bessthu-wa* Library on the planet *Puthubutiss*.

"It also has drawings, prints, and ancient artifacts," Su-povoi put in.

That got Olivia's attention. "Artifacts like the seed?"

"The seed?" asked Elder Two.

"Like the language sculpture the teelise presented to my people on your behalf." The very artifact that had convinced Olivia to come here in the first place.

"A Lore Seed," *Tassbewasspo* explained to the elder, "from Home—"

. . . *Tapuwathu* . . .

"—That's what they mean."

"Ah. That's not our area of expertise," Elder Two said.

"But the library could have things like that?" Olivia asked.

"It may indeed," said *Tassbewasspo*.

The prospect might have sparked excitement if she were less emotionally regulated. "Would it be possible to join you?" she asked.

"If that's something that would interest you," said Elder Two.

Olivia looked at them, turning the question over in her head. The old Olivia would never have flung her existing plans to the winds to visit a library with a group of strangers. But natal Olivia was intrigued by the prospect of an arts jaunt. "Well, before entertaining this admittedly enticing offer, I want to be sure I've first fulfilled my role here, such as it is."

"You've served your purpose here, to our understanding," said *Tassbewasspo*.

Elder Two confirmed this. "Unless we hear otherwise, your role as a stand-in for Max has been fulfilled. And as the spring in your home system is dormant for another two doza-cycles and two, we would *encourage* you to join them."

So that was really all that was being asked of her: a perfunctory appearance at the Zero Pole, and now she was good to go. Max would surely have had greater involvement with matters of state. She was getting off easy. And she wasn't complaining. This was her opportunity— one that might never present itself again.

"Well then, I suppose that's settled," Olivia said. "If you don't mind a guest."

"It would be an honor to have such an esteemed guest," said the assembly organizer.

"We won't let her miss her regression transfer," said *Tassbewasspo* over Elder Two's shoulder.

Regression. Their speciesism was anything but subtle.

"Someone from our transfer team will notify you with enough lead time for your return here," the elder said. "We'll issue you a hotfont so you can maintain instantaneous contact."

"A special communication device?"

"One that works within close proximity to the Fountain or its springs. From anywhere within this system, you'll be able to reach us without the usual transmission delays."

Into the unknown. She had found a way off Max's track—thanks in no small part to Max himself. It almost felt like she was making her own choices, an illusion that might have dissipated quickly if she'd turned their offer down. Still, now that it was decided, she was all too eager to get moving.

"So when do we leave?"

———

They needed to stop by the administration hub, Elder Two said, before she returned to her bead. To collect her hotfont, but also to meet up with a certain constable who wanted to follow up about a certain crime.

As the line runner sped them back to the hub, Olivia asked Elder Two if there was anything she should bring in the way of personal effects or supplies. "Maybe I need clothing? Something to insulate me from the local weather? Do I need to bring a gift for my hosts, or an offering for the library? Will I need personal identification, or . . ."

She stopped herself. Elder Two's skin had been growing mottled before Olivia had even finished. "No such hoard is required here," they said, sounding more concerned than judgmental. "As you find yourself in need, of course you will be provided for. Have you routinely been deprived of anything—"

"No, no, not at all. I was just . . . I just didn't want to be caught unprepared." But it did seem that the natals weren't big on personal possessions, since everything was accessible. That, or she was getting the red carpet treatment owing to her status and the general desire to keep her content.

Constable *Wass-wata* was waiting for them in the reception bead of the administration hub, as promised.

"We'll be right back," Elder Two said, darting out without pausing for pleasantries.

"Thank you for stopping by," *Wass-wata* said. "We only wanted to double-check a couple of items."

"Sure, anything I can do to help," Olivia told them, not for the first time.

Their questions were more conversational than the line of questioning she'd endured initially, but she had nothing to offer them that they hadn't already heard.

Was she aware of anyone who might want to cause harm to Max Mehdipour?

Had she overheard anything that might have led her to believe someone would sabotage his analog frame?

The secret meeting Max had had back on the Teelise Sphere came to mind, not for the first time. He'd never said a word to her about what had transpired in that room, but she'd assumed it was a legitimate meeting. Had someone threatened him? Could that be why he'd been so reluctant to say anything?

She glanced at the moth, now buzzing around the far side of the reception bead. If it knew anything, it was keeping silent about it. And though she couldn't be certain, her gut told her to follow its lead.

Satisfied with her answers once more, *Wass-wata* bid her safe journey, and exited for the fareline.

"This is the only thing you'll need," Elder Two said, entering the bead as if on cue. They handed her a slim handheld device, little more than a gel panel on a flexible frame. The elder explained to her the utility and operation of her hotfont, and about natal communication services in general.

Most importantly, between the local version of ambionts and her hotfont, Olivia would be able to reach anyone she'd come into contact with, live, whether in transit or at any standard transmission node.

———

The telltale fog of advancing torpor settled over Olivia as the moth zipped across her bead and affixed itself to the inner surface of her window wall. Only now did she realize how much of a toll the day's events had taken on her. But she couldn't cede to the siren song of her torpor hull, not until she gave Aleksi some indication that she was still alive.

She requested a transmission node, and the instruments emerged— panel and input strip both—from the wall at her side. As before, back in the Teelise Sphere, the only entry she could open was pre-addressed to Quv Vidalin, who would continue to act as intermediary and censor.

Staring at her six long alien fingers, she asked the bead, "Okay if I dictate?" As proficient as she was with her natal form, she didn't need to test her dexterity with a new input device.

"Whenever you're ready," it said.

Pulling a saddle seat over, Olivia settled in front of the interface, but found herself suddenly without a clear idea of how to start.

Just start.

"Hi, Aleksi."

Always a safe bet. She imagined him bringing her letter up in their lounge, Somtow at his side.

"I'm sorry it's taken me so long to say anything. Part of the reason is that there's only so much I'm *allowed* to say . . . which is especially diffi-cult when there's so *much* to say."

She took a breath as she sifted through the topics in her head. Aleksi didn't know about the mandatory mind transfer process, which made painting a clear picture nigh impossible. He knew only that she had trav-eled to the *Bebetathubutiwa* system, or Beringia as they called it. And as for Max . . . there was no way she'd be able to get that information past Quv. She'd just have to talk around the specifics.

"I'm doing well—surprisingly well, given how different things are over here. In fact it's hard to describe just *how* different."

Could she be any more vague? Perhaps it would be easier to just let fly and let Quv and the SA clean up after her.

She shifted to a more comfortable position in her saddle seat. "So, what's going on right now? Well, the multispecies assembly—the reason Max and I came here—takes place on a shellworld construct in the natal domain. The remote domain. That's where I am right now. I'm in my room. They call it a 'bead.' Outside my window it's similar to Vaix in some ways, with rolling countryside, and commercial centers, and civic centers . . . only it's all on the inside of a sphere. Which means, yes, it all defies gravity. Meaning that the natals employ some kind of localized gravitation to hold it all together. And it's amazing. It's *disconcerting*, for sure. If you keep your eyes focused on the immediate, it's no problem. But when you take in the full vista . . . *whew*. But they've really done it, you know? It's beautiful and jarring.

"On top of all that, their relationship to electromagnetic fields is profound. The fields' orientations influence their architecture, their language, even their perceptions. Imagine feeling the wind in your face, only . . . anyway, I can only imagine. The natals operate in a very different perceptual space from humans. Think of birds, I guess. Or sharks.

"I'm just getting started, but you can see how those qualities of the environment, pervasive as they are, would color the whole experience. Not that it's unpleasant. I'm getting used to it. My orientation process has taken several days. Just being here with your eyes open can be an overwhelming experience. But there's also a coherent internal logic to the way things work here. It's not haphazard, or perilous. Cosmetically it's different, but . . . it's smart, too."

She sighed and gazed out the window from her saddle. From a distance the panorama before her might not have looked out of place on Vaix. It was up close that the illusion of familiarity fell away.

"I feel like I'm not really doing it justice, but . . . well, this is as much as I can share. And what you're getting is probably a lot less than I just dictated. The rest of it . . . Aleksi, there's so much I could say. But I guess it'll have to—"

A polite tone sounded, and she turned to find the console's screen dark, with a message at the center in Interlish:

```
Intercession State
Message to be reviewed by First Seat core prior
to transfer
```

The First Seat? So not only was the SA monitoring her exchanges, the natals had their own filters in place as well. But what had triggered the censor? Was it something specific she'd said, or perhaps the merest suggestion that she might be withholding details?

Olivia attempted to review her message, but it was nowhere to be found. And she hadn't even gotten to talk about her excursion to the library on *Puthubutiss*. She'd try Aleksi again once she was planetside. Maybe the restrictions would be looser there.

As she dismissed the transmission node and prepared herself for torpor, Olivia probed her thoughts for any hint of excitement about tomorrow's journey. But her emotional inhibitor allowed her only the dimmest satisfaction. Natal Olivia could neither fully experience nor fully express the breadth of her experiences. But her thoughts and perceptions, she was sure, remained hers. Whatever essential thing that made her who she was was still intact.

I am still myself.

SEVENTEEN
DAY 33-34

THE NIGHT BROUGHT with it a vexing chatter, ceaseless electrical blooms across nerve endings Olivia was helpless to shield against. The ambient purr of the habitation hub was no match for the whispering, so clear now that she could pick out pieces of it.

She sat up, struggling to steady herself within the netting, and glanced at the moth, which was still affixed to her window, seemingly in a dormant state. But for her, torpor seemed out of the question.

Stilling herself, she listened. Though perhaps it wasn't *listening*, exactly. She reached out using whatever sensory apparatus this body of hers was outfitted with. And the signal tickling over her—through her—was definitely not random noise. It had a natural rhythm, ebbing and flowing, like a conversation would.

Olivia extracted herself from the torpor hull, and the whispering grew even more distinct. Could it be directional then? Could it be coming from something nearby?

She headed for the portal. The least she could do was find out—or try at least—what was causing it.

Allowing herself to be guided by the chatter in her head, she followed the fareline out of the habitation hub and into the close night air. The fareline's fleshy surface, a ghostly ribbon among countless others, emitted a gentle glow, and it was enough to navigate by as she made her way around a whorl that branched off into a sharp switchback. There the whispering was the loudest, far stronger than it had been in her bead.

But the fareline was deserted, stretching out ahead of her into an unknown gloom. The sphere's distant overhead interior surface formed the night sky, and its stars were the colored lamps of hundreds of other hubs.

The whispering continued.

. . . ddeshaa-ssylesh-approach-the-other-mysshouth . . .

Something was here, close by.

Following the sound, Olivia peered over the railing. She saw them on the landing below: three natals huddled together. They were too far away to be heard, but she had no trouble at all sensing the sequences of their electromagnetic signals. It *had* to be coming from them.

What exactly were they doing? If this was an alternate means of communication, she hadn't witnessed anyone else doing it. Their sequences used the same "channel" as the whispering, but they were more immediate, more distinct. This was an ongoing discourse, varied and verbose—and as foreign to her ear as the body she now inhabited.

Elder Two would have had a conniption. *The fetish of charlatans*, they had called it.

Staying out of sight, Olivia listened in. Most of the natals' words— assuming that's what they were—had no meaning to her, and her transliterator was of no help with this form of language. But occasionally she sensed a familiar turn of phrase, or the odd word, or—

. . . max-mehdipour . . .

The shape of the man's name was so foreign in electromagnetic form that it almost got by her.

Foul play, Elder Two had said. Could these natals be behind Max's death?

Only as the thought occurred to her did Olivia notice them looking up at her—first one, then all three. They'd spotted her, somehow. Or *sensed* her. She hadn't been careful enough, and now . . . nothing. She watched them watching her from the landing below. And after a moment their electromagnetic pulses picked up again. And she had no doubt she was sensing them when she detected her own name:

. . . natrush-ohllivia-jeyllani-ahlassann . . .

142

The rest of their exchange danced just beyond intelligibility. But she wasn't hallucinating. And she wasn't afraid.

"I can hear you," she called down to them, feeling the dull pang of doubt only after. Had that been a bad idea?

They went silent and watched her as if to see what she might do next. Or maybe they simply hadn't understood. Maybe they could *only* speak in that electromagnetic tongue. Maybe she could do the same, signaling her name back to them using—

"Olivia?"

She nearly jumped out of her skin.

It was Elder Two, making their way down to her from the opposite fareline. "We didn't expect to find you here. Were you not in torpor?"

"I was, yes. But then . . ." What could she tell them that wouldn't make them freak out like they did last time? "I couldn't sleep, so I came down here. And I was chatting . . ." She looked back over the railing, but the fareline below was deserted.

"Speaking with someone?"

"To some fellow night owls, I guess." Someone none too eager to be seen by officials of the state.

"A nocturnal creature," said Elder Two a second later. "We understand your meaning." They did nothing to mask the vaguely negative maze-like pattern on their skin. "It's quite late. But since we're both awake, how about we accompany you back to your bead?"

She chanced a glance at the landing below, somehow knowing the people she'd encountered were no threat to her, and yet knowing just as clearly that she couldn't trust those feelings.

"Yes," she told the elder. "I would appreciate the company."

———

Back in her quarters and suspended once more in her torpor hull's netting, Olivia couldn't keep her run-in with the three whisperers out of her thoughts. By some unknown means those natals had communicated in a way that resembled *Watiwabe's* ambient babble, adding their inscrutable patterns to the torrent. She and Max had clearly been in their thoughts. Who were they? And why had they been skulking around under cover of night?

In the darkness of her bead, her instinct was to tell someone of her encounter. But to what end? The investigation into Max's death would be pursuing all avenues, but that didn't mean that every utterance of her name was material evidence.

If she thought to do so, maybe she would mention the natals to *Wasswata*. But later. All she wanted to do right now was look ahead to *Puthubutiss*.

She lay in her netting, her mind adrift, the ambient whispering washing over her, its obscure poetry a constant companion, seemingly unknowable to her.

She listened.

Until she fell into torpor.

PART THREE
APEX

EIGHTEEN
DAY 34

FROM THE OBSERVATION port of assembly organizer *Tassbewasspo*'s shuttle, Olivia watched as *Watiwabe* receded against a sea of foreign stars. From a distance the immense construct bore almost no resemblance to the Teelise Sphere; instead of smooth skin, it featured complex swirls and layers upon glazed layers, as if it had been suspended in motion. The sight of it almost made her feel wistful. But something else, too: a gentle tug around the back of her head and down her torso. Not emotional, but a physical sensation that coincided with the whispering's own ebb.

She shifted in her saddle in an attempt to alleviate the mysterious malaise.

"Yes, it's always uncomfortable," *Tassbewasspo* said, sidling up in their articulated armature. "But the strain won't last long. Once we're clear of the structure's influence, your ampullae can acclimate to the flat response of our reliable transporter."

She noted that the assembly organizer had no signature now. Apparently there was no whispering without the modulated electromagnetic fields of *Watiwabe*.

"Ampullae?" she asked. "Is that a natal word?"

"Hard to say, since we can't hear what you're hearing. But they're your electroreceptors. You can actually see them here and here." They indicated their own face, minuscule divots in the skin running down into their neck. "There are some who find the third Case construct's embrace to be oppressive. Ourself among them."

At least she wasn't the only one feeling the unpleasant shift. Maybe this was the natal equivalent of some people liking hot weather while others preferred cool.

"If I may ask," Olivia said, "what are you wearing on your legs?" The framework looked polished and sleek, but strong.

"How do you like it?" *Tassbewasspo* said, their skin gone marbled with gratification. "It's a little augment for this old body."

"Well, it's impressive. Almost sculptural."

"For a common prime, you have a good eye," they said. A backhanded compliment?

Before Olivia could inquire further, the natal departed without elaborating.

———

Olivia dozed for a bit in the common area beneath a grand glassy dome. She awoke to an endless spray of stars, save for a bizarre aberration near the dome's top, like an image with a tear at the center. Was this a projection then, and not a transparent membrane?

The moth settled on her leg as if summoned. Olivia shook it off. "You really are a space invader, aren't you?" It hovered over her, its own little aberration. "You're too reticent to be perching on me." She waited, but her criticism elicited no response. "Nothing to say for yourself?"

The device issued only a *burst-tap-burst-tap* of doubt.

"You don't say."

How long had she been asleep? Suddenly curious, she went through her sling bag and retrieved the hotfont. The words on the translucent film resolved as she scanned them: *Steady connection.* The knowledge that she could still reach *Watiwabe* was reassuring, at least.

"Look, there," said Su-povoi, suddenly by her side.

"Hello," said Olivia, stowing her communicator. The Silu-dou was pointing up at the dome. "Yes, I'd noticed that too. A micrometeorite fracture, maybe?"

"No, that's the Fountain."

Olivia looked again, more carefully. The artifact had grown until its edges positively coruscated like a knife's edge caught in a beam . . .

She had to look away.

"It's difficult to look at, isn't it?" Su-povoi said. "Especially the first time."

"So that's how I got here? How we all got here?"

"All save for our hosts."

Su-jinda had now joined them, taking the saddle chair beside her colleague. "Enjoying your view of the mother of all the springs, I see."

"It's an odd sight," Olivia said. Even so, it was difficult *not* to stare at it. The edges of the anomaly were so distorted that she was sure she was looking at herself from behind, peering into yet another iteration of the Fountain.

"Do you see what I see? How does it do that?" Was the Fountain watching her watching it?

"I couldn't begin to tell you," said Su-povoi, his skin displaying wavelets of reassurance.

"I mean, is it a natural phenomenon?"

"The Fountain we see now," Su-jinda said, "is the product of generations of technical development. But yes, its core essence existed long before the natals came along." She gazed up at the dome, seemingly unfazed. "The story goes that it was a spacetime anomaly that vexed our hosts for most of their history, until—"

. . . *murmur-whir hiss-wave* . . .

"—came along."

The Silu-dou's sudden expression of electro-phonemes was as crisp and immediate as anything else she had said, seamlessly integrated into her speech. She had whispered just like the three strangers in the night. And she'd assumed Olivia would pick it up.

Muwhi-hiwa?

"Is that the name of a natal?" Could she parrot it?

"Their signature," Su-jinda corrected. "And they were one of the most honored natals in history, across their cultures. Because the—"

. . . *Muwhi-hiwa* . . .

"—project led to . . . well, what we see before us."

"But we all reap the benefits of their work," said Su-povoi.

"It is rather astonishing," Olivia said. "But it hurts to look at."

NINETEEN
DAY 36

TASSBEWASSPO'S SHUTTLE reached *Puthubutiss* in the dead of night, and the planet's terrestrial whisper announced itself, to Olivia's surprise, well before the shuttle had landed. In fact, the whispering was even stronger here than it had been on *Watiwabe*. She was just going to have to come to terms with it. Fortunately, other conditions on *Puthubutiss* seemed rather pleasant. The gravity was somewhat lower than it had been on *Watiwabe*, the air reassuringly soupy. And though Olivia could make out little of their surroundings from her vantage point at the open airfield, she could appreciate the mixture of foreign fragrances on the warm breeze. The air was redolent of fruit and honey, spiced with a minty tang that might have made her giddy if not for her emotional inhibitor.

Oh shit.

She'd meant to ask Elder Two to disable the inhibitor before she left *Watiwabe*, but had been too distracted by her midnight encounter. She would have to remain cool and distant for the time being. Still, she didn't need to feel excitement to appreciate her present circumstances. Being aboard *Watiwabe* had been a singular experience, but now she stood upon the soil of an actual inhabited alien planet. The first human to ever do so.

Even if it's not with my own feet.

She and the members of her party were met by a small team of hospitality stewards who provided directions to their accommodations. On the ride to their habitation cluster in an open-air shuttle long enough to accommodate their entire party, Olivia realized the moth was not with them. It had vanished into the shadows as they crossed the spaceport tramway, and had not returned. All the better if she didn't have to see it again until they returned to the spaceport for their final departure.

As they rode, *Tassbewasspo* supplied Olivia with information about their accommodations, including where and when her party would meet tomorrow morning. Apparently she would have to acclimate to an earlier start.

Tassbewasspo explained, "Unlike the Symbiotry Sphere—"

. . . *Watiwabe* . . .

"—the high moment will signal a little earlier here, due to seasonality."

She took their meaning without understanding the mechanisms behind it. The natals certainly seemed closely bound to the particularities of their environment. Maybe that explained why, despite having slept on the shuttle, she was already feeling drowsy.

———

From the privacy of her torpor bead, Olivia fought off her growing fatigue to contact the constable *Wass-wata*. She sensed their electromagnetic signature as soon as their mirage sprang up from the gel surface of the hotfont—a clever technological trick.

"Common prime Olivia."

"Constable. I hope I'm not catching you at a bad time."

"Bad?"

It was impossible to tell which concepts would fail to translate. "Um, you said I should reach out to you if I ever had pertinent information with regard to the investigation."

"Yes."

"Well, there is one thing."

"One thing?"

"Yes. On my last night on the Symbiotry Sphere, I overheard three strangers, out on the public farelines. They mentioned Max by his name —by his title. And when they saw me they mentioned mine."

"Mentioned it to you?"

"Not directly to me. They were . . . I wasn't that close to them." Too far to overhear. "They were communicating with each other."

Tick-tick.

"What was the context?"

Was the constable already annoyed?

"It was night. I couldn't sleep, so I left my torpor bead, alone, for a walk out on the farelines. I saw three strangers on another fareline, but I couldn't hear what they were talking about. I only understood when they used our titles."

"You didn't recognize them?"

"No."

Wass-wata looked away briefly, whether to organize their thoughts or to engage a colleague she couldn't tell. "And how did you say you came across these three strangers? So we're clear."

"Just . . . randomly. They were standing together, talking I assume, when I saw them below, on a separate fareline."

"And you were out for a walk?"

"Because I couldn't sleep. Right."

Their head flicked away again. "We'll put in a request for your whereabouts that night and see what other point traffic was in the area."

"Thank you." Well, that hadn't been so bad.

"Olivia, did you not think to mention this to us *before* you traveled to the second planet of the Inceptive Expansion?"

She would have winced if such a thing were possible. She glanced down at her skin: calm, even stipples. "I meant to contact you, but . . . there's been a lot going on."

"Yes, including your colleague being dead."

What could she say to that? Nothing. "I hope this is helpful, constable."

After several quiet seconds, they said, "We'll see. Do you know when you'll return?"

She told them she planned to stay for several hexa-cycles. "Should I contact you when I get back?"

"Unless you have another encounter, there's no need. If there's anything we need, we'll contact you."

The connection was severed before she could respond.

TWENTY
DAY 37

OLIVIA HAD FAILED to keep her hopes about the Chronicle Library in check, and her first impression from its grand entrance did little to diminish her expectations. The place was a marvel of engineering. Its soaring frame celebrated *Puthubutiss*'s particular electromagnetic lines of force, with its aerial exhibit hubs arranged radially around a central concavity, like a vast droplet's liquid crown.

When it became clear that the others were here only to ogle the extravagant grounds, Olivia made an excuse to go out on her own. For a while she wandered from exhibit to exhibit—mainly early manuscripts and decrepit sculptures—accompanied only by the ever-present whispering. She hoped to find insights about natal languages—or better yet, a Lore Seed, like the one the teelise had given to humanity.

But when at last she found one, it was an immediate disappointment. Tucked in a back corner of one of the older exhibits, it was so poorly lit and haphazardly arranged as to appear forgotten. And indeed it was little more than a husk now, the strands of words around its partially shrouded inner core having long grown inert, if they had ever been in motion to begin with. A creation she had effectively crossed a galaxy to see had been all but discarded by the people who had devised it, like a used-up carnival curiosity.

Her search for sources of actual research proved fruitless. It seemed the library's store of actual books was minuscule, in favor of *sculptures* of books, plus innumerable busts of famous authors and scholars. The Chronicle Library, hailed as a monument to natal literature, was more like a mausoleum, the literature itself regrettably absent, nothing left but the secret yammering in her head.

In the end, she wandered the grounds aimlessly, until she found herself outside, walking a perimeter path around the complex. The exotic local fauna seemed far more varied than what she'd seen aboard *Watiwabe*. For a time she watched a flock of six-legged feathered starfish made quick work of a lawn covered in purple down. Her feet eventually followed voices to a back patio, where a group of young natals were playing a complex counting game with their long, tapered fingers. The rules were inscrutable, but watching these youths was oddly reassuring. *They* didn't mind that a significant portion of the history on display within was fading, so perhaps neither should she.

———

After spending half the local day cycle at the library, Olivia met up with *Tassbewasspo* and Su-jinda, plus a few of their colleagues, on a walk along a greenway teeming with life. She couldn't have imagined a greater contrast to the library, so much so that she only half-heard the conversation on the way. Fortunately the discussion did not call on her participation, leaving her free to watch the hypnotic sway of bejeweled whip plants, and the turtle-like land jellies carving paths through dewy moss grove.

A hoarse whimper shook Olivia from her meditation. She turned to see *Tassbewasspo* on the ground, legs splayed. And making a hasty retreat —darting now into the coppice—was another natal, who appeared to have a considerable portion of *Tassbewasspo*'s exoframe slung over their shoulders.

Without thinking, Olivia leapt off the path and pounded after the assailant. This was madness—sprinting through unknown vegetation, possibly protected or poisonous—but the thought didn't trouble her. And, she realized, she was closing the distance—perhaps because the natal was slowed from lugging the extra hardware. She was actually going to catch up to them.

And when she did? Then what?

The natal ahead of her was small—an adolescent, perhaps. Hopefully they weren't armed, or willing to do something stupid in front of the dozen or so other natals watching from the garden path. With luck, the thief, once caught, would simply hand over *Tassbewasspo*'s armature, and she could carry it back with her.

When Olivia was close enough, she used a sweep of her frontmost leg to send the smaller natal tumbling. She wrested the augment from them as they struggled to extricate themself from a knot of fibrous weeds. She had no intention of engaging them any further, and yet she didn't immediately depart. Something kept her there, standing up to her second knee joints in black flax and spore-venting tubules, transfixed by the sight of the thwarted mugger.

"Sun-blind ship rotter!" they cried, livid, but already shrinking back. Indeed, their assessment of her was written plainly across their flesh— not the strobe of anger, but a new reaction, something Olivia hadn't seen before: a clashing spray of stains, like spilled ink.

Fear.

"Knocking over an old man is your idea of fun?" Olivia asked.

"*Swag taker!*" The smaller natal gave her a gesture that required no translation, then dashed away.

Olivia watched until they had disappeared into the foliage, leaving her with only the pounding, coursing heat, as well as a new emotion of her own, one almost powerful enough to overcome her inhibitor and put her off balance. And with her heart's unrelenting thrum came the electric prickling of adrenaline.

It was . . . *intoxicating*.

A shout of excitement from the direction of civilization reminded Olivia of the burden she had hanging from her arms. Hefting the still-warm framework, she trudged back toward the greenway, to the general plaudits of her party as well as several passing strangers who had witnessed the incident.

"Are you okay?" Olivia asked *Tassbewasspo* as she handed them the missing portion of their exoframe.

"All is well," her host said, less to her than to the onlookers, who went on their way, realizing the show was over.

Tassbewasspo took some minutes to snap everything back into place—perhaps the device should have been more securely fastened to begin with—and made a show of testing everything to make sure it was sound. "Assault was a small price to pay for the pleasure of watching Olivia chase down the perpetrator."

"That was truly impressive," Su-jinda said to Olivia. "You'd already jumped into action while I was still trying to assess what had happened."

"It wasn't planned," Olivia said. Which was what made it so unfamiliar. It had come naturally, hadn't it? The old Olivia would have just watched it all play out along with the others.

"We must confess," *Tassbewasspo* said, "that we're glad to have you by our side." Then, to the others, "Come, let's not delay a moment more."

————

Evening brought the spiced winds Olivia had first smelled on the night of their arrival, and a chorus of call-and-response voices that sounded more like stringed instruments than insects.

Beneath a diaphanous net that pitched and swelled between the soft patio and the deep turquoise wash of sky, *Tassbewasspo* held their gathering at a table decked with arrangements of flavor strips, the natal version of digestifs. The natal's friend *Powhita-himu* was in attendance, as were Su-jinda and two other representatives from alien domains, introduced to Olivia as Gundetukesp and Albannaruu.

The topic of the evening was the theft *Tassbewasspo* had endured in broad daylight, and Olivia's quick thinking—and quicker sprinting—that had brought the incident to a tidy resolution.

"We can't say we were surprised. What else but obdurate banditry could anyone expect from this decaying sump?" *Tassbewasspo* asked the group, their skin indicating not revulsion but a dirtier turbulence. Was that arrogance? "It's been in decline since our early evangelist circuits."

"Worse than that," said Gundetukesp, "word is the common primes here are losing the use of their distal digits."

"Did you catch their stench?" *Powhita-himu* asked, the pattern playing across their skin now mirroring that of their host. "That desperate fetor is something you would smell only here, be assured."

Tassbewasspo rapped on the table. "That should only make it easier to find where the rest of them are hiding!"

Olivia occupied herself with a flavor strip that, on contact with her soft palate, exuded a savory, meaty flavor. Maybe the indelicate banter at her table was a salty local custom. The thief had struck her as more blundering than monstrous or sub-natal. Maybe she was missing some key context.

"My friends," said Albannaruu, "let's not burden our guest of honor with our fanciful scenarios."

If they had sensed her quiet, at least now they might be ushered to less charged topics.

"The only burden is ours," *Powhita-himu* said, "because we'll never know the thrill of such a clean catch."

This was met by a murmur of approval.

"I'm just glad no one was hurt," Olivia said, adding, "and that there's nothing to detract from the many wonders we've seen today." If she could have made it a toast, she would have.

"Modest *and* generous," said Albannaruu, their speakers unencumbered by the myriad flavor strips hanging from their lips. They turned to *Tassbewasspo.* "Where *did* you find these delicious morsels?"

"From beyond the Local Knot—"

. . . *Bepumu-wabemu* . . .

"—like all the most enticing delicacies."

"I'm more curious about our friend from the Second Seed Whorl—"

. . . *Mupobuta-!hiss* . . .

It was a signature Olivia hadn't sensed before. The alien must be talking about galaxies now.

Gundetukesp leaned conspiratorially close to her. "Is everyone so *quick* as you are in the domain of humanity?"

"I don't know. I didn't know I *was* that quick. I've never run before." *Not in this body.* "Honestly, I don't know what I was thinking, chasing after them like that."

"Nonsense," said *Powhita-himu.* "If anything, your performance will only make us mourn your absence at the 'Just Cull.'"

"Oh, now that would be a sight!" Gundetukesp said.

"The what?"

Powhita-himu's skin betrayed their excitement. "On the moon of Bright Core's Second!"

. . . *CLICK-WAve-MUrmur-HIss* . . .

The sequence had begun with the electromagnetic equivalent of an alveolar click, a sharp pop still used in some of the oldest human languages—and often transliterated as an exclamation point in Interlish. She would think of the signal as *!Wamuhi.*

"Where the tanthids roam!" Gundetukesp said.

The word failed to translate for Olivia. "Sorry, I need more context."

"It's quite the lively moon," *Powhita-himu* said, "with myriad attractions for all. But the lure of the Just Cull is what separates it from lesser destinations. The local flora, the tanthids, are the moon's most agile creatures. But not harmless! Sure, the bantam members are manageable enough, but the primes . . . they're best avoided."

"Although we might make an exception for our xenogenous friend," Albannaruu said.

"It would be an even match with this one," said *Powhita-himu*, "judging by their display today."

What were they talking about?

"When you talk about a cull," Olivia said, "do you mean . . . thinning out a population?"

"Well, naturally," said *Tassbewasspo*. "But keeping in mind they are lesser entities, the tanthids. Overgrowths, really."

Fractal-like curls all around the table.

A hunt, then.

"Well, I'm more inclined to write a poem about hunting," she told them, "than to actually kill something myself."

"I don't believe that for a moment," said *Tassbewasspo*.

"Your size gives you away, see," *Powhita-himu* said. "You can't hide your ridge flares. I can see them from here."

Olivia looked at herself, pushing away the defensiveness before it showed on her skin. The sockets where her shoulders met her torso did broaden at their crests. Was that remarkable? A glance around the table gave her some indication: smaller shoulders, smoother joins.

"She wouldn't know," *Tassbewasspo* said to the others. Then, to her, "The outgrowths are nothing to be ashamed of. It happens. And it's not something you'll be able to hide."

It seemed the natals were reveling in a bit of discrimination at the expense of their naïve guest. It was plain in their skin patterns, which indicated various levels of amusement, but also something else. Was it . . . admiration? If they were smaller than she was, the difference was slight.

"Why don't you tell me more about these tanthids?" Olivia asked, keen to move the focus away from herself.

"Well, the main thing," *Tassbewasspo* said, "is that it's *not* a hunt. The tanthids are plants."

"Plants?"

"They grow up from the earth, yes."

"But *mobile*," Gundetukesp said. "Very much so. Sentient? Not at all."

"We're trying to reassure you that a cull participant isn't committing genocide," *Tassbewasspo* said.

"Unless one kills the heart mother that gives an infestation its drive," *Powhita-himu* added, "there is no pain involved. Not as we understand pain."

"Okay," Olivia said. "So like plant gathering rather than a hunt?"

"Not so passive as gathering," said *Tassbewasspo*. "The challenge is that the heart mother senses the entire field of play, but the participants see only what's in front of them."

"It's a structured event," *Powhita-himu* explained, "where participants are segregated by skill, and each field is strictly monitored. After the tanthids have been specially prompted, the resulting frenzy can last for the better part of a cycle. It's that survival display that makes them so fascinating."

"You would never be in danger," said *Tassbewasspo*.

Because she would never consider going.

Only that wasn't strictly true: she'd been picturing herself on some alien tundra with every word of their description. She'd never hunted, nor had the slightest curiosity about such an undertaking. But another thought was keeping the question open. Her sure-footed interception of the runaway natal had reawakened a sense of herself she hadn't felt for . . . how long? How long had it been since she'd felt anything close to physical mastery, not just of some grand feat, but of mere *movement*? Her early dance career had been cut short by uncooperative bones and ligaments. Her achievements since then, artistic and intellectual, may have been just as rewarding, but never in quite that *visceral* sense.

"It doesn't sound like anything I've seen before," she said. "You've all participated?"

"It's a popular local pastime," said Su-jinda. "Even Su-povoi entered the park several circuits ago."

"Would you consider it?" *Tassbewasspo* asked. "Joining us? Delaying your return?"

"Even the neophyte course provides an unparalleled boost to one's confidence," *Powhita-himu* said.

Olivia's answer—*old* Olivia's answer—sat at the edge of her speaker as the rest of the table went silent. What if, this time, she didn't turn the invitation down? Nothing technically precluded her from taking a small detour before returning to her post. Why forgo a truly novel experience just because the old Olivia couldn't have—*wouldn't have*? For fear of—

No, this would be an act of pure, demonstrative agency, the very thing to prove to herself that she *was* still herself. For once, the less she behaved like the old Olivia, the more Olivia she still was.

"I could go," she said, her voice hers, yet not. "At least to spectate. Assuming Elder Two—"

. . . *Ssputhu-buta* . . .

"—cleared me to go."

"They mean their transfer steward," *Tassbewasspo* explained to the others, "to whom they've forged a formidably close connection." They sounded almost disparaging, though Olivia saw nothing damning on their skin.

But they hadn't been embroiled in a murder investigation. They weren't waiting for the portal to their home system to reopen.

Was she?

"That's okay, they're being careful," said Su-jinda. "It's sensible."

"We can file an inquiry with the Affairs Chancery, to be sure," *Tassbewasspo* said. "But your transfer steward shouldn't mind. It is worth going, even if only to observe."

"See something new," said Su-jinda. "Expand your horizons."

"Okay," Olivia said, less a decision than an admission. "Why not?"

———

Before they went their separate ways for the evening, *Tassbewasspo* walked Olivia to a secluded branch of the greenway. They seemed none the worse for wear, or maybe she was more keenly aware of the stature of the other members than she'd been before.

"If you do join us, know that your hotfont won't work out on the moon of Bright Core's Second."

. . . !Wamuhi . . .

"It's too far from the Fountain."

That's right, there was some essential link between that instant communication device and the anomaly lurking within the natal system.

"Thanks for reminding me. I'll speak with them before we leave."

As they continued down the path, *Tassbewasspo* was silent, save for the muted staccato of their exoframe. Was there something else?

"Let me thank you again for stepping in earlier," they said at last.

"I'm sorry it happened."

"For all my big talk, I was discouraged." But their skin went from frustration to acceptance. "You'll find that it's tough work being old. The fact is that I need my augments."

"It's good you've kept your independence." *Hypocrite.* If Ran could hear her he'd never let it go.

"Oh, there are better ways to go about that," they said. "This ostentatious rig of mine is pure ego. Pure vanity. I have it polished every night."

Olivia displayed amusement.

"I could transfer to a new frame, sure. But I want people to know that this form, most sanctified, is a *survivor.*"

"You know, I can relate," Olivia said. "Back home I lived in almost constant pain, due to a genetic disorder. But I refused to let it win. If my body was going to betray me, it would be on my own terms."

Tassbewasspo's skin flashed several patterns that were hard for Olivia to get a read on. "Well that's hardly the same thing, is it?"

She didn't know how to respond.

They put a hand on her arm. "Your baseborn form is not sanctified." Then, to Olivia's surprise, they departed.

———

Back at the habitation cluster, Olivia found two messages waiting for her on the transmission node in her bead, the first from Aleksi, and the second from Ioor Volkopp.

Pleasure first:

```
Hey, Liv. I was glad to hear you're having such
a good time in that exotic world you describe.
You're right that it's hard to imagine, so I
appreciate your trying to paint the picture.
Something else is still hard for me to imagine
though—I got to thinking about this after
reading your message. I was trying to remember
when was the last time you sounded so serene.
It's been too long, I know that much. Maybe
being around your father is actually a healing
thing for you?

I don't want to make it sound like I'm not
happy for you. Your name will be in the annals
of history forever, first for poetry, and now
for your aliens. That's quite a trajectory.
Quite a dynamic range. It's inspiring, for
sure. Maybe try to hold on to this moment, this
time, for when it's over. It will always be
yours.

Enough esoteric rumination. "Wonderful Disar-
ray" is still in review. I shouldn't be
surprised that it's in limbo now. The team
aren't waiting around though. I've had an idea
```

in mind for a while. As soon as I get back to
Vaix I'm going to start blocking out the beats.

Meantime, France was nice, and we hopped up to
Vaasa afterward since we were Earthside anyway.

We?

It seemed smaller somehow, unfortunately. Or at
least less divine than I remember it. I'm not
saying I'm too big for it, just that it can be
hard to see the same things with different
eyes. Maybe you'll see what I mean when you get
home.

Speaking of, I should get home. Somtow and I
have been camping out at the Village dorm,
since it's close to our project's volume. And
he hasn't been feeling tip-top, so it's a nice
treat. Anyway, I'll give you a better update
next time. Gotta run.

Olivia stared at the words for several minutes afterward. She went
back to find the one word he'd used. *Serene?* Had she really come off that
way in her last message to him? Had she made it sound like she'd discovered a fantastic wonderland? Had Aleksi read nothing in her words about
how much of a challenge it had been for her?

But she was fixating, reading far too much into what was, by any
measure, a perfectly fine letter. Words could be misinterpreted.

After some moments of silence had passed, she opened the second
message:

Good day, Ind. Jelani, from the entire foreign
relations council. I know we haven't said so
until now, but I wanted you to know, person-

ally, that we couldn't be prouder that the two
of you are paving the way for future exchanges.

"The two of you," eh?

So please take our stand-back approach as a sign
of confidence in you both—but if there's
anything you need from us, please ask. In return
I would only ask of you that you remember the
sensitivity of your mission, especially as you
correspond with your loved ones. There are times
when we may place a hold on certain particulars
of your experience, which all fall under its
Restricted classification. But we want you to
know that we do so with the utmost care, and in
time many of these redactions may be released.

In any case, in the meantime we hope you are
having great success. It's hard for us to even
imagine what it must be like for you. But all
in good time.

Oh, before I go, the plan we detailed for Max
did call for regular updates. Time can
certainly slip by when you're fully immersed in
something new, but . . . still, if you could,
please do give Max a nudge when you can. Remind
him how eager we are to hear his perspective on
this . . . I was going to say "new frontier,"
but I'll think of something better.

So the SA head of mission was still a few details short of a full
picture. Was the Affairs Chancery waiting until they had their story
straight before informing the home office of their envoy's demise?
Presumably it would be better to tell them before the delay itself became

part of the story. But whatever the reason for the state secrecy, it was clear that the Sovereign Alliance and the natal Affairs Chancery were cut from the same cloth.

So be it. She would toe the line until the fog cleared—her field reports would remain free of controversial intel. If her hosts didn't want her tangled up in matters of state, who was she to protest?

Moving to the window, she activated her hotfont and hailed Elder Two. The transfer steward responded almost immediately, their image superimposed over the florid grounds of the guest dormitory outside. After pleasantries, Olivia got to the point of her call.

"Any new developments?" she asked them.

"Yes, today in fact. The operations ward have confirmed their earlier suspicion that Max's death came as the result of criminal intent. They said it was carried out by someone who knew their way around our security measures. As a result, our receiving bead has been closed to all incoming traffic for the duration of the investigation."

Olivia waited for the emotion to hit, but . . . no, her inhibitor was keeping her imperturbable. On the other hand, would a display of emotion even be called for right now? For whom?

"I don't suppose this sort of thing is common?"

"Certainly not. Across our entire career we've never seen anything like it."

"I can't imagine why someone would do this. It's not like Max could have enemies, not on this side."

"Maybe not Max specifically," they said, their hesitation spelled out in tightly packed bands across their skin.

"Meaning what?"

"Purely speculating, of course."

"Right."

"That this was about what Max represented."

Olivia let the words bounce around in her head. Suddenly the crime had a more personal edge, an immediacy it hadn't had before. Could it really have been political? Ideological? Could this have been not just a murder, but an assassination?

"Humans aren't even official members of the Empyrean Symbiotry yet," she said, thinking aloud. "How could we have inspired such a violent act, sight unseen?"

"Olivia, we're only a transfer steward. The transfer rites have been one of the key focuses of the external affairs body for generations. But you should know . . ."

Olivia didn't dare to interrupt the quiet that followed. Whatever weighed on their mind might not be for her ears.

"Not everyone appreciates the work we do," Elder Two concluded.

"I don't under—"

"That's all we can say right now."

It took every ounce of her willpower not to press the issue. She didn't want to get them into trouble. *Ssputhu-buta* must be telling her as much as they dared to. But what was she supposed to think? That there were "purists" among the natals who would rather not sully their "clean domain" with the taint of the baseborn?

"Do you think I'm safe?" she asked.

"We would advise you to contact the operations ward for a better assessment of your safety, as well as direction on whether you should return."

"I was in touch with the head constable—"

. . . *Wass-wata* . . .

"—yesterday, and they said they'd reach out to me if they needed to. Right now I'm asking you."

The elder's skin pattern transitioned to reassurance. "I think, for now, you're where you need to be. Even if someone knew who you were, there's no way for them to find you by the usual means, not with your analog frame. Anyway, it's not like you're down there making yourself conspicuous."

No fear registered within Olivia, of course. But that didn't mean *Ssputhu-buta* was being candid. They were being diplomatic. And perhaps overly optimistic.

A sound at her door made her jump. The moth buzzed into her bead, hovered for a moment, then parked itself on her window. Where had it been?

"Anyway, when you do return," Elder Two continued, "even though we're not processing new transfers, we'll still be able to conduct your regression transfer as soon as we have springstir."

"Actually," Olivia said, "that's one thing I wanted to talk to you about."

———

Immediately after her call, Olivia found herself reflecting not on the two letters she'd received, but on her conversation.

Elder Two had been impressed by her news that she'd be joining *Tassbewasspo* and several of their friends on some remote moon. They agreed that she shouldn't have to wait around with hotfont in hand, as long as she made sure to return before the Sol-side spring became inert again in a little over a month. That gave her more than enough time to explore some of the natal outer reaches. She had to take advantage of the time she had left here. She was only just becoming comfortable in her own skin.

Now, as she prepared for torpor, the moth roused itself and set to flitting about her bead in its inscrutable formations. She waved it away.

"Don't you have bad timing? We can play tomorrow, if that's what you're interested in."

But the drone centered itself before her and issued an electromagnetic approximation of Interlish she could barely understand.

. . . *soon* . . .

. . . *patience* . . .

Olivia froze. "What?" The drone held steady. "If that was you, say what you said, again."

. . . *soon* . . .

. . . *patience* . . .

She regarded the moth with a cool appreciation, though if not for her inhibitor she would surely be experiencing a range of emotions. The device had been playing close to the vest, but something had changed.

"What does that mean, 'soon patience'?"

The moth only repeated itself.

Had it been learning to communicate? If so, how? And more importantly, *why*? Max had refused to tell her anything, but now she was being counseled by a drone to be patient . . . presumably with the promise that more information was incoming?

"Just so we're clear," Olivia said, "I don't know who assigned you to Max, or whose interests you serve." Its origins had been a source of enduring conjecture. The Integrity Polity had assigned it to Max, so she'd first thought. But then it surely wouldn't be tagging after her. And the natals, if anything, seemed to find the moth just as irksome as she did. The drone was universally tolerated by all, yet claimed by none. And given that the constabulary had evaluated and released the drone, it must not have yielded any useful details to them. "I'm truly sorry you lost your custodian, but I don't think I'll be able to help you."

The moth circled her, and ended up exactly where it started.

"Okay, fine," Olivia said, putting a hand up. "Soon patience it is. Take all the time you need."

TWENTY-ONE
DAY 38-46

FOR THE JOURNEY to *Titassstihi*'s moon, Olivia joined *Tassbewasspo* aboard a much larger cruiser than the transport shuttle she'd taken to planet *Puthubutiss*. The journey was to last just over a week—*Powhita-himu* measured the duration as "one hexa-cycle and two"—which was Olivia's only indication as to the distance. By her estimation they must be traveling faster than a human ever had, at least in relativistic space—the spring gate didn't count.

More than one of her crewmates confessed traveling to *!Wamuhi* for the so-called Just Cull, which explained the general interest in fitness; the ship's abundance of onboard fitness facilities had caught Olivia's attention early on. But though she still had her doubts about her own participation in the popular pastime, she could hardly pass up the opportunity to subject her body to more rigorous challenges than she'd yet experienced. Her physical therapy sessions back on Vaix—a time-honored regimen of rote tortures—had been a fact of life, a sort of dance without creative expression. Now she was in a position to pursue a more deliberate regimen, one that should prove more gratifying.

It was with some hesitation that she entered one of the ship's recreational theaters after the high moment on her first full cycle. She didn't know what to expect, but taking her cue from her more experienced shipmates, she started off with basic limbering and strength-training exercises. She marveled at the adeptness of her body—muscle, bone, joint, limb. It responded to each new movement as if she'd been training her whole life. Was her sense of accomplishment warranted, or was it all down to the guidance of a motility actuator buried somewhere deep within her head?

Did it matter?

By her third cycle she'd gained enough proficiency to split her routine between strength-training contraptions and a series of gravity-defying obstacle courses. The deep satisfaction she got from scaling a wall—using her limbs to brace and balance and support her body—felt both familiar and altogether foreign. More than once she found herself reflecting on the rigors of her early dancing days. It had been so long since she'd truly felt powerful in her own body.

Maybe Elder Two had been right about her natural talents. With each passing cycle she found herself paying less attention to the individual positions of her limbs. She had gained a better sense of what a full sprint *felt* like, and how the rhythm of six pumping legs drove her to push ever farther. And as her confidence improved, she found herself eyeing the more advanced arenas.

The squad-based competitive matches took place within an arena encased in electromagnetic fields, meant to simulate that of a planet. The game was a straightforward enough variant of capture-the-flag, similar to the early games Aleksi had worked on. But if Olivia had hoped the simple rules would lead to a quick win, she was sorely mistaken. In fact, despite her overall competence, she was routinely caught off guard by her rival counterparts, and played an instrumental part in her team's initial defeat.

This was an altogether new challenge. For a time she sat out the team matches entirely, retreating to the observation stands as a spectator. But as she watched the interplay of the teams, she found herself watching not the individual members, but something hidden in plain view. A new dynamic.

The natals' movements hewed closely to the underlying electrical fields, as racing yachts used myriad dynamic forces—including air flow—to drive themselves forward. And further, if she opened her ampullae to the interference patterns the opposing team was causing in those fields, she could anticipate how their members would move from moment to moment.

On the day before planetfall, Olivia rejoined her old team and, using her new insight, managed to be in the right place at the right time with unparalleled regularity—so much so that Su-jinda suggested to her in private that she consider easing up on their overtaxed rivals.

Her team secured their victory on the final match of the trip.

TWENTY-TWO
DAY 47

OLIVIA WAITED with her group at the East Fen Harbor port, awash in *!Wamuhi*'s powerful electromagnetic fields. After debarking, her group had avoided the squat fractal of the terminal altogether, and she'd followed *Tassbewasspo* across the tarmac, through the moon's oily, light-diffracting atmosphere.

The sensation of physical saturation was like nothing she'd experienced before. On *Watiwabe* the orientation of the electromagnetic fields had been regular, if complex; they'd exhibited a predictability that prevented them from becoming overwhelming. But *!Wamuhi*'s ethereal chatter was akin to being buffeted by turbulence from all sides. Already *!Wamuhi* was more alive, unpredictable, unfathomable. And it was exhilarating.

At least it would have been, if not for the moon's oppressive atmosphere and fierce gravity. To idle here would have been to fall entirely flat. *!Wamuhi* must be incredibly dense to be exerting so much pull. This moon was far more like a miniature planet. Even the internal mechanisms of her moth whined against the strain as it flitted off to parts unknown.

"This way," *Tassbewasspo* said, ushering them to a makeshift, origami-like ground transportation stand.

Olivia stood with legs rigid and body low as they waited under the watchful gaze of the parent planet *Titassstihi* above—and the serpentine, stubby-winged creatures that filled the sky. Her breathing was heavy, her muscles strained, but she found her awareness of her body's active resistance entirely agreeable. Good thing *Tassbewasspo* had the benefit of their exoframe. She watched them in silence as her party awaited their transport in the shade of the stand's awning. Was the old natal actually smaller than they'd been back on *Puthubutiss*? Maybe it was the press of gravity pulling them down. Olivia definitely appeared to be standing taller than most of the others in her party.

"Our group's accommodations are at Haven Hub," *Tassbewasspo* told her as the muffled groan of an oncoming vehicle filled the air. "It's closer to the tanthid culling grounds than the tourist hubs, about two hours away by autotrack."

Maybe she was imagining the derision in their voice at the mention of the "tourist hubs." But the relative remoteness of their destination would surely discourage the casual sightseer.

———

The autotrack was a sturdy, gravity-hardened continuous-track buggy that reminded Olivia of the long-extinct pachyderms of old Earth. The ride in it to the Haven Hub was bumpy and uncomfortable, but at least she got an unimpeded view of *!Wamuhi*'s impressively lush and marshy wilds. Among the low-lying scrub were bloated mobile forms that resembled downed clusters of woolly balloons. The terrain was almost entirely flat and covered in flora that consisted mainly of mushroom-like trees with thready buttresses stretching out from caps of crimson or orange. When the rippling sunlight caught the landscape just right it was like she was looking at a field of fire.

By the time the lights of Haven Hub dotted the dark expanse before them, they were deep in *Titassstihi*'s shadow, the day snuffed out in under a minute.

"How long are the days here?" Olivia asked *Tassbewasspo*. She held on to the handrail as the vehicle jostled its passengers.

"That depends! There are charts you can consult, or a formula to calculate it if you're so inclined. But we couldn't guess—"

"Because *you* don't pay attention to the Tide," *Powhita-himu* interrupted, dark bolts of admonishment flickering across their skin.

"And my mind is clearer for it," *Tassbewasspo* said. "We don't relish the thought of such bodily intrusion."

At that assertion, *Powhita-himu* made a show of admiring their exoframe.

"Well you might have answered them already if you weren't admiring our legs," *Tassbewasspo* shot back, not without some amusement.

Olivia might have been overhearing a conversation that had been going on for several decades. What was the Tide? Was it like the whispering?

Powhita-himu turned to Olivia. "The local cycle is roughly a fifth of a standard Home cycle."

"Our home planet," *Tassbewasspo* explained.

. . . *Tapuwathu* . . .

"But we suspect you're asking about sunlight," *Powhita-himu* said, "which is a factor of the local cycle plus our orbit around Bright Core's Second—"

. . . *Titassstihi* . . .

"So the day that just ended was one hundred twenty-two standard moments. The next local day will be less than half that, followed by a day of two hundred. We're not tidally locked, so the days and nights here are in constant combat."

"But the days, such as they are, are like none other!" said Su-povoi from several rows back.

"I don't know about you," said the Qlin they'd introduced to her as Lyfilnagee, "but on Qlin the days are relatively long—even compared to the harsh moon of Bright Core's Second—"

. . . *Titassstihi* . . .

"So the best method to cope is to let go. Forget what time it is and hew only to the posted schedules of events."

"Better yet," *Tassbewasspo* said, "*we'll* let you know when you need to be somewhere. If you do need anything, invoke assistance from your bead or any designated node. You're already registered."

"What about transmissions to the Symbiotry Sphere? Are there nodes I can use, in case I want to communicate with Elder Two?"

"You're welcome to use any transmission node for that," *Tassbewasspo* said. "But the transmission time is four cycles each way. We will have left by the time you could get a response back."

Olivia exhibited her understanding. They'd traveled at half the speed of light to get here—a feat that would take her some time to wrap her mind around—but would be staying for less than a week. The thought of being offline for the duration had a certain appeal.

———

The Haven Hub was a single-story facility with connecting satellite pods, all within a thick-walled enclave. The structures were constructed of a fibrous latticework, with stump-like stilts to keep them raised from the marshy floor. At the center of it all was an open-air courtyard, its periphery filled with projected advertisements for cull-related products and services, including optical accoutrements, and colorful baubles for the spectators. The air was filled with music that sounded majestic to Olivia's ear, but with an unfamiliar instrumentation that evoked the calls of insects.

Olivia's party crossed the atrium beneath the baking sun—*Tassbewasspo* and *Powhita-himu* to the fore, and Su-jinda, Su-povoi, and Lyfil-nagee behind her—and as they approached the reception area, the ubiquitous electromagnetic fields converged. The local fields must have been tuned to direct guests to that spot. At the registry desk she took her cue from *Tassbewasspo*, identifying herself and her status as the natal's guest.

Afterward they proceeded as a group to a crowded interior commons whose ceiling was low enough for Olivia to touch. Fortunately the air within was in constant motion, dispersing the heat—and the smells—on refreshing currents. *Tassbewasspo* stopped at the edge of the hall, where several connecting walkways split off.

"This is where we must part ways," they said.

"Are we not together?" Olivia asked. Maybe her hosts got the deluxe rooms.

"This is a clean domain, we're afraid." They indicated a posted sign depicting a sun with six radiating flares. On either side of the entrance, as if to drive the point home, were natals wearing white garters on their forelegs.

So that was it. Only those born into natality. No baseborn transfers allowed.

"But we're sure you'll find your beads accommodating." *Tassbewasspo*'s skin showed no trace of derision.

"They'll be fine," *Powhita-himu* said, coming around to stand next to their old natal friend. "This isn't about idle comforts anyway. They're here to *fight!*"

———

Olivia found herself surprisingly relaxed in her bead. The layout was not dissimilar to her *Watiwabe* accommodations, with the torpor hull positioned at the center of the area where the electromagnetic fields converged. On *!Wamuhi* though, or at least in this region, the fields continued to be noticeably less ordered. Strong, but disarrayed, with the occasional superficial irritation of knots adding a sense of turbulence to an already unique experience.

A series of sculptures on a side table caught her eye. The metal-formed figurines appeared to depict the local fauna: spiky things with protruding orbs around them and fearsome mandibles at the front. The individual members were arranged small to large, like nightmarish nesting dolls. At the center of them was a stump-like object with its roots protruding from the top. The card in front of the display resolved to: *Tanthid Ring*.

So this is what all the fuss is about, Olivia thought.

Suddenly she was looking forward to seeing these plants in action.

TWENTY-THREE
DAY 48

OLIVIA and the more soft-spoken of the Silu-dou, Su-povoi, watched several rounds of an exhibition cull from an expansive observation platform. The trail to the games park reminded her of those that snaked through the wildlife sanctuary in Vaix's Uchronia Park canton. Only this was no sanctuary. Here high barriers rose up in defiance of the harsh gravity, and only these scattered overlooks offered views down into the muddy paddocks, lush plains, and sprawling maze of sunken trails.

Despite the unsophisticated, fly-by-night appearance of the Haven Hub facility, the operation itself, by Olivia's estimation, was first-rate.

The only downside was that, within that first-rate operation, she was clearly second-class. During her survey of the Haven Hub campus, she'd found much of it restricted to transfers. The so-called "clean realms" were everywhere. Though Olivia had been given a natal body, she would never be seen as a true natal by natals. Yet the truth was, she *was* a stranger here—one whose every need had been met without hesitation—and some exclusivity along the way was to be expected. If the symbiotry's other member races had learned to make their peace with it, so could she.

"I never asked you how long you've been here," Olivia said, staring down at the pasture, currently unoccupied. "I mean the Silu-dou."

"My people were the fourth to be admitted to the symbiotry, some three biqua-circuits ago, by Home—"

. . . Tapuwathu . . .

"—standard reckoning."

Olivia didn't know how to translate the figure into anything meaningful. Her transliterator had only provided her the words.

"But I've been here for four circuits," he continued, "or nearly so. I met Su-jinda during an ambassadorial function shortly after my arrival, and we fell in together. As much as that's possible here."

"I see," she said, more out of habit than anything. Was he suggesting physical intimacy? How would that even work in borrowed bodies? "And how have you found it here, overall?"

"Well," he began, then stopped. "That's . . ." He turned to her. "Some context is probably necessary to provide a meaningful answer. I don't know about the culture you come from, but my background is rather modest among my own people. Su-jinda razzes me about it, but it's true. We've been a spacefaring people for many dozens of generations, but I didn't participate in any celestial excursions until my late adolescence. And . . . I have no idea if any of that will make sense to you. Suffice to say that my role in this partnership exchange mission has been a life-defining one."

Su-povoi's passion gave Olivia pause. Suddenly now didn't seem the time to probe for his take on institutional xenophobia among their hosts. "Well," she said, "*I* find your story inspiring."

His skin pattern showed appreciation. "And you?"

"I've only been here for . . . a dozen-plus cycles, so it's all been a bit of a blur."

"A fun blur, I hope?"

"I'm trying to fit in as much as I can before I return," she said, satisfied that the conversation had come back around to something she could manage. "And this promises to be the most exotic junket yet. Tell me again what we're looking for?"

"I think we'll soon see some action," he said, turning back to the field of play. "This neophyte round isn't officially part of the cull. You've probably heard of the austerity regimen applied to each of the season's tanthid rings to bring about the frenzy. But . . . now, if my ears tell the truth, I think we're about to get our first—yes, *there!*"

The form that emerged from behind the support strut of the far observation platform looked nothing like a plant, though Olivia saw its resemblance to the stylized figurines back in her torpor bead. *!Wamuhi*'s brutal gravity had yielded a lifeform unlike any she'd seen in the Sol system, with sinewy shoots for legs—this one seemed to have at least ten—and gas sacs at each segmented joint. Additionally, its central abdominal sac must have provided some lift. Rising from behind that main blister was a spiny trunk that somewhat resembled a scorpion's tail.

"That's the reason we're all here," Su-povoi said.

"A tanthid."

"Just a sprat, but yes."

A young specimen it might have been, but it didn't shrink from the much larger natal that approached it, matching baton clasped before them. The scene playing out before her—orange-sleeved hexapod versus balloon scorpion—was as exotic as anything she could have hoped for, with no Sol analog.

"You said you've participated in the cull?" Olivia asked. She wouldn't have thought it. Not only was Su-povoi's sanctified form on the small side, he was quite mild-mannered.

"The neophyte course, yes. The beginner grounds are sparse, with bantam tanthids putting up just enough resistance to force participants to watch their backs."

As Olivia watched, the natal was set upon by the tanthid, the latter proving surprisingly limber for all its tricky structure. Its movements were deliberate and almost predictable until it was in range, at which point its two frontmost limbs split down the middle, revealing themselves as pincers. Fortunately for the natal, they had the advantage of size, and the tanthid's pincers could do little more than grab at its opponent's legs. But as they tussled, three additional tanthids—each as small —came around from behind, resulting in a miniature ambush. At this, the natal's skin went fractal, little curls of amusement playing out as they did their best to dodge the barrage of snapping runts.

"Something about the way they move is mesmerizing," Olivia said, unable to look away. Though the tanthids weren't quick or even graceful, their undulant unity evoked the coordination of dancers moving to some unheard music.

"It's the gestalt intelligence," said Su-povoi. "Remember that a tanthid isn't just one of its members, it's all the siblings at once."

The natal got serious then, stomping two of its assailants while tearing a third into ribbons. The remaining tanthid darted off the opposite way, using its gas blisters to push itself out of reach—not quite flying, but making good use of the thick atmosphere.

In the end the natal's greater speed and agility proved too much for the indigenous flora. The tanthids had meted out plenty of cuts and abrasions—Olivia could see the wounds from where she stood—but they were superficial. For a beginner, this must be more about mere participation than an actual demonstration of one's mettle.

"So what do you think?"

Olivia looked at the other transfer, unsure. Participating in anything like this in her own body, with its unreliable joints and aching bones, would have been out of the question. But no such distress registered now, other than the press of gravity. This body was more than a reprieve from her afflictions; it was a living fortress. Humanity had never experienced such physical potential.

She had to see what this body could do. What she was capable of. If she were to remain on the sidelines now, it would suggest that in a way her limitations had always been self-inflicted, and nothing to do with any physical malady.

"I think I should give this a try," she said.

Somewhere deep down, the old Olivia was pleading with her not to get involved. But unlike the whispering, that voice was all too easy to muzzle.

———

That evening Olivia passed by her bead and kept walking. Her legs wanted to move, despite the moon's harsh gravity. She was filled with a feeling of accomplishment—one that was as yet unearned. She hadn't done *anything* yet—except make a decision. If that was enough, what did that say about her?

And what did it say about her that old Olivia's voice was still objecting?

You're the poet girl with the disorder, and if you lose that—

Ran's words had stung that old Olivia to the point where she had rejected them outright. But with her emotional inhibitor in place, they now struck her as worthy of meditation. Had he been making a point she couldn't see then? Maybe some answers could only be seen from the other side of the question.

. . . pulse-tap-tap-tap . . .

The moth buzzed before her as if she should be impressed that it had found her. Where had it come from?

"Out for your daily constitutional?" she said.

By way of an answer, the damned thing landed on her foreleg, and with a prickle secured itself there with its static setae.

"What the . . . ?" Olivia gave it a shake, which did nothing but loose a burst of electromagnetic energy, turning the background whisper into a shrill wail.

We want to meet with you, said a voice in her head, using a form of communication between speech and wave.

Throwing her view wide, Olivia shot glances down both ends of the hallway at once. "Who's 'we'? Where *are* you?" No one was in sight. No one was here but her and the device affixed to her arm. It was the moth. The message had to be coming from the moth.

Or through it.

She ducked into the nearest open bead, barely larger than a closet. She tucked herself toward the back, in the crook between two humming machine cabinets.

"Are you still there?"

For a moment she sensed nothing. Because she'd imagined it. The constant whispering was finally getting to her, working its way into her thoughts. Soon she wouldn't be able to tune it out at all.

But another string of signals finally pulsed through her cells, untangling themselves into words.

We're here. And we'll explain, but only in person.

"Okay." She peered out into the hall. If someone found her here she'd have no explanation. "Why the secrecy? Why like this?"

For good reasons we can't get into now. We're sorry it took us this long to reach you, but this channel is unique to your makeup, as Max's was to his.

"Max? You spoke to Max like this?" And look where that got him. "I need to know who I'm talking to. Now."

We'll answer all your questions and more. But not here.

"Did you kill Max?" A shot in the dark.

We selected Max Mehdipour as the human Special Envoy to the natal domain. We needed them, and their death was a bigger setback than you can know. So now we need you. In a roundabout way, we're the reason you're here, Olivia.

That wasn't necessarily a clear-cut case for trust, even if it was all true.

"You had a reason to select him specifically?"

Yes.

"Why?" She asked knowing full well they—whoever they were—wouldn't answer.

For a moment she sensed nothing. She looked at the moth, inert save for a subtle glow along the ridge where its top and bottom shells met.

Meet with us so we can tell you why you're here.

Olivia might have laughed if it were possible. "Are you nearby?"

Close enough. Can you meet?

"When?"

Tomorrow.

"Tomorrow . . . no, that's . . . I'm busy tomorrow." *Busy weeding.* And they didn't get to barge in and set the terms for their engagement.

The next cycle then.

She was flying blind. But how was that different than anything else for the past two weeks?

"Fine. Sure, let's meet." She had to know what was going on. "Tell me how to find you."

TWENTY-FOUR
DAY 49

AFTER THE MORNING feed with *Tassbewasspo* and the rest of their coterie, Olivia joined them on the walk out to the observation area. Her moth—which had been flitting around since the high moment—was nowhere to be seen. She would have been glad for its absence before last night, but now she couldn't help wondering what it was up to, and who was behind it. More than once she'd had the distinct feeling of being watched. Or maybe that was just the flux between the magnetospheres of *Titassstihi* and *!Wamuhi.*

Unlike yesterday, when the observation areas were sparsely attended, today the raised platforms teemed with fans of the cull. As if in response to the gathering, a squall of exotic cries issued from behind the barriers. Haven Hub might be out in the hinterlands, but suddenly everything thrummed with life.

"I won't be joining you, of course," *Tassbewasspo* announced to the group, "but I'll be cheering each of you on." They approached Olivia. "You have your entry chit?"

"Right here," she said, pulling the card from her sling bag. She'd found it that morning in a pouch hanging outside her portal. The beautiful grid of glyphs resolved to Interlish as she glanced at it again:

```
Far Thorn / Late Thorn — Season 33,267 House
```

Tassbewasspo looked it over. "That seems to be in order."

She'd have to take their word for it—she could barely make sense of it.

"Follow the signs, you'll do fine," said *Powhita-himu*.

"We can watch your tote?" *Tassbewasspo* indicated her satchel.

"Right," Olivia said, sliding it off her shoulder and feeling suddenly naked. She was sure the terror of what she was about to face would be overwhelming if not for her inhibitor.

"Glory in sanctity!" *Powhita-himu* shouted, to rousing calls of agreement and chain-like patterns across flesh that Olivia read as broad assent.

"We'll see you after," said *Tassbewasspo*, before retreating into their exclusive seating area.

Olivia, it had become clear over the past cycle, was the only member of their group who had never participated in the Just Cull, and despite her willingness, she was out of her depth. The location of the culling ground entry points seemed arbitrary at best, and the signage had her going in circles. When was the last time she'd traveled beyond the guidance of an ambient? Even Earth's backwaters enjoyed universal coverage. *!Wamuhi*'s whispering was a poor surrogate.

Powhita-himu had already dashed off to join a private team, and the others were starting their rounds from other landings, leaving Olivia on her own. Lyfilnagee squeezed through the press of bodies to get to her.

"Will you be okay?" the Qlin transfer asked.

"Right now I just need someone to point me in the right direction."

———

After the Qlin told her what to look for, Olivia set off into the crowd in search of the Yellow Division Landing, grateful that she was half a head taller than the majority of the gathered attendees. She caught sight of a pylon with a label her eyes translated to "Meridian:117" and headed in that direction, but apparently it was only a marker, not a direction indicator.

"This must be part of the game," she muttered to herself.

"You look lost."

A diminutive natal wearing multicolored bands had approached her. Emblazoned on their left band was the insignia she'd seen at Haven Hub's central courtyard.

"I'm new at this," she explained, and showed them her chit. "I'm a participant. I was looking for the entrance. I think I'm getting closer though."

"Sorry, no," they said, looking up at her. "It's not surprising you'd get turned around. And you're late for your round—"

"Oh!"

"—but we can get you in."

"Yes, good. I'd appreciate that." She'd read no signature from them— no whispered name at all. Were they not natal, or were they truly nameless?

"Follow us, please."

Finally.

The natal with the colorful bands led her away from the throng and down a long ramp to a door in the side of the barrier. The sign on the door translated to "Service: Limited Access."

"This is it, really?" She never would have found this on her own.

"It's not where participants usually enter, no. But the main gate is locked now, and this . . ." The natal opened the door for her, using three fingers against a recessed touchplate. "This gets you to roughly the same place. Congratulations to you."

"Thank you, I *owe* you," Olivia said, leaving them with a bemused look on their skin.

Beyond the door was a cramped space lined with foul-smelling containers and shelves loaded with piles of the orange pikes like the one the natal had brandished at yesterday's exhibition. She pulled one loose and tested its heft in several of her hands. *Only for defense,* she told herself. *Just in case.*

A gate in the inner wall suggested her entry point, and a single call from somewhere beyond the barrier seemed to confirm that. Olivia grabbed hold of the metal latch and pulled. There was no handle on the opposite side of the gate; once she was through, that would be it.

"No turning back," she said as she ducked through.

———

For the first time, Olivia's points sank into the damp loam of *!Wamuhi*. The enclosure was expansive enough that the far barrier wasn't visible to her. The open field before her appeared to be free from tanthid and natal alike, but she remained on her guard to avoid being ambushed. Based on what she'd seen yesterday, the tanthids could use one of their numbers as a lure, then go for the numbers advantage.

Where to start? Maybe the thicker flora ahead of her could provide some cover—not only from roving tanthids, but from the spectator swarm suddenly buzzing overhead. She might have mistaken the gnat-sized constellation of remote viewers for native life if not for their tiny outboard impellors and orderly formation. She had her own audience.

Dammit.

She remembered the arrays of displays back at the Haven Hub. But was the feed strictly closed-circuit, or would her antics be cast to farther reaches?

Ignore it.

Facing any potential opponents would be challenging enough without worrying about how she'd look doing so.

Olivia set off in search of a better vantage point from which to survey the landscape. The going was slow, as the soft earth forced her to exert herself in a way she hadn't before in this gravity. She could lope along fairly well by making her body weight work for her, moving herself forward by mashing her six legs into the marshy soil one after the other. It felt unnatural, but that must be part of the point of this event.

Where was everyone? Shouldn't there be other natals? She saw no signs of life as she made her way along the periphery of the grounds, doing her best to ignore the swarm of tiny watchers flitting around in the stifling muck of *!Wamuhi*'s atmosphere.

A particularly strong flux line pulled at her as if something was drawing her in that direction. She turned with pike raised, fully expecting to find one of the local flora approaching from the thicket.

"You're bold riding that high!" said a natal wearing a brown sash across their abdomen, their flesh speckled with curiosity.

. . . Hibebemubutass . . .

Their signature marked them as a true natal, and a stranger. How had they sneaked up behind her? She'd thought she was being careful, but apparently not.

She lowered her pike, feeling silly. "I'm riding what high?"

Instantly the natal's skin was emblazoned by clusters of surprised sparks. "You're a *transfer*?"

Was it her accent? "I am."

"Well . . ." They took a moment to scan their surroundings before turning back to her. "That you've managed to make it this far is truly impressive—and we welcome you—but you should know how to release your shoulders for an improved stance."

"I don't . . . can you show me?" She'd thought the other natal was small, but their limbs were only slightly shorter than hers, and they'd merely positioned themselves low to the ground.

They came around her and placed their hands against her mid-legs at the third joints, pressing gently outward. It was all Olivia could do to stand her ground. "Look," said the natal. "Feel your weight here, along your arms, and where the bones join at the shoulder. Can you feel how you're working against the gravity even as you're standing still?"

"I think so," she said, not sure if she understood or not.

The other natal backed away and did something to its joints, one after the other, until it was standing at nearly her height. "Now, if you flare out quickly, like this, then shift the muscles down—pull here and here—then reengage."

With a series of meaty pops, the natal compactified themself. It looked as though they had dislocated several joints in rapid succession, and locked them at unusual angles.

"Give it a try," they said, pointing at her two mid-shoulders. "Here first."

Was she really about to pop her joints out of place for a stranger, when she'd been trying to avoid much the same thing for decades? Then again, with all her experience she should be a pro at this.

Olivia set her pike down and followed the stranger's directions, first flaring her mid-legs outward, allowing the bones to strain against their joints. Instead of resisting, she pushed farther . . . until something snapped. It wasn't pain she felt, but a sense that she was now using muscle alone to support herself, and if she let go—

"Now lower yourself and pull your shoulders back just before you hit mud."

As easily as her shoulders had dislocated, they locked back into place. She tested her two limbs and found them entirely unimpeded, except their range of motion was more horizontal than omnidirectional. At the same time, she was using far less resting energy to support herself.

Olivia repeated the process for her other legs, by which point she had lowered her center of gravity significantly, adopting the natal's crablike stance.

"Looks like you've got it," *Hibebemubutass* said. "Well fated to you, apex!"

Was that a good thing? "Thank you. Well fated."

The natal left her alone—peeling off half the accumulated spectator swarm in the process—but Olivia couldn't bring herself to follow. The other natal was more experienced and knew what they were doing—not to mention they would make a good ally in a fight—but . . . something held her back. Not just intuition, but a sense, almost tactile.

She turned around and felt the way forward in the pores of her skin. The lines of force all led in the same direction, into the thicket-lined glen ahead.

———

Attaining a gravity-defying gallop—pulling herself forward and pushing from behind—was possible only after Olivia had worked out how to manage her balance over the uneven terrain. Despite the thick air, the strange low stance, and the press of gravity, she finally felt unhindered.

The buzz of excited onlookers reached her from somewhere close by as she followed the electromagnetic fields, continuing along the shallow gulley to the foot of a knoll. Here the land was thick with crimson mushroom-like growths as tall as she was, each cap trailing a fall of tinsel, like a jellyfish. She climbed the hillock until she was high enough to survey the rest of her enclosure. A movement far below caught her attention, down where the spur of a raised embankment met the thicket's edge. It was the stranger with the brown sash. Olivia's heart ticked slowly as she watched them come face to face with something even larger than they were. It certainly displayed most of the markings of the tanthids she'd seen so far, but on a dramatically larger scale. Its pneumatophore was outsized relative to the rest of its body, probably to compensate for its mass, and it moved through the heavy atmosphere entirely without grace. Yet the quick natal appeared to be in trouble, jerking and flailing at something she couldn't see.

What?

She saw now that *Hibebemubutass* was covered in their own blue-gray ichor, and they were moving erratically—nothing like the smooth gait they'd demonstrated only minutes prior. It soon became clear that the natal was attempting to dodge something—projectiles of some kind, too small to make out from this distance.

They stumbled and fell to their knees, giving the tanthid time to close the distance between them. With one of their legs noticeably dragging, the natal managed to scramble far enough away to score a temporary reprieve. Olivia watched as they circled the slow-moving brute in time to land a horrifying blow, puncturing one of the creature's gas sacs. The tanthid wheeled around with surprising speed and threatened to flatten the natal, its spiny pincers snapping shut with a muffled report, but firing no shots this time. Maybe it was depleted, or more wounded than it looked.

Something was disturbing the fields around Olivia, putting her on alert. The disruptions continued, rhythmic, like the hammering of a frightened heart. And as she looked on at the battle below, one thought came to the fore: *This is not what I signed up for.*

Not in a regretful sense, but a literal one. She would never have been put in position to face this level of opponent. She stood no chance here.

This is the wrong arena.

Had she gotten the wrong ticket? Or had that natal with the multicolored armbands—the one with no signature—been trying to get her killed?

And yet she didn't flee, and she didn't hide. Regretting her decision even as she made it, Olivia abandoned her sanctuary. She kept as low as she could as she pulled herself through the overgrown tangle, edging ever closer to the skirmish below, until her senses started filling in more of the picture. It was the electromagnetic fields again, only this time the *thud-thud-thud* of the projectiles had given way to something altogether less localized. Something more *enveloping*.

What was she not seeing?

Olivia held her position among the low scrub and concentrated, willing her ampullae pores to open fully. She imagined reaching out with her perception as if she were plunging her hands into a raging stream, feeling the downstream currents, the cold water setting every nerve ending alight. And what she sensed was far more than the most immediate lines of force. She suddenly become aware of an entire new panorama, beyond sight, beyond sensation. It formed in her head like the details of a room materializing before dark-adapted eyes.

The energies seething around her enveloped not only the tanthid and the natal, but also something behind the hill *Hibebemubutass* was backing toward even now.

Olivia would join him. Surely together they would stand a better chance of—

Agony.

Everything went white.

Her muscles tight.

Burning.

For several seconds there was nothing but that all-encompassing deluge. Had she pushed herself too far?

But her body was released to her once more, and she was back on the ground, mouth pressed to dirt. She pushed away the last of the pain and rolled to her side in time to see another tanthid towering over her.

Fuck!

Had it been stalking her? For how long?

The field lines around her shifted an instant before something shot past her eyes. She jerked backward and managed to dodge the grip of the tanthid's pincers. She was only grazed across one of her legs, but the sting was a painful reminder that this was no longer a spectator sport. These things weren't playing a game. She had to focus.

No more mistakes.

Olivia scrambled away from the tanthid, heading in the direction where she'd last seen the wounded natal. If they teamed up together, dispatching their stalkers would be easier.

A path through a stand of cactus-like plants offered her an escape route. She shifted her view behind her, but her pursuer was no longer in sight. *Hibebemubutass* had moved on too, so there was no reason to linger. Creeping forward as carefully as she could, she considered the sheer size of the native roving flora. If it came down to it, could she really kill one of those things? If it became obvious how unqualified she was for this, would the Just Cull officials intervene?

If not for her emotional inhibitor she'd be delirious with fear.

Olivia came upon *Hibebemubutass* in a muddy clearing, their brown sash draped haphazardly around their remaining legs. Their head and torso were charred black and still smoldering, spicing the air with a smell she hoped never to encounter again.

They were dead.

So much for hoping the officials would intervene.

A shadow fell over her like a stain. Without thinking, she sidestepped and spun around to keep her back to the mushroom thicket. One tanthid had approached her from behind as a second bounded toward her from the direction from which she'd come. Its latticework legs made quick work of the distance between them.

They were crowding her, forcing her onto the defensive. Only then did she realize she had no pike.

Shit.

She'd left her only weapon in the muck, back when *Hibebemubutass* was showing her how to adjust her stance.

Olivia drew away from the tanthids, watching her back as well as her front as she positioned herself far enough away that she could keep them both in her sights. As they both watched her—biding their time, planning their next move—she turned her attention back to the curious undulations of the electromagnetic field. These weren't arbitrary shifts she was sensing. The fields were as responsive to their choreography as a banner in a gale. Except . . . that wasn't quite true. Step by step, the fluctuations she was sensing *preceded* the movement of the two tanthids.

If she paid attention, the beasts were actually telegraphing their intent.

Olivia flinched as a burst of energy broke across her electroreceptors, but she managed to dig her points into the mire and push herself free of the projectiles' path. She threw a glance at the tanthid on her left.

"Nice try."

In the distance, the oddly choral cheers of the natals rose over the high walls. Was that was the sound of approval? She couldn't be sure, but—

She let it distract her, and almost missed the telltale tremor in the electromagnetic fields that announced a new influence.

White.

Hot.

Agony.

It shot through her, lighting every fiber aflame, leaving behind only a consuming numbness.

The tanthids wasted no time. A crushing weight fell across Olivia's hindmost legs, pinning her in place as a great form rose before her. The image resolved as her eyesight returned, revealing two tanthids approaching from the front, their clacking pincers moving fast enough to blur under the wan sunlight.

But her most immediate problem was still pressing her legs down into the mud. If she couldn't free herself, she was done for.

The tanthid behind her—well within her expansive field of vision— had one possible vulnerability, even if the only way Olivia could find out for sure meant damaging her own body. Gathering her will, she waited until the pain across her legs was almost too much to bear. Then she pushed herself back, hard enough against the tanthid's pincers to nick the flesh of her foremost shoulders. Using her mid-legs for support, she arched back and, in an act of cruel choreography, punched with both forelegs, aiming for the thing's gas sacs.

One of her pointed wrists found its mark, puncturing the thin membrane, while her other slid harmlessly off its spiny carapace, opening a new wound across the back of her wrist.

The tanthid issued a fusillade of electromagnetic ticks, and its weight shifted just enough. Olivia was free.

Favoring her mid-legs and forelegs, she scrambled down into the network of gullies, ceding the high ground but making it impossible for the tanthids to close in on her the way they must have done with *Hibebemubutass*. The electromagnetic fields could give her the upper hand if she stayed focused and ignored the throbbing in her limbs, the brutal gravity making her feel every bit of her weight on them. She couldn't see the fields as such, let alone sense them from any great distance, but with time, and if she kept moving, she might be able to build a mental picture of them and sense the directions of their flow.

From the base of a shallow but soggy culvert, Olivia chanced a peek over the embankment. Her adversaries had scattered again. Two of them were still on the far side of the labyrinthine gulch, headed her way.

She headed the opposite direction, feeling the lines of force alternately resist her then relax, like a buffeting tide. She altered course, moving as the contours of the fields dictated, as if she were following her own internal fareline. Now she was getting somewhere: the lines of force were converging. She was on the right path, as long as—

A warm wind whipped up around her as if heralding an oncoming storm. She spun around, sure that one of the tanthids had managed to creep up on her again. But she was alone.

Alone, but being pursued.

A great shadow swept across the overgrown terrain, swallowing the tanthids. Beyond the yellow sky, the leading edge of *Titassstihi* edged up toward the sun, its sweeping umbra accompanied by a gale that set every branch and blade to murmuring. Another of *!Wamuhi*'s fleeting nights approached, quickly, and Olivia was determined to avoid crossing the tanthids in the dark. Her best bet now was to reach the border wall, where she hoped to find an open exit waiting for her.

As the darkness engulfed her, Olivia started back toward the habitat's edge. But the fields, pulling to one side, dragged her attention to a figure that stood alone—a solitary tanthid nearly twice the size of the others. It stood still as a statue, the skin of its great gas sacs fluttering as the winds kicked up.

Where did you come from?

And then it was gone, along with everything else, lost to the darkness of night.

As Olivia waited for her eyes to adjust, she contemplated her strategy. That massive tanthid had to be guarding the so-called heart mother—which, if the figurines in her room had been accurate, resembled an inverted tree stump. But she'd seen no sign of it, at least not from this distance. Could it be buried, like a root? And if she could keep following the electromagnetic map in her head, she might actually . . .

No, stop it!

She was letting it go to her head, letting herself grow delirious from a moment of quick-witted insight. But the impulse to entangle herself further in this frivolous contest would pass as quickly as the false night.

Just get to the exit.

Except—as she could now see once again—that monstrous specimen was actually closer to her than the far wall. Was that important? Was she really contemplating this?

She threw a glance over her shoulder ridges. The other tanthids would be in striking distance in less than a minute unless she fled with the hope of waiting out the darkness. Or unless she could actually find the heart mother and—

A dart shot by her left set of eyes, close enough that she could almost feel it displace the air. Keeping her legs locked in the low position, she pulled herself forward, away from her pursuers . . . and toward the final guard.

No thinking. Only running.

Olivia hauled herself through the buffeting air and straight toward the gigantic tanthid.

Just once.

At speed, she should be able to knock it from its position with the force of a small bus.

Just go.

If her theory about the mother was correct, she should be okay.

Go.

Because its true target was obvious.

She plowed into the tanthid, leading with her shoulder ridges, knocking the wind out of her, but not before she'd gotten a full mental image of the hidden mother's guiding fields.

Olivia scrambled for purchase as the toppled tanthid, perhaps stunned itself, went about the complex task of righting itself. The mother wasn't directly beneath its guard tanthid, as it turned out, but offset by nearly a meter—a clever bit of misdirection.

As Olivia got back on her points, the floundering tanthid's pincers clamped down around her abdomen and two of her legs. This time Olivia turned her focus away from the tanthid's assault; it was only a distraction, though a useful one. Leveraging the tanthid's brutal grip, she stomped her free legs into the damp soil, pushing downward as the breath was squeezed out of her, probing for something that might yield to her before she lost consciousness.

The bones of her wrists met some resistance, and she gasped with effort as she drove her wrists down and down.

. . . IMPOSTOR . . .

The single word—a desperate condemnation—filled the space around her, lighting across her every nerve ending as the tanthid's other pincer grabbed her across the torso and *pulled*. The pain was absolute, dulling all other senses. But Olivia was no stranger to pain.

Enervated, she thrust through something fleshy with her remaining strength, until a new warmth pushed up around her limbs. The tanthid's grip faltered for the first time, and Olivia tightened her fingers around her forelimbs to expose the forward edge of her wrist bones—and fell forward with all her weight until the heart mother's signals were silenced for good.

Olivia's world went white once more, and for a moment she was lost. She'd been needled by one of the tanthid's charged darts, maybe, but instead of pain there came a great empty gulf.

Then the vise grip around her body, having already slackened, fell away entirely.

Her perceptions had fragmented. What was going on? Was that monstrous tanthid returning for a second round? Were its smaller siblings angling for an ambush in her compromised state?

But the fields around her had quieted dramatically.

And the shimmering behind her eyes faded enough to let the sun's light shine through once more.

Then there were the voices.

Natals.

"Go around to the other side!"

Hands, wrapping around her torso, hauling her backward, until her legs pulled from the soil with a great sucking sound. Her fingers were coated in something viscous, smelling of fruity cheese.

"Are you okay?"

Strangers around her, vying for her attention.

But her eyes found the alien titan beyond her helpers, now wandering the arena like a lummox, no longer interested in her, or anything.

Lobotomized it.

The thought made her sick.

What had gotten into her?

The spectator swarm—invisible now in the sun's glare, but almost loud enough to drown out the whispering—was a frenzy overhead.

To see the carnage.

It had been self-defense in those last moments, but it was all so needless. This wasn't like her at all.

She'd gotten carried away, wrapped up in the moment.

She wasn't herself.

"They'll be fine," someone said. "Get them to the clinic."

———

"That was a glorious performance!"

An arena official—accompanied by their whispered signature *Whiss-wass-be*—had come into the clinic where a teelise was now diligently patching up Olivia's legs and back. The gathered crowd beyond the clinic doors showed impressive restraint by not bursting through. Beside her was *Tassbewasspo*—for moral support she supposed, or perhaps to soak up some of the spotlight.

"Truly remarkable," *Whisswass-be* continued, "the way you charged directly *at* the guardian."

They were right about that, but probably not for the reason they thought. She shouldn't have killed the tanthid heart mother—shouldn't have been *able* to. It had been so out of character that it already seemed like an act she'd watched her body carry out, rather than one she'd performed.

Committed. That's the apt term.

"Thank you," was all she could manage.

"And with no experience," *Tassbewasspo* said. "You weren't slated to be in that arena, if we recall correctly."

"It was kind of a last-minute thing." She wanted to tell them it was the result of a conscious act on someone's part. But what of the ramifications of telling them someone might want her dead? Now wasn't the time. If there was a connection to Max's assassin, she should know after her meeting tomorrow.

"Well, your feat has already swept the Tide," the official said, invoking that mysterious channel once again. "A nice buff to your reputation, we think you'll find."

IMPOSTOR.

The memory made Olivia stiffen enough that she pulled her rearmost leg from the teelise's hand.

"Please relax yourself," it said, holding its hand out as it waited for her to return her wounded limb to its place beneath the operatory light.

"Sorry."

She held still as the teelise continued suturing the deep cut in her flesh.

"Needless to say," *Whisswass-be* said, "as far as our participants go, it's seldom that we're honored with an apex. Let alone one whose name appears nowhere in the sodality records."

"A what? Apex?"

"They who embody the divine, and who instill the divine in others. As you have done today!"

Outside, night fell once more, and the sounds of pugilism rose up in the distance from somewhere beyond the barriers.

"It's an honor to be recognized," *Tassbewasspo* said, as if answering for her.

"Well, flattered as I am, I'm not an apex," Olivia said. She ignored *Tassbewasspo*'s flickers of admonishment.

"But you are, clearly," said *Whisswass-be* as it finished up and gathered its instruments. "Or perhaps we mistake your meaning?"

Olivia stood and tested her legs, and another thought struck her, which she quickly tucked away for later. "I mean, I'm not even a natal to this system. I'm a transfer from Sol."

"The Olivia Jelani!" someone shouted from the crowd outside.

At the mention of her name, sounds of jubilation shook the cloth walls of the clinic like a drum, even as many of those gathered chose that moment to leave. Her mere existence here had to be controversial . . . but were there some who saw her as a threat?

"We admit that we had no idea this was possible," the arena official conceded. "But it explains why you wouldn't know. So we'll tell you: your sanctified form has developed all the hallmarks of an apex."

———

"You look as though you've received a grim diagnosis," *Tassbewasspo* told her on the easy walk back to the hub.

"It wasn't enough that I was a transfer," she said, still trying to sort out her thoughts. "Now I'm an apex. Whatever that means."

"It's a physical truth in your case. But here it's just an honorific. And something to be celebrated."

Why should something like that bother her? She was only borrowing the body, after all.

The sun had peeked back around *Titassstihi*, which was now low in the sky. But as *Tassbewasspo* tried to make small talk with her, Olivia found herself distracted. It wasn't the throbbing of her flesh, which had already diminished greatly, thanks to the teelise. It was what she had done. More to the point, it was what she had *become*.

It was easy to accept the potency she was feeling as her own, and not some stolen attribute of the body she inhabited. And perhaps some of it was; she had accomplished something, after all, albeit a feat of dubious merit. But there was no way to tell where she ended and the natal began.

Her physical prowess was as alien to her as anything she'd felt on this side of the spring.

Yet . . . certain truths could not be dismissed. She was powerful, objectively. And it must be evident, based on the looks she was getting from others along the path, as if she were some kind of celebrity. Yes, there was a deference she hadn't noticed before—not here, nor in Sol system.

And then there was her physical size, which had grown. She'd initially rationalized her height relative to the locals as a result of their response to high sustained gravity. But even *Tassbewasspo* seemed smaller than they'd been when she'd first met them. When that had happened, she didn't know. Which meant *she* must have kept growing after her transfer. She might be growing still . . . but into what?

She saw in her mind's eye her legs covered in warm ichor, and the lines of aversion crossed her skin before she could push the thought away.

IMPOSTOR.

"Did you intend to play at the master level?"

Tassbewasspo's question cut through her distraction, as was probably their intent. But in their voice she heard something, as if they only needed her to confirm their suspicion.

"I was misled."

"Hum."

"Either my invitation was wrong, or the official who led me to my entry gate was."

"You didn't recognize them?"

"No." She didn't trouble *Tassbewasspo* with the fact that they hadn't had a signature.

The natal was silent for a moment. Then, "The word of your father's fate has been circulating."

"Oh."

"Yes, and one of the reasons your elder—"

. . . Ssputhu-buta . . .

"—suggested that you leave the Symbiotry Sphere—"

. . . Watiwabe . . .

"—was to get you away from the threat."

"I know that."

"But now—"

"Now I may be compromised here. I need to watch my back. Or . . ." *Tassbewasspo* wasn't thinking about her, were they? "Or I need to leave."

"We don't think that's a bad idea, and perhaps sooner than later. Especially given that *!Wamuhi* is technically outside of this domain's law commons."

Olivia looked at them, but their skin was calm and even. Had she unwittingly sought refuge on an anarchist moon? Someone might have mentioned that to her before now.

"So then I assume notifying the authorities—"

"Would not be a good idea here," they said, and this time their skin went blotchy. "One of the reasons you would leave would be to draw attention *away* from Haven Hub."

Was this an illegal operation? Or just frowned upon in certain circles? She couldn't bring herself to ask. But regardless, the passage back to Sol should be open again in just over a week, if Elder Two's estimation was accurate.

"I'll find a way to get back."

"Very good."

They continued in silence until the Haven Hub came into view through the squat foliage. Onlookers seemed unable to keep from staring at Olivia, but held their distance, perhaps because of her chaperone. However ambivalent their relationship, she was glad they'd accompanied her.

"Out of curiosity," *Tassbewasspo* said finally, "how did you pull it off? That encounter of yours could have gone very badly. Killing the tanthid heart mother is something even the adepts seldom do. So tell us."

I had a temporary leave of sanity, she was tempted to say. *A sudden bout of invincibility.*

"Mainly it was the fields."

"Fields?"

"The electromagnetic fields all around us."

They didn't understand.

"The tanthid mother distorts the fields when she communicates to the siblings," Olivia said. "Which meant I could track her back to her hiding place."

Tassbewasspo's skin conveyed confusion. "You're talking about farelines and belts? But that's not something one sees."

"Well, not *see* exactly . . ."

"If you speak about an orientation medium as if it's a beacon in the darkness," said the natal, "we're afraid you've interpreted it all wrong. That's like saying that . . . that your hunger told you a story. It's nonsensical. No, the sweep of these energies should be little more to you than a reassuring ambiance."

Olivia couldn't think of a thing to say to that. She'd just received a haughty reprimand. Yet she wasn't sure whether *Tassbewasspo* simply found her talk of the fields as vulgar, or whether they truly could not sense the fields as she did. The topographies and undulations of electromagnetic fields suffused natal architecture, even their language, yet they seemed to possess an aversion, or an ignorance, to embracing any sense of them beyond the superficial.

"You know," she said, "my people have a saying: 'beginner's luck.' I don't know how well that translates, but it describes a neophyte's accidental success, one that may never be repeated. I think that's as fitting an explanation for my achievement today as we're likely to find."

"Beginner's . . . yes, I can see that. You were in the right place at the right time."

"Or in the wrong place at the right time." All that and she hadn't even broken a sweat. Thanks to her inhibitor implant, she'd been calm and keen-eyed throughout. That, too, might have been what saved her. Though if someone really was after her, a bit of fear might be useful.

As they came to the back entrance of Haven Hub, Olivia asked *Tassbewasspo* if there was a way she could dial down her emotional inhibitor, or have it removed entirely. "It's making me too cool, too distanced from my own feelings. I think I'm taking more risks than I would otherwise."

That made their skin break out in fractals of amusement. "Of course your elder—"

. . . *Ssputhu-buta* . . .

"—would have already deactivated your assistants before you stepped point off the Symbiotry Sphere—"

. . . Watiwabe . . .

"That is procedure."

"That can't be true," she said. "I'm never this collected. This . . . *untroubled* by things. Something's different."

"If that's how you are, that's how you are. What is there to dispute?"

TWENTY-FIVE
DAY 49-50

OLIVIA'S FLESH was heavy in her netting. She was awake. Not just awake, but *awakened*.

"Hello?"

What had changed? Even beyond the hot, healing throb of her wounds, something felt off. She tried to shift, tried to get up, but her body didn't respond correctly, her limbs refusing to cooperate. Had her injury on the field been more grave than the teelise had recognized?

Something moved against her.

She wasn't alone. Someone had broken in while she was in torpor.

Someone was on top of her.

"N-no! Get the fuck—"

She tried to maneuver out from under them, but her limbs were no longer her own. She was too uncoordinated to get to her points.

"Lightslights*lights!*"

Through the blinding glare she saw only a tangle of limbs.

"Get off!"

What was seeing? The creature occupying her torpor hull had affixed itself to her.

A parasite.

And it was . . . working her legs like a puppet?

Or she was hallucinating.

She had to extricate herself from her bedding. Had to get help. But as she pushed backward with the hope of spilling out of the hull, two of her legs separated along a new seam, then detached themselves from the rest of her entirely.

Her body must be dying. This was organ rejection at a dire scale. A goodly section of her own body had just separated from her . . . except it was anything but dead. It was lively in fact, and moving independently, as if to get as far from her as possible.

Had she . . . given birth?

"Oh shit."

The head. She hadn't noticed it at first, but it had a head—like a natal head, only flattened, misshapen. During the separation it must have taken two of her legs and split the hindmost two from shoulder to knuckle, leaving them each with four legs total.

As Olivia watched in shock, the creature that had just separated from her made its way out of the basin, crawled into the darkest corner of the bead, and pulled its four limbs in.

And there it parked itself, still, like a piece of sculpture.

"What the *fuck*."

She maneuvered herself so her abdomen—her true abdomen—was exposed to the light. The area from shoulder to hip was now a vastly reduced hollow, the delicate skin there moist and gray and tender to the touch. The intruder must have been fastened to her since she'd first awakened after her transfer. Now it had separated from her, taking her mid-legs in the bargain, leaving Olivia with an exposed gap between her forelegs and now-diminished hind legs.

Something wasn't right. Natals had six legs, and now she'd been left with four . . . not to mention a sense of imbalance, and a curious feeling of loss.

She needed help. What if this was just the first stage of a process? She had to track down someone knowledgeable before any more of this borrowed body decided to jettison itself.

Tassbewasspo.

Olivia clambered out of her bead and staggered into the empty fare-line outside. With one hand to the wall for support, she alternated between two- and four-legged walking. But the natural rhythm of her legs had gone, and her muscles strained under the unrelenting pull of gravity.

Her moth, on the other hand, was flitting in the air over her as if it relished this midnight stroll.

"Hope someone's enjoying the show," she muttered.

She found her way out to the common area, deserted at this hour. Good. She hoped to make it to *Tassbewasspo*'s torpor bead without being seen. Perhaps the old natal would know what to do, or know who would.

She located the radiating sun sign—the marker of a clean domain—and made a beeline for the restricted side of the house. But as she crossed some unseen threshold, the overhead lighting became garish, and an attendant emerged to confront her, only averting their eyes at the last moment.

"I need to talk with *Tassbewasspo*." Could they understand her? "Uh, my sponsor. The assembly organizer." The lack of proper names wasn't going to make this any easier. "I don't know if you know who I mean, but I need to find them."

"The Olivia?"

"Yes, I'm Olivia." *Let the celebrity through.*

They made a sound she couldn't decipher. Then: "This is a clean domain."

"I know that, it's just . . ." She pointed at the hollow of her abdomen, which only made the natal recoil.

"This is a special occasion . . . ?" they asked.

Special?

"Yes, it's very special." Amazing. Something about her condition had them completely turned around. "Can you take me to their bead?"

The attendant's skin flashed, displaying a loose distribution of spots. Was that embarrassment?

"We'll leave it to you," the bouncer said, and stepped out of her way. At the same time, a strip of lights pulsed repeatedly down the gentle curve of the fareline, showing Olivia the way.

———

Olivia stood before *Tassbewasspo*, suddenly not sure what to say. "So this happened," she began, indicating the space where her mid-legs had been. "Look at me."

At first the natal appeared unsteady in their exoframe—she had surely roused them from torpor—but then stiffened as they realized what state she was in. *Tassbewasspo* averted their eyes, now fully awake. "What are you doing? That's not *tick-tick* . . . this is not *tick-tick* . . ."

"I agree, it's not. But I don't know what to do."

"That's not appropriate."

"Appropriate? A piece of me *came off*."

As *Tassbewasspo* stood before her, their silence was as opaque to her as the door they stood behind. But something she'd said must have gotten through, enough to evoke a display of delicate spirals over their skin. Curiosity? No.

Amusement.

"Give us a moment."

They disappeared into their bead for several seconds, leaving Olivia to her thoughts. What a ridiculous state of affairs. Her body was molting, reproducing, or dying, and all *Tassbewasspo* could say was that it wasn't *appropriate*.

The natal reemerged and joined Olivia in the fareline. They looped an arm around hers and drew her back out the way she'd come in. "First we need to get you back to your quarters. If someone saw you it would be unseemly."

The matter-of-factness of their voice provided some comfort at least. Whatever was going on, they didn't appear to believe her condition was a mortal threat.

———

They made it back to her bead without encountering anyone else. *Tassbewasspo* pushed her inside and shut the portal behind them. "Now where is your gamant?"

"What?"

"The part of you that *came off*," they said, using her words.

She pointed at the far corner, and saw only then that one of the bandages the teelise had applied to her after the cull was on that thing's leg. "There."

Tassbewasspo approached the figure and gave it a prod. It pulled in its leg, growing even more compact, but was otherwise still.

Seemingly satisfied, the natal turned to Olivia. "It's the male."

"The male?"

"It's not a perfect analogy, so you'll forgive us. But we're sure you can understand us."

"The male what?"

They approached her. *"Every one are two."* Clearly quoting something.

"What's that?"

"An old song. A song for . . . children." As if to illustrate, they touched their own torso to the side of the ribcage and ran their fingers along a seam so subtle Olivia would never have noticed it otherwise. They had their own gamant, yet they moved as one. Just as she had. Why would she ever assume otherwise? She'd never had the sense that something was *attached* to her. Indeed, she'd felt everything her gamant had felt, and had been in full control of its limbs.

"We're complete pairs, each of us," the natal said. "Including your own sanctified form. At least . . . you were."

How was this possible?

"Once mature," *Tassbewasspo* explained, "the prime and gamant remain whole for most of our lives, save for reproduction rites, for medical reasons, or . . . in various perverse circles. Which is why you wouldn't want to be seen in a public space as you are now. Alas, we are too advanced in years for a proper exchange, if that's what you'd—"

"No, I get it," Olivia interrupted. "Basically this is indecorous."

"If we take your meaning." Their skin affirmed it.

"So . . . why? Why did this happen to me now?"

"We don't know." They peered at the gamant's bandaged leg. "It could be the damage you sustained yesterday, or perhaps something related to your transfer. Or he could be having trouble acclimating. That's really not our area of expertise."

The compact form in the corner looked so small, almost frail. But it was his leg that had punched through the soil to the tanthid heart mother yesterday.

"Is he a full other person?" Olivia asked.

Swirls of amusement across their skin again. "We wouldn't go that far. A free gamant couldn't survive long on his own. Nor want to."

"Are they independent?"

"Enough to ball up in a corner if they feel threatened. You're right to think this shouldn't be happening. We'll get you a physical review after the high moment. But we would advise against leaving your bead in your present state."

"It would be unseemly, I get it. What do I do until then?"

"You'll be fine physically. Do nothing. We'll get this seen to first thing after the feed."

TWENTY-SIX
DAY 50

THE *THUMP-WAVE-SSTATIC-THUMP-WAVE-STATIC* SIGNAL for the high moment beckoned from the ether, but though she was famished, Olivia abided *Tassbewasspo*'s advice and sat out the feed.

Though she now required extra attention to walk, Olivia detected no difference to her sense of self, her sense of completeness. She was still herself, *all* of herself, even if one third of her was now huddled in the corner.

She approached the pale skeletal form. "You okay there, buddy?"

He was inert.

"Was it something I said?" she asked, reaching out and giving his leg the gentlest of touches.

A chirp drew her attention back to the center of her room. Her moth hovered there, expending an audible amount of energy to counter the gravity. She was supposed to meet with whoever was on the other end at some secret site, but that wasn't going to happen now.

"I'm in no condition to meet."

No response, save for another chirp.

Communication with her moth-speaker required physical contact. Olivia didn't bother to hide her anxiousness as she walked over to the moth and invited it to come to rest on her shoulder. Its setae gave her a tingle.

"Can you hear me?" she said.

Yes. Are you ready?

She explained her condition, and that she planned to remain in her bead until the matter was resolved. Surely they would understand.

The timing is bad.

"I agree," she said. "It wasn't by choice, but I'd rather not be seen like this."

It's really not as bad as you think it is . . . except maybe on the Moon of Bright Core's Second.

Meaning what? Was she talking to a member of one of the "various perverse circles" *Tassbewasspo* had mentioned?

"While we're talking," she said, "there's something you should probably know." If they'd come all this way just to reach out to her, they'd surely want to know what had happened to her at the Just Cull. She recounted the highlights of her ordeal out in the field. It earned her antipathy instead of accolades.

Needless brutality. You might have spared us the details.

"My *point* is that I think whoever tampered with Max's analog frame was trying to dispatch mine, too."

Only silence from the other end.

This is something we should discuss in person.

"Can it be tomorrow?"

It must *be tomorrow. After that—*

"I can do tomorrow." Only, what if her gamant was happy where he was? What if she was destined to be forever a quadruped? The gravity was already getting to her. But the stranger gave her the time and place of her pickup, and the moth disengaged. So it was settled.

Olivia shot a glance at the gamant. "Are you trying to get me in trouble?"

Above the moon's eternal whispering, an isolated signal was like a flick to the ear.

. . . tick-tick . . .

She approached him once more. "Is that you?"

"Me."

Pulsing dots of excitement broke out across her skin, an emotion he did not share. His skin remained a waxy taupe, utterly without emotion.

"To be honest . . . I thought we made a pretty good team."

No response.

"Do you remember that?" she asked him. "The running, the fight?"

"I hurt." Now he moved, carefully, deliberately. He placed a hand by the gauzy dressing on his leg, as if to show her where.

"I'm sorry about that, friend."

"Sorry," he repeated. Then, "We fix."

The guilt hit hard. "We'll get it fixed, I promise you."

Silence.

"Okay?"

"You are question," he said.

Question? "Curious, you mean?"

What could she really say to him? This was probably as weird for him as it was for her. Should she invite him to rejoin her? Would that count as a kind of infidelity? Could Aleksi understand something like this? Maybe, in one of his games.

She touched the gamant again, and it didn't pull away. Its flesh was . . . warm.

When someone finally did show up at Olivia's portal, two hours later, it was a medic.

TWENTY-SEVEN
DAY 50-51

AFTER SPENDING her day in isolation, Olivia woke that night to find the gamant back in her netting with her.

The medic had called on her for only a few minutes, long enough to assure themself—and then her—that there was nothing wrong with either her or her gamant. A disruption, physical or otherwise, was sometimes cause for separation. So they'd told her. And, not for the first time, she'd found herself thinking of the gamant and Aleksi at the same time.

Now something like adrenaline coursed through her as the smaller form moved against her. He moved carefully, as though to avoid startling her, and she remained as still as she was able. From what she could see in the darkness, he was reaffixing himself to her.

It was oddly moving, to be deemed a fitting partner after all.

She allowed the coupling to complete, adjusting herself only as he needed, until he was still once more. Minutes later the feeling of being close to someone else faded entirely, and once more she could feel all six of her legs. All six of *their* legs.

And even as she lay suspended in her netting, that sense of strength, temporarily lost, returned. Their pairing had brought with it a cool confidence.

Everything was in its right place.

TWENTY-EIGHT
DAY 51

DESPITE HER REINCORPORATED FORM, attending the morning feed might have been a mistake. As Olivia tried to concentrate on the skewered cuts of ropy protein—was it tanthid?—strangers, one after the other, made a beeline to her dining patch to congratulate her on her victory.

Though Su-jinda, Su-povoi, and Lyfilnagee were in attendance, none had seen *Tassbewasspo*. That was a shame. Olivia wanted to show them she was back to her fighting form.

"We missed you yesterday," said Lyfilnagee. "But I assume you'll be participating in the final cull today?"

Olivia demurred. "I've made some other plans, since this may be my only chance to visit here."

"A shame," Su-povoi said. "You represent the baseborn well."

Olivia couldn't tell if they were joking, owing to the arbitrary patterns on their skin. But there was no disputing that she was the spectacle of the hour. The last time she'd been recognized to such a degree was a decade ago, for her prizewinning poetry collection. Which accomplishment had been more deserved? Maybe she didn't need to know.

The moth came to rest at the edge of her patch and issued an electromagnetic blip.

"Okay, just a minute."

"Your reliable friend is back," said Su-jinda, pointing her tongs at the device.

"It's a fearful unit, it turns out," she said, flashing the Silu-dou tight curls. "Needs constant reassurance." She ate quickly so she didn't miss her taxi.

———

Olivia was jostled about in the driverless autotrack requisitioned by whoever was on the other end of the moth. Not too far from Haven Hub, they'd promised. But the causeway was at times nearly overgrown as it carved through the wilds. If she happened upon a tanthid out here, how would she fare? Then again, the specimens in the wild wouldn't be driven to frenzy—at least not unless the news of her killing blow had spread among its other circles.

The autotrack plodded through the marshlands until it reached a perfectly camouflaged cluster of huts standing among a dense copse of squat mushroom-trees. Awaiting Olivia's arrival were three natals. Though whether or not they were *truly* natal, or baseborn like her, Olivia would have no way of knowing until she got a little closer. They were definitely smaller in stature than she, but most were.

As the vehicle pulled to a stop, her moth alighted from her shoulder to hover by the trio. They could keep that glorified intercom as far as Olivia was concerned. She stood, not sure what to say, and one of the three—

. . . *!Ti!watawa* . . .

—took a step back. "Another apex," they said to their colleagues.

Another?

The natal in front—

. . . *Buwhi!buti* . . .

—ignored the comment. "Olivia Jelani," they said, with no trace of the aural overlap Olivia had gotten used to from her transliteration bud. Whoever this was, they were speaking in Interlish. "We're glad you could make it out here, especially given how little you know of us."

Olivia stepped down onto the moist loam. The fact that she was hearing EM signatures told her they were true natals. Yet one was speaking in Interlish. Curious.

"We'll start with names," the natal continued. "We are Oscar."

. . . Buwhi!buti . . .

Proper names? Maybe an attempt to be extra accommodating.

"And our colleagues are Emily—"

. . . !Ti!watawa . . .

"—and Langston."

. . . Bessbessta . . .

"Poets," Olivia said after a moment. "You've named yourselves after poets. Clearly you know more about me than I know about you."

"We should," said Oscar.

"I appreciate the gesture—giving yourselves names," she said, and her ego took it from there, "but I can also sense your electromagnetic signatures." She attempted to approximate Oscar's signature by thinking it as loudly as she could: *BUrst-WHIr-click-BUrst-TIck.*

The natals exchanged glances, and their skin told her enough.

"You learned this yourself?"

"I sense it. There wasn't much learning involved."

"That's unusual, especially from a transfer," Emily said. "But discretion will serve you best."

"So I've learned."

"It's not an issue here," said Oscar, "but out there . . ."

Time to get on with it. "You said you're the reason I'm here," she said.

"Indirectly, yes," said Emily.

"And you're the reason *we're* here," Langston added.

"We thought you might find it more agreeable," said Oscar. "We're sure you're eager to learn who we are and why we've contacted you."

"You could say that."

As if on cue, night—*Titassstihi*'s shadow, really—fell across the land.

"Let's get inside, if you wouldn't mind," Oscar said. "Our remoteness has its uses, but it also makes us vulnerable." They didn't elaborate, but somewhere in the overgrowth a series of long, low hoots—first the call, then the response—filled the darkness.

The interior of the designated hut was spare but comfortable, with a spongy bench running around the outside of the space, and a case of some sort at the center. It all looked modular and haphazardly arranged, as if they'd set everything up only moments before her arrival. Emily shooed several natals out of the hut—other poets?—and Oscar pointed Olivia at an open space on the bench. After shutting the door, they each took a seat. Olivia was reminded of a similar meeting she'd had with SA officers on Heliopolis. Another lifetime.

"You're not an easy person to track down," Oscar said. He was clearly the leader of the outfit.

"So tell me why you've gone to the trouble."

"Because we—the entirety of the natal domain—find ourselves facing a new threat. An existential threat. It's why we expedited the process of inducting humanity into the Empyrean Symbiotry. Why we initiated your induction, and played a key role in the selection of your emissary."

"Max was unaware of the reasons they were chosen," Emily said. "We made our introduction to them on the Teelise Sphere, briefed them much as we're about to brief you, then issued them the remote deeplink." The moth. "It was tuned especially for them, so we could communicate directly, without raising awareness."

She thought back. "That was *you*? That group I saw in that room—the *humans* I saw meeting with Max?"

"Not us specifically, but members of the Fifth Sun, yes."

"The transfer rite is much the same in either direction," Oscar added.

Disguised natals. Such were the lengths they would go to to remain covert. Human Olivia might not have stayed to listen. People who bent the truth weren't worth her time. But the despair in these natals was palpable, even across the divide.

"What do you mean by 'existential'?" If natality was facing some existential threat—genocide? apocalypse?—why had she heard nothing about it before? Why would an existential threat not be met by public outcry, and a vast rally of resources to meet it? "And not to be insensitive, but how does it relate to humanity?"

218

"The way it relates to *you*," Oscar said, "is that these are circumstances that a human may be uniquely suited to helping us address."

"'Us' being . . . all of natality?"

"More immediately, 'us' being the members of our small group, known as the Fifth Sun. We made the trip to talk to you because we're running out of options, even more so than when we made our case to Max. All we can do today is give you the context you need to decide whether you'll help us."

A hoot issued from somewhere outside, followed by muffled echoes in the dense air, the rustling of foliage, a volley of barked shouts and short shots. Then, finally, silence. Olivia's three hosts waited it out as if they'd heard it all before. After nearly a minute, Oscar continued.

"Let's start with the Fountain," he said. "We don't know how much you know of its history."

"I was briefed about it before I came," said Olivia, "but only in passing. The central singularity that all the springs lead into, yes?"

"Yes. But that wasn't always the case. The Fifth Sun have recovered scraps of ancient sequences—electromagnetic remnants, mostly faded now—that describe an early version of the anomaly we now call the Fountain. They describe it as a passage that once provided our people with a connection to the domain of a powerful race, or entity, referred to only as the 'Thirsty Pool.'"

Olivia sat in silence and forced her nervous hands to remain still.

"When we say the Fountain had a connection to the Pool, we mean that in the earliest days there were no springs leading to any other systems—the Fountain led *only* to the domain of the Pool. And that was a problem, because it seems that the Pool, by its very nature, was inherently destructive to organic life. Every account we found indicated that the Pool was not a lifeform as you and I are. Where ordinary matter is made up of atoms and molecules, this sentient anomaly was essentially made up of topological objects, topological *defects*—field vortices in quantum fields."

"Where was this Pool?" Olivia asked. "Where did the Fountain lead?"

"We don't know where the Pool's domain exists relative to our system. But we didn't need to know that, did we? For the first time, location didn't matter, distance no longer mattered."

"At least, that was the Fountain's promise," Emily said, "if we could properly harness it."

"Which we did," Oscar said. "As we gained an understanding of the Fountain's mechanics, we eventually managed to decouple it from the Pool's domain and co-opt it to our own ends. We developed stable springs—branches of the Fountain—and incorporated the Fountain into our commerce, exploration, and warfare. The Fountain provided us unprecedented access to the wider universe."

"And the Pool?"

"Once the entry to the domain of the Pool had been severed, the entity faded from the public consciousness. It became the stuff of mythology. Of superstition."

"Thanks to those in power," Emily said, "the Fountain has become a symbol of our virtuosity, superiority, and strength. Any who raised this more comprehensive accounting of history are deemed traitors or apostates, and excluded from larger society."

So that was who she was talking to. "Is that why we're meeting way out here?"

"It was never our goal to prowl in the shadows," Emily said. "But to ensure the survival of our species, we're forced to conduct our business in secret."

The words left Olivia with a chill, and her own questions stilled.

"Almost all of our people deny this history ever happened," Oscar said. "Dismiss something for too long, and it is lost to time. And in time the ignorance that loss yields may be exploited. And now . . . that's exactly what's happening."

"Exploiting—you mean someone is exploiting the Fountain's connection to this Pool," Olivia guessed.

Langston reached down and did something with the case on the floor. A moment later the space between them filled with the visage of a human, along with a list of details in Interlish.

"Have you ever heard of a Cole Quinlan?" Oscar asked.

"Should I have?"

"The first human to reach our system."

What? "Before Max and me?"

"They arrived in our domain nearly twenty-eight years ago, by Earth standard reckoning." That would be right after the discovery of the Teelise Sphere. "Cole located the spring the sphere had used to travel to Sol—before it consumed itself—and slipped through."

Emily indicated the information hanging in the air before them. "This was taken from Cole's public profile."

```
Cole Quinlan, M 55 (2912-2967)

Cofounds Slip Trade (trading/shipping) with
Leta Heftiba in 2954, when Cole is 42. Primary
operations in Main Asteroid Belt, with
subsidiaries throughout populated system. As of
2994, Slip Trade is the second largest trading
organization within the Sovereign Alliance.

In 2967 Cole is reported missing by his partner
and is presumed dead after system-wide searches
turn up no trace.

Surviving family: none.
```

"I've never heard about this," Olivia said, then thought about it. "Wait, I thought the whole reason for the transfer process was because no one could pass through the springs except natals. The teelise assured me that was true." They and Quv Vidalin, who had insisted that pouring her and Max into alien bodies was the only way forward.

Oscar's skin showed agreement. "Cole might not have attempted it if they'd known the physical cost. They surely sustained critical damage during the passage, and would have perished had someone not transferred them to an analog frame in time."

"It would have been a hasty and radical procedure," Emily said, "since there was no knowledge of human physiology."

Langston leaned forward. "And extrajudicial, given that there was no mechanism in place for a diplomatic process. Those who performed that transfer weren't part of any appointed body. A human's transfer, then, would have been an experiment in brutality."

Olivia pushed the image away. The official process had been grueling enough.

"We've found little to suggest why they would abandon their life," Emily said, "let alone risk approaching an unknown singularity. What we do know is what happened after. In their new natal form, Cole integrated with greater society, taking advantage of the anonymity a host body would afford them. But three circuits ago they got our attention through their association with a group called 'Unity,' based on Home—"

. . . Tapuwathu . . .

"—where this image was captured."

Emily waved a finger, and Cole's profile was replaced by the projection of a natal. They had only the four legs, being apparently free of their gamant. But most curious was their skin, which was either draped with some sort of adornment, or suggested a malady Olivia hadn't seen before.

"We know this is a lot to take in all at once," Oscar said, "but these are the things you need to know in order to understand why we're all here. Sometime during their circuits beyond our records, the human Cole Quinlan became obsessed with the Pool, the Pool's relationship to the Fountain, and the Fountain's relationship to natality."

"That's where Cole's group—Unity—comes in," said Langston. "Unity is attempting to restore the link between the Pool and the Fountain. All while our people stand proud and oblivious to it, blind to our own vulnerability."

"The Pool still exists?"

Oscar issued a *tick-tick*. "Based on our intelligence, the Pool is anything but extinct. It lives on in isolation. For now. If Unity did succeed in opening the Fountain to the Pool, there's no telling what harm they could cause to our people."

Olivia sat back in her saddle, and would have pushed back out of the hut and through the wilds back to Haven Hub if she could have. She chose her next words carefully. "Don't you think that someone with power and resources should know what's happening? If it's a matter of telling others what you've told me . . . I mean, if they knew—"

Oscar raised a hand. "They would do exactly as they've already done, and condemn us, vilify us. You don't think we've tried? That we're still trying?"

222

"Olivia," said Emily, "our home domain is made up of grosses of realms, principalities, states. However you wish to define them, they're spread across a dozen systems. We have appealed to anyone who would listen to us. We've been strategic about it, persistent. The Fifth Sun as it stands today is made up of all those who would listen. We have grown our numbers, but nowhere quickly enough."

"Every suggestion you can think of—including infiltrating Unity ourselves—we've tried," Oscar said, sitting forward to close the gap between them, "or are trying still. What we *haven't* tried yet is to get someone from Cole's own people—a human—to get close to them. That is why we are speaking to you."

"I'm no Max." She'd looked the man up prior to boarding the teelise shuttle. He had a background in conflict prevention, mediation, and peace negotiation. That made sense if they were counting on him to confront this Cole Quinlan. But based on what they'd told her, this wasn't just a question of expertise. "Besides which, how could any one person—much less a single baseborn *human* person—be of help to you on an existential scale? Unless you think I bear some responsibility because Cole and I share human backgrounds, what is it that you want from *me?*"

Langston's skin was a tricky labyrinth of disapproval, but Oscar and Emily were giving her space, as if that might help her come to terms with what they were asking of her.

"Just because I'm human, that doesn't mean I'm qualified to just . . . to march up to these people and tell them to cut it out. I have no authority, let alone influence."

"Maybe not," Emily said. "Maybe we came to you in a moment of desperation. But since then you've shown us something new, something we first witnessed on the Symbiotry Sphere."

The natal trio she'd encountered the night after Max's death. Members of the Fifth Sun, no doubt scrambling after Max's death.

"You're a human as Max was, yes," Emily continued, "but you also have talents that Max did not. Specifically, you appear to be highly EM-sensitive. And if Cole succeeds in reaching Pool space they'll be relying on EM signals for communication with the entity. That might give you certain unique insights into their methods and intentions, if we could get you close enough to them."

Olivia couldn't let her pity register on her skin. But she had nothing to offer these people, nothing that would be of any help to them, let alone natality. If they were right about Cole—and the implications of a restored connection between their Fountain and the Pool—they were truly beyond help. They could only hope that Cole would fail.

"I'm sorry," Olivia said. "I know you hoped there was something I could do to stop—"

"We know we're asking the impossible," said Oscar. "We're already taking all other measures we can, but if there's a chance you can help . . . we can only ask."

An electronic bellow shook the air, rising in tone until it evoked an animal in distress.

"What's that?" But Olivia sensed it before they could answer: an uncomfortable fluttering across her pores, like an insect stuck in the ear.

"The end of our meeting," Oscar said.

———

The encampment was scrambling when Olivia followed the poets back out onto the dirt path. Emily and Langston hurried off to help the others pack up equipment, and Olivia worked to take it out to the yard.

"Thank you for taking the time to hear us out," Oscar said. He stayed by Olivia's side, but the patterns on his skin were in flux. Distraction, anxiousness.

"You're all leaving, just like that? I'm not going to have time to decide anything."

"And there's still more to tell you," Oscar said. "But our sentinels have given us the signal to mobilize—you heard it. With each passing moment we risk drawing the wrong kind of attention, beyond even the local fauna. We'd like to give you a better understanding of the situation back on Home—"

. . . *Tapuwathu* . . .

"—but right now . . . we're in a compromised location, even out here. And we can't risk any of our small team being incarcerated, not with Unity making such progress toward their ends." A natal carrying a bundle of portable gear bumped into Oscar, and they stooped to help them steady the stack. They turned to Olivia. "We need to leave here. Not just the encampment, but this moon. There are things here far worse than the tanthids. And you can't slaughter *them*."

The words stung, but she deserved that.

"Come," they said, "it's time for you to return."

As the natal escorted Olivia back toward the autotrack, she saw weapons at the ready, and lookouts peering through the stout foliage. She did her best to suppress her rising anxiety, but the fluttering across her electroreceptors was already stronger than it had been before. What exactly was out there?

"Your autotrack will take you back to the Haven Hub," Oscar told her. "You should be fine as long as you keep heading in that direction. Now go."

Just like that. As she stepped up onto the running board, she turned back to the natal. They looked small. They looked *weak*.

"I wish there was something I could offer you," Olivia said. "But this is all completely outside my experience." She was about to say this wasn't even about her, but stopped herself.

"None of us are here because we want to be," the natal said, and the gridlines of acceptance on their skin took Olivia by surprise. "We've given you enough to make your decision. But don't take too long to decide. If you'd like to try—if you're serious—we'll meet you on Home—"

. . . *Tapuwathu* . . .

"Contact us there. Your deeplink will work from there."

The moth. She scanned the autotrack, and found it affixed to one of the support struts. Meanwhile, the fluttering had become a roar. Was she sensing one thing, or a hundred?

She turned back to Oscar to respond, but they had already left.

TWENTY-NINE
DAY 51

OLIVIA HAD NEARLY WANDERED ALL the way back to her bead before she stopped herself, listening. The fareline was empty, and in fact she hadn't seen anyone since her return. Had the denizens abandoned her during her field trip? It was later than she'd anticipated, so maybe—

A clamor erupted from somewhere nearby: a swell of voices chanting something in unison.

With her thoughts still fragmented after her meeting with the three poets, Olivia backtracked to investigate. As she rounded the corner to the central courtyard, several of the gathered onlookers locked eyes with her. This must be the closing ceremony she'd heard about, a tradition to celebrate another successful cull.

From nowhere *Tassbewasspo* was by her side, and with surprising strength they ushered her through the crowd, straight into the atrium, and right up to the natal who stood at its center, proudly adorned in a rainbow sash with fine silver filigree.

"The Olivia Jelani," *Tassbewasspo* said, just loud enough to be heard over the din. Then, to Olivia, "This is Haven Hub's master of ceremonies—"

... *Musstahiti* ...

"—and its leading sponsor for a generation."

A lull swept the crowd as Olivia looked out over their heads. What had she wandered into?

The emcee looked her up and down, evaluating her, then spoke.

"We have before us a player of keen instinct and natural cunning," *Musstahiti* said. "As formidable—as *fierce*—as we've ever hosted here at the Haven Hub!"

The thunderous ovation that followed—harmonic whistling and claps to forelegs—became tactile, exciting the thick air enough to drown out the whispering entirely.

The emcee then produced a small black amulet and made a show of presenting it to Olivia. Dangling at the end of a delicate link chain was a figurine in the form of a stylized tanthid.

Olivia accepted the offering and held it aloft for the pleasure of the crowd. "I'm honored," she said.

With one hand on Olivia's foreleg, the emcee waited until the courtyard was silent once more. "We hold that every season presents us with a surprise. Something that reminds us why we're here. We hope this season's trials have given you all what you come here for, cycle after cycle, circuit after circuit: the challenge of this most primal contest, of testing your mettle . . . or, for the spectators, the thrill of increasing your standing."

Appreciative patterns appeared all around, *Tassbewasspo*'s most vibrant of all, even if they'd sat out the games.

"This season's cull was special though," *Musstahiti* continued, "as many of you witnessed yourselves, or in echo. Because this season, the Olivia Jelani slayed an apex tanthid's heart mother!"

Discordant cries rose from the atrium, none of it touching Olivia. She had drifted and could only watch from far away.

"Which brings us to this season's surprise—because that, my most devoted, was *not* the surprise. No, this year's surprise stands beside us right now. Stands *over* us. And they're a bit of a curiosity, aren't they? Our new friend here, this sanctified form—a paragon among us, some might say—is *xenogenous*! A transfer from the human domain!"

The fields reverberated with excitement, not all of it positive.

"Ah, many of you didn't know, did you? But yet!" The crowd quieted.

"Though they were indeed baseborn, none here would dispute that the Olivia Jelani—the only apex we've hosted in five seasons—is a figure of fearsome proficiency. And there's a reason we mention this, because it gets to something that should not be a surprise to anyone. Which is that the perfection of our form is truly transcendent. Demonstrably so. It perfects . . . *anyone it touches*. Don't take us at our words, friends: witness the truth before you!"

That sentiment was one that the gathered seemed to appreciate universally. Every skin in sight registered approval. And why not? Olivia's accomplishment, such as it was, was a testament to *their* greatness. But she found herself hugging her own arms, as if that might mask the dark lines across her skin.

And just then, she did another thing the old Olivia never would have done.

She exited the gathering.

———

"See anything challenging out there?"

Olivia recognized *Tassbewasspo*'s voice and turned from the alien vista to find them approaching, accompanied by Su-jinda.

Olivia had stopped by her bead, but seeing the message from Aleksi waiting for her on her transmission node, and nearly a dozen from her friends at the SA, forced her out of her bead to walk off the sudden wave of guilt. It had been far too long since she'd provided an update, let alone given Aleksi a simple "hello." She'd escaped that responsibility the way she'd escaped her own body, left it all behind in another system for someone else to worry about. The more things changed, the more they stayed the same. Now her casual negligence had become a burden even to think about, and that called for an extended stroll keep her self-judgment at bay. So she'd made her way to a quiet overlook with an undisturbed view of the low marshy steppe, its mushroom-trees stretching out as far as she could see.

"I think my hunting days are behind me," she said.

"That would be a shame," said Su-jinda, joining her at the balustrade.

"I'm enjoying the view," said Olivia. "And the quiet."

Tassbewasspo moved to her other side, then locked his rigging. "You left the final observance swiftly."

"I was surprised to be the center of focus."

"But you can understand, surely. The master of ceremonies—"

. . . Musstahiti . . .

"—was truly impressed by your performance the other day."

"I know."

"Which is saying a lot. They were an archon in the High Legion for eight doza-circuits."

"That's . . . something."

"So it's quite an honor that they would take notice of you."

Olivia turned to face them. How much emphasis had they put on "you"? Their skin was neutral, but there was no mistaking the edge in their voice.

"I appreciate that, I do."

The natal placed a hand on Olivia's mid-leg. "We've been around for a long time, Olivia. Despite your myriad gifts, we've sensed in you a resistance to the light of your sanctified form. Are we correct?"

"I don't know," she said, being honest.

"Whatever you had to crawl through to get here, it can be difficult to appreciate just how far you've come, since the process is so gradual. But take our advice: make the effort to stop and take stock. Embrace the gifts you've been given. Here you can be anyone you want to be—and we don't just mean in the Empyrean Symbiotry."

Were they offering her something? Or was their appeal simply woven from the threads of their natalist inclinations?

Su-jinda moved next to the natal. "When I first arrived on Home—"

. . . Tapuwathu . . .

"—two doza-circuits ago, I was quite unsure of myself. In some ways you remind me of myself then."

"The transfer can be a shock for some," *Tassbewasspo* agreed.

"As it was for me. But I'm talking about my life in the Silu-dou. I was a commerce minister. I still am, I mean. I was strong-willed—I had a strong personality. But it shook me when I arrived here, because the person I was so sure about was so far behind me."

"So far *beneath* you," the natal added.

"You tease, but I couldn't see that then—that I had become perfected as a person without realizing it had happened. It was . . . intimidating."

"You intimidate yourself," Olivia said, fighting to keep her skin neutral as she endured the vainglorious sales pitch.

"In a manner of speaking. Which is why I can assure you that I understand. I've been exactly where you are now, with the existential questions, trying to knit together who and what you are, that internal struggle. But this is a singular opportunity. In time your present incarnation will make sense, not because you will it to be so, but because you've accepted your reality. That's when any muddle in your head will finally subside."

Su-jinda must have thought she was being helpful, as *Tassbewasspo* must in their own way. They wanted her to join their elitist club. And who wouldn't want to be a member of that club? The six-legged dress code was compulsory, but she couldn't deny the outfit was extraordinary. Then again, if this lot was so sure of their superiority, why had they abridged such a significant chunk of their own history, as the poets had alleged?

Her next thought threatened to send spirals across her skin.

"I've been thinking a lot about what the natals have accomplished throughout their domain," she said, choosing her words carefully.

"It's a lot to consider," said *Tassbewasspo*.

"Going all the way back to your first encounters with the Pool."

"Pool?"

"The Thirsty Pool, at the other side of the Fountain. I've been looking into that, into your history, and if you go back and look at the connection between—"

tick-tick

Tassbewasspo's skin was emblazoned with that muddy labyrinth of disapproval. "Who have you been talking to? That's nothing but vagrant superstition."

"No, but I've heard of it," Su-jinda put in, failing to take the natal's lead.

"Have I misunderstood something?" Olivia asked.

Tassbewasspo made a dismissive sound.

"It's natal mythology, right?" she pressed.

Now they unlocked their exoframe, and it hissed as it released them. "That was . . . an old story, meant to scare us away from mastering the Fountain. Nothing more than a crude fable to explain the travails of our earliest pioneers. It has no place in modern life." Having spoken their piece, *Tassbewasspo* moved back toward the inner hall. "Please, this is a night for celebration. Let us dispense with the quaint folk tales."

"I didn't know," Olivia said, playing the innocent.

"Whoever these people are who put such ideas in your head," *Tassbewasspo* went on, as if gleaning her thoughts, "they only want to drag you down, to take advantage of your naïveté. A *mature* natal would know better."

Oh, would they? So the much-ballyhooed apex Olivia was also an easy dupe who was prone to asking the wrong questions. No matter—she'd succeeded in derailing their jingoistic spiel, and that was worth a little exasperation on her host's part.

As *Tassbewasspo* and Su-jinda left the overlook, Olivia turned and let her many eyes become defocused. Dusk had fallen over the marshlands, and as she stared through the gloom her thoughts returned to the appeal of the natal poets. They'd told her that no one in position of power or authority had believed that a transferred human was attempting to renew forgotten pathways to an ancient entity. And hadn't she just gotten a taste of that herself? She could almost see herself returning to visit their home planet out of spite. Or maybe she was just playing down her own interest. Because at the center of the poets' concerns was a question Olivia couldn't easily dismiss: why was the only other human in the system so interested in the Fountain?

What did Cole Quinlan know that she didn't?

———

Back in her bead, Olivia was too keyed up to rest but too fatigued to keep ignoring Aleksi's waiting message. Putting it off had only made it easier to keep putting it off.

Rolling her tanthid amulet between her fingers, she brought the message up on her transmission node.

> Hey, Liv.
> I hate to tell you like this, but Somtow died.

Olivia scanned the sentence several times, until the words traced around the first edges of loss. It was hardly different in her natal body—the alarm and the ache of it. The basset hound had already lived half his life when she and Aleksi had retrieved him from the sanctuary in the neighboring Laelitu canton, a trip that marked the first anniversary of their relationship. And Somtow, with all his tender companionship, had come to symbolize to Olivia all the good their relationship could manifest when at its best. Children had never been part of the plan—to the extent they had a plan—but Somtow had been theirs just the same. And now Aleksi was grieving alone.

> Sorry to open with that, but I've already
> recorded this message several times. I'm a
> little talked out at this point, so this is
> what's left over. It was pretty bad for a day
> or so, but his pain blockers kept him from the
> worst of it. I'll go into detail later if you
> want, but right now I'm glad to have it over
> with. The manor seemed too quiet, so I've been
> staying with friends. Tomorrow maybe I'll
> gather his toys, et cetera. The grown-up stuff.

> "Wonderful Disarray" got pulped. We'll still
> get author credits, but no one will experience
> it as we meant it to be run. For the new
> project, I've started collaborating with a
> storyguide whose work I've been following for a
> few years. It's weird, because her creativity
> is kind of at an oblique angle to mine, as far
> as how she sews ambiguity into her narrative to
> give it more focus. I've always thought of
> ambiguity as a kind of soft lie, and you know
> how I approach things. Or maybe you don't.

Anyway, it's work. And it's nice to have something to disappear into for a while.

I feel like I'm talking without saying much.
It's hard. It feels kind of like I'm talking
into a void. Maybe if you

The paragraph just ended that way, and a new one began:

They tell me the spring gate will be opening
back up soon, in under two weeks. That'll be
good. We can talk about things then.

What had the Sovereign Alliance cut out? Something Aleksi was
about to say about her. Something they thought might upset her? She sat
with it for a moment, marveling at how far away the concept felt, like one
of Aleksi's stories she had once subscribed to. Could his words reach her
here at all?

She sensed old Olivia's guilt for thinking in those terms. And that was
fair. But in a very real way, natal Olivia—*apex* Olivia—had never met
Aleksi Tsang, nor any other human. Right now, even more than her physical attributes, that was a source of freedom.

Her eyes went to the remaining messages in the queue, all from Ioor
Volkopp. After a moment she dismissed the transmission node with a
gesture and readied herself for torpor.

THIRTY
DAY 52

HAVEN HUB WAS a shadow of its former self. The crowds of the previous day had been filing out since daybreak—the first of several intermittent dawns already—and the staff had been hard at work removing promotional signage and stowing furnishings.

After a quick feed, Olivia tracked down her cohort to see whether any of them were leaving for the Home system. By her estimation, the Sol's springstir was about a week out, and if she left immediately she would arrive in *Bebetathubutiwa* a day or so after that. But then what? If she delayed her trip home to help the Fifth Sun—and ostensibly all of natality —with Cole Quinlan, she risked missing her opportunity to catch the Sol-side spring before it went dormant again.

But first things first. Assuming she could find transport at all, there was time enough to decide on her path forward.

"You're cutting things pretty close," said *Tassbewasspo*, who had spent the entire morning feed talking to their equally natalist colleague *Powhita-himu*. *Tassbewasspo* was still acting demonstrably cool toward Olivia.

"I know," she said, "but I may not get another chance to visit the cradle of your people. I can't help wanting to know more about my hosts."

Their skin showed little enthusiasm. Now that she had dared to ask about the Pool, the shine was off the apple.

"We wish you luck," they said, and turned to leave.

"Home—"

. . . Tapuwathu . . .

"you said?" *Powhita-himu* asked. They waved their colleague on—*don't wait for us*—then informed Olivia they were headed there as well. "You could come with us." *They* hadn't soured on her, at least.

Unfortunately they were even more insufferable than *Tassbewasspo* themself, with that oblivious, bigoted jocularity. Then again, Olivia had managed to take a trip with Max, so how bad could this be?

"My group has commissioned a transport ship," they continued, "that runs back and forth between Bright Core's Second—"

. . . Titassstihi . . .

"—and Home."

. . . Tapuwathu . . .

"I hope it wouldn't be an imposition," Olivia said.

"We would be honored to have a true apex aboard." Someone at the entryway caught their attention, and *Powhita-himu* flashed them the interlocked chains of agreement. To Olivia they said, "You'd have to leave with us now though. We're on our way to the East Fen Harbor port—our autotrack is leaving. If you can catch the next one, we'll wait for you there."

———

On the ride to the East Fen Harbor port, Olivia allowed the din of the whispering to wash over her. Soon enough she would be free of it.

. . . impostor . . .

"Oh, you shut up," she snapped, earning her glances from several nearby strangers. That word had infected the very fields around her, a vindictive, whispered reverberation.

"Were you saying something?"

She looked at the natal sitting across from her—

. . . Bubepusstass . . .

—a stranger with a woolly shoulder bag stretched to capacity. She imagined them stuffing away Haven Hub paraphernalia before making their hasty getaway.

"Sorry, just . . . intrusive thoughts."

"Interesting! Is that an apex practice?"

Oh shit. The last thing she needed was someone taking an interest in her. A new admirer. "No, I just have a lot on my mind."

"We're sure. Well don't mind us, we feel safer beside an apex."

Hate to disappoint you, friend. But she kept her silence and did her best to match the friendly glimmering mosaic on the stranger's skin. Once she was free of *!Wamuhi*'s gravity well she could go back to being anonymous.

She stared out at the red-capped mushroom trees, feeling puzzled at her vague sense of nostalgia. She should have an image of this to take home with her, but had nothing with her to capture this moment. Only her memories—

"We're not a fanatic, you know."

Olivia turned back to the stranger. "Sorry?"

"The only reason we mentioned your stature at all is because we're a biologist."

"Oh. Well, so you know, this stature of mine is a fairly recent development, and no one was more surprised than I. I started off the same as anyone. The same as any other transfer."

"That's not unheard of. Within any natal colony, apexes aren't born, they're developed."

Like the queen in a bee colony?

"You're a transfer, right?" the stranger said.

"Yes."

"Well, there are any number of factors, internal and external, that may give rise to these morphogenetic processes in adulthood. But whatever your specific conditions, we can assure you that you are quite the—"

"Yes, thank you," Olivia said quickly.

"We hesitate to use the word *magnificent*, but . . ."

"That's . . . fine."

Olivia turned back to the window and studied the view, determined not to turn around again.

———

Powhita-himu was waiting for her as promised at the East Fen Harbor port. With the muted roar of nearby launches conducting through the floor and up her legs, Olivia followed them through the crowds to their private landing pad. There the two of them boarded a bulky but modestly appointed transport ship bound for the nameless planet the natals referred to as Home.

PART FOUR
COLE

THIRTY-ONE
DAY 60

OLIVIA SAT in the transport ship *Hi!posswhi*'s tiered gallery with several dozen other passengers, watching as they made their final approach to the natals' own *Bebetathubutiwa* system.

Her status as a so-called apex had had its plusses and minuses, owing to her reputation as a fearless hunter, which had followed her from *!Wamuhi*. Among her fellow passengers it had earned her both reverential genuflection and scornful glares. But whether intimidated or repulsed, most had given her wide berth over the two hexa-cycle journey, an unexpected gift.

Nagaraket was an exception. The environmental scientist from a domain known as Ketumunik had a wit sharp enough to slice through the absurdity of their condition. They'd met in the gallery, a pair of stargazers brought together by chance. But they'd met there every cycle since, until Olivia found in that routine a comfort that had proven difficult to come by otherwise.

Now, as the glowing dot of the Home system's sun appeared on the projection panel above them, Nagaraket compared the natal transfer program to an institutionalized form of shared psychosis. "I'll add," she said, "that it's a state elevated to ceremony by the most accommodating yet least tolerant people I've ever known."

Such was her candor that Olivia couldn't help but look around to see if anyone else had heard. How many of them were transfers? And of those, how many of them felt truly at home among natality, let alone in their borrowed skins?

"I've talked myself into some tight spots," she said, "but I think people cut me slack because of my physical presence."

"You're truly a biomimetic prodigy." Nagaraket flashed nonsensical patterns across her skin to make clear her jest.

But Olivia sat with the comment as she watched the stars outside. Nothing about her was human, save her thoughts and memories. "Sometimes, even though I know it's not permanent, this body feels like a test of my resolve. As if I might lose a piece of myself if I relax enough to settle into it. But then . . . I *have* forgotten myself a few times, and more often lately. I've forgotten to think of this as *foreign*, I mean. And it's like when you dream in another language for the first time, you know? I haven't become something *not* me, but something *more* me. A me I couldn't have accessed from the human side. Maybe?" Or was she rationalizing? "Maybe that's what I need to think, to survive."

Nagaraket's skin showed rippling chains of agreement. "Survival is one of the driving forces behind biomimicry. In a given ecosystem, a foreign specimen will strategically adopt traits of one or more of the surrounding organisms to survive, surrendering some of its own uniqueness in the process."

Surrender. The word didn't feel so threatening in that context. "So are you still you even if you're no longer the same?" The enduring question.

"I suppose it depends who's asking." Said with curls of amusement playing out across her skin. For a non-natal, she was impressively emotive.

"I'm going to have to think about that one for a while."

"Anyway," the scientist said, leaning close as if confiding a secret, "tell me who in the universe is the same from one cycle to the next?"

Two things happened at once: Olivia's forever-attendant moth darted into the chamber to *pulse-tap-tap-tap* at her, and the hotfont in her utility sash issued a trill.

"You're popular," Nagaraket said.

The Fountain, Olivia thought. They must be back in range, close enough to activate the communication device that relied on it.

"Sorry, I should probably . . ."

"I hope we speak again."

The sentiment gave Olivia pause. The first time for anything could also be the last, especially here. But some moments laid bare the tragedy of that eventuality.

"Me too," she said. As she left the gallery, she pointed at the moth. "You wait."

It hummed as if in response, but didn't dare to issue another *tick*.

Outside, Olivia found a secluded branch of the fareline, and there activated her hotfont. It was a hail from *Ssputhu-buta*, still active. With only a moment's pause, she said, "Elder Two, I'm here."

"Olivia Jelani, you look well," they said, apparently in the middle of some procedure, judging by the hygienic garb over their mouth and hands. "We're surprised you've waited so long to return from your excursion."

"Sorry, yes. There was a lot of ground to cover." And more to cover still.

"Well no matter: the Sol-side spring became active yesterday. You may return now for your regression transfer. Naturally the Affairs Chancery will brief you about . . . the case as it now stands." They were still choosing their words. "As well, you'll attend the compulsory debriefing to cover messaging and that kind of thing."

"Is there anything you can tell me now?"

"All in due course."

So, no.

Olivia eyed the moth as it wobbled in the air before her like an over-excited dog. It was fully capable of remaining still, but no, it had to demonstrate its impatience with every passing moment.

"Actually, I'm headed to Home—"

. . . Tapuwathu . . .

"—now."

That got the elder's attention. They stripped off their scrubs and took a seat. "You're remaining in this system?"

"There are a few things I need to do—to see, I mean—before I leave for good."

"You understand that Sol won't remain accessible for long."

"Yes, I am aware."

"In less than a doza-cycle the Sol-side spring will become—"

"Yes, I remember, Elder." They remained silent. "I'll return to the sphere—"

. . . Watiwabe . . .

"—as soon as I'm done planetside."

"Fine." Elder Two's skin flashed reserved acceptance. "We'll be waiting."

———

The moth was centimeters from her face. It must have a message for her from one of the poets. Who else could it be?

A group of small natals passed her by, their eyes lingering on her and the deeplink a bit too long. Or she was imagining it.

"Come on," she said, hurrying back to her bead. As soon as the portal closed, the moth settled on her shoulder and began its translating.

Olivia, this is Oscar. All planet-bound traffic from Bright Core's Second will be setting down in the Northland Republic, at North Belt 3.

They weren't wasting any time. Were they giving her directions?

That is close to a field hub we maintain, so you'll want to take the line runner to the Grand Ward—

MUrmur-BUrst-THUmp-MUrmur-SStatic

It's a ward known for its international flair. Ask the Tide to direct you to the Fleet Lobe on North Belt 8. It's . . . a good place for us to meet.

Mubuthumuss. She could remember that. As for the rest . . . she'd be lost.

"Shit."

Can we help you?

With a start, Olivia looked at the device affixed to her arm. "I thought this was a recording."

It is, but with a lexical tributary.

She thought of Aleksi's self-propagating fictions.

Did you have a concern?

"I have no access to this 'Tide' I keep hearing about, so I hope I don't need that to find you."

The Tide is optional. The information is ambient. Your deeplink can provide you guidance. Or ask any belt guide wearing the neutral armlets.

"Neutral . . . as in white?"

Neutral as in colorless.

Why were the simplest things the most challenging?

Remember that it's the Fleet Lobe on North Belt 8.

"Got it," she said. Then, out of curiosity, "What if I change my mind about coming?"

I'm sorry, I don't have a response to that.

Meaning, as far as they were concerned, the prospect of her ducking out of this Cole mission entirely wasn't even in the realm of possibility.

"No problem. Thank you." Was it polite to thank a script?

She waited, but sensing nothing more, she pushed the moth off her arm.

THIRTY-TWO
DAY 60

OLIVIA WATCHED from the window of the line runner as the city sped by like a strange diorama. Something about *Tapuwathu*'s atmosphere caused the scenery, from urban centers to vast stretches of country, to shimmer like a mirage. The orange-yellow sun above wavered as if she were underwater—giving her an appreciation for the effect *Watiwabe*'s artificial sun was meant to evoke. Elder Two was right: this was the superior experience.

After debarking she'd said her goodbyes to *Powhita-himu* and Nagaraket, then used a guide kiosk to point her in the right direction. Now she was alert enough, but how much longer could she hold out? She hadn't done this much traveling since her university break, and her torpor had been fitful. Was she dependent on the natal version of adrenaline to remain upright?

Her eyes followed the skyline of architectural twists and whorls, spires, and incurvate blades. Among them was not one rectilinear form. Indeed the buildings themselves—if that's what they were—resembled a sun's coronal mass ejections, tamed with some calculated intent, then finally captured in solid form. It evoked the videos she'd seen of Earth's aurorae at night. The view was a welcome change from the squat, utilitarian constructions on *!Wamuhi*.

Far less welcome was the whispering.

Here the cryptic chatter was even more intense than she'd experienced elsewhere—or perhaps she was continuing to grow more attuned to it. Without concentrating she could make out entire phrases, disjointed sentences that bore no resemblance to Interlish nor to the underlying languages the natals had used in her presence. These were subvocal stimulations closer to turbulence than to speech. Had the poets implied that her sensitivity to it might be advantageous to their cause, and not just a constant torment?

"They'd better be in the mood for questions," she said to herself. Sitting back in her saddle, Olivia let the line runner's gentle thrum lull her.

———

Olivia waited in a sunlit garden at the center of a Fleet Lobe open-air market. Something small landed on the back of her hand, perhaps an insect, so light that she couldn't feel it. She raised it for a closer look: two yellow lenses connected by glimmering filaments. It had no head or tail as far as she could see, but it was clearly alive. The fluid within the two spheres was swimming with glitter-like flecks, and delicate white probes reached out to touch her skin. When she noticed her skin darkening around the bug, she couldn't help but shake it off, and the pigmented spot immediately cleared. The thing must have triggered her chromatophores.

As she took in the peaceful but strange environment, her thoughts drifted to Aleksi. What would he have made of the crowd here? Six-legged spider orchids with cuttlefish skin went about their business, meeting up with friends and family, the smaller ones giving chase to each other underfoot. Organized athletic demonstrations in the park. Old friends reuniting with a complex embrace. A hushed song from a passerby. A physical altercation. A martial unit walking in formation. In some ways it was all so mundane, but the full pageant of it would have dropped his jaw.

She needed to send Aleksi a message. But where to begin? It was too much to fit into a single correspondence. That had been part of the problem. She could never hope to tell him everything in a way that made sense.

But she could aim a little lower.

Stop putting it off.

Olivia left her spot in the sun and found a bank of free transmission nodes at the edge of the atrium. She took the one on the end and waved a hand before it, hoping she could figure out how to get it to work. But she needn't have worried—the panel lit up and immediately displayed her standing message queue, which was a stack of messages from Ioor Volkopp. Beneath them was the familiar entry form, already addressed to Quv Vidalin.

She ignored the messages from Ioor, and all the quite reasonable questions they no doubt contained. Her priority was Aleksi, not the Sovereign Alliance. Let them pore through her private message to her partner and uncover what they could.

"Hi, Aleksi," she said, and waited for the words to appear on the form. Everything seemed to be in order. "I've been the worst correspondent, I know. But even though it's been—" Had it really been almost a month since she'd last written? "Time gets away from you here. It's not like Vaix where time is Earth-centric. Here the ships and planets—and moons, too—are all on their own, and you have to . . . It's like when you're in the ocean for a while, and when you finally look back at the shore your blanket is half a kilometer away."

So far she'd managed to tell him nothing.

"I'm not trying to make excuses. It's just an explanation. I've been doing a lot of travel. I . . ."

What could she say that wouldn't be censored? She'd murdered a tanthid heart mother? Been interviewed by a secretive group of would-be saviors?

"I'm on a little jaunt to the natal home world—please change that to 'remote' home world—which they call . . . Home."

No way was she going to try and explain *"Tapuwathu."*

"They're not big on names here, so they rely on roles, or physical relationships, or historical references—which is kind of nice, because you get some context. Well, usually. Home is just 'Home.' Anyway, I landed here about an hour ago, so I've barely seen any of the city yet. It's so hard to describe things here. It's like a fantasy. I wish I could show you. It could inspire your games. Even their architecture—"

"Olivia Jelani?"

She turned to see a single natal coming toward her across the plaza. Their signature tickled over her nerve endings a moment later:

. . . Buwhi!buti . . .

"Oscar?"

They approached her. "Glad you made it."

"Yeah, I . . . Sorry I wasn't in the main square."

"You're hard to miss in a crowd."

Right.

"Anyway, we're connected to your deeplink." Oscar pointed up at the moth, which was hovering several meters overhead, so still that she almost missed it.

"I thought I'd send a message home," she said, "since I was here."

"We'll let you finish."

"Okay, just one moment." She turned back to the node and read over what she had so far before continuing.

"Anyway, Aleksi, hopefully I've painted some of the picture for you. I'll fill in the gaps later. Pretty soon, I guess. For now though, I just wanted to tell you that I'm so sorry about Somtow. Our little pup. I miss him. But I hope you're hanging in there, and doing well otherwise."

She scanned the text. Awkward? Perfunctory? It would have to do.

"Okay, well . . . Love." She would send him something more substantive—something less rushed—once she'd gotten her bearings. "Uh, go ahead and send."

"Was there anything else you needed to do while we're here?" Oscar asked.

"No, no," she said, standing. "I'm only here to meet with . . . you."

Keep it discreet.

"Fine. This way, please."

———

They left the market area with the moth in tow, and the farelines provided gentle resistance as they moved through them instead of with them. Oscar was ignoring the city's underlying configuration as defined by its magnetic fields, like walking against the wind.

"Did you feed?" he asked.

"I felt the high moment as we were disembarking, but I didn't want to risk being late." Olivia had forgotten to be hungry, until now.

"We have some extra food."

We. "Emily and Langston?"

"It's all of us; all of us in—"

murmur-burst-thump-murmur-sstatic

"—at least." He paused. "You sensed that?"

"I can feel the signature, yes." Oscar had produced the signature without hesitation, as if testing her, and its echo was already reverberating in whispered form:

. . . Mubuthumuss . . .

Perhaps the practice wasn't as taboo here. She'd have to ask them about that.

"We're going to one of our smaller hubs, just outside the local belt."

Judging by the crowds in the walkways and parks, the natals here were far more varied than she'd seen elsewhere. Some clusters wore head-to-points clothing, some walked free of their gamants, and others were so small that they must be children. Sitting by a fountain at the center of a plaza was a group of natals with ornate pictures playing out across their skin—3D geometric forms and glyphs and pictures. That had to be the work of augments.

"It's so different here," Olivia said.

Oscar hardly broke his pace. "Different from . . . ?"

"The other places I've visited in this domain." She wasn't making sense. "I mean the other places were more similar to each other. Here it feels more . . . progressive. Maybe more alive?"

"It's not like *!Wamuhi*." They didn't elaborate.

Ignoring ranks of motorized transport, Oscar led Olivia to a sparkling canal teeming with colorful narrowboats. They briefly followed a fareline along the water's edge, but soon enough they were going against the flow once more. The additional impedance took a toll, like pressure on Olivia's eardrums that she couldn't alleviate, only across every inch of her skin.

Consequently, the traffic here was far lighter than it had been at the open market. The entire city was a reflection of the underlying fields, so it stood to reason that fewer people would congregate in areas that "felt wrong." Olivia didn't much care for the feeling either, but at least it was waking her up.

The buildings along the waterway were far less extravagant than those in the city center, trading gravity-defiant engineering for practicality. The soft-shelled forms almost resembled waves slouching ever toward the waterway. Oscar ducked under a low awning and held open a flap in the front of an unmarked edifice. The empty space within was cooler, and resembled an office carved according to some sinuous grain. The floors rose outward from the entranceway, banking in various whorls like the entrances to separate funhouses. Managing the furniture had to be a nightmare.

"Are you okay?" Oscar had stopped halfway down one of the passages to look back at Olivia. She'd been gawking.

"Yes, I . . . I'm taking everything in. Maybe I'm just hungry."

"This way."

———

From several levels up, the building's glass wall provided an expansive view of the canal below, as well as the vista beyond the city limits. As they waited for the other poets to arrive, Olivia fed on a fibrous savory stalk that Oscar had retrieved for her.

Tap-wave-tap-wave-tick

Two natals had entered the bead. The one on the right—

. . . !Ti!watawa . . .

—flashed the pattern of recognition as they saw Olivia, clasping the hands of their forelimbs together.

Coming over from the window to join them at the shallow base of the soft floor's gentle concavity, Olivia returned the gesture. "Emily."

"That's right. And this is Maya."

. . . Whititita . . .

Maya had only four legs—no sign of their gamant—and their skin displayed none of the usual patterns. They couldn't be a transfer, not with a signature like that. Maybe they had a reason to suppress their chromatophores.

"Good to meet you," Olivia said.

Oscar produced Maya's signature as he greeted them: *WHIr-TIck-TIck-TAp*. "It's good to see you again."

Several more natals filed in, and with each of them, Olivia sensed the attendant plucks and warps in the surrounding fields. A few of those gathered wore sashes, but they didn't appear to be security. They positioned themselves close to the window, like the audience to a new performance. The thought of it brought to mind one of Olivia's first public readings, where one of the attendees had interrupted her to ask if she was okay. She hadn't realized she'd been crying, not because of her poem—which she could have breezed through on autopilot—but because her knees were in agony.

That was old Olivia though. Natal Olivia was an apex, not subject to idle pains. And though she'd come all this way, natal Olivia had made no one any promises—yet. First she'd need to know more about this Cole Quinlan. She scanned the faces of those present, saw them watching her, perhaps with expectation, and found herself unconcerned. Even if her emotional inhibitor was inactive, her prevailing attitude was an ever more insatiable curiosity. She might well be in over her head, but natal Olivia was exactly where she wanted to be.

———

"An apex," said Maya. "No one mentioned this to us."

Once again, Olivia was the largest person in the room. If she grew any more she'd make a spectacle of herself just being in public.

"Was this an attribute your people requested for the transfer?"

Had that even been an option? "No," Olivia said. "It happened after."

"As with Cole," they said.

"Maybe it's something about their species," said Oscar.

Maya approached Olivia, giving her a thorough look. "Were you a warmaker prior to your arrival?

"I was a poet. A lecturer."

Silence.

"Early in life I was a dancer," she offered. She imagined what it might be like to watch a six-legged natal dance—or to dance, herself, in this body. She could, now that the pain was gone. But that life seemed so distant now . . . as did many things.

"We teach engineering," said Maya. Satisfied for the moment, they turned to Oscar and Emily. "Are they prepared to carry out Max's role?"

"Olivia lacks his training," Emily said, "but Max had no sensitivity to the ursprache."

Maya's skin remained blank, which only made clear how reliant Olivia had become on the emotive patterns. Without them she was at a severe disadvantage.

"They are sensate?" Maya asked.

"Surprisingly so," said Oscar.

After a moment of consideration, Maya waved at Olivia's moth, and it buzzed away. When it was gone, they looked at Olivia and produced a sequence of whispered signals that Olivia could barely keep up with, but which were as clear as any articulated words.

"What's that?" she asked. Was she supposed to reproduce that sequence herself?

Maya ignored the question and repeated the sequence again. It was nothing like the whispered beats and pops Olivia had been sensing, though each part still registered like a tickle across her pores. She focused on each part in turn, until Maya was silent.

"Now show them," Oscar said. "Like you demonstrated for us on the Moon of Bright Core's Second—"

. . . *!Wamuhi* . . .

"Right," Olivia said. The parts of the sequence were fading fast from memory. No time to deliberate. She held the first part of the sequence in her mind, then willed it outward through means unknown even to herself:

. . . *mysshouth* . . .

That was the first part, wasn't it? Maya gave her no indication, so she moved on to the next parts.

. . . *sellassash* . . . *llyllannann* . . . *trushym* . . .

Afterward Olivia regarded them both. She hadn't expected to be tested, not least on this. "I think that was it, but I don't understand it." And her transliterator could do nothing to help with the whispering.

"We were asking you if you sensed the words," Maya said, "using our native dialect. Which you can." They turned to the other poets. "How is this possible for a transfer?"

"A particularity of their analog frame," said Oscar, "or their own influence on it."

For a moment they were all silent, either considering the person they'd brought into their secret lair, or perhaps waiting for her to say something.

Oscar went to the table by the window and enlisted several of the silent bystanders to help him clear it of papers and equipment. One of them brought out a tray of what Olivia guessed were drinking vessels; each one resembled a comical cross between a pipe snifter and a pitcher plant. With these set at each place, and the saddle chairs arranged, Oscar beckoned for Olivia to sit at the head of the table.

"It's time to finish the conversation we started on !Wamuhi."

Olivia sat, and the others took their places. Once they'd settled in, Oscar gave the table a rhythmic tap.

"Let's first ascertain your level of commitment."

Weren't they past that? "I'm sitting here, aren't I?" Olivia said.

"We appreciate that. But you are far from home, and the task before us may be demanding."

Were they concerned that she'd miss her window home? "I was told I had a doza-cycle or so to return to Sol."

"That sounds correct, since Sol's spring activated yesterday," Emily said, not tripped up by the proper name. In fact the members of the Fifth Sun seemed conversant with a number of human idiosyncrasies—and much less hostile than other natals when it came to matters beyond their immediate domain.

"We do need to acknowledge the risk that, by the time we see this undertaking through, your spring may very well have closed again," Oscar said. "This would be an inconvenience for you, Olivia, given your family and obligations, but far more important, your extended absence would raise questions in your team, and possibly even trigger tensions between our peoples."

What questions was Olivia *already* raising back in Sol system? She'd allowed her communication with the Sovereign Alliance to lapse for countless cycles, and their unanswered hails had filled the transmission node's display. She didn't have to read them to imagine the questions within: *Are you both okay? Why are neither of you checking in? Where is Max? Why haven't you returned?*

Maya sat forward. "Then again, a misplaced emissary might be a *good* thing, as far as getting attention."

"Not if we're not in control of the response."

Olivia cut in. "If there really is something I can do to help here—and I haven't made you any promises on that front yet—I could always make up an excuse for wanting to stay. Your Affairs Chancery hasn't told my people about Max's death yet, and he's supposed to be reporting in regularly, so . . . I'm not sure how I'd explain his failure to return as well. But I'm going to need a lot more information about what this whole thing entails before I'm going to even think about any of that."

"We will tell you everything you need to know," Oscar said. "But then we'll need your answer."

———

Taking the vessel before her, Olivia put the thin glassy tube to her lips and drew the fluid upward. The water was fresh and unexpectedly smooth, a bit like cream.

"How much do you know about the ursprache?" Oscar asked.

Olivia looked at Emily. "I heard you say the word earlier. I don't know what it means."

"But you already know it," Emily said. "You understood the signature Oscar used for the Moon of Bright Core's Second."

. . . CLICK-WAve-MUrmur-HIss . . .

"You're talking about the electrical patterns." *The whispers.*

"That's right. It's the proto-language of our people."

"Our common tongue," Oscar said. "The language our ancestors spoke as we first came to realize who we were in the world. Rather than resonant tones in the air, the ursprache is made up of patterns emitted

from electrocytes in our abdomen and back, and detected by our electroreceptors."

What was the word that *Tassbewasspo* had used on the trip to
Puthubutiss? "Ampullae," Olivia said.

"The same. But the reason for this biology primer is because in order
to talk to you about Cole, and what we think they're doing, it's necessary
to discuss the ursprache . . . and its various applications." They took a
pull at their snifter.

Now that she was getting answers, Olivia found she had a taste for
them. For too long she'd suppressed her questions about the whispers,
starting back at Elder Two's initial dismissal.

"So this ursprache," she said. "It's the whispering I always sense?"

"What are you referring to?" asked Emily.

"The chatter all around us."

The natals looked at each other, their flesh showing confusion, and
Olivia pushed away a sinking feeling. They *had* to know what she was
talking about. Didn't they?

"The echo?" Maya asked at last. "You sense that?"

"Are we not talking about the same thing?" said Olivia.

"*We're* talking about a means of communication," said Oscar. "What
you're referring to is . . . an application of that language, also long abandoned. This 'whispering'—what we used to call the echo—is no longer
accessed by any except historians. Researchers. Religious scholars."

"How about poets?"

"Possibly, yes."

"The echo was once a medium of knowledge and enlightenment," said
Emily.

"Similar to the Tide?" The cull official on *!Wamuhi* had told her that
the news of her feat had swept the Tide, which had made it sound like a
public channel. Then, earlier that day, Oscar had suggested she consult
the Tide for directions to the Grand Ward.

"No, not like the Tide," said Oscar. "The Tide is utility," they tapped a
point on their head, "a meshed device to achieve an end. But the whispering is much older, a dedicated carrier infused into the very fields
around us, self-propagating, rooted in the ursprache, but with its own
emergent insights."

"Emergent . . ."

The term—used in a technical context at least—was one she'd heard Aleksi use when discussing his immersive fictions. He still authored some of his content directly, but most of his authoring involved complex milieu or character systems that would allow a fiction to emerge from internal dynamics.

"That means . . . the whispering I sense isn't just repeating stored messages. It's adapting over time."

tick-tick

"Think of it more as a latent space," Oscar said. "The echo was the distributed constellation of accrued knowledge. The more history a location had—and the stronger the fields there—the deeper the echo in that location. At least that was the case when people still actively contributed to it."

"So it's a technology? It's not some intrinsic property of the world that I've been picking up on?"

"It was a thing of our own creation," Oscar said. "And some would call it our crowning achievement."

"Not the Fountain?"

That earned her a quick *tick-tick*. "The Fountain is *not* ours," Maya said. And though their skin remained entirely blank, they stood from their saddle and set to pacing. Olivia was half tempted to apologize.

"The echo's sequences once yielded epiphanies," said Emily. "It could provide insight, in the way the subconscious might."

The idea brought something to mind Olivia hadn't thought of since school. "Like the old Earth term 'satori.'"

"Satori?"

"The path to enlightenment."

They took a moment to consider the word—or perhaps to look it up in their Sol lexicon. "Yes," said Emily, "that's apt."

"And you call it an echo . . . why?" Olivia asked.

"The sequences within it are constructs perpetuated by the ancient fabrics," said Oscar, "but they fade with each passing circuit. Very much like an echo that degrades over time."

"Only because larger society has turned its back on the ursprache, allowing it to become ever more incoherent," Emily said. "Electromagnetic signatures still exist for named things, but in time they'll be forgotten too."

"Not just forgotten," Maya said, sidling up behind Olivia. "There are genetic modifications to engineer the ampullae out of some castes. Bright-born fools."

Olivia's aversion was plain on her skin, and she didn't bother to try to suppress it. "Not you though," she said. "You've *embraced* your proto-tongue."

"Why wouldn't we?" Oscar's skin was stippled, either to present their own calm or as an appeal to the other Fifth Sun members present. "Think about it. Why would we have put so much effort into bringing about something so esoteric?"

"I don't know."

"It was devised in desperation, after those in power severed the connection between the Fountain and the Pool."

"The mythological thing at the other side of the Fountain?" That had come out wrong. "Sorry."

Oscar didn't admonish her. "The Pool communicated to us through some electromagnetic means—something at least superficially similar to the whispering."

"But while those in power made sure that the Pool was relegated to mythology," said Emily, "the echo didn't always adhere to political expediency. Those who listen today may still hear certain discarded truths."

"Such as the fact that there were those who saw the Pool as a source of insight," Oscar added, "while others saw it as a target for exploitation."

"Always the same two sides," Maya grumbled.

So it was all related, if circuitously—the whispering, the Pool, and Olivia's keen sense. But that didn't mean she could be of any use to the Fifth Sun. "How does Cole fit into all this?"

"This, unfortunately, is our primary focus right now," said Oscar. "Because Cole is driving Unity to reopen the Fountain to the Pool's system, no longer do we have the luxury of time to preserve the historical record, to restore damaged works of art, to raise public awareness about our cultural heritage. Indeed, within the last circuit we received evidence from a field operative—"

"That hasn't been verified," Emily put in.

"But there's a strong *possibility* that Cole's group has managed to open a conduit through the Fountain that's been closed off for a dozen biqua-circuits."

"How long is that?" Olivia asked.

"About thirty generations."

How long was a natal generation?

"Approaching two of your millennia," Oscar said, anticipating the question. "We haven't been able to get close enough to verify this, but we have noticed a lot of traffic—a lot of *inconspicuous* traffic—moving through that aspect of the Fountain."

"If Unity has gotten that far unchecked," Maya said, finally taking her seat again, "that alone would be enough to warrant an intervention."

"If the ancient stories are true," Oscar said, "contact with the Pool— an entity whose very existence is the patterned perturbations of space-time—would spell disaster for biological life. Based on accounts in the earliest chronicles, quantum field disruption of the type the Pool effects can result in the decoherence of matter."

"Fortunately," said Emily, "those earlier accounts also make it clear that the Pool, for whatever reason, was never able to make use of the Fountain, nor its springs."

"Then . . . what's the problem?" Olivia asked. "If the Pool can't pass through . . ."

"When we say Cole wants to open the Fountain to the Pool," Oscar said, "we mean that they're working to make that passage possible."

"That makes no sense," Olivia said. "If it's going to destroy all life— break apart matter itself—how could anyone stand to benefit from bringing it here?"

"It's *pure delusion*." said Maya, rapping the table. "We've heard them speak of allowing the Pool to 'finish what it started.' That's not just some romanticized poetic notion. They'd throw open the floodgates to chaos to usher in some fantastical *awakening*."

Emily put a hand on Maya's foreleg.

Olivia let them settle back into their saddle before continuing. "Aren't there safeguards in place to prevent someone from making this passage possible? We're talking about a known existential threat to every living organism in this system."

"There *were* safeguards in place . . . at first," Oscar said. "But once the general public were allowed to forget about the Pool, safeguards fell aside and restrictions loosened. Why guard an unmarked path?"

"Security through obscurity," said Olivia.

"Except not everyone did forget," Maya said. "And now Unity has found that ancient route."

"This is a lot to wrap my head around."

"Wrap your head . . ." Oscar flashed agreement. "Yes, that makes sense. It's almost too much to understand."

"Given all this, aren't the rest of your people willing to help? Why is it just a handful of us meeting—and secretly at that?"

"Because no one else believes it," said Emily. "To them, we're talking about an obsolete folk tale."

"Our best hope, to be honest, is that Cole fails in this effort," Oscar said. "The Pool was never able to gain access to the Fountain before, so who's to say Unity can solve the puzzle? But it's difficult for us to assess that from a distance, and getting close to them has proven a challenge. Which is why we've come to you."

"You mean, simply because we're both human, you think I can not only connect with him, but get him to stand down." That sounded more than farfetched.

"Just get close to them," said Maya, leaning into the edge of the table. "And then you will know what to say. You are the same. You have the advantage of understanding how a human might operate."

That wouldn't matter. She'd been here for just over a month, and the line between human Olivia and this ever-whispering skin had already grown diffuse. Cole had been a natal for thirty years. The odds that he would operate "like a human" were slim to none.

"And you have the other advantage," Oscar said. "If you manage to insinuate yourself into their operation, perhaps you can gain insight, through your electromagnetic sensitivity, into how they're employing the ursprache to reach back to the Pool."

"The survival of your race *can't* be all down to me," Olivia said. The words sounded ludicrous coming from her speaker flaps, but the absurdity of it had to be articulated.

"Of course it's not," Oscar said. "You're our plan A."

She looked at the three of them, almost afraid to ask. "What's your plan B?"

Maya left the table and moved to the window.

"A bit more drastic," said Emily. Then they got up to join their colleague.

After that reaction, Olivia was hesitant to push for details. And when Oscar, too, got to their points, she followed their cue.

"Come," said Oscar. "We'll continue tomorrow."

THIRTY-THREE
DAY 61

OLIVIA AWOKE in her webbing feeling almost weightless. Judging by the pinkish light filtering in through the windows, it must be early, before the high moment. But already the street outside sounded like that of any city she'd traveled to.

Keep still. Stay here.

But this moment of peace was illusory, and would last only so long as she kept the details of yesterday's conversation at bay. Already the weight of their plight threatened to reassert itself, like gravity on the approach to some previously unseen body.

Olivia's only distraction was the whispering, which saturated the air around her, fairly lapping at her nerve endings, beckoning her attentions from torpor's too-brief respite.

"Dammit," she said, allowing her room to come into focus.

Through the high frosted windows she saw crowds of pedestrians making their way past on the streets outside. The Fifth Sun seemed to have an open account at this place, and it was perfectly serviceable, even if there was a bit of a smell to the room. Not to mention the fields, which didn't even converge—

A tone sounded behind her, and she scrambled to gain purchase enough to turn. "What is that?"

"You've received an additional note from Ioor Volkopp," came the

voice of the natal ambiont, annihilating the pronunciation of his name.
"It's marked urgent."

The display in the corner of the bead lit up, and the unread stack of
messages was visible from where she stood.

"How many unread messages are there?" She didn't want to know.

"There are eighteen messages total," the ambient said, its voice free of
judgment. "The most recent three are marked urgent."

A tribute to her dereliction. Such were the lengths she had been
willing to go to to avoid having the conversation about Max.

Before she could decide against it, she crossed the room to the transmission node and opened the newest message.

```
Olivia, by now we've said everything there is
to say. There's no action we can take from
here to coax you into providing some clue as
to your wellbeing, but once more we must
express our disappointment with both you and
Ind. Mehdipour. Which only deepens now, since
we'd been looking forward to your return, and
yet there's still no communication from
either of you. Have you established alternate
plans? We have reached out to your hosts for
information, continually, and though we under-
stand that the Empyrean Symbiotry convention
went well, they leave many questions
unanswered.

Anyway, I repeat myself. Please return at your
earliest possible convenience. Or, failing
that, please respond so we can sort this out.
At the very least we need to know that you're
both well.
```

Dismissing the message and the display would have been easy.
Instead, Olivia opened a fresh pane and replied.

"Hi, team. I'm fine. And I'm sorry I haven't been better at maintaining a consistent line of communication. The fact is that I've been doing a lot of traveling, and messaging can be a challenge, even here.

"But speaking of, I'm trying to squeeze in as much . . ." She thought about it. "As much sightseeing as I can before I return. So, my apologies again for losing track of time. It's easy to do when time itself is measured differently. I promise to try to be more mindful. I'll be in touch again, and send will a note to Max to do the same. All is well."

It was vague, flirting as it did with outright deception. But at least it shouldn't rouse suspicion. She needed to hold them off for . . . how long? Eventually she'd need to tell them *something*. Or she could become inaccessible for a while—go to ground and shift the burden to the First Seat to explain her absence.

Meantime, there was nothing from Aleksi. Of course he had a lot going on, what with the new project. Still, this silence felt off. Could Somtow's death have sent him off course? Olivia sat back in her saddle. They'd brought the puppy home on their first anniversary, in a fit of confidence about their future. Now their dog was gone, and she was feeling every light year of distance between them.

A knock at her door gave her a moment of hesitation. No one knew she was here but the Fifth Sun operatives. She crossed her bead and encountered a familiar signature before she got to her door:

. . . *Bessbessta* . . .

AKA Langston.

She opened the door, and the small natal issued the usual *tap-wave-tap-wave-tick* greeting. "We're glad you found the day," they said, laying a friendly hand on her shoulder as they entered the bead. Their geniality was a change from their usual reticence. Either the prospect of her support had already lifted their spirits, or they were keeping on their best behavior to ensure she made the desired choice.

"Thank you. Were we going together?"

"We have a lot of ground to cover, so we'll accompany you for the high moment, then after to the field hub."

"Sure. Great." At least she wouldn't have to navigate alone. "Let me get my sling bag."

"There's a feed stand we know that you might enjoy, if you want a good example of the local fare."

"I'd like that."

As she went to the other room to find her sling, her moth landed on her arm with an abruptness that made her recoil. She lifted a hand to bat it away, but the drone's setae were already tickling her skin.

Don't speak, or they'll hear you.

Olivia stood stock still.

We've already sent someone to your bead, so find a way to stay put. And do not confront Langston.

There must be an explanation. But the best way forward was with a cool head. "I'll be right out," she heard herself call into the other room. "Just need to clean myself up."

The moth had already alighted from her arm and was zipping toward the open clerestory window when Olivia heard a *pop*. A black dot opened in the skin of the deeplink, and the moth dropped to the floor, inert.

Langston stood before her with a device of some sort in their hand. "You made a good show of deliberating the question, common prime. But you can drop the act."

Olivia stood with her sling still dangling from her hand. Too much was happening at once.

"I don't know what this is about." They'd killed the moth. And now they were accusing her of . . . what? Of being a spy?

"Your plans end today, as Max's did. Your infestation is over."

"*Bessbessta*, my plan is your plan. We're on the same side!" This lunatic was about to put a hole between her eyes, and no one was going to stop them.

Bessbessta raised their hand—

Without another thought, Olivia threw herself into the natal, slamming them to the ground. She pinned their weapon-wielding hand to the floor, sending the device skittering into the corner. They thrashed beneath her, but against her superior strength *Bessbessta*'s struggles were to no avail. All she had to do was hold them down until . . .

No.

Something was wrong.

The natal had ceased their thrashing and now stared calmly at her, their skin stippled, static.

A tidal wave of nausea overtook Olivia, her muscles all seizing at once, pulling her into a compact ball that contracted ever tighter. She fell into a white-hot agony, all-consuming and insatiable.

Her body was rejecting her. And Langston must have triggered it somehow. She couldn't get air. Did she have lungs? It didn't matter now.

She was dying.

And then *Bessbessta* was on top of her. She was the one on the floor, and the natal—their skin an even mottle of calm—was holding her down.

Olivia fought the pain with all her might, but every joint sang in a way that was all too familiar. Except this pain went beyond the pain she'd endured for decades—it was a more volatile agony, more insistent. And that was exactly what *Bessbessta* wanted to see. They were watching her die as she—

A blinding flash filled the bead.

The world went dark.

———

All that remained of the pain was a body-wide tightness that held Olivia fast. Her eyes locked on the figure crouching beside her as an acrid smell registered on her high palate.

"What happened?" she asked, her voice little more than a rasp.

"Allow the antidote to finish circulating," they said. Oscar. Of course. "You'll make a full recovery."

As her head cleared, she noticed Maya, plus some of the others she'd seen in the field hub. Langston's body was on the floor halfway across the room. Only their two mid-legs—the two under their gamant's control— were still moving.

"We need to examine their wounds," Maya said, pushing Oscar aside. "Help me with them."

The two of them placed several of her hands beneath Olivia's legs and, with the help of another natal, Olivia got back onto her points. She let them guide her back out into the front area of her bead, where the light made it easier for her wounds to be attended to.

My poor gamant.

"Hold still," said Maya.

"Sorry," Olivia said, trying not to think of the dead body in her bead.

266

Until recently she'd gone her whole life without seeing anyone dead. Well, except for Ran. She caught Oscar's eye. "Langston—"

... *Bessbessta* ...

"—mentioned Max. I think they were involved somehow."

"That's no surprise," Oscar said.

"I think they killed him and his transfer steward."

"No, Max did that."

"He . . . how?" Olivia asked.

"Hold *still*," Maya urged, still patching up her leg.

"*Bessbessta* used a nerve agent on them," said Oscar, "not unlike the one they used on you. Max would have experienced the side effects over the course of a cycle, starting subtly, but by the end . . . well, the ferocity of his behavior was the result of a specific agitant with hallucinogenic properties. Max was certainly not to blame for the result."

Olivia had seen it herself that first day, in Max's ungainly progress and general lack of focus.

"Better?" Maya asked.

Olivia inspected her leg. It was shaking. She was shaking all over. But at least she could move again. The contusions had been minor compared to the full-body trip to hell she'd undergone. Now only her sore muscles remained, plus one dead body.

"How long have you known?" she asked.

"We began to suspect something on *!Wamuhi*," Maya said, "when we lost track of *Bessbessta* for part of a cycle. By chance another of our operatives caught sight of them at the Haven Hub complex—a flagrant violation of our clandestinity directive."

"I ended up in the tanthid pen—"

Maya issued a *tick-tick* and glared at her, flickering bolts of admonition forming and dissolving across their flesh.

Olivia put up a hand. "I was hanging out with the wrong crowd, okay? I didn't know that then. My point is, someone led me to the wrong enclosure—someone without a signature. And it could have cost me my life."

"*Bessbessta?*"

"Like I said, I couldn't get a read on them," Olivia said. "But now I think . . . yes."

"We didn't put everything together until today, when *Bessbessta* left to meet with you alone," said Oscar. "It was the echo that helped us to draw the last connecting line."

"Straight to here," Maya said, gently touching her foreleg. Olivia winced at the sting. "Right here," Maya repeated to Oscar, and showed them the blue-brown lump there. "That's where they applied the agent."

"Not subtle," Olivia said.

"But effective, as you would have found out if we'd gotten here a moment later."

Olivia sat on the edge of her torpor hull. "I don't get it. The Fifth Sun's plan stands to prevent a catastrophe, and you came to me for help. So why would someone from your own organization make an attempt on my life?"

Oscar and Maya looked at each other as several of the other natals murmured among themselves.

"What am I missing? Was *Bessbessta* aligned with Cole?"

"Maybe *Bessbessta* held a misplaced antipathy toward humans," Oscar said. "Specifically *because* of Cole."

The thought caught Olivia off guard. Was the idea so farfetched? *Bessbessta*'s only experience with humans was in association with a plot that threatened the existence of their entire race.

"Does anyone else in your group feel the same way?" She looked at the others, but saw on their skin only wavelets of reassurance.

"It's fair that you'd ask the question," Oscar said. "None among our group will threaten you further."

How could they be so sure? "Well, finding Cole might be a way for me to redeem myself."

"We aren't here to judge or to redeem you," said Oscar, "but we'd be glad to have your help."

One of the other natals came in from the other room holding *Bessbessta*'s weapon in one hand and the dead moth in the other. "We found these."

"We'll take them with us," said Maya.

In the other room, Olivia caught sight of Langston's gamant, shuddering as it was pulled away from the ruins of their body, then collapsing to the floor.

Oscar moved to block her view. "Why don't we attend the high moment now, if you feel you're able. Then we'll reconvene at the field hub."

In other words, they didn't need her help here. "You'll notify the authorities about this?" she asked.

"It's best that you're not involved with these matters."

Fine. She didn't need to know what would happen to *Bessbessta* or their gamant. Plausible deniability was a universal concept. Or maybe she was rationalizing to let herself off the hook. If she had simply returned to *Watiwabe*, *Bessbessta* would still be alive.

Impostor my ass, she thought, recalling the tanthid heart mother's final judgment of her. *Craven is more like it.*

How easy it was to distance herself from her own responsibility. She'd been clinging to the excuse that she wasn't herself and thus shouldered no moral burden—but that was a coward's argument in the end. She'd *chosen* to be here, for better or worse.

This was who she was now.

————

At the high moment, Olivia found herself unable to eat more than scraps. The intricately decorated multicolor puffs were said to be a savory local delicacy, but she could only stare at her food, and her corner of their shared slate was left nearly untouched. All she could think about were consequences—all the ripples that fanned out from a single inciting action.

She looked over at Maya. "You said yesterday that Cole was delusional, that he wants to allow the Pool access no matter the consequences to life here. How has he gotten any support?"

"They've surrounded themself with likeminded fools," Maya said, her voice modulated below the conversational hum around them. "And they've shielded themself from easy discovery. They are as bent on achieving their end as we are on stopping them, and undeterred by the potential consequences. We've seen it. We've worked at their side. The knowledge of what may happen only emboldens them. They *want* it, for what they believe will come after."

"Last night you called it an *awakening*." Olivia once more stared down at the pastries before her. They were gradually losing their cottony texture, glistening as their inner contents leaked through. "As if anything *new* is necessarily *good*. I mean, cancer is new."

Oscar waved a dismissive hand. "If you believe the system is diseased, you look for something new, for the *cure* would necessarily be new. It's down to perspective."

"These people sound like fanatics. No, zealots. I don't see how I'm any better positioned to get close to them than the rest of you."

"There are more similarities in your backgrounds than there are differences," said Maya.

Olivia looked at them. It hadn't been meant as an insult, she was sure.

"Your insights may show you how they got to this place," Oscar said. "And thus the path out of it."

"I don't know," she said. "From everything you've told me, the man sounds too far gone."

"Would that stop you from trying?" Oscar asked. "Given the stakes?"

She couldn't argue that. Cole might very well be a psychopath, but that would only make this mission more of an imperative.

The hall had already begun to clear out, and Olivia found herself restless—not because she knew what to do, but because she had no clue. And her muscles were still tight from the morning's trauma. Had the body in her bead already been removed?

"They're either contemplating a way to decline our plan," Maya said to Oscar, "or they're worried about failure."

Olivia held her words. Maya's dismissive tone was performative. Maybe they thought they knew something of her—as *Bessbessta* had—through some association with Cole.

"We face failure if we do nothing," Oscar said. "What else can we do but seek ways to avoid it?"

"What could I possibly have in common with someone willing to bring this threat to an entire species?" Olivia asked Maya. She was going to nip this in the bud right now.

"Even we have shared many of their ideals," Maya said, to Olivia's surprise. Where had that come from? "The Fifth Sun originally formed around an idea of reconnecting with the Pool. The idea is . . . compelling. From a certain perspective."

"But Cole is different," Emily said, "because there's something that pushes them to continue."

Olivia considered the three natals sitting across from her. She knew more about who they *weren't* than who they *were*—a people defined by the line they'd drawn between themselves and a rogue human in natal camouflage.

THIRTY-FOUR
DAY 61

A SPECTRAL MINIATURE hung in the air among those gathered, the map of greater *Mubuthumuss*. It was zoomed in to a point by the canal that bisected it.

"Cole and several of their colleagues routinely visit open enclaves," Maya told Olivia, circling around the display. For now at least, they were taking Olivia's presence as a gesture of her willingness to help. The rest of the Fifth Sun's field hub appeared to be significantly less bustling than it had been yesterday, with only the three poets—those who remained—to walk her through the specifics of the plan.

"What is an open enclave? Some kind of event?" Olivia asked, following the image of the canal to a point of interest represented by a glowing circle.

"It's a festive gathering," said Oscar. "A bit under the Tide, where the only mandate is free expression."

An unexpectedly relatable concept. She'd attended her own share of such parties, though not in several decades.

"There's an open enclave scheduled for tonight," Maya continued. "If we become separated . . ." They pointed at the map, and a bright line followed the canal's edge, where it connected with a cluster of buildings. "You can find your way back to the field hub along here." Maya used a gesture to center the map over a prominent access built into a sloping bank. "The two of us will go in through the main port, here."

"I won't stand out?"

"You'd stand out if you didn't stand out," Emily said, the fractals on their skin visible even through the glowing illustration between them.

"Cole has used these events to recruit new members," Maya continued, "so we'll try to take advantage of that and get you an audience with them as an interested party."

"What sort of recruits would he find at an event like this?" Olivia asked.

"Don't get the impression that open enclaves are attended by social degenerates," Oscar said. "Those from the highest poles can be found in attendance, if you know where to look."

"Will I have some kind of cover story?"

"We've thought of that," Oscar said. "Cole has instituted a system of titles for all those they work with, a very human predilection. But presenting yourself as 'Olivia' would be the wrong approach."

"It would give me away," she said. "Unless you wanted me to come clean as a fellow human transfer. Sometimes it sounds like you want me to appeal to Cole on a *human* level, but if I came out as—"

Oscar gave her a *tick-tick*. "We'd like you to keep that information in reserve, in case it becomes useful later."

"Then what about my voice?" The transliterator was brilliant at removing language barriers, but the spoken words were always there in the background. "If I use my Interlish, Cole will know."

"Maybe you weren't told, but you can fully suppress your voice at will. And you'd better try it now."

"Then it's a good thing I thought to bring it up," she said, not bothering to hide her vexation from her skin. "So tell me how."

"Say something with the intention of masking your words."

"Oh." So it was a feature of her biomechanical assistant, a purely responsive interface by the sound of it. Such controls had the advantage of being unobtrusive, but at the expense of inscrutability. So how did one *speak* in this foreign body without being heard? Maybe it was like speaking under one's breath, only . . . all the way under.

"Does this work?" she said, doing her best to not actually speak. "Can you hear me?"

"Good, your voice is fully masked."

Glad I thought to ask.

"As for your identity," said Maya, "for you we've selected Holipzibey."

Olivia repeated the word under her breath until the foreign syllables sounded somewhat less foreign. *Holipzibey.* It wasn't a proper name, nor derived from the whispering tongue. Was it an aesthetic preference, or did Cole just need verbal handles to cope with natal society? Could he not sense the electromagnetic signatures as she could?

"It's an old word from Third Diaspora Territory," Oscar said, "on a planet known as the Plain Country. So it won't be transliterated for you. Holipzibey is a person who articulates."

Maya gestured to theirself. "We adopt the title of Manti-Ja when dealing with Unity. It's a generic designation from our family province."

"Manti-Ja," Olivia repeated. "Okay. Holipzibey and Manti-Ja. And what about my background?"

"Do you know of the Third Diaspora?"

Olivia attempted a *tick-tick* of her own, pushing the negative response out from thought to signal.

Oscar sensed it. "The people who live in that region are known for their discretion. They even eschew Tide access. So if it comes up, it would be fitting for you to speak little of your culture beyond that."

"Unity aren't organized enough to be doing thorough background investigations," Maya assured her. "Cole is guided by caprice. We first got an audience with them only because we attended the same technical institute as one of their deputies. Cole fancied our banter, not our offer to help Unity extend secure channels to their various interim hubs. That's something they're always in need of, by the way. Would you feel comfortable offering to do something like that with—"

"I would not," Olivia said, cutting them off. This was exactly what she'd wanted to avoid. A little pretense was fine—who hadn't started the occasional conversation with some creative self-marketing?—but she wasn't about to go in presenting as something she could be challenged on.

"That's fine," said Emily. "But you'll need appear to be valuable to them in some way. Once you're in, being of similar mind and in appearance should go a long way toward getting them to lower their defenses around you."

"In appearance?"

Maya dismissed the map and took Olivia by the arm. "There's something you need to know about Unity."

———

Coaxing her gamant to detach was a delicate ritual. Maya showed Olivia how to place the hands of her forelegs—the set that were fully hers—just so on his body while inviting him to ease himself away. At the same time she was to envision herself pulling back from him, but without slipping into antipathy, lest she hurt her gamant's feelings.

At least that was the clearest way to think about it. For some reason it hadn't set in till now that they were doing this right away. But of course they were. This wasn't something the Fifth Sun had the luxury of time with. They were worried that Cole was going to pop a hole in their universe.

Olivia's obligatory separation from her gamant, now that it was intentional, was a surprisingly intimate process, a bit like being watched while making out with someone. To their credit, Maya had asked everyone else to give them some privacy. Maya's own gamant, they'd said, was being cared for in a dedicated foster bead one floor below; Olivia's would be similarly cared for.

As Maya continued to encourage her, Olivia observed a seam along her abdomen, which darkened as her gamant slowly pulled away. A tingling along her torso was met by a shock of cold, then a rising warmth, as if nerve endings from shoulder to waist were scrambling to adjust themselves to their fresh exposure.

The part of her that was no longer her took one step forward, then another. And then he stood before her, his four points to her four, his head and neck like a flattened variation of her own, adapted to tuck flush into the concavity above his own ribcage.

I couldn't dream this up.

It struck her as a senseless cruelty. "Does Cole have something against gamants?" Was it something he demanded as a proof of some-one's dedication to the cause? Or maybe it was meant as a display of loyalty to Cole? No one in the market had given gamant-free Maya a second glance. Those loosened social mores might explain why he'd set up operations here.

"They've framed it in terms of a 'freedom,'" Maya said. "Everyone has an opinion, but it's a definition of freedom we don't share, any more than a freedom from your own limbs would be beneficial. Maybe it's a notion they brought here with them. This can be a traumatizing state for uncon-ditioned gamants to be in for extended periods of time. We hate to think where Unity has been keeping them."

Olivia approached the solitary gamant and gave him a gentle stroke. A moment ago, she thought, she would have felt that.

The gamant shifted on his points. "You go on a trip?"

Olivia couldn't hide her surprise. But sure enough, her gamant was looking up at her now, his face a simplified caricature of his host's own face. Why should she find his question so heartbreaking?

"A talker," Maya said, with a look of amusement on their skin.

"Yes, that's right," Olivia told her gamant. "I have to be away for a little while, but . . ." She hesitated to tell him she'd be back soon. Would she? And even assuming she did return, what would happen to him after she returned to Sol? They'd been through a lot already, perhaps more than most couples. Olivia thought of Aleksi. "You'll be okay," she told him. "You'll be with friends."

"Words," said the gamant.

She stroked his leg again, with no more words to say.

———

Olivia followed Maya—soon to be known as Manti-Ja—to the outskirts of *Mubuthumuss* proper, not just toward the canal, but down the embank-ment and along the waterline. The air here was moist and smelled of brine and, unexpectedly, mint. They walked in solitude by the water's edge, ignoring the natural orientation of the electromagnetic fields around them, and the resulting turbulence registered across Olivia's skin as a minor but sustained irritant.

"What's this?" Maya asked, cupping Olivia's dangling tanthid amulet in one hand as they walked. Back in her room, Olivia had thought it might be nice to show some flair for the occasion. Natals had no necks to speak of, so she'd slid the chain up around her foremost shoulder, where she'd observed the odd ornamentation in others. A stupid idea. It could only draw unwanted questions.

"Just a gift."

"It's strange."

"I'm not prepared for this," Olivia said, changing the subject.

Maya didn't break stride. "We knew far less than you do about Unity when *we* first approached them."

"But I don't even have access to your Tide."

"That is for the best. As we said, Holipzibey's culture eschews augmentation. You must proceed according to your character if you are to succeed in infiltrating Unity."

Infiltrate.

If someone had told her weeks ago—or even days ago—that she'd be *infiltrating* anything, she wouldn't have believed them.

Then again, hadn't her entire diplomatic assignment been one bewildered, ungainly infiltration?

———

The so-called open enclave was a barely concealed circus held in a massive subterranean labyrinth. Unlike the city above, which for all its sprawl presented as a choreography of architecture designed with some intention, here the constellation of arcades, walkways, and suspended terraces had ceded wholly to the chaos.

Myriad natals, some four-legged and some six, added their voices to the cacophony. Some had augmented their skin with multicolored bioluminescent chromatophores, making their spectral forms hypnotic in the relative gloom.

"It's overwhelming," Olivia said, her voice practically lost in the din. For the first time, the whispering had competition.

"It is a spectacle," Maya conceded.

They shepherded her over to a natural alcove between the outer wall and an old support structure, onto which had been grafted a tangle of soaring ramps leading to separate levels. At least the music—a syncopated staccato of vocal barks lashing out over a blanket of arch strings—was somewhat muted here.

"The open enclaves are a natural consequence of *Mubuthumuss's* prevailing orthodoxies. People need a place to express themselves without concern."

Some behaviors must truly be universal.

Olivia leaned in close. "How do we find Cole in a place like this?"

"They're usually easy to find." Maya peered into the cavernous darkness, then keyed in on one of the ramps. "Come."

The ramp hewed close to a curiously rhythmic electrical field that must surely be generated by artificial means. The result was a heady lightness in the air, like an intoxicating current beckoning Olivia ever deeper into its coruscating depths. On their way down, Maya ran into someone they knew, another four-legged natal, whose signature Olivia failed to resolve.

Got to focus. She'd need to stay present if she had any hope of ingratiating herself with Cole and his people.

Maya and their colleague conferred without inviting Olivia to join them, and she did her best not to listen. All she overheard was, "I wouldn't waste my time trying to convince them." It was a phrase she might have heard anywhere, only here it was juxtaposed against an almost theatrical excess of alien pageantry.

How far she'd strayed from her intended route. Were there some detours from which one might never return? She might find out. The Sovereign Alliance had certainly put too much faith in her. *Impostor*, she thought. No matter who she threw in with, there was no getting around that basic fact. *Even the tanthid heart mother saw it.*

"Okay, this way," Maya said, giving her leg a gentle tug.

Olivia followed.

"My friend told us where Cole was last seen."

They passed a solo gamant on the ramp, notably smaller than Olivia's own. He was emitting a signature that was impossible to read as anything but distress.

"Are you okay?" Olivia asked him.

"Not right one," he said. "Not right."

A large hand pushed her aside. "You leave him alone, *bebethuti*." Olivia gazed up at another apex, their face decorated with gauzy leafwork that ran along the contours of their features. "Unless you're vying for possession?"

"I was making sure he was okay," Olivia said, suppressing a chill.

They ignored the gamant, who was wandering as if lost. "We think you've lost your way."

"Maybe."

"Sorry to bother you, bright-born," Maya said to the stranger as they hooked Olivia's foreleg in their own. Then, over the confusion of multiple sources of music, she snapped, "Please, stay with us."

When they were safely out of range, Olivia apologized. "I'll be more vigilant."

"Your accent gives you away," Maya said, finally letting go of Olivia's leg, "and there are those here who . . . Not everyone is equally accommodating of the broadest range of social variation."

"Even here? This is a hell of a place for someone to show their bigotry."

"To the contrary," Maya said, "this is a place where very little is concealed." They took the left fork at the terminus of the ramp and continued downward. "*We* don't think that way, understand, but some do."

"Of course."

They left what passed for a fareline—though the fields were too dense here, more like a muddle—and into a den whose geometry might actively have been shifting beneath their feet. Was her mind drifting again? No, she was right: the floor here was so soft that it was like walking into a living organ.

Maybe it is.

A natal came up to her just then—

. . . Tabubetibe-poss . . .

—and their hands immediately wrapped around Olivia's forelegs. "Come play. *Come play!*" Like Maya and herself, they had only four legs.

Maya placed a hand on the stranger's legs and pried up their fingers. "Not here, boon. Fleet away now."

After a second of hesitation, they let Olivia go, and rewarded Maya with a disparaging maze pattern before trotting into the crowd.

"Friendly," said Olivia.

"All eyes open."

"Right."

———

"That's different," Maya said. Olivia followed their gaze down to a lounge-like public area carved into a well-appointed concavity. There, a company of four-legged natals in black leggings were positioned like pieces on a game board. "They're surrounded by security."

At the center of the arrangement was a natal unlike any Olivia had seen before. Or rather, the small projection of Cole that she'd seen back in that jungle hut on *!Wamuhi* hadn't done him justice. He was more than an apex, maybe more than a natal. Bony growths protruded through his flesh, giving the appearance of some calcified exoskeleton. The result was anything but elegant, and might even be painful. He looked overgrown and . . . dirty, somehow. As though he had some kind of residue smeared over his body. What had happened to him?

Yet despite Cole's aberrant appearance, wasn't there something about the way he moved that suggested he wasn't natal? Or maybe Olivia was reading too much into it.

"How could a human presenting as a natal inspire such ardent followers?" she asked. "Is he not seen as the outsider he is?"

"It may even help," Maya said.

Olivia's skin became mottled with puzzlement.

"Cole's message holds a certain appeal for those who feel themselves on the outside," Maya said, peering down into the lounge area, where Cole was holding court with two much smaller natals, one whose skin was solid black. "As an outsider, Cole's message can be their message. And Cole's drive can be their cause." They looked at Olivia. "But they're also an agitator. Cole grooms them, sharpens them."

Like a grain of sand in the oyster. But what black pearl was he forming?

They followed one of the many twisting ramps down to the ground level, the alternating electric fields across Olivia's receptors like the ebb and flow of some secret tide. She couldn't have appreciated—nor anticipated—such a thing from above. It was as close as she'd come to moving through permeable walls, a shadow architecture that lent a supplementary structure to the space around her. As they moved through the fields toward the salon pod, an unbidden giddiness rose up in her, so acute that it almost tickled.

"Do you feel that?" Olivia asked.

"What?"

"All around us, like the electrical fields are . . . playing with us." Like a funhouse without the mirrors.

"That's a tumult."

"It's . . . intentional?"

"Meant to heighten the experience, yes—though not all will be sensitive to it." At the base of the ramp Maya stopped her several meters from the domed entrance, as if she might otherwise tumble forward. "From what I've seen, Cole is entirely EM-insensitive. Not just to the ursprache, but to any fields at all, locational, positional, and degree. But we think that's why they employ these artificial fields, to draw those like you."

Olivia wasn't *drawn* so much as she was feeling vaguely inebriated. She'd have to summon her wits when the time came or she was liable to do something stupid.

Two natals stood by the entrance, perhaps standing guard, or waiting for their turn with Cole. But if they were meant to be intimidating, it wasn't working. Olivia almost giggled at the thought. The feeling was less like joy and closer to that tickling sensation, and her concentration was off as a result.

"We're at the edge of the eddy current," Maya confided. "That's what you're feeling. For all the work it took to set this up, it will all be gone tomorrow."

Meaning, Olivia suspected, that this might be her best and only chance to get close to Cole. "So now what? How do we proceed?"

"Now we introduce you."

Maya took the lead, walking them to the lounge entrance. Maybe it was that easy. Maya was already known to Unity, after all.

The two natals posted by the entrance moved in front of them, blocking their way. They glanced at Maya, but both seemed taken by

Olivia, looking her up and down. Still, whatever they say wasn't enough to sway them. "Sorry," said the one on the right. "Private audience only."

"We're with Unity."

"Manti-Ja, correct?" asked the natal on the left.

"Yes."

"We know who you are. You're not cleared."

Olivia glanced over their shoulders at Cole, and only now was the severity of his malady apparent. What she'd taken for smudges were in fact growths, like black moss, or some fruiting flora. His ridge swellings were serrated, uneven, painful to look at. What was this affliction? Would the same fate befall her if she remained here, in this borrowed body?

"Let us explain," Maya said. "Our consociate here, Holipzibey—"

Olivia clasped her hands together in greeting.

"—has been interested in our cause for quite some time. We see Cole is busy at the moment, but maybe after—"

"No," said the other guard, "we're not here for that tonight."

"They mean I can help the cause," Olivia said. It might mean more coming from her. "*We* can, I mean."

"What?"

"We only ask for an introduction." Maybe it was the euphoria of the tumult giving her too much courage. But they needed to see that she wasn't just someone off the fareline. "As an outsider from the Third Diaspora Territory, we suspect we would have much to—"

"You don't sound like you're from the Third."

"Why do you speak that way?" asked the other one, moving closer.

"What way?" But of course she must have an accent. Perhaps one like Cole's.

"Come, Holipzibey," Maya urged, "we'll try again later."

"There won't be a later," said guard-left.

"If we can explain—" Olivia stopped herself. What could she explain? They were already shutting her out. "We have a facility . . . with the electromagnetic fields. With language, we mean. With the ursprache and the echo. We know that's something Cole has—"

"You *know*?" Guard-right, the larger of the two, walked her up against the wall, not so much pinning her there as using their body to bump her away from the salon pod's entrance.

Shit.

"Whatever you think you know, you picked the wrong time for intimidation."

"That's not what we—"

"Whatever you've heard, forget it."

"You've misunderstood us. We were trying to provide some context." Just as Maya was trying to pull her back toward the ramp.

"Well here's some context for you. Cole decides who they're going to meet with in advance. Manti-Ja, you should have known better."

Maya dropped Olivia's arm. "We don't know either of you, but we've been working with Cole for the last circuit."

"Not anymore."

"What? You don't have the authority—"

"Unity is no longer in need of your services," said guard-left. "Please make your way back out, and enjoy the enclave."

"Unity is our cause too. You don't speak for—"

Guard-right moved quickly, and Maya shrieked. Had the guard struck them? It had all happened so fast, and now Maya was down on two knees. Olivia helped them back to their points, only then noticing the blood on their left hind-leg.

"You okay?"

"You don't want to make a scene," guard-left answered for them.

Olivia caught Cole's eye—he was indeed looking in their direction—and she sensed, for the first time, something like a signature, whispered as a distinct but baffling sequence.

. . . !ss!ss!ti!ss!ss!hi . . .

Cole's signature was little more than a corruption of the ancient channels, nothing like the natal signatures she'd been immersed in for the past cycles. This was a debasement.

Guard-right moved in front of Olivia and stood tall, blocking her view. "Cole will no longer be in need of your services. See your way out, or we'll be forced to insist more energetically."

So it had come to threats. How had things taken such a turn?

"Come on," Maya said, and left Olivia standing outside the lounge.

Olivia hurried to catch up.

THIRTY-FIVE
DAY 61

AT NIGHT the *Mubuthumuss* ward was a symphony of mechanized velocipedes and line runners, barking street vendors, and some creature whose brays sounded to Olivia's ears distressingly similar to human lamentation.

Oscar and Emily, along with several others from the Fifth Sun, had met up with Olivia and Maya back at their unmarked building by the waterfront to reunite her with her gamant and get their post mortem. The music and merriment outside lent their entire dour recounting a regrettable incongruity. Not only had they failed, now Maya had been ousted from Unity, setting the Fifth Sun's cause back. They needed time to reassess, to weigh a fresh infiltration versus their unspoken fallback plan. Olivia had asked about that plan, but Oscar had been loath to tell her anything.

Until he did just that. "We'll return the Fountain to its dormant state."

She ran his words through her mind. The entire Fountain, deactivated. Could they do something like that?

A chill settled over her, either at the prospect of being a natal for the rest of her life, or because Oscar would only have told her out of a sense of grim inevitability.

Now back in her old torpor bead in North Belt 8—which the Fifth Sun had thoughtfully cleared of dead bodies—Olivia stared up at the night sky through the open clerestory windows. If the Fifth Sun shut the Fountain down, Cole would certainly be forced to find a new hobby. But Olivia would need to return to Sol system before that happened.

She thought about Ran, who, after his "accident" seventeen years ago had undergone full-body systemic revision. He'd suffered a reaction to the procedure, and the result had been brain death. This left only his cranial omni to salvage, that neural black box with its indelible record of his thought patterns and memories going back to infancy. Once his medical team had dutifully initiated his Second self, they had called upon Olivia to help with his reorientation. Help it how, exactly? she had asked. And those words had left a mark because of the ones that followed: Help *him*, they had said, by giving him something familiar to fix on. Just be there.

But she hadn't gone to Ran, or whatever lay recuperating in his virtual recovery bed. She'd had no interest in entertaining whatever crude parody they'd made of her dead half-brother. Instead she'd gone to the nearest mod shop and had her own omni removed. The desecration committed against Ran would never be visited on her. Her body might have its flaws, but at least it was *hers*.

Nils, when he'd found out about her rash deed, had compared it to suicide. That characterization had struck Olivia as a grim, poetic irony.

Now, staring out the windows, her mind millions of light years away, she was once more being asked to "just be there," to offer Cole a bit of familiarity, to find out what he was thinking, and perhaps guide him back to something familiar. The difference was that *she* was a Seconder this time. Though she didn't feel like one. In fact, she was more *herself* now than she'd ever been, in this alien body. And maybe it was the same for Cole.

Maybe it was curiosity, rather than civic duty, that had made her agree to this mission. And maybe . . . maybe curiosity was an intrinsic driver for a Seconder? Freed from the moral burdens of one's first life, one could explore other possibilities. Olivia never would have entertained thoughts like these before, let alone intercede with a possible terrorist.

As the ever-present whispering spiced the night air—an echo, forgotten, dismissed—Olivia gazed out at alien constellations. She could cross that gulf and return to her quiet life.

But what would she do if she could do whatever she wanted?

What if she tracked Cole down on her own?

———

A single tone issued from the transmission node, snapping her out of her reverie. A short, text-only message from Ioor Volkopp was waiting for her:

```
Where is Max? Please send update.
```

"Shit."

Her last reply to them must have made it clear, finally, that her extended silence was one of personal choice rather than some extenuating circumstance. So—gone was the pleasant banter and the gentle coaxing.

What was she supposed to say? The words of Ioor's colleague Quv Vidalin came to her: "We want to have a holistic plan in place before we tell the public." She couldn't argue with that logic.

Stay as close to the original mission as possible.

Olivia cleared her throat before composing her reply.

"Sorry I haven't kept you in the loop," she dictated. "I've befriended a great number of the natals—the remotes. And now that I've fulfilled my primary role, I'm debating how much more time I'd like to spend with them. There are a lot of factors to weigh. As for Max, you'd have to ask him. You know we were never close."

And even less so now.

THIRTY-SIX
DAY 62

THE MARKET DISTRICT was positioned along the quietest part of the local electromagnetic belt, free of distraction or interference from outside fields, and thus refreshingly mild. The relative stillness opened Olivia's senses to the aromas of food from myriad vendors, the peculiar instruments of street buskers, and the diversity of the crowds.

Under the rippling yellow sun she strode along the fareline, following the currents of foot traffic along the canal . . . and trying not to think of the new message from home that had been waiting for her at dawn. How long had it been since she'd been free of someone else's plans?

. . . *thump-wave-ssstatic-thump-wave-static* . . .

The call of the high moment gave direction to people's step, and Olivia found a bistro teeming with natals. But as she fed on some sort of stuffed succulent that tasted of spiced cheese, this morning's message replayed in her head unbidden. It was the first visual message she'd received, and from a man she hadn't recognized at first, even though he'd been sitting in her lounge, on her couch. Indeed, it hadn't dawned on Olivia who she was looking at until the moment before he spoke.

"How do I look?" Ran had asked her.

He looked vaguely like Ran, only with a stylish touch of gray in his close-cropped beard. It was as if he'd sensed her thoughts about him last night.

"Nothing fancy, but age-appropriate at least." She hadn't seen him—not in the flesh—in almost twenty years. If this could be called seeing, on a video volume projected over light years, and seen through alien eyes. "Maybe you inspired me to make the leap." He had no idea. "I was afraid for so long that maybe having a body would lead me back to where I was before. Which, for better or worse, you've called me out on. And I can't live in that kind of limbo, with that fear hanging over me. So," he put out his hands, "here we are."

The shock of seeing him had almost obscured the foremost questions: Why video? Why now? But it wasn't hard to guess. It was an overture from the General Polity, as meaningful as Ran's own: *Don't forget where you come from.*

"I can't wait to meet you again," he continued. "And let me reassure you, Olivia, lest you still doubted it: you won't be meeting me for the first time."

She stared at his face, familiar but not.

The image tracked as he stood, went to the deck, and squinted against the pale sun. "I'm sorry about Aleksi." *What?* "Of course it hurts, especially when you're so far away. But . . . I don't know, maybe there's a positive side to it, too."

Oh. Shit.

He'd done it. He'd taken his cue from her absence; her *silence*. And . . . how could she blame him? But the sting was dull—dulled by distance, and by something else. She was no longer where the pain was. It could no longer find her.

"It seemed like things were pretty cold between you for a while, but sometimes it's about timing, too. I feel like I'm filling in your half of the conversation. I can imagine you saying that, but . . . honestly, I don't know.

"Anyway, I know how limiting communication lines have been. But your pals at the SA are trying something new here, as an act of good faith. So they tell me. It would be nice to hear something from you, now that your return date has come and gone. Can you tell me *anything*? It's not just my own curiosity. Dad's been asking, and Whistler. And others who are, I guess, less Aleksi-aligned. They've been coming to me for some reason. Like you and I have a special line."

Like we used to.

Ran signed off with his characteristic abruptness—as sure a sign that he was still Ran as any—leaving Olivia with too many questions, and with the sun barely above the horizon.

Now she looked down at her fingers, covered in savory paste, and tried to conjure the illusion of a holiday. But she couldn't run away from her responsibilities, even here. It wasn't such a stretch to imagine that Ioor Volkopp and his Sovereign Alliance cronies had sanctioned a video message in an attempt to get her to communicate again. And as far as that went, it wasn't a bad strategy. They weren't wrong.

. . . *!ss!ss!ti!ss!ss!hi* . . .

Olivia's eyes darted from mat to mat.

Cole Quinlan—that had to be his signature—was somewhere close by. At least close enough that she'd sensed the unique disturbance of his signature. The whisper couldn't mislead her, could it? It was an echo of the truth. How had Oscar put it? The whispering was rooted in the ursprache, but it could offer its own emergent insights.

Leaving the remainder of her breakfast, Olivia headed back outside and assessed the market. The vendor stands danced like a living mirage in the dense air, but there was no sign of an oversized natal in the crowd. But though Cole's signature had been fleeting, something of it remained. The fields around her had changed somehow, more accommodating, as if they might yield to her purpose. No longer was she adrift like a leaf in a stream. Suddenly there was . . . a right direction.

She turned, slowly, until the path before her cleared, then she set off in that direction, proceeding into the plaza.

. . . *!ss!ss!ti!ss!ss!hi* . . .

The signature again, more distinct than before. Closer. As long as she gave herself over to her natal senses, they would show her the way forward.

Ignoring the crush of natals, she crossed the plaza toward a cluster of trade establishments and workshops. There she moved more deliberately, as if tasting the air for a new type of spice, stopping only when she stood outside what appeared to be an old resource hub. The signature was difficult to sense through the eddies of convergent fields here, but it was just as unwavering.

Has to be here.

She headed inside.

———

The resource hub was similar to a library, only with aisles of artifacts in sealed cases, and research pods with interconnected tables, where natals were conducting quiet studies. For Olivia, the silence only intensified the whispering, almost to the point of distraction, but it didn't seem to bother anyone else.

Cole's signature was distinct even above the echo, and Olivia let it guide her toward the back of the close-stacked farrago, moving her way past warm bodies and toward the human hiding in their midst. She found him at a workstation that somewhat resembled a transmission node. His myriad overgrowths were impossible to ignore, and might even have looked like some accessorized ornamentation from a distance—a crown on his head, fancy livery along his arms and shoulders. But close up the bulges and protrusions were undoubtedly disfiguring and malign.

Don't stare.

She had to find a way to approach him without raising any flags. Circling around the bead, she feigned an interest in the collected works on display, stealing glances at Cole's handheld panel only when he slouched forward to read it. Unfortunately the glyphs were too far away to resolve, but the format appeared to be that of a list . . . or perhaps lyrics?

She made her way to the aisles behind the man, where she had a much better look at the display. Her hunch was correct: the words were definitely—

"It's edible, you know," said the giant, sitting up until his rear eyes were aligned before her like two rows of dark beads. Cole's voice was surprisingly soft, though she was the only one within earshot.

Shit.

She hadn't been thinking of the natal's nearly panoramic field of view. She only extended her own field out of necessity, and usually kept her focus forward.

"Pardon me?"

290

"My crops." He shifted in his saddle seat to face her, and plucked off a patch of the dark fleshy growth with his somewhat gnarled fingers. "Few can resist the urge to gawk, so I try to be generous and offer my admirers to partake."

Had he lost his mind? "Oh, no thank you," she said, and only then remembered her natal pronouns. "We weren't gawking, we promise."

He bobbed forward and back—a very non-natal head nod—and returned to his panel. "I believe you. As an apex yourself, I suspect you've seen stranger."

Olivia wasn't sure what to say. *Had* she seen stranger? Cole was like a beached cuttlefish half covered in black barnacles.

A botched experiment.

And he hadn't shied away from using his singular pronoun. For whatever reason he hadn't deemed it a risk. But she couldn't afford to tip her hand.

He allowed the scrap of material to drift to the floor. "Forgive me for the crude prank. It's one way I deal with this malady of mine, but my humor, as a friend once told me, is frequently lost on others."

"We're . . . sorry we gave you the impression we were being rude," she said, coming around to his side. *Now or never.* "We couldn't help but notice . . . you're researching verse?"

He considered the words anew. "Well, I hadn't thought of it as verse."

"Are you not a poet?"

"Yes," he said, "I am not. In fact if there was anyone who was the *opposite* of a poet, that's what I'd be."

"We'll have to keep that in mind, and not get too close."

He sat back on his saddle to face her. "You mean . . . you actually are a poet?"

"On a good day," Olivia said, her skin flashing fractals of amusement.

"Well! A poet *and* an apex. I'm not sure which is more rare."

Olivia considered her next words carefully. "You sound a little like a *bebethuti.*" She was careful to produce the final electrical signature as clearly as possible.

"A . . . ?" He fluttered a hand over his ampullae. "Sorry, I'm deaf to the proto-tongue. But I suppose I take your point. It's my accent?"

"We like it," Olivia said quickly. "It's somehow fitting." So he had no sense of the ursprache at all? No echo, no whisper? If that was true, maybe she wasn't destined to suffer his progressive ailment after all.

"Well," he said, "if there's one thing I've always liked about the Grand Ward—"

. . . Mubuthumuss . . .

"—it's the variety of people drawn here from far and wide. As large as the Home system is, I haven't always found it to be so eclectic."

He had a point.

"We didn't mean to interrupt," Olivia said. "Your work caught this outsider's eye, since it does resemble verse." Would he bite? Now was his chance to dismiss her, to get back to whatever he'd been doing before he'd caught her staring.

"It's really a kind of puzzle," he offered.

"Some poems can be puzzles." She edged closer. "At least at first. This is your own work?"

Now Cole was hesitant, neither giving her room to move closer nor pushing her away. His skin provided no clue as to what he was thinking.

"We apologize—we ask only because of our facility with language."

"A facility, eh?"

"It's been recognized."

"Formidable," he said, relaxing a bit. "Any token of recognition I might have heard of?"

"Possibly, though we don't know how well it would translate."

"What is your native tongue?"

Revealing she was human seemed like playing a card too early. Withholding that information might be of dubious value, but there was no need to offer it immediately. "See if you can tell."

He seemed game, turning to face her fully.

Great. What should she share? She had no fear of him being familiar with anything from her oeuvre. But she found herself timid anyway. This was a bizarre scene. Two aliens. Two impostors. One reciting poetry, the other planning the demise of the system.

"We wrote this about our brother," she said.

"One's departure is sometimes a return.

The lie suits so nicely — a guest, a stranger,
whose face we once loved — and do still. Except
for the truth, at last, shining through this new,
perfect show, reminding us how one left."

After a polite amount of time had elapsed, Cole gave her a quiet clap, another un-natal practice.

"It goes on from there," Olivia said.

"It's not a sunny poem, is it?"

"It was a trying time."

"Well I appreciate your sharing that, in all sincerity, even if I don't have a clue about poetry. Which may be my problem today. To answer your riddle though, a poetry reading is probably not the way to guess someone's natal dialect. But it sounded appropriately poetic to my ear."

"We're from the Third Diaspora Territory," Olivia said, pleased with herself for using her cover story as intended.

"I see. Sorry, I don't know it."

"We tend to keep to ourselves," she said. Loath to kill their momentum, she moved closer. "But you said you're having some trouble with your project?"

The human natal paused for a long while, during which Olivia remained silent, all too aware that she had no backup plan. But at last he relented and backed away from his handheld panel to show her what he'd written. She peered at the words scrawled on the display.

```
Echoes, echoing. Echoes.
Fear the far, remote, distant.
Fear the far, quiet, solitude.
Echoes, echoing the thought,
echoing the word, echoing the deed.
Fire to notion, the burning thought.
Fear the near.
Fear the all.
```

"There's more to it," Cole said when she'd finished reading, "but this is as far as I've gotten."

"It's . . . evocative," she said, hoping her feedback wouldn't be met with the dismissive bark it deserved. The writing was bad, to be sure. But she'd learn nothing by dismissing it at the outset. The goal was to get close to him, not to challenge him.

"There's something to it, you're saying?"

"Well, it has a certain suggestive prosody." If her work colleague Siti could hear her now, she'd mime a silent retch. That kind of benign feedback was usually deployed to shield the egos of those who were writing for the wrong reasons. Olivia looked at Cole closely, but nothing about him gave off any guile. It was in his voice: he wasn't testing her, he was asking. "Have you been working on this for some time?"

"In all honesty, I translated it," he said, "at least in a way. So it's new, but I didn't exactly compose it."

Translated from what? Pressing him on that was a needless risk though. This might not even be important, save to him.

"Tell me what you meant before, about prosody."

If that was what he wanted to know, she could improvise. "It's in the way the words play, the way they repeat. That's called *anaphora*. And there's a self-referential quality in the echoes, the way the echoes echo themselves, which makes the reader, the observer, part of the echo. See? It brings you into it." She took a breath. "It's not at all complex, but there's still an evocative sense, an interactive quality. It's not passive. It expects the participant."

Cole had been looking down at the words as she spoke, as if they might blossom there before him. When she'd finished his gaze lingered for a moment more before he finally said, "You've already gotten more out of it than I've been able to."

Now she was curious. "Is this what brought you here?"

"I don't have access to the Tide, so I came here to check for literary matches. Didn't find anything. So next I'll check the archives. Either way it's a good excuse to visit this resource hub. I come here sometimes to concentrate."

"Concentrate? Here?" It was all she could do to keep the whispering at bay.

"Why shouldn't this be a good place to concentrate?"

He must have heard something in her voice. She had to be careful if she was going to set the pace. "Just that it can get pretty busy."

He said nothing, but it was all too clear that he wasn't buying her explanation. Maybe some trace of human body language remained.

He let it go. "So you definitely think this is poetry?"

"I don't know about that." *Pronouns!* "*We* don't. Our first thought was . . . well, maybe it's best if we didn't—"

"Tell me." By now she had his full attention. "I've been going around in circles, and this is a nice distraction."

"We were going to say, it put us in mind of a test pattern."

"Like . . . ?"

"Like when you're calibrating a piece of equipment, and you test its registration based on a known pattern." She thought of the baseline set design Aleksi had used for his performance volumes: their own home, complete with one reference—Somtow. If the model was convincing, the theory went, then it would be that much easier to trust in the calibration of whatever wild set he was currently designing. At least that's how he'd described the practice. As time had passed, she'd sometimes found herself wondering how far reality had drifted from that idealized instance.

"I must say this is the most intriguing conversation I've had in some time."

"Sorry to hear it," she said, hoping the humor would translate. "You said you thought of it as a puzzle though? Why?"

He looked at the words again, but remained silent for a long while. "When I see something like this I think of it as a challenge. Like . . . a test."

"A test? Like the writer is testing you, or . . . ?"

"Maybe. If they were, how should I respond?" He slid the panel in front of her. "Assume this is a test. What comes after?"

A test within a test.

Was this natal interpreting poetry at the back of a library the same one who would leak a destructive entity into the system? Did the Fifth Sun have that right? He'd given her no indication that he was planning for the downfall of natal civilization. So why not humor him?

"Well you could take this and try to run with it. Use it as the basis for what comes next."

"Okay, but that might be a challenge, given our lack of context. I don't want to make a mistake."

"You said you translated this?"

"That's right. Think of a song that has never been notated."

She considered it. "Well . . . maybe, then, present it as is."

"I don't follow."

"Meaning . . . your transcription itself could *be* the test. Your involvement in the process, like I said. So read it back to the author as is."

He got that. "Like setting a baseline."

"Maybe, if you have to start somewhere." Was there a correct answer, or was he testing her willingness to participate in the thought experiment?

"Have we met?" He hadn't looked at the poem for several minutes by now.

She'd gotten his attention. But best not to mention their near miss at the open enclave.

"We don't think so."

"It's just that there's something . . . I don't know. I hesitate to say *familiar*."

He wasn't talking about the open enclave now, but something more essential. For a moment she was sure his eyes could see through her disguise. But no, that was just—

A natal was behind Cole now—another one with no discernible signature—whispering something into his ear as they gave Olivia an unbroken stare.

"You'll excuse me," Cole said. "Thank you for the pleasant distraction."

She stood as he did, as a politeness. He was at least a head taller than she. "Yes, well . . . good luck with your poetry. Good luck with your *echoes*."

She read a moment's confusion in his stance. Then he got it, and held up his panel. "Right!"

And he left her with her thoughts, their conversation circling around in her head. Only then did it occur to her that she'd forgotten to give him her name.

———

Back in her bead that afternoon, Olivia used her transmission node to get in touch with Oscar. They'd surely appreciate that she'd taken the initiative to track Cole down herself—after all, it shouldn't harm whatever else they were doing to get closer to Cole in the wake of Maya's ouster.

After filling them in on her encounter, Olivia suggested that she return to the resource hub the next day to see if he might be there again.

"Olivia, we thank you for contributing your energies to this cause." *Uh-oh.* "But we must tell you that there's been a lot of deliberation about the path forward—and it's not because we lack confidence in you. It's because the price of failure is too high, and the Fifth Sun's two paths forward are not compatible. The second option precludes the first."

"You're talking about closing the Fountain completely."

"You should return to your home now."

"Oscar, why not let me at least try?"

"Because the only way to get closer to Cole is by helping them. And that gets them closer to their goal while guaranteeing us nothing."

"I only have to *seem* to be helping him."

"They would know."

"He *won't*." Was Oscar calling the shots unilaterally now? Or had the group already decided she was out? "I've had a conversation with him now. There's something about that poetry that's important to this process somehow. Something they haven't yet figured out. And I think that could be my way in." She leaned closer to his image. "It can't hurt to try, right?"

"We're not done trying," they said. "But it has nothing to do with you. You should return to the domain of humanity while you still can."

THIRTY-SEVEN
DAY 63

OLIVIA WAITED for her shuttle at the North Belt 3 Transportation Hub. In an hour or so she would be well on her way back to *Watiwabe*, then finally through that strange anomaly, and back home.

And she would leave the natals to their fate.

Stop that.

The crowds hurried along the concourse to catch their own flights, or to make their way out into the sun. Small groups in colorful costume, a couple with skin strobing with synchronized fury, and a hundred others with their individual hopes and destinations. They may have been born to a different star, but they weren't so different from her. What would become of them if some unimaginable force did manage to leak through the Fountain?

Stop.

This would be the worst of it. The guilt. But what could she have done? Good intentions weren't enough. She wasn't a coward for refusing to get in over her head in a fight that wasn't even her own to begin with. She could be of no help to the Fifth Sun, no matter how much she wished she could. And she was skeptical of the Fifth Sun's "Cole-will-destroy-our-galaxy" story anyway.

Well-intended, ill-equipped.

She nearly missed the trill of her hotfont in the susurrus of the bustling hub. She patted her sash and the device pulsed under her hand. Had Elder Two discovered her flight plans? Surely they had better things to do with their time. Or maybe they didn't.

Removing the device, she found a hail not from the elder, but from "Principal Trader." If not for the accompanying image of the apex natal—bony growths jutting from his every contour—she wouldn't have a clue who was calling.

She allowed the connection, but failed to recall the standard natal greeting. Was there one? How had she been greeted?

"Well fated," she said, sure that was wrong.

"We met yesterday at the resource hub," said the diminutive mirage. "My title is Cole."

"An unusual title. And yes, of course we remember." If she were playing her role to the hilt, she might ask what a Cole is. But she couldn't bring herself to do it. "How did you find us without knowing our title?"

"As you probably noticed yesterday, I don't always have all the answers—but I've always been able to find the people to help me get them." More bluster than an answer to her question. Was he trying to impress? "Sorry, I didn't mean that to sound arch. Have I caught you at a bad time?"

"Not at all."

"I wanted to tell you how much I enjoyed our conversation yesterday. Your insights were . . . useful."

Could poetry be useful? He seemed pleased about it at least. "I'm not sure how you mean that, but it's good to hear."

Shit!

She'd let her pronoun slip. Maybe he hadn't noticed.

"Right, so I was wondering if you'd like to meet. That poem I was working on . . . there's more to it now. So I thought, maybe I could give you some more context and we could look at it together."

Could Cole read the muddle of emotions that played as noise across her skin? She should say yes and not overthink the question. Saying yes wasn't committing to anything other than finding out what was going on. Finding out how this poem—which seemed to have more significance than she'd thought—tied into Unity's scheme.

Except the Fifth Sun had already decided to go another way.

And so had I.

But here was an opening no one could have anticipated. She wished Oscar or Maya were here beside her.

"If you're interested," Cole said, breaking the silence.

"We admit we're intrigued." *Answer now, think later.*

"So let's meet. No strings attached, nothing weird. Sometimes it's good to get another row of eyeballs on something when you don't quite get it." Cole told her where and when. So this was really happening. "Oh, and what do I call you?"

Old habits, as Maya had informed her. "Do you mean our title?" The name *Holipzibey* sat inert behind her speaker flaps. Maya had used her given handle at the open enclave, just after they'd been blocked from entering Cole's exclusive grotto. Using it now seemed a needless risk.

"As I mentioned, I'm imperceptive to electromagnetism. So if you give me something I can articulate . . ."

"Right, sorry. We're from the ministry of poetry research, from the Third Diaspora Territory."

He appeared to think that over. Finally he asked, "Would you answer to 'Poet'?"

———

As soon as Cole severed their connection, Olivia contacted the Fifth Sun. Emily answered her hail, and Olivia asked if they could delay whatever plans might already be underway.

"At least wait till you hear back from me," she said. "I think I've found a way in with Unity."

It was hard to believe the words were coming out of her own speakers. Then again, that voice wasn't really hers anyway, nor anything else about her. Not technically. But what about that tiny spark at the center, driving her actions? That singular impulse? Was *that* still Olivia? The question was a constant companion, like a moth she could never fully bat away.

"How did you manage it?" Emily asked.

"Cole hailed me directly," she said. "I don't know how he tracked me down, but it must have been important enough to him. From what I could tell, it's all about that poetry. I guess he liked what I had to say about it."

"Which was what?"

Olivia filled them in on the details of their conversation the other day, then ran through it all again once Oscar and Maya showed up. Even Maya could provide little insight about why it might mean so much to him.

"We know they were planning on establishing communication with the Thirsty Pool," Maya said, "but we were never able to get more detail than that."

"So maybe the poem is Unity's first attempt at formal communication?" Olivia asked.

"If it is, they're farther along than we'd feared," said Oscar.

"I can tell you that he's fixated on it," Olivia said. "I . . . could help you find out why. Try to." Saying it aloud made it seem possible.

"It would be good to know more," Emily said, as much to Oscar as to her.

After a moment of silence, Olivia gave voice to the words in her head. "I'm willing to see it through."

"Do what you can to get yourself in the same bead as them," Oscar said. "But if we were right—that your involvement would only serve to accelerate their progress toward their goal—disengage. Let us know. Then you can redirect your focus on your returning transfer."

"As long as you're sure."

"Sure?" said Oscar, and Olivia saw fear on their skin. "If we had a better plan, we'd be doing it now. But the only other plan we have is far *worse*, even if it's probably inevitable. So go now. Find out anything you can."

After their conversation, a calm settled over Olivia—not one of relief, but one of cool resolve. She barely recognized the feeling. The old Olivia would have thought she was losing her mind. Maybe that's what this was.

THIRTY-EIGHT
DAY 64

AFTER ABANDONING HER FLIGHT, Olivia returned to her torpor bead. Her goal, if everything went to plan, would be to find out what Cole wanted of her, then provide the Fifth Sun with an update afterward.

Waking well before the next morning's high moment, Olivia nearly left her bead on her sixes, forgetting that Unity appeared to go about their business sans gamant. With great care, and a litany of apologies under her breath, Olivia separated once more from her long-suffering "other half," then contacted the Fifth Sun to request that they look after him.

Now she was back at the North Belt 3 terminal, doing her best to ignore the attention she attracted—if it wasn't her gamant-free state, it was her imposing stature—as she crossed the main concourse. She made her way past the travelers, the families, the vendors, and the officials in their colorful sashes. It was the maintenance hub she was looking for.

She found the entrance just where Cole had said she would, and was greeted by a stranger—

. . . *Timubu-be!ss* . . .

—who was on four points, like her, and wearing black leggings similar to those she'd seen at the open enclave the other night.

"Whom do we find?"

The question threw Olivia for a moment. "Oh, we're . . . the Poet."

The natal issued a *tap-wave-tap-wave-tick* of greeting as they clasped their hands before them. "Our title is Athena."

Athena? Olivia suppressed her amusement from her skin. The name had Cole written all over it. What did a people without names think of being labeled?

"Please follow."

Athena led her into the bowels of the terminal, remaining silent as they went. Olivia offered that she'd been enjoying her stay in the *Mubuthumuss* ward, but Athena only replied that it wasn't her ward. Apparently they weren't one for small talk.

The flat, sparse service halls had none of the flourish of the architecture outside, and displayed no alignment to the pervasive EM fields. It could almost be a Sol-side facility if not for the overhead lighting, which took its cue from the yellow, diffracted light of *Tapuwathu*'s sun.

They passed a number of natals on the way down, all of them free of their poor gamants. Was this entire area under Unity's purview? And where *were* all the gamants? In some room together, huddled and afraid? Or maybe they had it better off, left alone to do whatever gamants did together.

As Athena left Olivia alone outside an unlabeled door, Olivia couldn't help but wonder about her own gamant. Did he miss her?

"Poet?"

Olivia looked up at the natal poking their head around the open door.

. . . *Sswhi-!hithu* . . .

"Follow, if you please."

————

The inner offices were entirely misaligned with the prevailing fields, giving everything an unsteady feel. As a consequence, keeping her focus on Cole—and not on the undercurrent of her restlessness—required some effort.

"Sorry about the mess," he said.

His colleagues appeared to be packing up—carrying cases, wheeling equipment, and generally giving the two of them wide berth as they sat across from each other in an otherwise emptied side office.

"You're moving?" Olivia asked.

"At the moment I'm taking a breather, so thank you for that." Was he slouching, or was she imagining it? Carrying that much weight on just four points must take a toll, not to mention the burden of his condition. "But yes, you've caught us in transition. Having dedicated space right in the terminal has been a luxury, but it's time for us to move on."

"Congratulations."

He gave her a human-like nod. "And that kind of brings us to . . . well, *us*. 'Us' being Unity, in this case. That's what we call our little outfit here, for reasons I'll get to. But before we get to the business at hand, I wanted to ask you a question."

"Of course."

"Why did you help me the other day?"

"Oh." It was a fair question. Had it been pure serendipity? "We thought we were just having a conversation."

"I don't think that's the entire truth, Poet."

"Also because we like puzzles."

"Language, you mean."

"No," she said, calculating the risk of an appeal to ego. "*You.*"

He contemplated that in silence.

"We find you working in the resource hub," she said, "and can't help but wonder who this person is, so fixated on a cryptic collection of words."

"And what were *you* doing there?" he asked. "Half a moment before you found me I mean, what were you doing?"

"We were around the corner, feeding, at a little spot we found."

"Right." His skin provided her no insight. "You told me that your facility for language had been recognized."

"Yes."

"Well." He stood then, with some effort, and Olivia followed suit. "It's been recognized again."

"How do you mean?"

"Have you ever heard of the Thirsty Pool?"

Wow. So this was really happening now. He was letting her in. "The Pool, as in the myth?"

"No, as in the truth." He beckoned for her to follow him back out to the busy commons. "Come."

She pictured him leading her to a natatorium like her own, only with a pool that was a void of unfathomable black. Instead he led her to a storage closet stacked with crates.

"What are these?" she asked.

"Provisions." He gave the nearest one a rap. It sounded solid. "Most of these are packed with a stabilized protein base."

"Food?"

"Eventually, maybe." He lowered himself and scooped one of them up in his forelegs. "Join me?"

She selected the crate by her side and lifted its bulk easily. Going from four legs to two was more of a challenge, but Olivia managed it. As they walked, they fell in line behind several other natals moving supplies down the service corridor. They passed a sign that read: *"Local Pole | Private."*

"What if I told you that the Pool is real," Cole said, picking up where he'd left off, "and that it's been trying to communicate with us?"

"With Unity?"

"That's right."

"We suppose we'd wonder if you were testing us."

"No test."

It also wasn't a secret, at least not down here; Cole was speaking loudly enough for anyone around them to overhear, and he didn't seem to care.

"Clearly there's a reason you wanted to meet with us here."

"And there's a reason you came."

"So why are we talking about the Pool?"

"The reason I'm talking to *you* about the Pool is because of something you said earlier, back at the resource hub. You said it was outrageous that I'd go there to study."

"Okay?"

"Because you're sensitive to electromagnetic fields, aren't you?"

Time for her to draw him out. "What do you mean?"

"Come on, Poet," he said, never breaking stride. "As I'm sure you can tell by my accent, I don't run with the aristocracy. You don't have to play it safe with me."

"Okay."

"And I won't play it safe with you."

"I'm not following you."

He set his crate down, and Olivia did the same. They moved to the side to make way for several passing natals.

"I'm sure it hasn't been easy sensing what you sense," Cole said, "and never being able to acknowledge it in polite company." He sounded . . . rehearsed.

"Are you selling us on something?"

"I'm trying to illustrate that we're both outsiders. Or . . . we're not, but we find ourselves on the outside because of circumstances that have nothing to do with us."

"I'm just wired up wrong," Olivia said, resisting the flow of his spiel just enough—she hoped—to force him to elaborate.

"That may be, but you're a lot of things. You're an apex, for one. And you don't speak like anyone I've ever met, at least from what I can tell through that transliterator you have on you."

"Fine," she said, wiping grit from her hands. "So once you've done that—once you've shown us how much we have in common—then what?"

"That's when I ask for your help, and maybe by then it won't send you packing because of the unorthodox nature of my work."

Was he enjoying this, or was she imagining it?

"Is it always this hard to get people to work with you?" she asked, perhaps enjoying herself too.

"No, but I'm careful. And I only want to work with people who want to work with me."

"So I'm being vetted."

"How about this: I'll tell you a little more about what's going on, and if it's too much on the side of fairy tales and mythology for you, then we part ways. You can go back to denying what's right in front of you."

"I like that," she said, because it was true. "So what's going on?"

They both flattened to the wall to allow the passage of a hulking crate on a dolly. When it was gone, they picked up their own crates and continued along the hall.

Cole spoke to her over his shoulder. "I've believed for a long time—and I'm not alone in this—that there's a reason our EM-sensitivity is so well developed. We believe this sense of ours was an environmental adaptation brought on by the Fountain, and more specifically, by the Pool. Because the Fountain is connected to the Pool—at least it was—and the Pool happens to communicate using patterned electromagnetic sequences. As our species evolved with the Fountain next door, naturally there was some benefit to being able to sense this channel. So we adapted."

"The Pool was real, you're saying."

"Have you not been listening to me? It *is* real, it's sentient, and it can communicate."

"Can, as in . . . presently?"

"As in continually. Right now."

"We're sorry to insist on clarity," Olivia said, "but this is all quite a leap. A folk tale come to life."

"Most folk tales are based on some aspect of our lived experience, don't you think? I'll be the first to admit that the Pool is still very much a mystery to us. But you believe in the Fountain, right?"

"What do you mean?"

"You've seen it. Presumably you've seen it being used."

"Of course."

"Okay, well we can actually tell a lot about the Pool by looking at the Fountain, by asking what the Fountain really is, and why it was a failure."

"Why it was—"

"And we can also tell a lot about the Pool by studying the message you saw me staring at. Because the Pool sent us that."

Olivia narrowly avoided dropping her crate. Unity was already communicating with some space entity?

"And we replied to it exactly as you suggested," Cole continued. "Now the Pool has responded in kind—with something even more interesting."

Meaning Olivia had already helped them, without even knowing she had.

"Just so I understand: you're saying you're actually in active communication with the Pool?"

"We are. The first thing we cast was the codex sequence, a key historical record of the echo, essentially an instruction manual that describes how to communicate using our long-dead ursprache. You've heard of it?"

"The ursprache? Yes."

"And what is the Pool saying?"

"Almost there," Cole said as they approached a set of wide doors. "Through here."

The doors pulled aside, and they entered a cavernous hangar occupied by a solitary cargo module, squat and gray, its hatches open. A small team of natals wearing rugged-looking safety gear was loading containers onto the module. They weren't just relocating; they were headed off-world. And by the look of it this wasn't just some excursion. They were moving their entire operation.

Two natals were suddenly in front of them, forelegs out to relieve them of their burdens. Once Olivia and Cole were alone again, she contemplated Unity's progress.

"Everything you've been telling me—*us* about, all this preparation you're doing is part of it."

"This is *all* of it," Cole said, the pride in his voice evident even through translation. "There's just enough room inside for the crew, given the amount of supplies we're packing in. Once this segment separates in orbit, we'll be docking with our survey ship, *Bäckahästen*, and thence to stranger skies."

"To what end?" She still had no proof that Unity intended to subject natal civilization to an entity that could swallow it whole. But for the first time she might be closing in on a definitive answer.

"There's the question I'd hoped you'd ask," Cole said, and once more Olivia thought she heard pride. If so, it was misplaced. "But you should know the answer, based on everything we've discussed."

"You want to learn something from the Pool?"

"What I want . . . No, the better question is what we can *give* the Pool."

"Okay. Which is what?"

"Access."

"Access to the Fountain?"

"Since the beginning Unity's goal has always been to mend the severed link between the Pool and the Fountain it spawned. That's what 'unity' means. And it not just about connecting one to the other, but granting the Pool the same unlimited Fountain access we've enjoyed for dozannia, so it too can travel through the Fountain. It was natality who severed the link, after all, then capitalized on our unfettered use of the Fountain, blocking out everyone who didn't look like us. So what we're attempting to do now has been a long time coming. Can you think of a better, more direct way of correcting an ancient injustice?"

All for unity.

The way Cole looked at her now, she was up against it: he expected a response.

"It's not a bad pitch, if we're being honest."

"I don't know what you have going on in your life right now," Cole said, "but I'd like you to hear for yourself what the Pool has to tell us."

Perhaps they were calculated, but Cole's words still managed to stir something in her. Was she so easily swayed by flattery?

"You barely know us," Olivia said, not meaning for it to sound as weak as it did.

Cole ambled toward the cargo module, and Olivia followed. If they got close enough, she thought, he might shove her inside and save his breath. Up close, the module's condition was more obvious. It was worn, its surface a patchwork. Olivia might have mistaken it for derelict save for the holds packed with myriad cargo containers. From this angle, Cole's initiative seemed more like a passion project held together by sheer force of will.

"I've built Unity by following my instincts," Cole said, running his hands along the module's hull. "And look what we've achieved. We're in touch once more with the Pool of old, and now I have a chance to set things on the right path."

I, not we.

Was that the old Olivia, looking for any reason to dismiss his offer? To call it esoteric and frivolous, a distraction from the real world?

But then, she wasn't really considering this, was she? For a moment she'd forgotten about the Fifth Sun. She'd even forgotten the question of whether Cole was a savior or a madman, or merely a lost soul in a metastasized flesh suit on some doomed vanity mission. She'd forgotten the real question at hand: How deeply could she infiltrate Unity?

"How long do we have to decide?"

"We're aiming to leave the day after tomorrow, I hope. And before you ask, I'm not sure how long we'll be away. It could take a day or a month. It could take longer."

"And in what capacity would we be joining you?"

He pulled her away from the natals loading the bays. "Come with me and listen to the Pool. Come and hear for yourself."

A simple proposition, and she wanted to say yes—whether as an infiltrator or a guest. But before deciding, Olivia would have to reckon with certain questions. Did she have a reason to go, beyond her own curiosity? Did she need one? Why did she still fear the Olivia who would make such a decision? Was there no coming back from such a decision?

"So?"

Cole had been waiting.

"You said that you've already heard back from the Pool," Olivia said.

He said nothing, just stood before her as if he realized she was stalling. But he wouldn't get an answer out of her, not yet, because she didn't have one. How could she when she couldn't even reconcile which Olivia she should answer for?

"Yes," he said at last, moving back around to the rear of the module, where the other members of Cole's group were walking the last of the crates up the ramps. "We did hear back from the Pool. But look, I have a dozen things to deal with right now."

"Right," she said, with some relief.

"We can meet tomorrow if you'd like. Or is this all a waste—"

"*No*," she said quickly. "Let's meet."

He considered her for a moment before responding. "Okay. Outside the terminal there's a statue, on the north side. A memorial to the vaunted High Pioneer."

. . . *Muwhi-hiwa* . . .

The natal who had first activated the Fountain. Su-jinda had mentioned them on the ship to *Puthubutiss*.

"I'll be there two moments after high," Cole said.

"We'll find you there."

———

"So we were right," said Oscar's mirage. A statement, not a question. In the background Olivia saw Maya with her blank skin, and several other of the Fifth Sun retinue that she couldn't get a reading on.

"Based on what I've learned so far, yes. Unity is in active contact with the Pool, and Cole has been doing his best to recruit me because he believes that I may have a natural gift for interpreting future communications."

"What is the Pool saying?"

"I only saw a portion of it," Olivia said. "But what I saw was kind of a logorrheic poem. I couldn't make much of it, frankly, but I think it was its version of the codex sequence that Unity shared with it beforehand."

"They're starting from where we left off," Oscar said, only not to her. "If the Pool proves amenable to Unity's plan—if they actually figure out how to grant the Pool passage—there's nothing we'll be able to do to stop it."

"But Cole only said he wants to give the Pool access to the Fountain," said Olivia, "not that he bears any malice toward—"

"Even *if* that's all they do," Oscar said, their focus squarely back on her, "the rest will be inevitable. Our ancestors knew this—or at least enough did to commit it to the historical record. They viewed the Pool as neither malicious nor benevolent, but they had seen with their own eyes that its very nature precluded ours. And we think Cole knows this full well."

If Cole was aware of that, it was something he'd left out of their conversations so far. "Then I'll ask him that directly when we talk tomorrow," Olivia said. "He wants me there by his side, so I'll make him work for it."

"You haven't already agreed to join them?" Maya asked. She then said something to the others that Olivia couldn't hear.

"I'm sorry," she said. "When Cole put the question to me today, I froze. But I agreed to speak with him again tomorrow."

Oscar gestured for the rest of their team to leave them alone. When it was just the two of them, they asked, "Are you okay, Olivia?"

Where had that come from?

"Uh, I think so. It's just . . . this isn't a decision I'd wish on anyone. It means missing my only way home for I don't know how long. Possibly forever." She pictured the view from her deck back home, Sol's pale light falling across Piosey's verdant foothills. "And I feel like I have to decide when I clearly don't have the full picture. The stories you've told me are horrifying, yet the way Cole tells it, Unity is aiming for restoration, not ruin."

"The two are inseparable, Olivia. And we can't wait on you for very long. Soon we'll have to take our final measures to ensure that Unity fails in its mission."

"I know." But she could still have it both ways—to find out about Cole's plan, and to make it home on time. The path hadn't closed for her, not yet. She hadn't lost herself like Cole had.

"Give me tomorrow," she said. "Let me talk to Cole."

THIRTY-NINE
DAY 65

THE FAUNA SANCTUARY was heavily wooded, with a network of soft biocrete trails connecting the scattered enclosures within. Cole had requisitioned a short trip on a line runner, which had them both away from the bustle of the city center and out to a lusher landscape.

That morning, standing in the shadow of *Muwhi-hiwa*'s statue, Cole had told her that the renowned natal, whose team had first activated the Fountain, had never once entered it themself. That idea, he'd told her, had always struck him as comic. Olivia couldn't help but wonder if the High Pioneer would have opened the Fountain at all, had they known what awaited them on the other side.

"Come with me, Poet," Cole had then said. "There's one more thing I want you to see."

Now, under an orange-crimson canopy, Olivia watched as a towering creature—a living scaffolding, its skeletal limbs raising it well above the tree line—combed over a tree using strands of sticky gossamer to pluck up some sort of morsels from the foliage.

"I've always liked watching the spoolers," Cole said, following Olivia's gaze. "So methodical, so committed."

"We've never seen them up this close," she said. That much was true.

"They're bigger in person, aren't they?"

"Amazing."

As they followed a sparsely populated trail, Olivia found herself thinking of Ran and Whistler, her father, and even Aleksi. What would they have made of the sanctuary's alien tranquility, the rustling of corkscrew fronds buffeted by the strangely undulant atmosphere, the myriad trills of beasts unknown? Would they have appreciated the familiarity of it all, despite its novelty?

"How do you feel about what we talked about yesterday?" Cole asked.

That's right, they weren't here just to disappear.

"We don't know," Olivia admitted. "It's a lot to take in."

"But you're getting a sense for why I'd want to reach out to you. Someone who is adept at language, but also keenly sensitive to EM signals."

Indeed, this enterprise of theirs could have been tailor-made for her. But maybe she was filling in the gaps in her knowledge with what she wanted to hear. There was so much she still didn't know . . . and this would be her last chance to find out.

"On the hotfont the other day," she said, "you told us there's more to the poem now. We need to know what you mean."

By way of explanation, Cole produced from his sling bag a panel, which he activated for her. Olivia had expected verse, but she saw instead a static line diagram made up of several geometric shapes. The most prominent figure somewhat resembled a virus, with a hexagonal head leading to a spine, and then to a waist from which three legs had sprung.

"What's this?"

"This is the pictorial we presented to the Pool, illustrating its connection to the Fountain in natal space." He tapped the display. "Here is the Pool, and the conduit to our system. Then we have the Fountain, and the three primary natal systems here."

"And the Pool understood what this meant?" She wouldn't have.

"Judge for yourself." Cole advanced the image, and the result was a rearrangement of the first diagram, with most the components superimposed. Now only the natal systems remained clear of the composite form. "This is what the Pool sent back, encoded in its particular electromagnetic patois."

"What does it mean?"

He pointed at the bottom of the display. "This was the message that accompanied the pictogram."

`All me`

Olivia repeated the words, as if they might impart some hidden meaning.

"How would you interpret that?" Cole asked her.

"Well, there's no more separation between the symbols. So that may indicate that the Pool perceives things differently."

"Or?"

"Or? Well . . . assuming the Pool interpreted the meaning of the original symbols, the merging of them here taken with the message could tell you—"

"That the Pool is the Fountain and the Fountain is the Pool. Right? *All me*."

"*Maybe*." The Fifth Sun had never mentioned that possibility, that the two might be linked still. "But even if so, this could be a statement of fact or a statement of intent. Or something else entirely. It's easy to read into something so vague."

"I don't think it's vague at all."

"Well . . . but it *is*."

"Okay, fortunately we're not completely in the dark. We have the archival records, and whatever remains of the echo."

The whispering. "Something to back up your assertion?"

Cole switched off the device. "I mentioned some of this yesterday, but according to records, the Pool sent cells out—parts of itself as we now know—into new systems, in an attempt to reach beyond its territory. Our Fountain is one of these cells. But the Pool's plan failed: despite the open connection that remained, the cells were inaccessible to it. After several dozannia, the visiting natals arrived on the scene, and so the Pool initiated communication through whatever means it thought might work, including gravitational waves, essentially strumming spacetime like a stringed instrument. And it worked. The Pool made its presence known, and within less than a circuit had managed to bridge the communication gap with natality, at least to some extent.

"Except . . . then something happened—an action or event we haven't been able to dig up, even from the archives. And the passage from the Fountain to Pool space was severed completely. Until recently."

There he stopped, letting the silence draw between them. As the chorus of the sanctuary rose to fill the space, Olivia replayed his words. Was he saying what it sounded like?

"You've gone to the other side?"

"Many times now."

"You're not just in communication with the Pool. You've already visited its . . . where it lives?"

"I assure you it's unlike anything you've seen before."

And Cole had lived to tell the tale. Unless he was telling a tale right now.

"The Pool is still there," he continued, "as it was when the historical records were first recorded. And now Unity is doing what our forebears failed to do: learning how to understand the Pool. Its basis for knowledge is far more alien than that of the biological species we know. It doesn't die, or even live as we do. It has no relationships or property. It seems to be alone in space. But its thirsts. It *wants*. And that's the key to understanding it. Because so do we. That gives us a basis for relating to it. And that's what we've been building on.

"Once we've reached a level of mutual understanding . . . then we can proceed to make our wants known to each other."

Olivia needed to sit down. She found a saddle-bench, and Cole joined her there.

"This is a lot," she said once more. And for a while, Cole said nothing —to his credit.

It was impossible to ignore the gulf between this bench in the middle of an alien sanctuary and the sectional in Olivia's lounge so far away. *Travel far enough*, she thought, *and it gets easier to forget . . .*

What?

The answer was elusive, dancing away from her as more vexing questions filled the gap. How had she found herself here, at the tail end of so many choices that weren't hers?

Were her own choices really hers at all?

She looked at Cole, the former human. He wasn't lost. This was exactly where he needed to be, right now. How had he found himself here?

"What about you?" she asked him.

"What about me?"

"What do *you* want, personally?"

"You go first, Poet," he said.

She'd discussed that very question with Oscar. Why would Cole think she had an interest in this? *Be honest*—that's what the poets had recommended.

Did she want anything? What would old Olivia say?

"We should know the answer to that, shouldn't we?" She thought about it. "It says something, maybe unflattering, that what we want hasn't been our primary motivator. Not since . . ." She looked down at her hands, still alien but now as familiar as her own. She'd seen what these hands were capable of; had put them to good use. But the novelty of physical reliability—of strength—had faded into a general sense of self-assurance. Of conviction. So why was it so difficult to answer her own question?

"We've felt limited for a long time, physical and otherwise," she said, testing the words for credibility. "We don't need to get into that . . . mainly because the limitations have now disappeared. Pain, constant pain, is like noise. And when it's gone you hear things you never knew existed. Things that change you in the listening. You talk about listening to the Pool . . . We've started listening to a whole lot more than that. It's like the most exquisite new music. And we'd follow that music . . . we don't know how far. But maybe we want to find out, even if it's a selfish pursuit. That's why we're here, now. Tomorrow we don't know where we'll be."

"That's not what I was expecting to hear," said Cole. "But I'm glad you shared it."

"Okay, now you," she said, trying not to feel self-conscious about her unintentional confession.

"Well, I've had my own struggles, of course. But generally what you see is what you get."

She could dispute that, but remained silent.

"Life was difficult for us, growing up," he said. "Food and shelter weren't sure things. We moved around a lot. It was a time of constant instability. But then things changed. I lost what little I did have—my family, our place, and any sense that I understood the world. I was placed in a communal safe harbor with some peers, and . . . it was *luxury* by comparison. Stable. I'd found a post-scarcity lifestyle I'd never known could exist.

"And I *hated* it. Life had never felt so . . . *irrelevant*."

"That's why you're here?" Olivia asked, still trying to figure out how all that turmoil added up to the twisted natal sitting next to her.

"In one way or another I've been searching for relevance my entire life, and a few times I thought I'd found it. But this—what I'm doing with Unity—is relevant, objectively. I knew it from the time I had the good fortune to learn of the Pool. We have an opportunity here, not only to right a past wrong and reconnect with the progenitor of the Fountain, but to give the Pool the stage to finish what it started."

"Yes, but . . ." She had to know. "Cole, is there something you're not telling me?"

"Is there?" He sounded surprised. "Ask me."

"You know the stories as well as we do. They allude to the danger of the Pool coming through that Fountain."

He waved the notion away. "The same stories devised by those who relegated the Pool to myth. What better security than our own superstitions? We lived by that Fountain for millennia, and even adapted ourselves to the Pool's mode of communication. Does that sound adversarial to you?"

Nothing he'd said raised any flags. Could the Fifth Sun simply be wrong about Cole's intent? Not to mention the harm the Pool might be capable of causing?

"You don't have to believe me," he said at last. "The proof is all around us. In fact, that's why I wanted to bring you here to begin with."

Olivia looked at the enclosures around them, at the interplay of flora and fauna, from the most massive tree to the smallest insects. What did any of it have to do with an entity on the other side of the Fountain?

"I don't mean to misrepresent you, but my understanding is that the Third Diaspora Territory is a bit self-isolating. Do I have that right?"

He must have looked into her cover story. Hopefully the cultural seclusion the diaspora practiced would provide her some cover. What was the name of her supposed home planet? Oscar had mentioned it. Something plain . . .

Plain Country.

"The Plain Country isn't completely cut off from the rest of the system," she said. "But yes, we do practice . . . deliberate quietness." Good enough.

"And I respect that," Cole said. "But it might explain why you're not seeing the full picture here. You'd never know it from the sparkling splendors of the Northland Republic—"

. . . Mubuthumuss . . .

"—but this Home planet of ours—"

. . . Tapuwathu . . .

"—by and large, is an ecological disaster, with declining animal populations on a global scale. Many of the species in this sanctuary exist only in captivity. But you know what else they have in common?"

"What?"

"Almost all of them are EM-sensitive. Isn't that interesting?"

"We didn't know."

"It's a fact, and it's not coincidental. Our magnetosphere does what a magnetosphere should do, but it's otherwise unremarkable. But the *Fountain*'s influence cannot be overstated. It's fundamentally changed the development of life here, behaviors, perceptions, even the way we communicate. The Pool's influence was profound. This is what I wanted to show you. The animals here, and even the plants, they're *all* natals. And when the Pool was cut off . . . well, that's when these populations began to suffer. Some more than others."

She considered what he was telling her. If he was right, then the devastation of the type the Fifth Sun had foretold had happened already. Could they have had everything backwards? Or was the evidence Cole was giving her circumstantial, taking advantage of her supposed ignorance?

The trouble was that she had little to sway her either way, and none of it was concrete. Only what she'd been told.

"Don't do it for you, in other words," Olivia said. "Do it for nature."

"If you were wondering why I've gone to such lengths to find a new relevance . . . well, this is all I've got."

"It is beautiful here."

"It was *more* beautiful, once."

Whether she was helping the Fifth Sun or Unity—or somehow both—the question lingered still: What did she want, right now?

The biggest surprise might be that her answer wasn't "home."

"We'd like to help," she said. She wasn't sure if it was her own voice she heard, or the voice of an agent of the Fifth Sun pretending to be an agent of Unity.

"That's a yes?" Cole asked, his voice almost disappearing beneath the plaintive cries of fauna and the whispering's own unyielding monologue. "No matter how long this takes, you'll join us?"

Casting herself into the unknown—a promising unknown—seemed like something new Olivia would do. A transfer turned apex, and changing still. *That* Olivia might find a place for herself in such a grand undertaking. More importantly, new Olivia *wanted* to. Out of pure, grim, selfish curiosity. She wanted to know what was out there . . . and for once, nothing was keeping her.

"Would you like to see it for yourself, Poet?"

"Yes," she said.

"Yes?"

"Yes."

———

As the afternoon turned to dusk, cool currents from the outer bay came in over the canal and mingled with the day's heat, intensifying the atmosphere's already dreamlike refractions. Olivia wandered the colorful farelines of the *Mubuthumuss* ward to clear her head, enjoying how the undulating air gave the city an underwater feel.

But even after taking the most circuitous route possible, Olivia eventually found herself back at that unmarked building by the waterfront. Fighting the urge to watch the city fall into night, she headed up to her torpor bead. She'd already delayed the inevitable more than she should have.

It was time to face her transmission node—or at least to take intentional action rather than trying to avoid things away.

Ioor Volkopp's latest message was at the top of a queue she'd never make her way through. She ignored it straightaway. He wouldn't have anything useful to say, and any reply she forced herself to compose could only serve to highlight her decided lack of interest in the original plan. Plans changed, but she wasn't going to get her SA handlers to understand that in a paragraph.

From Aleksi there was nothing, nor from Ran. In a way that let her off the hook, but the disappointment was unavoidable.

"Hi, Aleksi," she said, before she knew what would follow. The words hung before her. Maybe she should send them as is.

"I hope you're okay. Ran filled in some key details for me, so I'm not entirely clueless. Still, it would have been nice to hear it from you—how you were feeling, and what that meant for us. On the other hand, we've both been taking our own paths lately, so I'm hardly one to talk. Anyway, maybe you had a point—this probably isn't the best forum for that kind of talk."

Switching gears, she dropped a few harmless observations and platitudes before sending the note. The Sovereign Alliance would surely pick it apart for clues as to the state of her mental health.

Let them.

She started a second message.

"Hello, brother. It was good to see you. I was surprised that . . . I don't know. Maybe it's not surprising. We have so much to discuss. And I'm sorry I haven't been a frequent writer. But I wanted you to know that I'm well, and . . . also that I'm extending my stay. I can't give you dates right now, but know that it's all for a good cause."

She thought about that. Yes, despite the unknowns before her, she couldn't be surer about her decision to do this thing.

Before sending the note she asked him to send her regards to their father and friends. And after a moment of consideration she asked him to write back.

Then, before she lost any momentum, she found her sash and fished out the hotfont.

"I'm going to Pool space with Unity," she told Oliver and Emily when they appeared in mirage form before her. Who said the selfish decision couldn't also be the most helpful one? "Cole told me he'd found historical records that prove that the Pool and the Fountain are two parts of the same thing."

"We've seen that," Oscar said. "But you should know that it's a metaphor, not meant to be taken literally."

"He believes it literally." She recounted what she and Cole had discussed at the sanctuary that morning.

"We were right to fear the worst," Emily said.

Oscar addressed Olivia. "You should return to your home."

"I will, but *after* tomorrow's visit to Pool space. I know the Fifth Sun has been waiting for an opportunity like this, an opportunity to gain real insight into what Unity is doing."

"Our fear is that the only insight we'll gain is that we're already too late."

"Have you found an alternative?" Olivia asked. "One that doesn't risk the lives of everyone who relies on the Fountain?"

"We've never been able to get as close to them as you've managed to in just a few cycles," Maya said, materializing in the air next to Emily and Oscar. "Believe us, we would have brought this to a decisive conclusion if we had."

Was that a suggestion? That would be crossing a hard line. Killing the tanthid mother had been a one-time thing.

"How long does Unity plan on being in Pool space?" Oscar asked.

"As long as it takes to learn how to open the Fountain back up to the Pool," said Olivia. "Nothing led me to believe they think the process will be quick."

"Quick or slow, we *cannot* allow the Fountain to be opened to the Pool," Oscar said.

"I understand that. But Cole is going tomorrow whether or not I join him. He's going to proceed with whatever he has planned. The only question is, do you want eyes on him?"

"Go then," Oscar said. "But if Cole succeeds—if there's any indication that the Pool is actually on approach—we're going to do what we need to do. And you might never return to your home. There would be no more Fountain travel."

"It won't come to that."

"You can't know that."

They were right. But that only underscored the fact that this was something Olivia could never again experience. "Just let me be your eyes and ears." *And ampullae.* "I'll do what I can. And either way . . . you'll do what you need to do."

FORTY
DAY 66

"THERE'S A CERTAIN ART TO IT," said the natal called Ederzithel—so dubbed by Cole. Olivia watched the approach to the Fountain in miniature, projected as a mirage before them. So represented, the anomaly looked nothing like it had from the observation port of *Tassbewasspo*'s shuttle. In fact it was now a featureless black field visible only by the absence of stars behind it. "The exit point is essentially determined by the attitude and position of entry," the natal continued, pride apparent in their voice, "which is how access to certain destinations is controlled. But that leaves room for a creative approach, if one is discreet and knows where one is going."

Olivia got the gist of what they were saying. "You're not afraid of attracting the wrong kind of attention? If someone observed us approaching the Fountain from a prohibited angle, wouldn't that risk tipping them off that we're headed to Pool space?"

Her remark prompted starburst blooms of approval across the natal's skin. "Exactly so. Which is why we've implemented a relay system—"

"It's an art, as they say," Cole said, cutting them off. Ederzithel's pride would probably keep them talking for as long as Olivia pressed. "Our poet has better things to think about."

"Of course," Ederzithel said.

That morning Cole had sent Athena—*Timubu-be!ss*—to meet Olivia at the terminal, and they had escorted her to the multi-payload launcher platform located on the opposite side of the port from the commercial pads. Once the launcher had rendezvoused with the designated transfer station, Unity's section had separated, then made its way to the sleek survey ship *Bäckahästen*, where the crew treated her with deference, like she was Cole's own guest of honor. What had he told them about her? Had he described her as some glorified translator, or did her oversize stature speak for itself?

As she stared at the oddity in the projection field before her, she tried not to feel like an impostor. "The last time we saw the Fountain," she said, "it was a truly strange experience."

"It doesn't like to be watched," Cole said, "which is why we rely on sensors. You were looking at it . . . ?"

"Through observation glass." Like staring directly at the sun. Was it odd that she wanted to see it with her own eyes? "Would it be possible to look at it directly?"

The request gave Cole pause. But then he went to Athena, saddled at a display that showed an explosion of arcs all converging on their position. They must be watching their backs.

"Please take our poet up to the opticon," Cole said. Then, to Olivia, "Our security officer will show you the way."

"We appreciate it," Olivia said.

As she turned to follow the natal, Cole placed a gentle hand on Olivia's foreleg. "Just to warn you though, it's going to get a little weird."

———

As *Tapuwathu* diminished to a chartreuse dot, the whispering steadily ebbed, leaving behind a peaceful stillness. Olivia hadn't realized until the *Bäckahästen* was underway just how quiet the ship was. But of course there would be no electromagnetic field generators here—Unity was forever dedicated to satisfying Cole's personal predilections. His only interest in matters electromagnetic lay ahead of them.

As she followed behind Athena, Olivia ran her hand along the bulkhead as a kind of reassurance. Had she become so reliant, so quickly, on an external source of orientation? Or was this the ampullaic equivalent of ringing ears? A few years back she and Aleksi had chartered a private boat on Vaix's Cercegal Sea. For days after their excursion the phantom undulation of waves had persisted.

In time she would surely gain her bearings here, just as she had back then.

"Have a seat here and you can watch the entry," Athena told her once they'd reached the glass-walled bead Cole had called the opticon.

Several saddles were bolted to the floor before the thick glass pane, each fitted with a harness assembly. One natal, small in stature, was seated already, wearing an armature that ran from their back and down each leg.

"Poet, this is Massimo," Athena said. Olivia found herself anticipating their EM signature, but there was only that odd, incomplete stillness.

"Hello," Olivia said, sending a *tap-wave-tap-wave-tick*. Massimo offered the traditional salutation.

As Olivia mounted her saddle, Athena remained on their points, approaching the glass close enough to touch. Beyond it, the Fountain was as mystifying in appearance as it had been the first time. The great aberration appeared to be . . . a window into their own ship. Yes, if she angled her head just right she could see *herself*, from behind, as if from the back of the bead.

The Fountain version of her spun around the barest moment before she did the same. She half expected to see . . . who? But of course there was only the rear of the bead looking out into a featureless starfield.

She faced front once more to find Athena watching her. "It's a challenge at first, isn't it?"

Over their shoulder, the natal who was Olivia waved her hand.

"Try waving," said Athena, their skin flecked with anticipation.

Olivia complied, raising her foreleg and wriggling her fingers as her Fountain-self had already done. She was the one playing catch-up.

"Are you seeing the same thing we are?" Olivia asked.

"We all do," said Athena. "We've come to find it reassuring in a way."

Watching herself through the Fountain, Olivia could understand that. Was *that* Olivia feeling the same assurance too?

———

Time's passage seemed to quicken as *Bäckahästen* made its final approach. The exterior lights of a thousand ships merged into visible lanes—all of which would be halted if the Fifth Sun went through with their plan. A plan that seemed ever more unfathomable as the sheer volume of traffic became apparent.

Before merging with the nearest route, *Bäckahästen* broke away and took a more indirect approach, circling the anomaly.

Finding the one way in.

Within the Fountain's funhouse mirror, the image of Olivia was fracturing, ghosting, in a constant state of dissolution and resolution, as if it was seeing more than one possible Olivia at once. She saw several of her counterparts turn away a moment before she realized she would also turn away.

"You see the ripples now," said Massimo. Not a question.

"Whatever it is," she said, "I feel like a voyeur."

A tone echoed throughout the opticon. "Crossing the event horizon," came Cole's voice.

Olivia braced herself, grasping the rests of her saddle. But if she expected a shockwave, none came. Outside, the ripples—if that's what they were—only seemed slightly closer. At the same time a hollow choral harmonic rose up, seemingly from the bones of the ship, growing loud enough to fill the chamber.

"What's that?" she asked over the din—but her question silenced the chorus.

Another hollow chorus rose to meet Athena's reply. "Forward resonance. Less unnerving if you remain silent."

There was no getting used to it, even beyond the sensory disorder. What if she heard her own echo, then decided not to speak? The thought of it gave her a chill. It was too much responsibility.

Turning her focus back to the Fountain, that other version of their opticon had now grown close enough that she saw Athena and Massimo too, as if two image-reversing mirrors were coming together. She wanted to ask why this was happening . . . but she wouldn't, or she would already have heard the resonance. Was this normal? It *couldn't* be normal.

At last the Fountain was no longer strictly outside—it had entered the opticon itself, overtaking Athena and replicating her in a kaleidoscopic array. And then it took Olivia, too, until it was everywhere, all around her.

At that moment she was in all places at once, staring out at herself staring out. And she could no longer turn away, because she was around everything around her.

Too much.

No one should see this much.

Everything inside, outside, inside out.

Everything . . . was

FORTY-ONE
DAY 67

OLIVIA'S MUSCLES all responded at once, her legs driving outward as if she could ward off some force far greater than herself.

Only . . . she was bound.

No, tangled—in something soft.

The bead came into focus. She was on her back, suspended within a plain hull.

Torpor webbing.

She must have blacked out. She'd lost consciousness at some point. Maybe everyone had. But at some point someone—or *someones*, more likely—had conveyed her to her own torpor bead.

Clearing her eyes, she looked around. The space was far more stripped down and utilitarian than the torpor beads she'd grown accustomed to. Testing her limbs, Olivia found them reliable. She grabbed the edges of the hull and pulled herself upright, testing her weight on all four points.

"Welcome back."

Cole's voice, over the comm. Thoughtful of them to put a watcher on her.

"Did we make it?" she asked.

"Want to see?"

———

From the bridge of the ship, Olivia looked out beyond the other gathered crew members to the symmetrical formation etched across the infinite dark.

"What is this?" she asked. "Are we inside something?"

"Those are stars," Cole said, watching her more than the view. "And nebulas. And galaxies. Believe it or not, we're outside. That's space, only . . . in order."

It made no sense.

"We're no astrophysicist," Olivia said, scanning the view from one side to the other, "but how can everything be lined up like that?"

"For all we know, it's the result of a careful and conscious manipulation of symmetrons," he said. It was impossible to tell if he was serious. "But whatever the explanation, our only guess is that this is something the Pool has done just for us. The stars only align this way in this region. Move too far in any direction and you start to see the lines dissolve. It's breathtaking the first time you see it."

"You didn't tell me it was going to be like *this*."

"It is unique. We haven't been able to find where we are relative to the natal system."

Olivia looked from face to face, a few of which had been watching her as if to gauge her reaction. Who were these people rallied to Cole's cause? How many here knew that Cole was a transfer? Would it matter? Olivia had never heard him make mention of it, though he clearly exhibited profound physical differences from any of his Unity cohort.

"So . . . it's an illusion?"

"It may be some kind of exotic localized effect—but localized on a vast scale, mind you. Any direction you look, at any level of magnification, you can see that the stars are real. Relative to our position, they're truly, physically aligned to each other. But think of it this way: if space is infinite, maybe this is inevitable."

What would it take to create such a phenomenon? Such a grand display? It was unfathomable. It had to serve some purpose beyond being a kind of interstellar poetry.

"It has to mean something," Olivia said, almost to herself. "Maybe this place—"

"The Pool's signals are the strongest here," said Ederzithel. "Strong enough to interpret."

"That 'poem' you found me researching the other day," Cole said. "This is where we picked it up. And that was just a piece of it. Speaking of which . . ." He turned to Athena. "Have we sensed anything out there?"

"Not yet, Cole."

———

"First things first then," Cole said, and stood as carefully as he did anything. If he was in physical discomfort, he never let on, but Olivia found herself wanting to spot him lest he faltered. "We don't stand on formality here, but let's take advantage of this respite to make some proper introductions."

The strings of lights outside—many billions of galaxies—lent the moment a formality despite Cole's assertion. As he moved to the center of the bridge between the various stations, all eyes were on him. "As you see, Olivia, we are a skeleton crew. Everyone here has heard me speak of our new poet, who hails from the . . . ?"

Is this a test?

The name came to her readily. "The Third Diaspora Territory."

"Which is a first for us, I think."

Several of those present issued a *tap-wave-tap-wave-tick* of greeting as they clasped their fingers before them. So they weren't entirely EM-insensitive.

"But our backgrounds are diverse," Cole continued, "and here you'll find that our cycle-to-cycle roles are broad. Ederzithel and Athena, whom you've met already, both have backgrounds in research. Athena generally makes sure the operation is running smoothly, and Ederzithel . . . well, they do the opposite, making my life difficult."

"Cole would be out here alone without us," said Ederzithel.

"And here," said Cole, "we have Gregor, Napoleon, Coretta, and Vandana."

So many names you've given them.

But no signatures, and no whispering. It only underscored the stark silence around her. What business did they have in such a place?

"Researcher, researcher, historian, and systems first," Cole said. "As for the others, Massimo is usually hiding somewhere in engineering, and you may or may not see Tove, who prefers to spend their time with the cargo." He turned to her. "Of course Unity has other members on the Home planet, just as important to this mission, and in key positions. You may get to meet them after."

"We'd like that," she said.

"So, why a poet?" he asked, addressing all those present. "Partially because poetry is the highest form of communication, or possibly the other way around. And, not coincidentally, we now find ourselves with a communication challenge best suited, I suspect, to someone adept with the language arts." He looked at Olivia. "A linguist would have been nice, but a poet will do."

Olivia observed amused fractal displays among several of those present. "Well, my fields of study were creative writing and literature."

"I'm only kidding, of course," he said to her, as if in confidence.

This ease of manner he fostered must serve some greater purpose, or he wouldn't put so much effort into it. *We're informal here, we wear whatever hats are necessary in the moment.* Was it because the ramifications of their prospective success were so grave? Or did he truly view this as a moment of levity?

"The other reason I wanted the poet to be here—and possibly the more important reason—is because their electromagnetic sensitivity is quite strong. And that is a combination of talents that should be very useful to us."

"Can we talk about that?" Olivia said, surprising herself.

"The mission, you mean?" Cole asked.

"Since most of us are here . . ."

"Please, yes. Anything you want. That's why we're here."

Olivia's gaze returned to the formation outside, the stars literally aligned, the lines meeting at regular intervals, forming polygonal grids, as if the ship itself were caught in a net.

"You've mentioned this concept of allowing the Pool to finish what it started before. And now, seeing the stars out there . . . we guess we need a refresher. What does *finishing* look like? And is the Pool's vision of the future . . . can it be the same as ours?"

The natal that Cole had called Coretta spoke first. "We are the Pool's vision."

This elicited sounds of agreement.

"The Third Diaspora wouldn't have taught you our full history," said the one called Gregor. "The Pool sent us the Fountain. We were raised by it, we were raised *on* it, all under the Pool's supervision."

"That was the way of things for dozannia," Loretta said.

Vandana stood and came around her saddle to be by Cole's side. "The severing only happened a dozen biqua-circuits ago." Olivia tried to parse that out. Was that a thousand years? More? "Your third diaspora hadn't even happened yet. Look how quickly we've lost even the rudimentary senses we once had. In another few generations we may not be able to communicate with the Pool at all."

It was hard to reconcile the natal's words with the vast achievements of her people. "But we're an incredibly thriving culture already, independent of the Pool," Olivia said. "Look at everything we've accomplished, across multiple systems, and now with the Empyrean Symbiotry—"

"That denialist farce," Athena snapped. "They exist only to promote the lie that we're not shadows of our former selves. Don't your people see that, Poet?"

"They don't," said Gregor. "They're Third Diaspora new-realmers."

"That's not necessary," Cole interjected. "They're here now, aren't they?"

"Yes, but why?" Gregor asked. "Poet, we were a greater people in the Pool's radiance, and soon, regardless of whether you choose to believe it, we will be greater still. We can't think of a simpler way to put it."

Something in their words pricked Olivia's attention. This wasn't just about granting the Pool access to the Fountain. "Are you talking about some kind of uplift? That natality can somehow be improved by the Pool, or . . . united with it?"

"Something like that," Gregor said.

"Or maybe something entirely different from that," put in Athena. "Something we've never known."

Cole lifted a hand. "Poet, your hesitation in these final moments, if that's what you're giving voice to, is understandable. As I said, we all come from different backgrounds." If the rest of the crew only knew.

"Some live in contented ignorance, but many of us feel the burden of the compromise we've been forced into, and the sacrifice. Just remember one thing: you stand to benefit from the unification as much as anyone."

Olivia wanted to say something; to protest, or at least advise caution. But that wasn't her role—the last thing she needed was to be ushered to some makeshift brig for attempting insurrection during her team introduction. This crew were all true believers; just look how they'd bristled at her slightest resistance. There was no way she would get through to them.

"It's an ambitious plan, truly," she said, striving to keep her tone neutral. "I never appreciated how much until now."

Seemingly satisfied, Cole made his way back to his saddle. "Let's focus on our discrete goals here. Once we can communicate reliably with the Pool, we'll work together—Unity and the Pool—to open independent springs."

"Springs that are independent of the Fountain," Gregor explained. "Like miniature fountains, with their own variable destinations."

"All quiet out there," Ederzithel said. "No signs."

"So we prepare," said Cole. "Poet, this will take a while. Feel free to watch from here. Or tour the ship. Catch up on torpor. I'll call you when we need you."

She was being dismissed. "You're sure?"

"We've got everything in hand for now."

Maybe this was for the best. She needed to use her hotfont to send a message back to Home.

As she made her way out, she overheard Cole say, "Athena, Napoleon, let's get you ready."

———

The truth about her circumstances didn't fully hit Olivia until she entered her cabin. Cole had confirmed the Fifth Sun's worst fears about Unity, and with that Olivia's chances of returning to Sol had diminished significantly. She'd have to convince Oscar and company to hold off on their plan to close the Fountain until after she'd been transferred.

If not . . .

She stared at the bare walls of her cabin, imagining a fate that had, until recently, seemed farfetched. She should be terrified at the prospect of never returning home, of never seeing her friends or family, and of never really being *herself* again. Instead, that sense of calm—of *natal* calm—washed over her once again, and in the silence another question surfaced: Would it be such a terrible fate to live out her remaining circuits as an apex? Would it be such a dear price to pay?

Perhaps not.

But only if there was a system left to live in.

One that I haven't helped to destroy.

Olivia retrieved her hotfont from her sling pack. The risk of attempting to contact the Fifth Sun from *Bäckahästen* hardly mattered now. Oscar and company were now the only ones who could stop Unity.

But when Olivia raised the device, the words on its screen didn't look promising:

```
No access
```

The least exotic explanation was that they were simply too far from the spring for the hotfont to operate. But they'd just traveled to a place where all the stars aligned, so she couldn't assume the hotfont's failure was a factor of distance.

Olivia realized she'd been squeezing the device. She forced her fingers to relax lest she crush the thing. Now what? Walk off her anxious energy in the passageways? No, she'd already made a spectacle of herself on the bridge. She had to stay ready to set things in motion as soon as the channel was restored.

She raised the device again. "Can you let me know when you've reestablished a connection to *Bebetathubutiwa?*" She'd produced Home's signature without even thinking about it. Hopefully she wasn't being watched.

"I will," the device said.

Letting herself fall into her torpor netting, she set the hotfont at the edge of her hull and waited.

FORTY-TWO
DAY 68

TOO MUCH TIME HAD PASSED, as evidenced by the hollowness in her abdomen and tightness in her bowel.

Olivia sat up, her body swaying in the netting. She'd thought the lack of the whispering would mean a more relaxing nap, but instead it had only deadened her senses.

She glanced at the hotfont:

```
No access
```

Shit.

"What time is it?"

"Fourth hexad and seven, local," said the ambiont.

That didn't tell her anything. "How long have I been asleep, in hours?"

"About fifteen hours."

Shit!

———

Olivia entered *Bäckahästen*'s small bridge to find Cole exactly where he was when she'd left, precariously balanced on his saddle seat in the middle of the chamber as he conferred with Vandana. Or maybe it was Ederzithel. Without their signatures it was hard to tell from a distance. Or maybe Olivia was just hungry and groggy, despite all the sleep she'd gotten.

"As long as the module's a distance that demonstrates we're preparing our reply," Cole was saying. He gave Olivia a wave as she took her place by one of the instrument clusters. "We'll cast our response when we're in position."

"Transmission module will be initialized in three hexa-moments," said Vandana.

Olivia watched the displays. The main camera was trained on the payload platform, which resembled a theater stage just outside the ship. At its center sat a single mysterious set piece, a bulky module laden with a complex array of transmitters and receivers. It looked like it'd been turned inside out.

What was it they were listening for? Would she see lights in the sky? Would a burst of static announce the Pool's arrival over the comms?

"Can I ask how this works?" she asked. *Shit—my pronoun.* She resisted the urge to correct herself.

Cole gestured toward the display. "Napoleon and Athena are out there in our transmission module preparing our response to the Pool. Do you recall the snatch of poetry you saw me deciphering at the resource hub back in the Grand Ward? That's what we used for inspiration."

"You've already . . ." Why would they try that without including her? "But we thought that's why *we're* here."

"That's why I'm telling you."

"We need to look at that first poem again first, for context."

"You can call it up, Poet. But there's no need to put everything else on hold. Are you hungry?" He indicated an open bin of multicolored feed-sticks affixed to the back of the nearest console. "They're not bad." He grabbed one for himself.

Olivia ignored them. "What's 'everything else'?"

But surely *everything else* meant whatever they wanted it to mean. She could feel her skin betraying her.

"Making sure we understand this entity—and that it understands us —is just the first part of this," Gregor said, their skin pattern suggesting irritation. "Or haven't you been paying attention? Right now we owe it a reply, so we reply. Unless you have a better idea?"

"They're a poet," Cole said as he nibbled. "Of course they're going to be critical before they've even seen our reply."

"So can I see it?"

Cole pointed to a display by Olivia's side, and the words appeared there:

```
When the echo calls,
we will answer.
A brave answer to your signal,
to break the quiet,
and deliver you to your new home.
All will be—
```

Olivia didn't bother to finish. "Do you think this is the right way to present ourselves?"

"I know it's not prize-worthy, but this isn't a contest."

"We mean, is this the right way to approach the Pool?"

"The *right* way?" Cole adjusted on his saddle. "First of all, remember that we're not starting from scratch here. The early natals were in regular contact with the Pool. And we casted the full echo codex, as I said. You've already seen from its communications that it understands us, at least to some degree. So the purpose of this response is twofold. First, to show the Pool that we understand *it*. And second, to show it that we have a plan."

Olivia looked out at the transmission module again, a crude construct, improvised from scrap by all appearances. "And the ancient stories, about the Pool being incompatible with matter?"

"Didn't I debunk that particular superstition for you? Poet, the same way you make meaning with words, the Pool makes meaning of the universe. Where the void offers little more than quantum foam—a churn of fields popping virtual particles in and out of existence for all eternity—the Pool is about order. Look out there. You see it as well as I do. Not just order, but *purpose*. Not to mention that we are the living proof of that purpose."

"You have zero concerns—"

"We've taken every precaution, I assure you."

"The Fountain is part of the Pool," Gregor said quickly, before Cole could stop them. "If not for the Fountain, we would be very different. We are the Pool's lost children."

"Okay, Gregor, I think they get the point."

"Casting now," said Vandana.

Something might have hinted at the transmission, a faint flutter across her skin. Otherwise there was nothing but the purr of countless internal systems, including the thrum of her own vexed heart. She hadn't been able to articulate precisely why their approach was misguided, but the answer seemed frustratingly close, encoded in the beats of the Pool's own signal. And whatever the correct approach was, it certainly wasn't to be found in that insipid verse.

"Anything?" Vandana asked.

After a moment, a voice came over the comm. "All quiet." Not Athena. Napoleon, maybe.

"Maybe it's not understanding?" Gregor asked Cole.

"Or it's not here," said Ederzithel.

Or it has good taste.

A torrent of electromagnetic sequences saturated Olivia's every nerve ending, making her recoil as if she'd come into contact with a live wire. "Something's here," she said, unable to articulate what was going on. "Something's . . . talking. Something close."

"I knew it," Cole said. "That's the Pool. Can anyone else interpret what the poet is sensing?"

"Nothing that specific," said Vandana, "but the electromagnetic signature is similar to the one we read last time."

Indeed, the chatter was enough to set Olivia's mind abuzz.

. . .   *ss!bu!butibe!be!be-ssta!be!be!be-poss!po!po!poss-whitamussbethube-sswhihi!ta!ta!tass* . . .

And on it went, each burst and pop originating from somewhere beyond the platform. The thought of it formed a pit of dread somewhere deep within Olivia's alien belly.

"Try re-casting the echo codex to drive home that association," Cole suggested. "It should be able to parse anything we—"

"What's that?" Vandana asked.

The natal did something to widen the view of the transmission module. The entire section had a strange, diffuse quality that made it look sharp and blurred at the same time.

"Is something wrong with the camera?" Cole asked.

"No cameras, it's a plenoptic feed." As if to demonstrate, Vandana swiped at the image on their own panel, causing the view to orbit around the transmission module. No matter the angle, the section was clearly undergoing some localized alteration.

All the while, the electromagnetic sequence continued unabated, a chaotic string of indecipherable chatter.

"Status of our sensors?" Cole asked.

"Everything nominal."

"Comms?"

"Clear," said Ederzithel.

"Then what are we looking—"

He stopped.

Whatever was happening to the transmission module had intensified, causing it to bloom into a fuzzy approximation of itself. The light from the stars behind it glimmered through, warped as if seen through a lens.

"Hail them," Cole said.

"Napoleon, report," said Vandana.

Silence.

No response.

And no more electromagnetic signature. Had the Pool left?

"Napoleon, Athena, please report your—"

The module strobed and flickered, going from solid to spectral and back again, as if its very atoms were phasing in and out of existence.

Then it was atomized entirely, and with it the two natals inside.

FORTY-THREE
DAY 69

DESPITE ATHENA'S and Napoleon's unceremonious obliteration, the crew's general mood had become, if anything, even more resolute. According to Vandana, the crew hadn't lost two of its key members, but rather had established a connection to the Pool unseen since the times of ancient natality.

Were we watching the same display? But if anyone noticed the dread imprinted on Olivia's skin, they said nothing. Neither did they notice as Olivia left the bridge, nor attempt to stop her in the passageways as she walked aimlessly, struggling to sort through the disarray in her head. Only when her legs began to cramp did she realize that she wasn't getting closer to any new insight. She was as lost here as Unity was.

She found herself following Cole's voice, not to the bridge but to a spacious supply hold stocked with rations containers and a multipurpose food processor. It was the closest thing to a galley she'd found aboard *Bäckahästen*. Cole was engaged in an animated conversation with Massimo and Coretta, two of the quieter crew members.

Olivia grabbed a slate from a supply rack and loaded it, her hands trembling, with various foreign morsels and pastes—several of which she now recognized well enough to lament the reconstituted quality of the local fare—and sat down to eat.

Why had the Pool obliterated the transmission module? Except maybe out of miscalculation, desperation, or ineptitude? Or perhaps it had been given the wrong idea about Unity's intent, after being subjected to that amateurish poetry. Most likely it would have expected something far more basic, like a social mirroring exercise, to make sure everyone was on the same wavelength.

Which is what I tried to tell him from the start.

The man knew what he wanted, but he hadn't the faintest clue how to get there.

She didn't need to wait for an opening with Cole; he took the saddle across from her while she remained focused on her food. Did she warrant such priority treatment over his regular crew?

"I was worried when you disappeared," he said.

She looked at him. "We don't think it's *our* disappearance you need to worry about."

"Every single one of my crew understands the risks and the promises of this venture. As I think you do. Maybe you just weren't prepared to see—"

"We don't know *what* we saw," Olivia said, placing her spatula by her slate, her appetite ceding to fury. "But we know it's *not* something we need to see again."

"I'm not giving up," he said. "Ask yourself why them and not us. What happened to the transmission module was instructional, like it or not, and if we don't learn from it then it was a lesson wasted on us. You understand why we need to try again, don't you?"

"Take us back," she said. With her hotfont out of commission, her only hope of reaching anyone lay on the other side of the spring they'd arrived here through.

"I couldn't if I wanted to," Cole said with a cool finality. "There's no way back until we've accomplished what we set out to do here."

He meant it literally.

"What are you saying?"

"I mean that we have everything we need here now," he said, waving a hand at the stacked crates around them, "including provisions to last us many circuits, which you helped us to load. Plus now we have you."

"You clearly don't need us," said Olivia, "as you've demonstrated already. So we're asking you to let us go back through the spring."

"I *closed* the spring. That's what I've been trying to tell you."

"*What?*"

"Leaving the door open behind us would have been a crutch. Now we'll have the incentive to actually—"

"So this is . . . so you resort to *kidnapping*?" That was enough to draw eyes: Ederzithel, who'd just wandered in, and Massimo and Coretta, now out in the passageway.

"Poet, we're on the verge of communicating with an ancient entity the likes of which no one's seen for dozannia. Going back would have been a failure, a retreat from every one of our driving goals."

"But we're *stranded* here!"

Cole leaned in close. "I'm committing us to the one goal that will allow natality to travel *anywhere*, at any *time*. That is the *opposite* of being stranded."

He took advantage of her stunned silence to stand and make his way out of the galley. Just as well—there was no penetrating the man's magical thinking. He was beyond logic, and the crew had long ago bought into his fallacious vision. Olivia had been a fool to come, to think she could accomplish anything here. Nothing she did now could stop them.

In fact, if she was to have any chance of returning to Vaix, she *needed* Unity to be successful.

She found Cole in the bridge, watching over Gregor and Vandana as they monitored some sort of involved reconfiguration out on the payload platform.

"What this?" Olivia asked, afraid she might be too late.

Cole turned to her. "I got to thinking about why our first approach ended the way it did. It was the transmission module itself: it got in the way of our message. It was an unnecessary abstraction, something the Pool has no direct connection to."

It sounded like so much conjecture.

"The Pool needs to connect with us directly," Cole said.

Olivia looked at the payload platform on the display. "Meaning what? That you're sending someone out there to hold their breath and wait for the best?"

"That's a funny image. But no, I mean *I'll* go out to the payload platform. By myself. I'll be safe within an effector volume, but exposed enough that the Pool can understand who it's connecting *with*."

"Who it's *connecting* with? Cole, that's . . . it's suicide."

"The Pool would not harm one of its children," Gregor said.

"Shall we ask Athena and Napoleon for their opinion on that? Do you hear yourselves? That's baseless." She turned to Cole. "You're not even a natal *natal*—"

"*No* natal is what they could be," Cole put in, without missing a beat.

Olivia looked from natal to natal, but none present showed even the faintest trace of surprise or revulsion that their captain was from a foreign shore.

"You should know better than to encourage this kind of thinking," Olivia said. "Talk about superstition."

"Help me and I'll get you your spring—directly back to Sol system if you want."

Shit.

She'd called him out, and now he'd done the same to her.

Had they known all along?

She hooked him by the foreleg, and he allowed her to pull him to the far side of the bridge. "How long have you known?"

"That you're a human, like I was? For a little while." He looked over her shoulders to the others on the bridge. "We're not like them at all, you know. The two of us. We can't pass just because we look like them and sound like them. But I have learned a lot from natality, in a way I never could have if I hadn't walked a mile in their shoes. Idioms like that are a dead giveaway, by the way."

"Cole, you're a *human*. Somewhere in there you're as human as I am. So what does any of this Pool business have to do with you? Why is this mission so important to you? What's in this for Cole Quinlan?"

"You've only gotten the slightest whiff of transformation, and look where it's gotten you. Humans *are* apexes, Poet. Whoever you were back in Sol, you're an apex now. What does that tell you? Now imagine if that was just the start. I *have*."

"Cole, you keep talking about transformation. But was the transmission module's annihilation your idea of productive transformation? Is that what you want to see on an even larger scale? I can't imagine what would happen if the Pool deluged the entire natal domain. Also, I don't know if you've looked in the mirror lately, but you're—"

"It's only a deluge if it's not *controlled*—if we let it find its way to the Home system on its own. We have the matter well in hand, and will be good shepherds."

She fell silent as she searched for the words to respond.

"Sorry," he continued, "but inaction isn't the moral victory you think it is." He pulled away from her. "We can do what we came here to do, or we can die out here, stranded."

Because he had orchestrated it that way. In which case—thanks to Cole—Unity might very well be the last people Olivia ever saw.

"Fine," she said, "let me tell you what I think."

"Finally, she's ready to help?"

"As I've been trying to tell you for I don't know how long now, you're not communicating with the Pool correctly."

"I'm listening."

"I think—no, I'm sure—that the Pool was looking for a far more literal interpretation of the classic 'call and response.' First you translated what it had said, then you tried to collaborate with it."

"I'm not following."

"Repeat the original sequence exactly as you received it."

"You know we already did that, at *your* suggestion."

"You *didn't*. You translated the Pool's signals into words, and then threw a codex at it. You should have cast the signal as you *received* it. That's the only way to establish a true baseline. Everything that follows will be based on that."

For a long while—perhaps to his credit—Cole remained silent. As the other natals gathered around their respective instrument clusters to enact whatever scheme Cole had dreamed up, he said to her, "That will be a problem. Not only am I EM-insensate, I can't speak in the natal proto-tongue."

"I can." She demonstrated by generating several of the signatures she'd picked up during her time in the natal domain, which drew the attention of the others. They might not be able to sense the wall of signals the Pool had casted, but she was coming through loud and clear.

Cole was oblivious to it, of course. "Did you do something?"

"They just used the ursprache," said Gregor.

Cole looked from her to his engineer. "Could we cast EM signals like that?"

"Of course."

"Mmm," Cole said, but nothing more. Blank skin or not, he looked like he had a lot more on his mind than he had moments before. "I'll be back."

Olivia followed him out.

———

"Hey. Cole." Though his gait was longer than hers, Cole had been moving slowly, carefully, as if his growths were impeding his motion. "Are you okay? Because I'm trying to figure out what's going on in that head of yours. What's really going on here?"

He stopped and placed a hand on the bulkhead as he caught his breath. "I've had better days, to be honest."

"Are you sick?"

"Sick? No. Just . . . a bit too big for my britches. I love being able to say things like that around someone who'll understand." He grabbed hold of one of his knobby leg joints. "This syndrome of mine is untreatable. My initial transfer was a rush job. Corners were cut. Long story short, every growth you can see grows *inside* as well as out. It takes a toll."

"I'm sorry," Olivia said, and meant it. Her transfer had been a kind of escape, but Cole's sounded more like a cruel trap.

"You know," he said, wringing his hands as if to loosen the joints, "if I had to guess, I'd say you actually *are* a poet. Tell me that much is true."

"I was, once," she said. "And I was recognized for it."

"You see? Some truths just come out, don't they? So why didn't you tell me you were xenogenous?"

"That word again."

"Ah. Yes, natality is adept at hiding its epithets in plain sight. As they do their guests."

Could he know about her connection to the Fifth Sun? She certainly wasn't going to volunteer it now. Let him think that she'd tracked him down on her own, from Sol to this place, using her own canny wits.

"I'm curious," he continued, "why the whole cover story about the Third Diaspora. Did you think that was some ace up your sleeve?"

She didn't have to search too deep for a plausible answer. "What I told you in the sanctuary that day about my own struggles was true. I'd pushed against my physical afflictions for decades, and had made a pretty good life for myself. But it wasn't until I came here that it dawned on me that . . . maybe being human was its own limitation." She wasn't about to implicate The Fifth Sun's part in her extended deception. Let him think she was just being cautious. "So when I first suspected that you weren't just different, but human yourself . . . well, my own background wasn't something I was going to rush to spell out."

"Okay, in the spirit of our new openness, can I tell you something?" He allowed himself to lean fully against the wall. "I'm scared."

For some reason this revelation only made her want to throw up her hands.

"But sometimes," he continued, "doing what you set out to do—what you *must* do—is scary."

"Then I can only wish you luck," Olivia said. "I need you to succeed, because as much as I'll miss being forever pain-free, I still want to get home."

"Where is home?"

She took a breath. "Vaix."

"I know it well. The Sovereign Alliance was a good customer of our little outfit, once upon a time. So why are you here now?"

"You know why. I came with a diplomatic mission, to—"

"No, Olivia, I mean why are you *here* now. With me."

Without the Fifth Sun's help, why *would* she be here? *Give him something that's true.*

"Because you're a human interfering in the affairs of another race." He would buy it because it was direct and to the point. And also, possibly, because he couldn't deny it. "After seeing what happened to the transmission module, I have grave misgivings about your success."

"In what way am I human? For that matter, in what way are *you* human?" He stood straight again—as straight as his body would allow in the cramped passageway. "No, I'll tell you why you're here now. Because of a series of choices and a set of beliefs. That's all. And I think that we must have a lot in common if we're both in the same place at the same time."

He turned and continued heading wherever he was heading.

"That's a tidy reductionist picture you paint," she called after him. "You're putting all of natality at risk because of some fantasy that you'll be able to control what happens after you open your new spring. I can't condone it!"

"Maybe not. But unless you want to live your last days here you'll need to help me. See you tomorrow."

FORTY-FOUR
DAY 70

OLIVIA WATCHED Cole's plan unfold from the bridge. He stood at the center of the shielded payload platform as the solid barriers around it receded. The image on the display was stark: a single natal standing before the staggering tessellation of a billion fiery suns. None among the crew had taken issue with this reckless scheme, though no evidence suggested physical exposure to whatever was out there would better serve the mission.

But despite her relative safety, a curious feeling of weight fell over Olivia, enough to make her grab the lip of her saddle for stability.

"Are you ready?" she asked Cole. Could he hear her? "Everyone, hold on."

"You get something?" Cole asked, his miniature form peering out into the black.

"A kind of pressure, just now. Subtle across my skin."

"All sensors open," said Gregor.

"A signal?" Cole asked. "A message?"

"No words. It's more like . . . when you feel someone staring at you."

Silence.

Then, "I'm not seeing anything."

And that's how things remained, poised for action, but settling into a state of heightened stasis. Cole shifted uneasily on his points but held his ground. The crew monitored their respective stations, issuing occasional status updates almost in a whisper. And Olivia waited for any indication that they weren't alone.

No one wanted to scare away the ghost.

———

Holding herself in a state of prolonged receptivity, Olivia found, was hard work. Phantom signals manifested themselves in the currents of ventilation systems, or in the twitch of a muscle.

"So you found me all on your own?" came Cole's voice, abrupt enough to make Olivia jump.

It took her a second to realize he was asking her.

"What?"

"I looked you up, Olivia Jelani. A new initiation into the Empyrean Symbiotry is quite the cause célèbre, as you might expect. Only it seems that things didn't go quite as expected, what with your colleague—who is also your father—suddenly ducking out of the festivities for undisclosed reasons."

"I'm flattered."

"Then you go to ground for a couple of doza-circuits, by my calculation, before surfacing in a ward in the Northland Republic. And there you come face to face with the only other Sol transfer in the entire system. Was it fate?"

Coretta and Gregor were both looking at her now.

Olivia thought about the chain of events that had brought her from her own swimming pool to the bridge of this oddly named ship. It was a chain of events set into motion by Cole himself. If not for him, she would never have found herself here.

Is that fate?

"I came to *Tapuwathu*—to the Home planet—at the invitation of friends I'd made over here. I happened to accompany them to an open enclave—"

"Aha."

"—which is where I first saw you holding court among your coterie."

"Is *that* what I was doing?"

"The rest was . . . me following my nose." He didn't need to know any more than that. "What can I say? You do leave an impression. Also you don't really disappear in a crowd, do you?"

After some seconds of silence, he admitted, "No, I suppose you're right."

Convinced or not, Cole left it at that.

The signal, when it finally came, was not subtle. In fact, it snapped Olivia out of her waking torpor with the electromagnetic equivalent of an extended shout, powerful enough to leave her joints tingling.

HERE

It was real, and coming from all directions, shooting through her, making her head resonate like a bell. She slid off her saddle and stood as if she might bolt somewhere.

"Poet?" Vandana asked, standing up to peer over their station.

"Are you picking up something, Poet?" Cole asked.

"I just sensed a word—'here'—followed by a kind of . . ." The signal was incessant now, like a flood slicing through the ship. "It's a presence. Something is . . ."

Focus.

But there was nothing to latch on to until the sequence repeated. And there, again: the same complex sequence, set on a loop. The initial intensity had thrown her, but if she paid attention to the signal's actual structure, it wasn't beyond parsing.

"*Here?* That's all?"

"Now it's like a wall of words." On the display, Cole was inching closer to the edge of the platform. "They're not words I understand. But I'm sensing them."

"We are picking up something," Gregor confirmed. "The faintest oscillation."

Why was it so much louder than before? Had she become more attuned to it, or could it now be directing its signal *to her?* The thought made her feel lightheaded.

"Is it something you can repeat?" came Cole's voice. "Can you cast what it's saying back to it?"

That would have no effect, but any will she might have had to protest Cole's suggestion had left her. The signal was lighting up her every nerve; it would probably soon start to cause damage, physically or otherwise.

Returning to her saddle, she leaned into the amplification pad as Ederzithel had shown her earlier. Then she produced her approximation of the signal as accurately as she could.

The Pool went silent.

"It heard, I think," Olivia said, vastly understating what she'd been sensing. But for Cole it was enough.

"Okay," he said. "Is it still—"

. . . Echo remote, echo near . . .

"—speaking, or did it—"

"Cole, stop," she said. "I need to concentrate." She'd nearly missed the words under Cole's, but the signal was more modulated this time, the sequence as understandable as speech, but delivered silently.

The ursprache.

Olivia dutifully repeated what she'd sensed, conjuring the words in the form of an electromagnetic sequence, using organs she had no understanding of.

They waited then as the silence drew on.

What had the words meant? Had the Pool used "echo" in the generic sense, or was it talking about the codex that Unity had cast to it?

. . . Echoes, echoing . . .

"There's more now," Olivia said quickly.

The sequence that followed was familiar, because it was the "poem" Cole had first shown to her. She'd been right: the Pool must be leading them through this known sequence to establish a baseline, in a more immediate way than the codex was meant to provide.

"Repeating now," she said. "Give me a moment."

After producing the sequence perfectly, she indicated that she was done, and they waited once more. Several minutes passed, but Olivia sensed no response.

"This doesn't feel right," Cole said.

"Wait," said Olivia.

"Did you signal it exactly as you—"

"Yes, Cole."

"Try it again."

"What?"

"Exactly the same as before."

She looked around the bridge. All eyes were on her. "Fine."

Once more, Olivia signaled each phoneme as carefully as she could. When she was done, she peered into the nearest display. "Done," she said, looking for any activity apart from Cole's pacing. *A spark or a shimmer —anything.*

But if the Pool had signaled any acknowledgment at all, neither she nor the ship was picking it up.

Cole's patience ran out first. "I want you to tell it something for me."

"We should wait."

"I have a message for it."

"We don't know if that will help."

"We've made it this far. I have something to say."

She stared at his image. Why did it feel wrong?

"I'm the one standing out here, Poet. Don't you think it's rude if I say nothing?"

"What then?" she said. "Tell me."

Up on the display, miniature Cole made a low-grav hop to the edge of the platform. "I want you to tell it to come closer."

He had to be kidding. Did he want to whisper something into its ear? For all they knew the Pool was already surrounding them. Or perhaps it was nowhere at all.

"That's what you want to say?"

"I want it to approach, as close as it can come."

Her resistance was a fading mist. Who was to say one signal was worse than any other? "Okay, signaling."

She implored the creature of fields and darkness to please come as close to them as it could.

But if the Pool was there at all—if it had sensed and understood her signal—it gave no indication. It did nothing.

Cole did.

With a mighty leap, he propelled himself off the platform entirely, and out into space.

And before Olivia could comprehend what was she was seeing, the overgrown natal vanished from the display.

"*No!*"

———

Stranded.

That's what they were now. And not just stranded, but doomed, since the Pool—whatever it was—would keep picking them off one by one until there was no one left aboard.

Olivia appeared to be the only one thinking that way though, given the crew's reaction to her single reactionary shout.

"Are you okay, Poet?" Vandana asked, their fingers poised over their control interface.

How could she even answer such a question? Olivia looked from face to face. These people were delusional.

She stood. "Sorry, I can't do this." And she headed out.

Suddenly the passageways were all dead ends. There was nowhere to go, and nothing she could do to dig them out of the hole Cole had buried them in. Maybe she could reach out to the Pool directly, beg it for mercy. Did a lifeform made up of quantum fields have mercy?

"So you're like Cole?"

Coretta had caught up to her.

"What?"

Coretta the historian. Did she intend to put this all into perspective?

"The two of you, you're of the same people?"

Olivia stopped, as much to see what was going on on their skin as anything. Speckled curiosity was indicated there. Not existential dread or unbridled rage.

"We came from the same place," she said, humoring the natal, "but that's about the extent of it."

"Cole wants something better for us," Coretta said.

"Wants? You mean wanted. And that's debatable."

"But that's not why you're here."

"No." None of those reasons mattered anymore either.

"You didn't come here to help us."

"I didn't . . . Look, I came to natality on a diplomatic mission. And I ended up *here* because I thought I could . . ." But their disappointment was already written across their skin. "It's not relevant to what you're doing out here, but what else can I tell you?"

"Cole told some of us pretty early on they suspected you might be a transfer, like they are. We didn't care. We thought, no matter your background, that you would come to understand the opportunity we have here—especially as you're EM-sensitive. You can sense what's out there in your skin. But *still* you resist."

The true believer still believed.

Olivia turned and continued down the passageway, calling over her shoulders, "Why you'd place all your faith in someone who wasn't even natal-born will forever be a mystery to me."

"The fact that we're here now speaks well of our faith," Coretta called after her.

"You've seen what the Pool is capable of, twice. Yet you would have no hesitation—"

"A flame may assist life or extinguish it. But unlike the flame, the Pool may also learn."

Olivia turned the corner to the habitation block. "Sorry," she said under her breath. "I really don't have time for this."

FORTY-FIVE
DAY 70-71

ALONE IN HER CABIN, Olivia slumped into the webbing of her torpor hull, her mind swimming with disjointed appeals to reason. She would have to ask the Pool to help them if there was any hope of returning to natal space. But who or what would she be appealing *to*? What could she possibly say to an entity she could barely comprehend? Clearly there was a wrong way to ask, and judging from recent events, there were still some rough patches with regard to even the most basic of communications.

She was still turning the thought over in her mind when torpor finally overtook her—or maybe it was plain exhaustion. When she awoke, the cabin lighting was low, just enough to give it form.

Might as well be a coffin.

A weak trill made her sit up in her webbing. This wasn't the first time she'd heard it—indeed, the first signal had woken her from fitful sleep.

"Hotfont?"

Two chirps issued from the corner of the cabin, followed by a third trill.

Scrambling to her points, Olivia found her sash on the crate in the corner as the cabin lights rose. She pulled out the already active hotfont, sure that she must be dreaming. The hotfont was reliant on the Fountain to operate. Did that mean the spring to *Bebetathubutiwa*—the one Cole said he'd closed behind them—had been reopened?

The imager was blank though, save for the words: *Active connection. Port unknown.*

"Oscar?" she asked, guessing, hoping.

The device responded with a crackle.

"Elder?" she asked. "I'm having—"

"Olivia?" came a familiar voice. "This is Ran."

She nearly dropped the hotfont; nearly forgot she was holding it. This wasn't possible. And yet his voice had been unmistakable. *"Ran?"*

"Olivia, is that you?"

"Ran! Where are you?" Her thoughts were tumbling over themselves. "Did you come over?" But how would he have gotten here?

Her brother sighed. "Your friends told me I wouldn't be able to understand you. But I can hear you. I *guess* it's you."

What is he talking about?

"If it *is* you, that means you're close to the wormhole. Olivia, we need you to come home, okay?"

"Ran . . ." Where was he calling from? Where was *she*? "I'm not back at the Fountain yet. How are you talking through—"

"I don't know if that's you, but I hope it is. And I hope you can understand me. Please come home."

Had *Bäckahästen* somehow returned to natal space? "Show me the outside view," she said.

Instantly the cabin walls were replaced by the Pool's neat star arrangement, stretching out in all directions. All directions save one: blotting out the galactic latticework was a single void, apparent only in its absolute, glorious absence.

"*Hell* yeah. Ran, you probably can't . . ."

But the words on the screen read only: *No connection.*

———

"What's going on?" Olivia asked as she entered the bridge.

Gregor was there, hunched over their instruments. And Vandana and Coretta had been discussing plans. Plans were surely a good sign, no matter what they were about.

"Cole succeeded," Coretta said. "Cole and the Pool."

"Where? How?" She saw no sign of Cole on the loading platform.

"It's a new spring," said Vandana, pointing out the single pattern-free patch of space.

Cole couldn't have been right. Maybe the Fifth Sun had opened the spring from the other side, to give her one last chance to return before they shut down the Fountain.

It didn't matter.

"So we can go back now," she said.

"We can't leave Cole behind," said Coretta. "Nor the Pool."

"Cole is gone," Olivia said. "And the Pool—"

"We know what you think."

"The probe is approaching the spring," said Gregor.

Olivia watched the display, but saw nothing. "What are you doing?"

"This is the first spring the Pool has ever spawned," said Vandana. "So we must test it for stability. A stable spring would mean the Pool should have full access."

Full access.

The words made her feel too light, as if she might float out of the bridge. But she couldn't just stand here and let them—

"Something's not right," said Gregor.

Good.

"Is it unstable?" Coretta asked.

"It's stable, but this spring doesn't link to the Home domain."

"Where, then?"

"We think it's . . ." They turned and looked straight at Olivia. "Astrography analysis indicates this spring is linked to the domain of humanity."

That was how Ran had contacted her. But that meant that Cole . . .

"We need to close it," Olivia said. "*Close* it. *Right now.*"

"Poet, can you please leave us? We need—"

"This was never the plan," she said, moving close enough to Coretta that she could pull them up off their saddle—close enough that Vandana stepped forward as if to shield their colleague. "This experiment didn't work. We *can't* leave that spring open."

The electronic call of a siren filled the bridge, as if set off by Olivia's fury.

"Activity on the payload platform," Coretta said from their instrument cluster.

Gregor switched their view. They were right, and this time Olivia saw it too: a single natal, overgrown, ungainly, making his way back into the payload bay.

———

Olivia galloped down the central passageway and burst headlong into several storerooms before locating the ramp to the cargo area. Cole had played her for a fool—had duped them all. Why hadn't she seen what was right in front of her all along?

She found him in the cargo bay, where a natal had just finished easing Cole into a thermal suit. For some reason the sight of it made her skin strobe with fury.

Throwing off her sash, Olivia grabbed the railing at the gangway's edge. "*Cole!*" He looked up at her, and her words went away. There *were* no words.

She vaulted herself over the rail, tackling him before the other natal could react.

"*What the fuck did you do?*"

"It's done, Olivia," came his answer, voice resolute, without fear.

"*Undo* it then," she said, driving his forelegs to the floor. "You close that spring, or . . ." Or what? She was going to kill him right here? Then what? "What have you done?"

"Exactly what we set out to do," he said without struggle. "The Fountain wasn't the Pool's greatest failure; the *natals* were. So we're giving the Pool a second chance."

"*Not in Sol!*"

"Why revisit well-trodden ground?"

She shook him, slamming his shoulders into the deck. "I won't let you. You can't destroy everything just to live out this pathetic uplift fantasy."

The other natal's hands were on her now—Tove, that's who it was. But he was small and weak. Meantime, the voices of the others were coming down from the main passageway.

"You have a myopic definition of destruction," Cole said. "Will this change humanity? Of course. Could it perfect them? From my experience, I'm already well on my way."

He's lost his mind.

All four of Olivia's hands were on Cole now, two pinning him down, the other two digging into the natal version of a windpipe. Her fingers might be slender, but they were fantastically strong.

Cole bucked, and his sheer mass was too much for her, toppling her onto Tove. As she scrambled for balance, Cole was already making his way, awkwardly, up the ramp. Coretta and Gregor were waiting for him at the top. Vandana and Massimo positioned themselves at the base of the ramp to shield their returned leader from Olivia.

Block a fucking apex, she thought, and pushed her way through them as if they were fern fronds.

Before Cole could reach the passageway, Olivia leapt to the gangway's support struts and clambered up over the edge, vaulting over the side. Swinging around, she brought Cole down hard against the bulkhead. "You don't get to do this!"

Shouts echoed in the background.

They had nothing to do with her.

"What are you going to do?" Cole asked her, his voice surprisingly cool given his position.

"Whatever the hell I want," she said, her mind blank save for the rage. She pushed herself against him like a compactor, until his lungs emptied with a hiss. If his bones gave, could she find the restraint to stop before she—

"Wait!" he croaked. He waved a single malformed foreleg before her to get her attention. She batted it aside as she butted him in the head with her thick skull, pummeling away until the blue-gray ichor bubbled around his mouth.

"Poet!" said someone behind her.

Hands were on her now—had been on her the whole time. She'd been oblivious.

"*Olivia!*" Cole cried out.

His voice was loud enough that the hands let her go. And in the silence that followed, as he sat up, Olivia let her own hands fall away.

He could have stopped her at any time, but hadn't. She'd underestimated him. And now, as she looked at him, it was clear that something had changed.

Fields.

She sensed the electromagnetic fields across her skin, not the Pool's din, but a new, more controlled signature. And they didn't feel like Cole at all.

Who is this?

"We'll need Cole's body," said Cole.

Olivia backed up a step, her hands shaking from exertion. "What?"

"We'll need him," he repeated, "or the new springs will be of no use to us."

New springs.

"No use to who?" But she already knew. Or, in this case, what. They had just told her.

"We are the Pool," Cole said.

She heard a murmur behind her. Surely the crew's most fantastic dreams were being realized, but maybe not as they'd foreseen them.

"Where is Cole?" she asked.

"Here, still. There's more we need to navigate, but for the first time in a long time we see possibilities."

"Don't take Sol," was all she could muster.

A dozen patterns flashed across his skin for the first time, a mishmash of emotions. Whatever was inside Cole was still getting acclimated. "Cole intends to lead us there." He—or they—stood. "But if you spare Cole, we promise to leave your system to you."

Either they were both in there, truly melded somehow, or this was some kind of sorry ruse.

"Take the shuttle, now, through the spring," Cole—it—said. "It's stable, and *Bäckahästen* is unarmed."

She shouldn't believe a word of this. She *couldn't*. But her body betrayed her, and the sensation across her skin told her his words were true. Indeed, that sense of truth was emanating from him now. Not a field of assurance or even of sympathy, but one of utter *clarity*. The Pool's precious Fountain was finally within reach; what did it care about a dead end like Sol, now that it had found a way, through Cole, to open springs to any destination it wanted?

The bloodied person before her, who was Cole, and a natal, and something else entirely, regarded her from across the floor.

"You'll let me return to Sol, and you'll stay away?" she said. "You'll keep Cole out of Sol?"

"We have no need of it. And neither does he. He knows that now."

There was more to that sentence, unsaid. Had he just had a change of heart? Or had Cole's mind been changed for him?

"And what will you do instead?" Olivia asked.

"Our only interest is to return to our Fountains."

Fountains, plural? A sharp chill rose in the air in the bay.

"I'll accept your offer," Olivia said, not quite believing what she was saying. "But only if you promise to close that spring behind me."

"We won't have to," said Cole.

"Yes you *will*," she said, taking a step toward the hulking natal before her.

"Olivia," he said, pointing out beyond the payload platform, "the spring is already closing."

FORTY-SIX
DAY 71

BÄCKAHÄSTEN'S SHUTTLE was little more than a featureless, pill-shaped pod from the outside. But though the vessel had no portable gravity field of its own, the cockpit was well appointed. It offered saddles for six, and interior walls that provided a full 360-degree projection of the exterior view.

As Olivia watched *Bäckahästen* recede, an odd fatigue began to set in. Her torpor had been light, and she hadn't fed properly in several cycles. But this was something different. More external.

Swiveling her saddle around, she turned her back on the ship to face the new anomaly before her. Cole had told her she would need to take no action—just sit back and let the guidance system fly her straight into the featureless black nothing ahead. And though she'd sensed he'd spoken truth, at the back of her mind Olivia was sure she'd been duped. All Cole wanted was to get the other apex off his—*their*—ship. If the spring closed before she arrived, she'd be sailing off into the depths of Pool space.

But it was too late to second-guess her decision. She had no choice now but to trust that Cole—and through him, the Pool—had bigger fish to fry. For now the spring was holding. The Pool might even be holding it open for her.

As it blotted out more and more of her view, she remembered her hotfont. She pulled it out of her sash, sending her tanthid amulet spinning weightlessly in the air before her. She snatched the keepsake and slid the chain up her foreleg and around her frontmost shoulder before returning her attention to the device. Hand poised over the imager, she hesitated before hailing Ran.

Wait . . . not thinking straight.

He wouldn't understand a word she said. Anyway, what would she tell him—or anyone? Instead Olivia attempted to hail the Fifth Sun, hoping beyond hope that the spring ahead of her might be able to relay through to the spring within the Teelise Sphere.

"Oscar?"

The device issued not even a chirp in response.

By the time Olivia looked back outside the shuttle, the spring's lensing effect had compacted the star grid into a shrinking sphere behind her. *It only gets weirder from here,* she thought.

At least it would be brief—

Traveling through a spring shouldn't have hurt, but the pain was all-consuming, like flames melting flesh from bone. Olivia's many eyes, through a fog of agony, showed her still strapped to her saddle, skin slick with blood.

She was bleeding out.

It was the spring. There must have been something wrong with it. And now . . . now her body was dying, with her trapped inside.

She peered out through the shuttle walls, out to constellations that looked once more like constellations, random and beautiful. Had she made it back to Sol?

Rolling her head around, the glimmer of something nearer caught her eye: the hotfont, on the floor beneath the saddle in front of her. She reached out, but the pain was a white-hot point that pushed everything else away.

Come on, Olivia.

Fucking apex.

Maybe now she could reach the Fifth Sun, through the Teelise Sphere. They would want to know what was coming their way.

As the pain turned into an enveloping numbness, her thoughts drifted to Elder Two. She should thank them for their patience with their ungainly human charge.

How much she had learned since then . . .

Making one final attempt at grabbing the hotfont, something inside her tortured body gave way, and the agony made the stars outside dance before her eyes. Every nerve in her borrowed body sang as though she was being microwaved.

But she'd succeeded, hadn't she?

Olivia looked down at her hand, at the bloody hotfont with its active display.

Fighting darkness deeper even than a spring, she sent a blind hail out into the universe.

FORTY-SEVEN
DAY 71

"I KNOW YOU'RE AWAKE."

Was she? It was so dark.

But the man was right—*Ran* was right. She hadn't realized it until he'd said the words.

"*Water*," Olivia managed, her voice . . . almost familiar.

Her eyes were gritty and tear-stung. But she heard her half-brother—her brother, really—leave her side and rifle through something as he got her a—

That's right: he had a body again, didn't he? And so, apparently, did she. Right now its mouth was dry. At least it was no longer in pain.

How long would it take her to reacclimate? She attempted to open her eyes, and was greeted by pale, indistinct blotches that suggested a bed, white, and a room, also white. Her field of view was so narrow as to be claustrophobic, her perception dull, as if filtered through some diaphanous veil drawn between her and the outside world.

Ran returned to her bedside and pressed a cup into her hand, helped her curl her fingers around it. It was cold, and Ran's hands were warm. And she had five fingers. Five *tiny* fingers.

She took a sip and let her throat do what it had always done. Some things, at least, could still function without her active participation.

"They said I could wait here with you," he said, sitting on the edge of her bed, where at least she could make out his face.

"Where is here?"

"You have your very own room in the post-critical care unit aboard Soutomaior Station." He craned his neck to peer out the window to the sea of dark beyond. "If you look out at the right moment you might even catch a glimpse of the sphere."

"You came all this way?" Was that really necessary?

Ran gave her a smirk. "It's been nearly a week, sister. The teelise didn't know how long you'd be in recovery. Your SA friends thought it would be good for you to wake to a friendly face." As she'd once failed to do for him. "And now that I have a physical face, why not show it off?"

"You know how I got here?"

"The SA was characteristically cagey about that particular detail, but my understanding is that a drone discovered your shuttle—which took a pretty good beating, by the way. Apparently it was floating derelict out beyond the Main Asteroid Belt. Authorities were notified, and I suppose they coordinated with the teelise to make sure nothing was amiss. As for how you got all the way out there from the sphere . . ." He shook his head. "No idea."

No, and that information would probably be locked away in a vault for some time to come. "That's . . ."

"A long story, I'm sure," he finished for her. "And I know better than to ask." He nodded pointedly toward the door.

"Have you talked to them? The Sovereign Alliance?"

"Oh, they are *very* keen, shall we say, to welcome you home. Officially."

Olivia had no doubt about that. The SA had to be beside themselves after her silence.

She breathed in the antiseptic air. If she told Ran about everything she'd been through, would he believe her?

"What the teelise *did* say was that you shouldn't rush anything," Ran said. "Your recovery will take as long as it takes."

"That's putting it lightly." He didn't even know that she'd been out of her body for . . . what day was it? "I feel like a scattered puzzle." She rested a hand on his leg. He was really here, physical, and heavy enough to sink into the mattress.

A knock on the door made her jump. Olivia could only make out a blurred suit. "We'll need to step in now, if you two could wrap things up."

"Just give me a few minutes with my sister," Ran said.

After a pause: "Five minutes."

Olivia smiled as she fumbled for Ran's hand. "It's good to see you, even if you're a blur."

"I'll take the compliment."

"How's Aleksi?"

"He asked about you. I think he's on some kind of vision quest."

"Ah. Nice." She'd had her fill of vision quests.

"I'll try to reach him while you're being debriefed or whatever. Give him the update."

"Make me sound heroic?"

He squeezed her hand. "I always do." He left her bedside, merging into the indistinct blur beyond.

"Where are you going? I can't see past the edge of my bed." Hopefully that was temporary.

"I'm coming right back." He retrieved something from the table by the door and returned with it cradled in his hands. It appeared to be a black statuette. "The teelise wanted to make sure I gave this to you."

He sat and held it out to her. The figure was identical to the amulet *Musstahiti* had given her on *!Wamuhi* after her victory. But no, it wasn't just identical.

This is *the amulet.*

Only now it was as long as her forearm and heavier than any jewelry, its chain dangling down well past her elbow. The natals were clearly larger than she'd assumed. She had thought the teelise had provided her some sense of scale, but no, they'd been purpose-built.

"A souvenir?" Ran asked.

A reward? A trophy? A memento of her brief stint as a predator? For some reason Olivia felt no great sense of ownership. "A gift for you," she said, putting it back in her brother's hands. "You'll be needing more than clothing and furniture now that you're out here with us again."

368

"Thank you," he said with a quizzical grin, turning the figure over for a better look.

Olivia took a deep breath, feeling the lungs in her chest. She could sleep for a week. "I'm not looking forward to being interrogated."

"Just think about after," Ran said. "I've booked us a cabin on the *Firmament to Fin* to get you back to Vaix."

She looked up at him. "You're coming with?" *Say yes.* Now that he was physical again, they should spend more time together. They had so much to catch up on.

"I can stay with you for as long as you want."

Olivia blinked the tears from her eyes, and suddenly her vision was sharp enough to show her Ran's face. It really was Ran's face.

He really was Ran.

But was she still herself? She'd spent so long living in fear of losing herself, avoiding change, even if it meant trapping herself in her pain. Now she'd swung the opposite way, so far that there was no telling what was left of the original Olivia. Who'd gone to sleep in that transfer hull, and who'd woken up here? Was she the same Olivia she'd been before, or just some poetic approximation?

Close enough.

Ran placed her hand back on her stomach before standing and stretching. "Ready to face your fans, sister?"

She pulled herself up and made a show of straightening her sheets. "How do I look?"

"Perfect."

PART FIVE
EPILOGUE

FORTY-EIGHT
DAY 94

THE EARTH SPUN below Olivia as she watched, the gentle undulations of her pool easing the pain in her joints.

The feeling of smallness—of frailty—had dogged her since her return. No longer was she the apex of her kind. What had the teelise done with her natal body? And her gamant? She would contact them and ask if there was a way for her to visit them. Or would that be macabre?

Neither could she contact Oscar, or Elder Two—let alone Cole Quinlan—for any insights into how natal space was faring in the wake of the Pool's newfound transportability. The Teelise Sphere had apparently lost all contact with *Bebetathubutiwa*; they were calling it the "Great Severance." The teelise at this end of the spring were now stranded and alone in Sol, just as Olivia had almost been stranded and alone in the natal home system. No wonder the Sovereign Alliance had been so hot to talk with her.

That, and the situation with Max. Just before the Great Severance, the natal's First Seat had finally revealed that Max had died under their supervision—though they presented it as an unfortunate medical incident, a rare occurrence but completely natural. And unless Olivia decided that the SA should hear the whole grim story, they would never know otherwise. Over time she might decide they should know more, but her instincts on the matter felt unreliable. It was a lot to process, after all: her father by blood, recruited by a secret society to intervene in the case of a renegade human expatriate, killed by a misguided member of said secret society lest he prove to be more of a threat than a solution.

And maybe Langston had been right. About Max, and about her. Thanks in part to her involvement, Unity had successfully communicated with the Pool. Merged with it. And for all she knew, the Pool was now assimilating other natals as it had with Cole.

It could have been worse.

She'd helped. She had to believe that much. She'd done the best she could—certainly better than she would have managed in her human form. She'd bargained with an entity made of space stuff, had been granted passage home, and had perhaps spared Sol in the process.

Yes, she'd helped.

Once more—whether because of the Pool or because of the Fifth Sun —Sol was on its own. She considered the planet beneath her feet. How would humans react to the news of humanity's first emissary to *Bebe-tathubutiwa* being killed by a member of the host race? Not that there was anything they could do about that now.

But something stuck in her head. Max had been an alien at the time of his demise, technically. So was it truly Max who had died over there? Not so long ago she'd feared that the transfer process itself was tantamount to execution—an end of one life, and a clever but calculated likeness carried forth thereafter.

Now she knew otherwise.

———

The water speakers issued a tone. Olivia pushed off from the bottom of the pool and surfaced, wiping the water from her face and breathing deep.

"What is it?"

"There's someone at your door," the ambiont said. "I don't have any information on them."

Ran must have stepped out to run errands. Who would be calling this early in the morning, before the high moment? She glanced at the time, her eyes fixed on the numbers. She hadn't surfaced for air for almost thirty minutes.

That can't be right.

"Uh . . . show me?"

Above the water's surface she saw the feed from the front door: a young woman in a single-piece green suit. Definitely not Sovereign Alliance. Olivia didn't recognize her.

"Can I help you?" Olivia said.

"Ind. Olivia Jelani?"

"Yes?"

"Our name is Stanford Glove," the woman said, her accent nondescript. "We were hoping to speak with you. If now is a good time?"

"Who is 'we'?"

"*I,*" she said. "I would like to speak with you."

"About what?"

The woman outside shuffled her feet as she cast a glance over her shoulder. "About . . . Cole Quinlan."

An old-fashioned adrenaline rush sped through her. She'd made no mention of Cole to her interviewers, at least not yet. As far as she knew, the man hadn't been on the Sovereign Alliance's radar. So who was this woman with the improbable name?

"Wait there," Olivia said.

———

"You've come a long way to meet with me, haven't you?"

Olivia couldn't stop staring at Stanford Glove's face. Not because it was artificial—which it certainly was. Seconders had taken the mystique out of fabbed bodies decades ago. It was because the person inside this woman wasn't human at all.

"The circumstances are not ideal."

"How many of you are over here?" she asked the natal. Was she really having this conversation in her lounge?

"We can't say."

"Meaning?"

"Meaning we don't know. *I* don't know. My team are six."

"Spies?"

"*No*, no. We are clandestine, but I am a social scientist." She looked at her teacup as if she wasn't sure what to do with it. "My project centers on cultural anthropology."

"The spring back to your home system is closed," Olivia said.

"But that may not always be the case. I must assume that my assignment is ongoing. Originally it was for two local circuits. Now . . . I don't know. That's why I'm here."

Olivia read no sadness or fear on the woman's face—assuming emotions would register there at all. She seemed composed. Focused.

"Who gave you your assignment?" Olivia asked. "Are you with the Empyrean Symbiotry?"

The woman's face went funny then, a show of emotion she hadn't yet gotten the knack for. "My work is with a small group very much *outside* of that body. My very presence here runs counter to their reverent, exceptionalist segregation." She held Olivia's gaze. "You know of the Fifth Sun."

"Yes." It seemed the Fifth Sun had longer roots than she'd given them credit for. "I had some involvement with them before I came back."

"I've been a member for many of your decades, when our primary focus was still on promoting the cultural heritage of my people. Humanitarian work. I have no interest in extracting state secrets from you, nor in political maneuvering. I am here only for the reasons I stated, and I can only hope, for my sake, that you'll take me at my word."

Olivia *could* take her at her word, but a spy might ask the same thing. Still, in that moment, she couldn't help but think how much this Stanford Glove reminded her of Oscar and the other poets.

"Besides me," she said, "who else knows you're here?"

"Only a small group of trusted experts outside of the Sovereign Alliance's field of view. Not even the teelise know. We are inclined—my team are inclined toward discretion, until we understand the implications of our circumstances."

Straight from the Fifth Sun's script.

"Look," Stanford said, "I know I'm not supposed to be here. But I need to know what happened to my home system at the end. And right now you're the only person who can tell me."

Olivia had heard much the same thing from her SA interrogators. More debriefing, that's what this was. Lacking contact with the natal domain, all eyes were on Olivia Jelani, glorified attaché.

Her thumb found the old tear in the couch fabric, opened by a dog's errant nail. She ran it idly along the frayed edge as she studied the strange woman sitting across from her. Did the tense frown on her face truly reflect her state of mind? Impossible to know. The truth could be different for different people, regardless of the mask they wore.

"Okay," Olivia said with a sigh. She settled back on her couch, letting her sore bones sink into the cushions. "First, tell me: what do you know about the Thirsty Pool?"

THANK YOU!

THANK you for reading *Whispering Skin*! If you enjoyed reading this book, I'd be grateful if you'd consider rating it or leaving a brief review to help bring it to the attention of other readers like you!

For info about my upcoming releases, book news, and more, sign up for my newsletter at https://jdrobinson-author.com.

ALSO BY J.D. ROBINSON

The Hole In the World (YA SF)

On the Loop (SF)

The Last Shadow (SF)

Broken Helix (SF)

Songs From the Void (SF)

ACKNOWLEDGMENTS

I'll say what I always say: many people provided me with invaluable information, obscure details, or inspiration for this book, including family, friends, and complete strangers. I was humbled by their generosity and insight. I must add, however, that I made adjustments and embellishments where necessary in support of the larger story. So any inaccuracies or misrepresentations that arise on the page are mine alone!

———

Mike Chadwick
Invaluable information about the roles and practices of international diplomacy.

———

Special thanks go to editor extraordinaire **David Gatewood**, whom I've had the pleasure of working with several times. His unrelenting attention to detail helped me make this story the best version of itself. I recommend him to any author out there.

https://lonetrout.com

———

The cover artwork design is by **Bastien Lecouffe Deharme**, an amazing artist who took my crazy cover concept and ran with it! Check out his portfolio.

https://www.shannonassociates.com/bastienlecouffedeharme

ABOUT THE AUTHOR

J.D. Robinson was born in the last year of the 60s, smack in the center of the United States— aka Tornado Central. He was quickly whisked to the East Coast, where he spent his formative Virginia days entering obscure machine code from the backs of magazines, reading science fiction books by nightlight, falling asleep over  his doodles in class, and attempting to write stories. Nothing came of any of it.

Well, that's not strictly true. He amassed notebooks and loose scraps of paper filled with unattached musings and thoughts. Each was like a solitary voice with—seemingly—no way ever to find its way into a coherent story. It wasn't until nigh upon his forties, after he fled to the West Coast, that a close friend suggested that they co-author a story. This was his first novel-writing venture. But, though that project never yielded a book, the spark had started something terrible.

"Terrible" may be too strong a word for it, but for better or worse, writing is now what he spends every free moment on. (And sometimes moments when he should be otherwise engaged.)

As of this writing he's completed six stand-alone novels.

J.D. Robinson writes intimate, humanist science fiction, speculating on the human condition as fallible characters face the most exotic existential questions. You know, the usual stuff. A reclusive nerd, he now lives in Northern California where he's waiting for the big one. The singularity, that is.

facebook.com/jeffrobinson.author
twitter.com/scamper
instagram.com/scamper
goodreads.com/jdrobinson

Made in the USA
Middletown, DE
26 July 2022

69866700R00231